The Gathering

The Gathering

C. J. TUDOR

MICHAEL  JOSEPH

MICHAEL JOSEPH

UK | USA | Canada | Ireland | Australia
India | New Zealand | South Africa

Michael Joseph is part of the Penguin Random House group of companies
whose addresses can be found at global.penguinrandomhouse.com.

Penguin
Random House
UK

First published 2024
001

Copyright © C. J. Tudor, 2024

The moral right of the author has been asserted

Set in 13.5/16pt Garamond MT Std
Typeset by Jouve (UK), Milton Keynes
Printed and bound in Great Britain by Clays Ltd, Elcograf S.p.A.

The authorized representative in the EEA is Penguin Random House Ireland,
Morrison Chambers, 32 Nassau Street, Dublin D02 YH68

A CIP catalogue record for this book is available from the British Library

HARDBACK ISBN: 978–0–241–48626–9
TRADE PAPERBACK ISBN: 978–0–241–48627–6

www.greenpenguin.co.uk

Penguin Random House is committed to a
sustainable future for our business, our readers
and our planet. This book is made from Forest
Stewardship Council® certified paper.

For Mum. Love you.

'Like many indigenous species, vampyrs have been demonized and terrorized by human settlers, to the point where only a few colonies remain in remote areas. Soon, we may live in a world where they are nothing more than a legend.'

— Extract from *The True History of the Vampyr* by Professor Benjamin Fletcher

'It is actually very rare for a vampyr to attack a human. Most exist happily on animal blood and have done for many centuries – a way of living which is no more barbaric than that of the average meat eater.'

— Dr Steven Barker, Head of the Department of Forensic Vampyr Anthropology (DFVA)

'Vampyrs are hereby decreed a protected species on the verge of extinction. Any culls must be authorized by the government and only in the interests of public safety. Culls will be approved when no other more humane option is available. Vampyr trophies are declared illegal.'

— Vampyr Protection Act, 1983

'No one is going to stop us hunting down the spawns of Satan. It's God's work. They are an abomination. And we will not rest until every last one of them is returned to the pits of hell.'

— Revd Colleen Grey, Church of the Holy Cross

I

It would be wrong to say that life had passed Beau Grainger by.

Beau Grainger had ambled along steadily, without excitement or drama (for the most part), but also without bitterness or rancour. He had always lived in the small Alaskan town where he had been born and saw no reason to move elsewhere. Most places became familiar after a time, like most people.

He had loved two women and married one of them. They had raised three children and seen them make their way in the world. A fourth they had buried before the infant could take his first breath. Funny how that was the child Beau wondered about the most. We always hanker after what we can't have. Human nature.

Beau had lost his wife, Patricia, to dementia ten years ago and she had been dead almost three years now. By the time she passed, Beau had finished mourning the woman he loved and buried a stranger.

Now, in his seventy-ninth year, Beau had a few good friends and few regrets. And that is really the best a man can hope for as he starts the final lap of life. That, and a swift and painless death. Beau was content. Or as content as anyone truly can be. But even a man like Beau, not given to introspection or sentimentality, had days when he thought too much.

Today was one of those days.

His joints ached, which they did sometimes in bad weather. His coffee tasted bitter, and not even a shot of whiskey helped. TV held no interest and books failed to distract him. He couldn't settle.

Beau wandered around his living room. Small and snug, with worn leather armchairs and a large, open fire. Above it hung Beau's trophies.

Beau was a hunting man. He loved nature, but he also loved the thrill of the kill. To be a good hunter took patience. And Beau had plenty of that. Watching, waiting for the perfect moment to strike. To truly know another beast is to look into its eyes as it dies.

Beau moved closer to the heads. Three of them, mounted on solid wooden stands made for him by Cal Bagshaw (dead almost a year now from throat cancer).

Beau stared into their glassy eyes, ran a finger over their pale, dry skin and around their sharp white teeth.

'Bite me,' Beau whispered, and chuckled. But a whisper of cool ice still drifted across his neck.

Okay, Beau-boy. But remember, the first cut is the deepest.

Beau backed away, and then told himself not to be such an old fool. He turned to the window. Black clouds bristled on the horizon. The white snow undulated like a vast frozen sea. A storm was coming, something foul on the air. Beau had smelt that smell and felt that chill before.

They were back.

It was about to begin again.

2

The cab driver was a talker.

Great.

Barbara guessed he didn't get a lot of business this time of year, so he was hungry for company. He lived alone. Probably always had. His heavy beard and food-stained shirt, plus the odour of BO, suggested long-term 'don't give a shit'. Not that she was suggesting a man needed a woman to take care of him. No, sir. But everyone needed *someone* to make an effort for. Without that, you got used to your own stench pretty quickly. She should know.

The driver's name was Alan, according to his licence. 'Call me Al,' he had grinned. 'You know, like the song.'

Barbara had nodded and smiled. 'Yeah.'

She hated that song. She wasn't so hot on the silver cross and rosary beads dangling from 'Call Me Al's' rear-view mirror either. But to each their own.

For the next few miles, she batted away the endless questions: *First time here? Yes. Sightseeing? Yes.* A lie, but it led to him giving her a rundown of the best tourist attractions in the area, which was pretty short yet somehow still kept him occupied for the next thirty miles or so.

The scenery swished by in a breathtaking gust of ice and snow. And it *was* breathtaking stuff, Barbara supposed. If you liked snow, forests, mountains, more snow, more forests, more mountains. Pretty. Sure. But get lost out there and you'd be a frozen corpse within minutes. Not so pretty.

She fought back a yawn. An early flight from New York to Anchorage, a nerve-shredding air taxi to Talkeetna and now an hour-and-a-half drive along the snowy AK-3 highway to her destination. Man, why had she agreed to this?

'You're our best forensic detective,' Decker had told her.

'What about Edwards?'

'Family commitments, which you don't have.'

'So I draw the short straw because I'm single and childless.'

Decker had leaned forward, stubby hands splayed on his desk. He was a short, stocky man with a Friar Tuck ring of black hair around a bald pate and a face that looked like he was permanently in the middle of a minor cardiac event. He'd been Barbara's boss for over ten years, and she still wasn't sure he knew her first name.

'You want me to pay you a compliment, Atkins? Tell you you're better than Edwards? Our foremost expert in the field.'

'That would be nice, sir.'

Decker had glared at her. 'Your flight is booked. Don't forget your garlic.'

He turned back to his computer, indicating that their conversation was over.

Barbara stood. 'Great, sir – should I cook them some dinner?'

'Good that you know your place.'

She had smiled. 'Sir . . . with all due respect, you're a real asshole sometimes.'

And then she had walked out without looking back.

4

On reflection, her sunny, easy-going nature might also be why she was being shipped out to Alaska.

'So.' Al was staring at her in the rear-view mirror. 'We don't get so many tourists stopping in Deadhart. I mean, we get a few of them Goth types; they all like to take a picture of the name, you know? But most don't stay long. Most head on back to Talkeetna. You plan on doing that?'

He had her sussed, Barbara thought. Never underestimate a cab driver, even out here. They saw all of humanity in the back of their cars. They knew how to read people.

'Maybe,' she said. 'I'll play it by ear.'

Al nodded, cleared his throat. 'I just thought . . . you might be heading that way because of the boy.'

Barbara felt herself tense. The local police department had been instructed to keep news of the death quiet for the first forty-eight hours, until she arrived to make an assessment. It didn't do to stir up trouble too soon.

'What boy?' Barbara asked carefully.

Her eyes met Al's in the mirror. The silver cross danced and dangled.

'The one that got killed,' he said.

Okay. So word had already got out, and if Al was chatting to his customers about it, that leak was pretty much a flood. Barbara just needed to know how far it had spread. Could she sandbag it? She debated. Best to be up front. Or at least appear to be.

'You got me.' She sighed. 'I'm here about the boy. What have you heard?'

She gave Al a little half-smile. He had been smart. Outwitted her. Now, she was giving him a chance to show how much more he knew.

5

'Look.' He lowered his voice a little, even though it was only the two of them in the cab. 'I know you want to keep it quiet. I'm not a gossip, okay?'

'And I thank you for that, sir.'

'I only mentioned it because my sister, Carol, she lives in Deadhart, see.'

'I see.'

'And she told me about the boy – and that some specialist detective was flying in.'

'Right.'

'You're obviously from out of town, I don't take many folks to Deadhart and, no offence, but you look like law.'

Did she? Barbara knew she was no beauty queen. Short with a barrel waist, thick legs and a nose that could sniff out a good steak from fifty paces. Solid. That was how people often described her. Good old solid Barbara. And getting solider by the day since she turned fifty. Age might bring wisdom, but it also brought indigestion and elasticated pants.

'Well, yessir. Well spotted. But I'd appreciate it if you didn't mention it to anyone else.'

'Oh, absolutely. You think you'll be here long?'

They were climbing now. To her right, steep hills bristling with dark spruce and spindly birch. To her left, the ground dropped further and further away. She could see the glint of water in the distance. The Susitna River. Barbara swallowed. She didn't like heights. Or water.

'Well, I guess it depends on what I find,' she said.

She glanced up and saw Al frown. 'No offence,' he said. 'But seems like it's pretty clear what happened.'

'Is that so?' She couldn't help the slight edge that had crept into her voice.

'Yes, ma'am. I get why you're here. You gotta tick the right boxes. But everyone in town knows one of them *Colony* killed the boy. Not saying they did it malicious. I mean, they can't help themselves, but it doesn't change the facts. A young boy is dead.'

She forced a smile. 'Well, I'm not much of a box-ticker, Al. I just want to find the person responsible.'

He carried on as if he hadn't heard her. 'Look, I'm no 'phobe or nothing. Live and let live and all that. But it's like an animal. I love my dog, but if she bit a kid I'd shoot her, no second thoughts. Once they get a taste of blood, they're gonna come back for more. Same thing.'

'And would you also kill that dog's pups and any other dogs in its pack?' Barbara asked.

'If I didn't know which dog done the biting, yes, ma'am.'

The cross swung to and fro. The land slipped further away. The road was precarious now. Barbara was suddenly very conscious of the icy snow beneath Al's tyres. They were heavy-duty snow tyres, and his cab was more of a 4x4, but still. One small slip and they'd be rolling down into the river's icy depths. She didn't want to distract Al, so she swallowed her retort and nodded. 'Well, I'm sure you're right. But I'm booked in here for a week, so if I find I've got some time to kill, what else do you reckon I should do?'

Al smiled, and he was off again. Barbara decided she preferred Al the tour guide. She sat back in her seat as the road started to descend. The car rolled along the highway, then turned on to a narrower track. The dark expanse of forest hugged the blacktop either side. Above them the sky had begun to ditch into darkness. Barbara checked her watch. Just after 3.15 p.m. A lot of darkness in Alaska at this time

7

of year. Further north, it would soon be the start of the polar night: twenty-four-hour darkness for a little over two months. Even here, in the central region, she'd be lucky to see five hours of daylight. That was why the colonies settled here. In summer, they spent more time hibernating. Sun wouldn't kill them, but it wasn't comfortable. Central still offered a decent amount of night, although some colonies moved in the summer, to areas with less midnight sun.

Up ahead, the cab's lights illuminated a makeshift wooden sign at the side of the road: **Deadhart. Population 673**. Underneath, some bright spark had added: LIVING.

Nice. Of course, the population was now 672, Barbara thought.

The car rounded another wide bend, the trees thinned, and the town came into view.

'What the –'

Although it was only early November, the town was lit up like a Christmas wonderland. Lights. Lots of lights. Every building along the small main street was adorned with row upon row of twinkling fairy lights. Windows glowed with shimmering stars and crosses. Trees had been strung with multicoloured bulbs. Some residents had gone for broke with sparkling reindeer and flashing 'Merry Christmas' signs. Incongruously, these were mixed with Halloween lanterns and more traditional mounted antlers and animal skulls. Atop the roof of the general store a huge illuminated Santa waved his hand up and down, except some of the lights were bust so it looked like he was rubbing something else, closer to his bulging sack.

Barbara blinked. 'Guess people really get into the festive spirit here in Deadhart.'

8

'It makes people feel safe,' Al said.

'They know that artificial light is no deterrent, right?'

'Yes, ma'am, but at least the lights mean you can see who or *what* is coming.'

'I guess so.'

'Where is it you want me to drop you?' Al asked. 'Hotel or police department?'

'Erm, you can take me straight to the Police –'

Her words were cut off. Al slammed on the brakes. Barbara bit down hard on her tongue as she was thrown forward against her seatbelt.

'Shit!' Al cursed.

There was a thud. Barbara glanced up. A boy stared at them through the windscreen, face white, eyes wide, hands splayed on the cab's hood.

Then, just as suddenly, he leapt up, clambered over the car's roof and vaulted off the trunk. Al flung open his door, yelling after the boy, 'You'd better not have damaged my car, you little shit!'

But the boy was gone, a blur disappearing between the buildings.

Al shook his head. 'Damn kids.'

Barbara climbed out of the back. 'Did we hit him?'

'You just saw him jump the car. You think he'd do that if we hit him?'

But Barbara thought she had heard a thud. She crouched down. Her eyes scanned the ground. A drop of bright red glistened in the mushy snow. Blood. She reached out a hand and her fingers touched something sharp. A jagged sliver of glass. Barbara picked it up carefully and looked back at the car. No damage. But blood and glass on the ground.

'I swear, we didn't hit him.' Al got out and stood by the driver's door, looking nervous.

Barbara straightened, her back creaking. 'You know that boy?'

He shook his head: 'Look, they're not bad kids here. But they get bored. Makes 'em do dumb stuff sometimes. Drugs. Alcohol.' He shrugged. 'Kids will be kids.'

Barbara offered a conciliatory smile. 'We were all young once, right?'

'Right.' Al's face relaxed. He climbed back into the driver's seat.

Barbara's smile faded. She looked after the boy thoughtfully. *Kids will be kids.* Maybe Al was right. But the boy hadn't looked drunk. Or high.

He'd looked scared to death.

3

Al pulled up outside a white clapboard building sand-wiched between DH Drugstore on one side and the Roadhouse Grill (and Hotel) on the other.

Barbara frowned. 'I asked to be dropped off at the police department.'

'This *is* the police department, ma'am.'

Barbara peered through the cab's window, and now she could just make out a hand-written cardboard sign stuck beside the door: 'DH Mayor and Police Dept.'

'They're getting a new sign made,' Al said.

'What happened to the old one?'

'Some kids stole it.'

Right.

Al grinned. 'Let me get your bag.'

As he unloaded her case, Barbara climbed out of the car. Now the rush of adrenalin from the near-collision had faded, she could feel the cold. Colder here than back in Anchorage. Not as many tall buildings to provide shelter from the bitter northerly wind that cut across the river and sliced at your skin like a million tiny razors. There was a smell it carried on it too. Familiar. Unpleasant. Spruce, dank water and fish. And maybe a drift of weed. It wasn't illegal here. Maybe someone was smoking inside one of the houses, although Barbara couldn't see any open windows.

She stamped her feet and clapped her gloved hands together, suddenly feeling hungry.

Al brought her bag around.

'That'll be a hundred and forty dollars, ma'am.'

Would it now? she thought. There was no meter in the cab, and she was pretty damn sure that the woman she had pre-booked the cab with had quoted her $120. But it had been a long day, and she wasn't really in the mood to argue. Now she was here, Barbara felt a familiar impatience. To start the job. To do what needed to be done and then get out of this place. Maybe it would turn out Al was right. Maybe she could just tick those boxes and go do some sightseeing. But even as the thought crossed her mind, she knew that it was unlikely. Barbara had never really been one for standing and looking at stuff. Your eyes could only tell you so much. And they could deceive you. To really get the measure of a place you needed to live it, smell it, feel it. Get your hands dirty.

She fished her cash out of her wallet and handed Al three fifties. Hopefully, enough to keep him quiet about her visit.

He nodded. 'Thanks, ma'am. Just give me a call when you want to leave – and keep an eye on the weather. If a storm rolls in, the air taxi won't run, the train only comes through Talkeetna once a month in winter and the trunk road gets impassable pretty quickly. You might find your-self stuck here a while.'

Great. Barbara looked around. Despite the lights, she could feel the darkness weighing in heavily all around her. The brightness of Main Street only seemed to amplify the wilderness surrounding them. This was a harsh place.

A wild place. 'Nature's got an appetite for the unwary,' her dad used to say, usually after a beer, or six. 'You gotta make sure you're the hunter, not the prey.'

'I'll bear that in mind,' Barbara said. 'And can I get a receipt?'

'Sure thing.' Al pulled a wedge of receipts out of his pocket and handed them to her. 'I'll leave 'em blank,' he said with a wink.

'Thanks, Al.' She smiled, even though she knew she would stick down the correct fare. Honest as the day is long. That was Barbara. 'Course, here in Alaska the days weren't so long.

She bade Al goodbye and watched him pull off, no doubt to drive home to his one-bed cabin, eat a ready meal and maybe jack off to some porn before bed. Or maybe not. Maybe Al enjoyed cooking, music, books. Maybe he didn't even own a TV. Maybe. Making assumptions about people was dangerous, but sometimes your gut just knew. If Al wasn't the type of man who kept a bin for tissues beside his armchair, she would eat her mittens.

Barbara turned and looked up at the police department building. Lights in the shape of prancing reindeer had been strung around the window frames, intertwined with miniature jack-o'-lanterns. The whole town was like some bizarre *Nightmare Before Christmas . . . nightmare.*

Small towns, she reminded herself. They had their ways. You just had to roll with it. She hefted her case and walked up to the door. It was locked, so she pressed the buzzer at the side. Nothing. She tried again, keeping her finger on the button.

An ear-splitting crackle reverberated through the intercom

and a muffled female voice muttered: 'Oh shit.' And then: 'Sorry – Deadhart Mayor's Office and Police Department?'

'Err, hello. It's Detective Barbara Atkins here. From the Forensic Vampyr Anthropology Department.'

'Oh, the Fang Doc. Hang on. I'll let you in. Come straight through.'

Fang Doc. Barbara rolled her eyes. It was going to be a long week. The door buzzed. She pushed it open and stepped into a short corridor. To her right a room had been converted to house two small holding cells. Basically, cages with a bed and not much else.

To her left, another door led to a room which she presumed must be both the mayor's office and the police department. Barbara could see several large filing cabinets and three desks, which was pretty much one too many for the room's size.

A small stout woman stood in the middle of the room. She looked to be of native Alaskan descent, with thick, dark hair cut in a short bob. Maybe mid-forties. She wore glasses and a colourful blouse with jeans. Barbara surmised that this was not Police Chief Pete Nicholls. The woman held out her hand as Barbara entered.

'Hi, Detective Atkins!' She paused and frowned. 'Do I call you Detective, or is it Doctor?'

Barbara smiled and shook her small hand. 'Barbara works for me.'

Although Detective and Doctor were both correct. She was a doctor of forensic vampyr anthropology and a homicide detective.

The woman's smile widened. 'And you can call me Rita.'

'Good to meet you, Rita.'

Instinctively, Barbara liked this woman. Her eyes were bright and direct, her smile genuine.

'You work here with Chief Nicholls?' Barbara asked.

A look of amusement crossed the woman's face. 'Kind of. I help out. We're waiting on a new officer to start on rotation soon. Till then I'm all Pete's got.'

'I hear my name being used in vain?'

Barbara turned. At the back of the room, where a doorway led to a small kitchenette, stood a tall, wiry man holding a cup of coffee. He wore a plaid shirt with the sleeves rolled up and dark jeans. His thinning hair was shorn close and he sported a neat moustache. Barbara guessed he was about her age, but better maintained. Instinctively, she sucked her stomach in.

'Chief Nicholls?'

He walked forward and held out a smooth, lightly freckled hand. 'One and the same. And you must be Detective Atkins, esteemed doctor of forensic vampyr anthropology.'

She shook his hand. 'But you can call me Fang Doc . . .' She winked at Rita.

Nicholls glanced at the other woman. 'Please tell me you didn't?'

Rita clapped a hand over her mouth in mock dismay.

'It's okay.' Barbara smiled. 'I get that a lot. In fact, it's one of the kinder things people have called me.'

Nicholls smiled, but it looked a little forced. 'Well, I've probably been called a lot worse in my career.' He moved to his desk and set his coffee down. 'Can I get you one? Warm you up a bit?'

'That would be great,' Barbara said, with some feeling.

'I'll make it,' Rita said. 'How d'you take it, Barbara?'

'Milk and two sugars, please.'

'Snap.'

'You're honoured,' Nicholls said to Barbara. 'Getting Mayor Williams to make you coffee.'

Barbara stared at Rita. 'You're the mayor?'

Rita waved a hand. 'Makes it sound fancier than it really is. Mostly paperwork, checking folk are okay. Keeping their gun licences and food hygiene up to date. I help the chief out here sometimes – *and* I make a mean cup of coffee.'

Nicholls raised his eyebrow. 'Then how come you never make me one?'

'I'm the mayor, honey.' Rita sashayed off, chuckling to herself.

Nicholls shook his head. 'Certifiably insane, that one. But the town loves her for it.'

'I can see why,' Barbara said. 'She seems like a hard person to dislike.'

She eased herself into a seat, unzipping her bulky jacket. It was warmer in the office, but not exactly toasty.

Nicholls regarded her appraisingly. She had only exchanged one brief email with him, and she wasn't sure what she had expected. He was probably thinking the same.

'So,' he said. 'You have a good journey?'

'Not too bad, sir.' She paused. 'My cab driver knew about the boy –'

'Marcus Anderson,' Nicholls interrupted. 'The boy's name was Marcus.'

Barbara nodded. 'Of course. I'm sorry, sir. But the point is – the cab driver *knew*. Got a sister in town, apparently.'

Nicholls clicked his tongue against his teeth. 'That'll be

Al Haynes. Sister's Carol. She works in the hardware store. Yeah, she's not known for keeping things to herself. But then, this is a small place. People talk. That's why I'm hoping you can wrap this up quickly.'

Barbara shifted in her seat. 'Well, I'll certainly do my best, sir.'

He sighed. 'We've not had a killing like this for twenty-five years –'

It was Barbara's turn to interrupt: 'With all due respect, sir, it's my job to determine *what* type of killing this is.'

Nicholls nodded slowly. 'That it is. But let me just lay the groundwork. This is a quiet town. Sure, we have the usual problems – drinking, drugs. Some of the kids get themselves into trouble every now and then. But we haven't had a murder here since the Danes boy. Not until *they* came back . . .' She saw his jaw tense.

'That would be just over a year ago, that the Colony returned, right?'

'Right. And I'll be honest with you, Detective, the whole town has been on edge ever since. Worried, wondering why they're back. Why now? Tensions are running high. A lot of folk aren't happy about waiting for you to call it.'

Barbara bet her dimply white ass they weren't. Towns like this always thought the law applied to other people.

'Sir, authorizing a cull is a very serious call. That's why it happens so rarely. We're talking about sanctioning the killing of a whole colony – men, women . . . children –'

'And *I'm* talking about the safety of a whole town – men, women, children.' His lip twitched beneath the moustache. 'The law states that a cull can be sanctioned when a colony poses a threat to human life –'

17

'I know what the law says.'

'A young boy is *dead*,' Nicholls continued. 'His parents are broken. People need to see justice done, one way or another.'

Barbara bristled. 'Well, I'm sure you've made *people* aware that the authorities are far less forgiving about unauthorized culls these days . . . especially those involving minors. We can't have anyone taking the law into their own hands.'

And it didn't hurt to let Nicholls know that she had done her homework. She knew all about Todd Danes's murder . . . and the aftermath.

Nicholls nodded. 'I'm just letting you know how it is.'

Barbara thought she already had a pretty good idea of 'how it was', but she bit her tongue.

'You weren't the police chief here when Todd Danes was killed?' she asked, deciding to change tack.

'No. That would have been Jensen Tucker. And then Ben Graves took over till he retired six years ago. That's when I stepped in.'

'Where were you before?'

'Seattle.'

Barbara raised an eyebrow. 'Heck of a move, if you don't mind me saying.'

'I was in need of a change.'

She waited, but he didn't elaborate.

'And what about you?' he asked.

'Me?'

'How did you get into . . . your line of work?'

She was saved from an answer by Rita's arrival: 'Okay, folks. One Mayor's Special for the Detective Doc.' Rita grinned and placed the brimming mug on the desk. The sweet aroma of rich coffee beans floated up into Barbara's nostrils.

'Damn. That *does* smell good.'

'I never lie . . . well, not about coffee anyway.' Rita chortled again. Then she eyed them both more keenly. 'I'm guessing you two want to chat some more about police business, so I'm just going to call it a day here. Nothing that can't wait till tomorrow.'

'No need,' Nicholls said. 'I'm sure Barbara would like to check in to her room and get herself washed up . . . after her coffee, of course.'

'Actually, I'd like to get started,' Barbara said. 'After all, you said you wanted to get this wrapped up quickly.'

Nicholls smiled curtly. 'I did.'

Rita beamed. 'You know, I think you two are gonna get along *real* well.'

Barbara reached for her mug. 'Oh, I think Chief Nicholls and I understand each other, don't we, sir?'

His gaze was stone. 'That we do.'

The girl sat in her room. Waiting. Listening. She was hungry, but these days she often was. She had become used to ignoring that constant gnawing feeling in her gut. Her Captor was strict with her feeding.

The door was locked. There was only one small, barred window, the glass painted black. The girl didn't mind that so much. It was necessary. And her Captor had hung a pink blind decorated with dancing unicorns over the window to make it look less like a jail.

Her Captor had also provided plenty down here to keep her occupied: from a radio and an old record player to cable television and a video recorder. She had a bookcase overflowing with paperbacks. There was an exercise bike for fitness. She even had a private bathroom with a large shower.

Her Captor was not a monster. They loved her. They told her this daily.

All of this was for her own good. To protect her. She understood that, didn't she?

Yes, she did.

And no, she didn't.

The girl wandered over to the bookcase. Her reading tastes had changed over the years — from the classics, crime, sci fi, horror, literary, poetry. She had explored most genres of fiction, even tried her hand at writing herself. But she found it hard to convey her emotions in such a limited way. There didn't seem to be enough words for how she felt.

Now she found herself more interested in non-fiction. Books about religion, philosophy, books that explored the soul, the psyche. Her Captor encouraged this. Told her it was good education for the day she could re-enter the world. The girl had also taught herself several languages, including Latin. The mind is a beast. It never gets full.

The girl sat back down on the bed. No books interested her today. No TV shows or games.

It wasn't just the gnawing pain in her stomach.

This was something new. Yet old. Half forgotten.

A sense that she was not alone.

A faint murmuring in her mind.

A scent, a tingling in her bones.

There was someone coming.

And like her, he was hungry.

4

'Why don't you tell me what you already know?'

Nicholls pulled open a drawer and placed a couple of dog-eared folders on the desk. High-tech stuff. But then, Barbara was old-school herself. She had a smartphone and a laptop, but the laptop was old enough to be steam-powered and she didn't use the phone for anything smarter than calls or texts.

She sat back, holding her mug. 'To be honest, I'd like to hear it straight from the horse's mouth.'

Nicholls opened one of the folders. Barbara sipped her coffee. She'd given him back control and she sensed that Nicholls was a man who liked to be in control. Not a bad thing. Not yet, at any rate.

'Marcus Anderson, fifteen, left his home after dinner on Friday, the 10th of November. He didn't return that night. His parents weren't too worried because he'd said he might stay over at his friend, Stephen Garrett's house. When he didn't show the next morning, his mom started to get a little concerned. She texted him. No reply. Then she called Stephen's mom, who said that Marcus didn't sleep over. Stephen said that he last saw Marcus around 9 p.m. They'd been hanging around an old hunter's cabin in the woods with another boy, Jacob Bell. A lot of the kids do that. They go there to drink and smoke and well, you know –'

'I think I can just about remember.' Barbara paused. 'And that was where you found him?'

Nicholls nodded and slipped out some photographs. The crime scene.

Barbara studied them. The boy was skinny. Lanky. That was the first thing she noticed. He'd obviously had a growth spurt and the rest of him hadn't caught up yet. At that age, they can't eat enough to keep on the pounds. He lay spread-eagled on the dirty wooden floor of the cabin, clad in just a pair of jeans and a sweatshirt. The jeans had ridden up at the ankles, exposing white shins and frayed socks. One boot had come off. Barbara swallowed. She wanted to tug the jeans down, to cover him, keep him warm. But the boy was long cold.

She studied his throat. A mess of torn skin and gristle. There was blood around his face and the top of his sweatshirt, but not enough for a throat wound like that. There should be blood everywhere. All over his clothes, pooling beneath him on the floorboards. But there wasn't. Which suggested it must be elsewhere. Removed, or ingested.

The reports were right. At first glance, this looked like a Colony killing.

Look again, Barbara. She could hear Susan's voice. *You think you've looked, but you haven't. You've just observed. Now look again and see it properly.*

She fished out her glasses and picked up each photo in turn. This time she concentrated her attention on the scene around Marcus. Several items on the floor had been numbered with evidence markers. Half a dozen joint stubs, three cans of beer, a cellphone lying beside Marcus's hand, and something else.

'What's this?' she asked, pointing at the small pink object.

Nicholls reached into his drawer, which seemed to be the stand-in for an evidence locker, and took out a clear plastic bag.

Barbara took it off him and peered inside. A small, jagged piece of pink plastic. She frowned. Hard to say what it was. It looked like part of something else, but she couldn't say what.

'Any clue?' Nicholls asked.

'Well, it's plastic. It's broken off something.'

'Yeah. I bagged it up, but I'm not sure it's relevant. Might have been there for a while.'

'Maybe, but it looks pretty clean. Rest of that cabin is dirty. You're right, though – might not be relevant.'

But these things often were. Barbara took out her note-book and wrote down: 'Pink plastic?'

'I'm just gonna grab myself another coffee,' Nicholls said. 'Call if you need me.'

'Thanks.'

Barbara peered at the pictures again. Despite the lack of blood around Marcus's body, the perpetrator wouldn't have been able to inflict those injuries without getting covered in blood themselves. The femoral artery was a geyser. They would have had to hide or dispose of their clothing. She made a couple more notes. There was something else about the clothing, she thought.

She looked at Marcus. Blue sweatshirt, jeans, socks and boots. But no jacket. The teens were hanging out in an old hunter's cabin at night. The temperature must have been minus five at least. No jacket. So where was it?

Nicholls walked back in.

24

'Did you find his jacket?' she asked.

'What?'

'Marcus's jacket. He's not wearing it in these photos.'

Nicholls set his coffee down. 'No. We didn't find a jacket.'

'Oh.'

'Oh?'

She looked up at him. 'Well, he must have been wearing a jacket. Did you ask his parents, friends?'

Nicholls looked irritated. 'Of course. And yes, he was wearing a jacket. North Face. Grey. Brand new, in fact.'

'So where is it?' Barbara prodded.

'I presumed the perpetrator must have taken it. Maybe as a souvenir?'

Barbara frowned. It didn't fit. If this was a Colony killing, then it was born out of rage, desire, hunger. They didn't take souvenirs. They'd got all they needed.

'Tell me about the other boys,' she asked.

Nicholls's jaw tightened. 'They didn't do this.'

The rebuttal was too fast. Barbara smiled pleasantly and reached for her coffee.

'I never said they did, sir. I'd just like to know a little more about them.'

He regarded her dubiously and sighed, again: 'Stephen is a typical teen. He's bright but easily bored. His parents run an outdoor-adventure business. His mom, Jess, grew up here. Dan, his dad, moved from Canada. He takes tourists trekking through the national park. Sometimes, Stephen goes with him.'

'So Stephen knows the area well?'

'Guess so. He's been in minor trouble, but then what

teen hasn't? The usual – drinking too much; he got into a fight with another kid once. But he's not a killer.'

I'll be the judge of that, Barbara thought. In her experience, for every misdemeanour you caught a kid for there were half a dozen you didn't know about. Conversely, in any group of kids there was a fall guy. The kid who threw the last punch as the cops arrived or couldn't hold their liquor. She would need to talk to Stephen to see which one he was.

'And the other friend, Jacob Bell?' she asked.

Nicholls cleared his throat. 'He moved to town with his dad about nine months ago.'

'No mom?'

'Divorced, apparently.'

'Why here?'

'His dad, Nathan Bell, grew up around here.'

Bell. Barbara had thought the surname was familiar.

'Wasn't he one of Todd Danes's friends?'

'Yes. But I wouldn't read too much into it. It's a small town. And Todd's killer confessed. There's no doubt what happened to Todd.'

No, Barbara thought. Maybe not. But there was doubt about what happened afterwards.

'Look,' Nicholls continued. 'I'll be honest, I don't much care for Nathan Bell. He drinks too much, doesn't seem to care if Jacob gets to school or has clean clothes, but that's not Jacob's fault.'

Barbara nodded but made a mental note. 'Can't choose your parents, right?'

'Right.'

'What about Marcus's parents?'

26

'Good people. Run the general store. Marcus was their only child. They're with relatives in Talkeetna right now.'

'I'll need to speak to them.'

'I know. They should be back in a day or two.'

Barbara nodded. She didn't relish that conversation. But it was necessary. Something else occurred to her.

'Are Todd Danes's parents still living in Deadhart?'

Nicholls shook his head. 'I heard they moved to Fairbanks with his younger sister not long after his murder. Wanted to make a fresh start.' He gave her a pointed look. 'If you can ever really make a fresh start when you have to pack up your child's ashes in a suitcase.'

Heard loud and clear, Barbara thought.

'Okay,' she continued briskly, 'So, Stephen and Jacob last saw Marcus at around 9 p.m.?'

'Yeah. Marcus was walking home with them when he realized he'd left his phone in the cabin and wanted to go back for it.'

'The others didn't go too?'

'These are boys. They don't stick to each other like girls do.'

'Well, girls wouldn't have to do that if it wasn't for boys, sir.' Barbara moved on before he could reply. 'So, we only have the boys' word that Marcus was alive when they left him?'

Nicholls rolled his eyes. 'You don't think we didn't consider that? A fight. A drunken fall-out. If it was, *with all due respect* . . . you wouldn't be here.'

'May I ask what makes you so certain, sir?'

Nicholls reached back into the drawer and produced

another clear plastic bag. Barbara could see it contained a cellphone.

'Marcus's phone?'

Nicholls smiled, self-satisfied. He'd saved this till last on purpose, she thought. Humouring her while she asked her questions.

He pushed the phone across the desk towards her.

'*Proof* that this was a Colony killing.'

5

The footage was dark and grainy. Less than a minute long. But it felt longer. It started with a view of the dirty cabin floor. Marcus must have grabbed his phone as he was attacked. A last-ditch attempt to record what was happening to him, perhaps? Somehow, he had managed to turn the phone around, and Barbara could see a figure on top of him, on all fours, pinning him to the ground.

Impossible to tell whether they were male or female. It was too dark, and the figure was dressed all in black. Jeans, a hoodie. They didn't look big, but vampyrs were strong.

Marcus squirmed and struggled. The figure raised their head. Barbara got a glimpse of sharp white incisors before they pressed their face to Marcus's neck. Marcus screamed. Barbara felt her heart lurch. The phone must have slipped from his fingers because now all she could see was the floor and a portion of wall. Marcus screamed again. The static image continued for another few seconds. Then abruptly stopped.

Proof.

That was what Nicholls had called this (and her boss, that fucker Decker, hadn't told her about it).

But she wasn't so sure.

For a start, who stopped the recording? Marcus, in his death throes? Or his killer? But then why not take the phone?

Something about it felt wrong. Something *niggled*.

'I'll need to study this again, properly,' she told Nicholls.

'Take your time,' he said, sounding smug. 'Tomorrow, you can look at the body. Hopefully, that will be all you need.'

Maybe. Maybe not.

Barbara couldn't take the phone with her, so she uploaded the footage to her laptop before she left Nicholls's office to check into the Roadhouse Grill and Hotel.

Barbara suspected the 'hotel' was an afterthought, and that kind of showed in her room. Not that it was a bad room. *Quirky* might be the best description. The ceiling sloped and she would have to duck to get into the sagging double bed. The bathroom was shared with the only other room, next door, and the ancient shower spluttered like a man trying to ask a pretty girl on a date. But the sheets were crisp and clean, the patchwork quilt reminded Barbara of her grandmother and the hosts had even left out some coffee, milk and a coffee pot.

The young girl who showed her up had given her a key-ring with two keys on it. *'One for your room and one for the outside door. Grill opens at ten. We don't do breakfast, but the café across the road serves from eight.'*

All in all, Barbara had stayed in worse. Much worse.

The Grill was exactly what Barbara had expected. Same place she had visited in a dozen different states across America. Bar down one side. Tables in the centre and booths along the other side. The walls were decorated with antique guns, animal heads and old photos of the town and its residents. Behind the bar there were other mementoes.

Large crosses, wooden stakes and a case of long, yellowed incisors. The beer pumps had handles made out of humerus bones. Antique, she guessed. Not illegal. Just distasteful.

But then, this wasn't cosmopolitan New York or liberal California, where such things would be viewed in the same way as hanging a commemorative noose or Klan hood upon the wall. Towns like these, they had their ways. Some might call them backward. But it was more that they were stubborn, digging in their heels while progress tried to drag them forward. It would happen, eventually. It always did. But they'd resent it every step of the way.

Still, at least the menu at the Grill wasn't too offensive (although a little heavy on wild boar and reindeer), and the food coming out of the kitchen smelt good. Barbara tucked herself into a secluded corner booth and ordered a cheeseburger, fries and a large beer from the same young girl who had shown her to her room. She was late teens, with purple hair shaved on one side, wearing a Pearl Jam T-shirt and ripped jeans (*progress*). She brought the beer over first and Barbara took a sip before pressing play on the laptop again.

Nicholls hadn't offered to join her for dinner, and Barbara guessed it wasn't just because he wanted to let her 'settle in'. She was an outsider, a *cheechako*. He didn't want to be associated too closely with her. Barbara's presence here was an unwelcome necessity. On that, at least, they were agreed.

The bar was about half full. Locals. This wasn't tourist season, and this wasn't a tourist town. Not like Talkeetna or Fairbanks. Barbara observed an elderly couple at another booth, a family with two kids at a larger round table and a striking woman with white hair sitting opposite a teenage girl wearing a conservative blue dress at a table for two. A couple of older locals slouched on stools at the bar.

They had all looked up as she walked in. Some covertly, some less so. Generally, Barbara didn't stick out too much in a crowd, which was a good thing in her line of work. But in a place like this she might as well have burst in doing the can-can wearing a sequinned leotard and feather boa. One of the bar-slouchers had muttered something under his breath as she walked past. Barbara was pretty sure it wasn't complimentary.

She had nodded pleasantly, 'Evening, sir.'

He'd scowled, picked up his drink and thrown it back before slamming his glass down on the bar. Make mine an old-fashioned shot of toxic masculinity, Barbara thought.

It didn't surprise her much when she saw him rise and walk, somewhat unsteadily, towards her table. In a way, she had been waiting for it. She closed her laptop, sat back and smiled.

'Can I help you, sir?'

The man looked to be in his late seventies, tall for his age and wiry. She guessed that beneath his checked shirt and windbreaker he was still defined, muscles not yet gone to flab. His face was carved with deep lines, eyes a watery blue (cataracts, perhaps), white hair thinning and cut military short.

'You the Fang Doc?' he asked.

Barbara kept the smile pinned ('Put a tack in it,' as her mom used to say) and held out her hand. 'Barbara Atkins, sir. Pleased to meet you.'

He looked at her hand like it was covered in crap.

'No offence, ma'am, but you're wasting your time here.'

And there it was. Barbara lowered her hand.

'Is that so?'

'We all know who – or *what* – killed the Anderson boy, and we know how to deal with it.'

'And how would that be, sir?'

'The last time one of those creatures killed a kid, we hunted 'em down and drove the rest away. Never had no trouble after that.'

Barbara nodded. 'I read about that. An unauthorized cull. Three of the Colony killed. Lucky no one was prosecuted.'

The man snorted. Barbara could smell the bourbon fumes. 'You don't prosecute people for exterminating vermin,' he growled.

'One of those vermin was a minor.'

He rolled his eyes. 'They're not *real* children. Some look like kids, but they ain't.'

Not true, Barbara thought. 'Turning' children had been outlawed by the colonies centuries ago. And vampyrs could breed. Most children in colonies were the vampyrs' own offspring. They might grow and age more slowly, but they were still kids.

'We *saved* those creatures,' the man continued. 'From eternal damnation. We did what was necessary.'

'Really? Was disfiguring the bodies necessary too?'

A flash in the cloudy eyes. His jaw tightened.

Another voice spoke: 'Is everything all right here?'

Barbara glanced up. The striking white-haired woman she had spotted earlier had approached the booth.

Unlike the rest of the clientele, who wore the small-town uniform of plaid shirts and jeans, she wore a long,

33

grey dress over tights and chunky black boots. An ornate silver cross hung around her neck.

'We were just chatting,' Barbara said to her.

The woman smiled. 'Well, that's good to hear.' She glanced at the man. 'Perhaps it would be best if you headed home, Beau. You wouldn't want Jess to have to come and fetch you again.'

The man looked like he might argue, and then sighed, the aggression leaking out of him like a punctured balloon. He nodded at Barbara. 'I didn't mean to trouble you.'

'No trouble. You take care now, sir.'

Beau walked back to his stool, picked up his jacket and meandered towards the exit. Without being asked, the woman took the seat opposite Barbara. As she did, Barbara felt the room settle, like an exhalation of breath. Conversation and movement resuming. Their little tableau had played out. Almost like it had been rehearsed.

Barbara smiled at the woman across the table. 'I'm –' she began.

'Dr Barbara Atkins, forensic vampyr anthropologist,' the woman finished. 'I know.'

'Guess word travels fast here.'

'About the only thing that does.' The woman stretched out her hand. Her nails were long and manicured. Not small-town nails. 'I'm Reverend Colleen Grey.'

Reverend. Well, that explained the cross. Barbara shook the Reverend's hand, conscious of her own bitten nails and ragged cuticles.

'Nice to meet you, ma'am.' She paused. 'I didn't realize they had a church in Deadhart.'

'I guess you could say I'm kind of a pioneer. I built the church here myself.'

Not with those nails, you didn't, Barbara thought.

Perhaps catching her sceptical look, Colleen added: 'I had some help from the community, of course. And it's not much. Pretty rough around the edges. But the town needed it. Needed me.'

The Reverend certainly wasn't short on confidence. The evangelical seldom were.

'How long have you been here?' Barbara asked.

'Coming up to three years now.'

'So practically a newcomer then.'

Colleen laughed. 'True.' She fixed Barbara with sharp grey-blue eyes. 'You sound like you know small towns.'

Barbara hesitated and then said, 'I grew up in a place not so dissimilar to this.'

Colleen nodded. 'I thought I got a hint of Midwest in your accent. Not much. But it's hard to shake.'

'You got me,' Barbara said, reaching for her beer. She took a slightly larger sip.

'Where are you based now?' Colleen asked.

'New York, Brooklyn.'

'Ah, the Big Apple. You live alone, or –'

Or . . . a whole heap of ambiguity in that one word. For a short while, there was an 'or', but Barbara sure as hell wasn't going to mention Susan to this woman.

She smiled. 'I like my own company, ma'am.' She glanced towards the bar. 'You seemed to know the gentleman who came over?'

Colleen nodded. 'Don't judge Beau too harshly. Stephen Garrett is his grandson.'

35

Barbara raised her eyebrows. 'Marcus's friend?'

'You can understand why he's upset. It could have been his boy, right?' She pressed her hand to the cross. 'People just want to see the right thing done.'

'Then we're on the same page.'

'I'm so pleased to hear that, Detective. Some towns-folk, they wanted to take matters into their own hands right away. But Chief Nicholls and I persuaded them to wait.'

Really? This was news to Barbara. But she wasn't unduly surprised.

'That's very decent of you, ma'am.'

Colleen beamed. In contrast to the rest of her polished appearance, her teeth were crooked and a little yellowed.

'Did you know Marcus Anderson?' Barbara asked.

'Not well. But he was a good kid.'

'Chief Nicholls said the boys sometimes met up at the cabin to drink and do drugs?'

'A good kid, not perfect. Teenagers experiment. It's part of growing up.'

Barbara glanced across to where the teenage girl in the blue dress sat, hands folded in her lap, silently staring into space. A little odd. Normally girls of that age were on their phones every second they could get.

'Do you tell that to your daughter?' she asked.

'Daughter?' Colleen frowned. Then she turned, follow-ing Barbara's gaze. 'Oh, Grace?' She smiled. 'She's not my daughter. She's my assistant.'

'Oh. I'm sorry . . . she looks very young.'

'Eighteen. Her mother died. I took her under my wing. She helps me with church business.'

36

Barbara glanced over at the girl again. 'Did Grace know Marcus?' she asked.

Something in Colleen's face changed. 'Grace doesn't associate with boys,' she said curtly. 'She's very devout.'

As far as you know, thought Barbara. In her experience, young people lived two lives. The one their parents or guardians knew about, and the one they didn't.

The purple-haired waitress approached, holding a tray of food. 'Cheeseburger and fries?'

Barbara's stomach rumbled. 'That'll be mine, thank you.'

Colleen rose smoothly. 'I'll leave you to enjoy your dinner.' She paused. 'You know you really should try the barbecue night here . . . if you're stopping that long.'

She smiled again and wafted away from the table.

The implication was not lost on Barbara. She *wouldn't* be here that long. Her job was to tick boxes so that the local law enforcement could get on with the cull.

The girl placed her plate of food on the table. 'You want to watch that one,' she said casually.

'Who? Reverend Grey?'

The girl raised an eyebrow. 'She's no more a Reverend than I am.' Then she tucked her serving cloth into her apron and walked away.

Barbara doused her fries with ketchup and stuck one in her mouth thoughtfully. Part of her already wanted to get out of this town as soon as she could. It was starting to stir up too many memories. *I thought I got a hint of Midwest in your accent.* And the accent wasn't the only thing hard to shake.

But there was still that niggle. She liked to do things right. If you're going to do a job, do it properly. No short cuts. They'll always come back to bite you (no pun intended).

Belt, braces and a full metal jacket, Barbara.

Another Susan-ism. Barbara lifted the burger to her mouth and paused.

There it was.

The niggle.

The jacket.

She put the burger down and wiped her fingers on her napkin. Then she opened her laptop. The grainy footage began again. Marcus lay on the ground. Sweatshirt, jeans, no jacket. Marcus wasn't wearing his jacket when the attack took place.

The phone slips from his hand, offering a view of the dirty floor and the cabin wall. Barbara paused the video and enlarged it. There. A faint grey blur.

The image was fuzzy but now she knew what she was looking at, it was obvious.

A jacket. Hanging on the wall.

'Grey. North Face. Brand new.'

Marcus's jacket. He must have taken it off and hung it up.

But why? Had he returned to the cabin for more than his phone? A sexual assignation, perhaps? But why remove his jacket? It would have been freezing.

Unless . . . Marcus *knew* he was going to lie down on the cabin floor. And he didn't want to get his jacket dirty.

Because it was *brand new.*

'Dammit,' Barbara whispered.

The footage wasn't proof. It was staged.

6

Tucker sat on the deck of his cabin, staring out into the forest.

It was dark and freezing cold, but neither bothered him. Never had. Even as a child, Tucker had never feared the dark. His stepdad worked nights. Once the door closed behind him at 8 p.m., both he and his mom breathed a sigh of relief. Even the house seemed to settle more easily. A peace that would last until the front door burst open at nine o'clock the next morning.

Heat. That bothered Tucker. He'd never enjoyed the sun. Mornings, when his stepdad would sit out on the deck, swigging beer, seemed full of hot foreboding. As the sun rose higher and his stepdad got drunker, Tucker would feel the heat rash prickle across his skin. That was when he would seek out a hiding spot in the woods or under the decking, in the crawl space beneath the house where no one could reach him.

Back when he was a cop, it wasn't during the long months of winter, with daylight barely scraping in an appearance for three hours a day, that he dealt with the most trouble in town. People were generally calm; they slept more and went out less. Summer, when the hours stretched longer and the sun clung to the blue sky, that was when the drinking and bar brawls began. When husbands remembered how they liked to beat up their wives for wearing a dress that showed a bit too much cleavage and underage kids got themselves doped up and lost in the woods, necessitating search parties and helicopters to the hospital. Heat. Sun. Tucker didn't miss it.

Most of the time.

Music drifted out of the cabin's open door. Nirvana. 'Come as You Are'. Tucker raised a glass to his lips and took a long sip. From the forest, hidden eyes watched. The pig he had slaughtered earlier hung from a butcher's hook attached to a sturdy tree bough. Tucker wasn't worried about it attracting bears or wolves. The animals here knew him, and they knew he would leave them the carcass. Tucker was relaxed about predators.

The furred kind, at least.

Something else was bothering him. He felt tense. That was why he was drinking, which he knew he shouldn't do. It disagreed with him, for several reasons. But tonight, he had needed the slow burn of a good bourbon, just to ease away his edges. Not that it was working so far. The anxious feeling remained. A hard knot in his stomach. Anticipation. But not the pleasant kind.

Something wicked this way comes.

It had started even before they found the boy. When the Colony returned. Tucker didn't need anyone to come and tell him they were back. He just knew. And now it was happening again. Twenty-five years later. Another killing. Another kid dead.

Something rustled in the undergrowth. Stealthy, soft. A person not so familiar with the sounds of the woods probably wouldn't have heard it. But Tucker's senses were more attuned to such things these days.

From the other side of the cabin, where he kept his few pigs and goats – now in their pens for the night – he heard muffled squeals. They sensed it too.

He slipped a hand to the side of his chair, where his crossbow was propped. Then he stood, eyes scanning the dense green foliage. He caught a flicker of twin amber discs. Eyes.

He raised the crossbow. 'I know you're there, so you might as well come out.'

Silence. Or as near as dammit.

Tucker waited.

The forest remained still.

Tucker held his breath.

Finally, a shadow separated from the other shadows and emerged into the faint light of the moon.

The girl was slight and pale, dressed in cut-off dungarees, tattered hiking boots and an oversized jacket made of stitched animal skins. Her blonde hair hung in two loose pigtails on either side of her heart-shaped face. A child. No more than nine or ten.

Tucker's flesh crept.

'I asked you to stay away,' he croaked.

'We did. But now we're back.'

'That's a mistake.'

'We'll see.' The girl cocked her head to one side and regarded him curiously. 'You look old, Tucker.'

'That's what happens. A few grey hairs won't kill me.'

'Not yet.'

He swallowed. 'What do you want, Athelinda?'

In a blink, she was on the deck, inches away. Like a gust of wind had swept her there. Tucker could smell dirt, age, death.

She placed a finger on the tip of the arrow. 'I want you to put the crossbow down, before I rip out your throat and bleed you dry like that fucking pig.'

Tucker lowered the weapon.

'Better.' She walked across the deck and sat down in his chair. Then she reached into her pocket and produced a small pipe. From her other pocket she took out a tin of tobacco and a silver lighter.

Tucker eyed her coolly. 'I'd say that habit is going to kill you, but . . .'

'I wish.' She packed the pipe with tobacco and lit it. Then she sat back and propped her boots on the wooden railing. 'We need to talk.'

'About the boy?'

'About how you are going to help us.'

'And why would I want to do that?'

'Because you owe me, you ungrateful fuck. And if you don't' – she smiled, revealing creamy-white teeth and two sharp gold incisors – 'I'll make sure the whole damn town knows what really happened twenty-five years ago.'

7

Barbara didn't like the dark. It seemed a fool-ass thing for a grown woman to admit. Right up there with believing in the Closet Monster and the Boogie Man.

But just because a fear was foolish didn't make it any less real. And it wasn't an irrational fear. It was primal. Darkness meant you couldn't see the predators coming.

In the city, it was easier. That old adage about the city never sleeping was true. There was always a haze of illumination. Bars, traffic, streetlights. Here, it was different. Night came down hard and fast. Even the town's omnipresent Christmas decorations couldn't ward it off.

She was back upstairs at just past ten thirty. She took her towel and toiletries and washed and brushed her teeth in the small bathroom. The tiled floor was freezing even through her thick socks, and she hurried gratefully to her room. Barbara wondered briefly if anyone was in the other guest room, then dismissed the idea. If they were, she would have heard them by now.

Once she was settled under the heavy quilt in bed, she plugged in her phone and set her alarm before turning out the lamp. Then she lay there, unable to sleep. As always. For someone who hated the dark, it was kind of ironic that Barbara spent so many hours staring into it. Her mind was in a free ramble. Churning over what she had learned today and that damn cellphone footage.

Marcus was dead. That was a fact.

But the footage was staged. She was certain that was also a fact.

Had Marcus intended to film his own murder?

But then, why worry about a dirty jacket?

Or was it a 'turning' that had gone wrong?

Like before, with the Danes boy.

Teenagers didn't change that much. They were attracted to darkness, flirting with the forbidden. Over the years, plenty had run away to join a colony. Being 'turned' seems romantic when you're young. Living for ever, being an outcast.

But while relationships between consenting adults and colony members were not illegal, 'turning' a minor was, even if the colony member was underage themselves. Turnings could easily go wrong. The process involved biting – *infecting* – the human, who then needed to consume vampyr blood plasma to complete the process. But it was risky. Like asking a starving bear to nibble your finger. For an inexperienced vampyr, the hunger was hard to control. There were many cases where humans bled out and others where they rejected the blood plasma, ending up in a half-turned state, neither vampyr nor human.

Of course, the danger only made it more attractive to some. Like Todd Danes.

Barbara needed to talk to the other boys. Find out what they knew. They were Marcus's friends. They had access to his 'other life', the one his parents were unaware of, or blind to. Talking to their teachers might be a good idea too.

She had a feeling that these requests would not go down well with Chief Nicholls, or the town. And then there was

44

Colleen Grey. An interesting one. Barbara would like to find out a little more about her role in Deadhart.

It wasn't so unusual for a small town like this to have its own chapel or pastor. A lot of towns near colonies did. Since the Vampyr Protection Act was signed into law in 1983, religious opposition had been growing. Churches had mobilized in protest against the 'spawn of Satan'. As with so many things in life, battle lines had been drawn, between the right-wing evangelicals who believed that vampyrs should be hunted down and killed (because that was what Jesus would want) and the 'woke' liberals who believed that minorities should be protected and respected. Age old. Barbara had seen it with race, homosexuality, women's rights, abortion, trans rights.

While the VPA was welcomed in most states, it was different in the small towns, the appropriately named Bible Belt. Barbara had some sympathy. She'd grown up in a small town herself (Colleen had been right on that one). And the fact was, colonies didn't tend to settle near big cities. It was easy to be liberal when the wolf wasn't at your own door.

But then, it wasn't Barbara's job to judge or theorize here. It was her job to make a decision. Was Marcus's murder a Colony killing or not? And right now, she just didn't know.

She sighed and checked her phone. After midnight. She should really try to get some sleep. She turned over and closed her eyes.

Something knocked against the wall next door.

Her eyes shot back open. Was someone using the bathroom?

She held her breath, listening for the toilet or shower.

Silence. Then two more knocks.

It could just be a drunk from the Grill. The stairs to the guest rooms were at the side of the bar. The rooms had locks, but anyone could walk up and enter the bathroom. However, the Grill closed at eleven. Even with stragglers, it should be shut by now.

She switched the lamp on and swung her legs out of bed. Then she pulled her sweater over her pyjamas and after a moment, picked up her gun. She waited. No more noises. Had the occupant gone, or were they waiting quietly inside?

She opened her bedroom door and padded out into the hallway. Dimly lit by a single dusty overhead bulb. She walked a few paces to the bathroom. The door was shut. Her turn to knock. She rapped against the wood with her knuckles.

'Hello? Anyone in there?'

No reply. Barbara twisted the handle. It opened into darkness. A grubby light cord hung down by the door. Barbara pulled it. The harsh illumination momentarily blinded her. She blinked and squinted. The small room was empty. Shower dripping slightly. *Tap, tap, tap.* Toilet seat down. Just as she'd left it.

Almost.

A mirror hung above the cracked sink. There was writing on it. Scrawled in red:

THE SUN WILL BE TURNED INTO
  DARKNESS,
AND THE MOON INTO BLOOD.

And just in case the message wasn't clear, the visitor had left her a present, hung over one of the taps.

A rudimentary cross on a leather choker . . . fashioned out of two sharp vampyr incisors.

8

The alarm went off at seven. Barbara opened her eyes. It was still dark. Sunrise wouldn't come till around 9.30 a.m. Another two and a half hours. Christ.

She hauled herself reluctantly out of bed. The wooden floor felt cold. There was a draught coming from somewhere. She stretched out a hand to touch the old iron radiator. Barely warm and it was already turned up to max. She grabbed the extra blanket from the bottom of the bed and wrapped it around her shoulders. Then she picked up her clothes and traipsed to the bathroom.

She had bagged up the choker for evidence, but the writing on the mirror was still there. Permanent marker. Barbara would have to ask the staff downstairs if they could clean it off with spirits. She'd taken a photograph last night, after checking the bar for the intruder. No sign of anyone. And no sign of a break-in. At least, no obvious sign.

She turned on the shower and shed her clothes. The shower was hot, for about thirty seconds. It turned cold in an instant, sending her scuttling for the sanctuary of a rough bath sheet. She dried her body and hair as quickly as possible before wriggling into her heavy jeans, a shirt and thick sweater. Then she brushed her teeth and retreated to her room.

Hair still damp, she made a coffee and sat down with it on the small chair next to the window. The chair was uncomfortable, and the coffee was dishwater, but Barbara sipped it gratefully regardless. *Something is always better than nothing, unless it's jail time.* Another Susan saying.

She skimmed her phone for messages. Mostly junk, a reminder that her renter's insurance was due, a curt message from Decker asking for an update and . . . she paused. A text from Susan. Like she'd known Barbara was thinking about her. But then, Barbara often thought about Susan. Perhaps if she'd done it a bit more when they were in a relationship, it wouldn't have ended.

'Hey. Heard you got shipped to Alaska? Hope you're wearing your thermals! Let's grab coffee when you're back. Auric sends his love.'

Auric. The goldfish they had bought together because it seemed less of a commitment than a cat or a dog (only to discover that goldfish can live for up to twenty years). Auric was now eight and had been living with Susan and her wife for over three years. Susan got the fish and the new partner while Barbara, well, she got 'let's stay friends' and a single room in a run-down hotel in Deadhart, Alaska. Big win for the commitment-phobe.

She replied to the text with a thumbs-up and a frozen-face emoji, pulled aside the curtains and peered out. The street was silent and still dark, except for the persistent twinkle of Christmas lights. Across the road, the illuminated Santa above the general store continued to merrily pleasure himself. Ho-frigging-Ho. She let the curtain fall. Her cellphone buzzed. Nicholls.

'Hello?' she answered.

'Hope I didn't wake you up, Detective.'

'No, sir. I'm up and enjoying my morning coffee.'

'That crap they put in the rooms?'

'Well, *enjoying* might be a stretch.'

He chuckled. 'Okay. Well, I just wanted to double-check that you're good to view the body this morning.'

'Yessir.'

'We can grab a decent coffee downstairs first. I'll meet you there at eight thirty.'

'I didn't think the Grill opened till ten?'

'They don't. They're opening up early just for us.'

'That's very kind of them.'

'Yeah, well . . . we're not there just for coffee.'

'Oh. Then what are we there for?'

'Because it's the only place in town with a freezer big enough to store a corpse.'

The coffee *was* decent. Barbara had to give Nicholls that.

A scrawny woman with short, bleached hair (an older version of the purple-haired girl) had served them, more with a scowl than a smile.

'This is Carly,' Nicholls introduced them. 'Carly runs this place with her husband, Hal, and daughter, Mayflower.'

Barbara smiled and held out a hand. 'Good to meet you, ma'am.'

The woman shook it, reluctantly.

'I think I met your daughter last night,' Barbara continued. 'Mayflower's a pretty name.'

'Thanks.'

'After the ship?'

Carly regarded her coolly. 'We're all pilgrims here. Trying to protect our land.'

Our land. Except it was the land of the Dghelay Teht'ana

49

first, Barbara thought. The earliest known humans in the region. The first non-Indigenous settlers here were vampyr, a few hundred years before the white men came.

She lifted her mug and took a sip. 'Good pilgrim coffee. Guess you have it shipped in?'

Nicholls cleared his throat obtrusively. 'Shall we head out back?'

'You know the way,' Carly said, which immediately made Barbara wonder how many bodies got stored here before being buried or taken to Anchorage.

Barbara followed Nicholls through the door behind the bar, still clutching her coffee mug, a small medical bag in her other hand. The walk-in freezer was at the back of the kitchen. They walked past grease-stained cookers and shelves lined with tinned goods and long-life products and up to a thick steel door.

'This is a pretty big walk-in for a place like this,' Barbara said.

'Well, folks here hunt and eat a lot of meat,' Nicholls replied. 'Plus, in winter the ground can be too hard to bury bodies, so we often have to store them here till the thaw.'

'Right.'

Barbara was pretty sure that storing bodies in a commercial freezer must violate several food hygiene laws, but places like this tended to be a law unto themselves. Still, it would have been nice to know before she ordered a burger last night.

Nicholls pushed down on the heavy handle and the freezer door swung open. A blast of cold air hit them. Barbara shivered. The body bag was laid out on a steel table to the left of the large room. Metal containers and hunks of wrapped-meat lined storage shelves on the other side. Their breath puffed out in small, icy clouds.

'Did anyone check the body over before you stuck it in here?' Barbara asked.

'Doc Dalton,' Nicholls replies. 'He's the local GP. Determined cause of death and approximate time, which you have in the report.'

Barbara nodded. But a GP was not a coroner. Marcus's body would still have to be autopsied back in Anchorage. Moreover, bodies were normally kept between minus 2 to minus 4 degrees in a morgue. Commercial freezers were kept at a minimum of minus 18. She remembered that from when she worked shifts in the local café as a teen-ager. Freezing and defrosting could compromise tissues and DNA.

Barbara sighed. 'It would have been better to keep the body somewhere cold but not deep-frozen till I arrived.'

Nicholls sipped his coffee. 'Well, I'm afraid we don't have anywhere else that's suitable.'

'What about the cells at the station? Turn the heating off. The room would stay cold.'

He looked a little awkward. 'People wanted the body kept somewhere more secure.'

'More secure than the cells?'

A hard look. 'The way they see it, frozen corpses don't walk.'

She stared at him, aghast. 'Marcus is *dead*.'

'And so are those creatures out there.'

Not true. Vampyr physiology was understood much better these days. Their hearts beat a minimal amount, but they weren't dead. Nor were they immortal. They aged, just very slowly over hundreds of years. They couldn't turn into mist or fly like bats. They weren't invisible in mirrors. They could recover from injuries that humans could not. But they were not invincible. A stab to the heart or decapitation would kill a vampyr. Just like it would a human.

However, to some of the folk here, that would probably be semantics. And Barbara wasn't here to win hearts and minds. That took more time than she had left on this planet. She was here to do her job.

'Okay,' she said. 'Well, let's unzip him and see what we've got.'

It never got easier. It was impossible to look at a young, deceased person and not think about all that potential unfulfilled. A waste. An overused phrase, but it was true. Sometimes Barbara could almost feel it. The unused energy humming around the corpse like an electrical field. She put her cup down on the floor and studied the youngster.

He was a pretty kid. Blond, probably tan in summer. Freckles on his nose. Now pale, almost blue. Skinny, as she had noted before. Ribs standing out like a toast rack on his exposed body, clad just in boxers (the rest of his clothes bagged for evidence).

But I bet you ate like a horse, Marcus. Bet some of the other kids ribbed you about your weight, too.

For some, imagining a body as a living human being made the job harder. For Barbara, it made her remember that she was dealing with a person who'd had feelings and thoughts and dreams, not just a slab of meat.

She glanced at Nicholls, who was sipping his coffee and shuffling his feet to keep warm.

'Let's wheel him out into the kitchen, where it's not sub-arctic.'

They pushed the steel trolley out of the deep freeze into the Grill's kitchen. Nicholls slammed the freezer door shut.

'This going to take long?'

'You don't need to stay if you don't want to.'

He grimaced. 'I'd rather be present, if that's okay with you.'

He didn't trust her. But that was his call.

'As you wish, sir.'

Barbara slipped on her glasses. Then she set a small Dictaphone on the side of the table and pressed record. She would use her phone to take pictures. Finally, she pulled on a pair of latex gloves.

She turned to the body.

'So, Marcus, I'm just going to take a look at the rest of you before we get to that nasty gash on your neck, okay?'

She sensed Nicholls raising his eyebrows. She didn't give a sweet dime. She examined Marcus's arms and hands, looking for defensive marks. No bruises, which she would expect if he had been violently restrained. From the video it looked as if the perpetrator had pinned him down to stop him struggling. But the lack of bruising would suggest – again – the attack was less brutal than it appeared.

She took several pictures.

'No bruising on the arms, which would indicate the victim didn't struggle.'

'Marcus was wearing a thick sweatshirt,' Nicholls interrupted.

'I'm sorry, sir?'

'That might explain the lack of bruising.'

'Maybe. We can come back to that.'

Barbara hadn't raised the issue of the staged footage yet. She wanted her ducks neatly lined up first. She raised one of the boy's hands. It felt stiff as a mannequin. No scrapes or torn nails, although they were a little long, and dirty.

'Did the doctor take any samples for forensic analysis?' she asked Nicholls.

'That's a little outside of his job description.'

'Of course.'

And he's lazy, Barbara thought.

She squinted. She could see a tiny bit of thread caught in one nail. She crouched down and delved into her backpack. She brought out tweezers and a small plastic baggy. Then she gently plucked the fibre from the nail and dropped it into the bag. She would send any samples back to Anchorage.

She moved back up the body to the boy's throat. The wound was ugly. Messy. To her practised eye, it looked like the teeth that had inflicted the damage had been blunt. That didn't discount a member of the Colony. It took a while for some vampyr's incisors to fully erupt. And some older colony members had been known to file down their distinctive 'fangs', still wary of persecution. But then, it didn't discount a human either. A human jaw didn't pack quite as much power, but our teeth had also evolved to rip and tear meat. She circled, taking photographs.

'Wound consistent with biting. Flesh has been torn, some flesh looks to have been excised, maybe swallowed.'

'He got his throat ripped out?' Nicholls said.

'In layman's terms, yes, sir.'

Barbara reached for another plastic baggy and a scalpel. She took a small sample of flesh from around the wound and dropped it in the bag before sealing it. Vampyr DNA was almost identical to human DNA. Unreliable as evidence, but it could still help back up a case. Finally, she took her moulding equipment out of the bag and started to place the malleable material around the throat wound.

'What are you doing?' Nicholls asked.

'Taking a mould of the bite. It might help establish any distinctive teeth marks.'

'What for?'

Barbara straightened. 'Sir, my job is to collect all the evidence. I would like to see an individual held to account, rather than a mass cull for no good reason.'

Nicholls looked set to argue. Barbara deliberately turned back to Marcus's body and carefully peeled the hardened mould off. She dropped it into another baggy. And then she paused. Something else had caught her attention. A mark on Marcus's shoulder. She frowned.

'Chief, can you just help me roll Marcus a little here?'

He sighed but acquiesced, gently helping her roll the stiff body to the right. Barbara peered at Marcus's back. The skin was darker and mottled here, where the blood had started to settle, but she could still make out a distinctive tattoo just above his left shoulder blade: two black stakes forming a cross over a pair of sharp incisors. Barbara's stomach turned.

'You see this?' she said to Nicholls.

'I see it.' His voice was tight.

'You know what it is?'

In an irritated tone: 'This is Alaska, Detective, not the other side of the moon. It's a Helsing tattoo.'

She nodded. 'A hate symbol. Supporting the genocide of vampyrs.'

'Kids get all sorts of tattoos.'

'Not like this. Far as I know, most tattooists wouldn't undertake this piece of work. Gets back to them, they lose their licence.'

The tattoo was a strong statement. Akin to a swastika. It troubled Barbara that a fifteen-year-old had a tattoo like this. She took several photos, then let Marcus's body roll back on to the steel table. She peeled off her latex gloves.

'Why wasn't this in the report?' she asked Nicholls. 'Surely Dr Dalton must have noticed it?'

His jaw tightened. 'The kid had a tattoo. Kids do shitty things to rebel, to piss off their parents. Doesn't mean he was a bad kid. It's not relevant.'

'It's not up to you to decide what is relevant.'

'Well, maybe I knew this would happen. You would judge Marcus, even though he's the victim here. Even though some creature tore his throat out and bled him dry, you're making it his fault.' Nicholls's voice had risen. He glared at her.

'That's certainly not what I intended,' Barbara said steadily.

'The fact is, this is a Colony killing. You said it yourself. You saw the video.'

'I did indeed, sir.'

9

'And though this world, with devils filled,
Should threaten to undo us,
We will not fear, for God hath willed,
His truth to triumph through us.'

A small crowd of about a half a dozen people stood outside the Roadhouse Grill. They held crosses and swayed as they sang; an old hymn Barbara recognized: 'A Mighty Fortress is Our God'.

At the front, leading them, a familiar figure: Colleen Grey, dressed not in grey today but in a flowing black dress coat over a crisp white high-necked blouse. Attire that wouldn't have looked out of place at the turn of the last century. Her assistant, Grace, stood beside her, dressed in a similar outfit but in pale blue.

Barbara wondered that they weren't both a matching shade of blue from the cold. The dress coats couldn't be that thick and Barbara was still chilly in a thick knee-length duffel coat.

'Let goods and kindred go,
This mortal life also.
The body they may kill:
God's truth abideth still,
His Kingdom is for ever.'

'Then you have all you need.'

'The video isn't conclusive evidence.'

'It . . . *what*?'

'I believe it might have been staged.'

'You think Marcus *staged* his own death?'

'That's not what I said. I said I think the *video* might have been staged.' She sighed. 'Let's put Marcus's body back and then we can sit down and talk through –'

The door to the kitchen suddenly swung open. Barbara and Nicholls turned.

Carly stood in the entrance, a cigarette dangling from her fingers, face grim.

'You better come outside. We got company.'

The singing finished. The crowd stood still, crosses aloft. Nicholls glared around at them, his gaze settling on the preacher.

'What are you doing here, Colleen?'

Not *Reverend*, Barbara noticed.

Colleen smiled. 'We came to give you our blessing, Chief. You and Detective Atkins. To share the strength of God and hope that He guides you in this difficult time.'

Nicholls scowled. 'Well, I'm sure we both appreciate that, but right now we have work to do.'

'When are you going to call a cull?' someone shouted.

Barbara turned in the direction of the voice. 'I'm afraid I can't discuss that, sir. Right now, I'm still collecting evidence.'

'We all know who's responsible.' A woman at the front. Grey-haired, worn face.

'Well, in that case, you have nothing to worry about, ma'am.' Barbara smiled.

'We could have had their heads ourselves by now,' a thickset man in a trapper hat and overalls muttered.

'I'm sure you don't mean that literally, sir.'

'*Damn vampyr lover!*'

This shout came from the back of the group. Barbara tensed. She had been in situations like this before. These weren't bad people, or at least she hadn't been given any cause to think so, not yet. But they were angry, and scared and grief-stricken. When all those things rubbed up against each other, like dry tinder, things could ignite. It didn't take much to turn an unhappy crowd into an angry mob.

'Well . . . why did no one invite me to this party?'

59

A ripple ran through the group. A short figure marched down the street, resplendent in a bright crimson snowsuit and matching bobble hat. Rita. She walked up to the front, placing herself between Barbara and Colleen Grey. Then she put her hands on her hips and looked around appraisingly.

'You know, as mayor, I should really be informed about organized gatherings in the town.'

Colleen smiled, but it looked stiff. 'The work of God cannot always stick to a schedule.'

Rita nodded. 'Well, the work of the police can. So perhaps all you good folks could get back about your business and let these officers get about theirs.' She cast an eye around the crowd. 'Maggie Dawson, I need to talk to you about my gutter later. See what sealants you got in stock. And Layton, you still need to renew your hunting licence for next year.' She raised an eyebrow. 'So, I'm sure we've all got plenty to be getting on with.'

There were mumbles and shuffling, and then, slowly, one by one, the crowd began to disperse.

Only Colleen Grey remained. Statuesque and statue still, seemingly unbothered by the interruption. Grace stood a pace or two behind her, eyes downcast, silent. If it wasn't for the singing, Barbara might have thought she was mute.

'I'm sorry if our gathering has caused a problem, Rita,' Colleen said steadily.

Rita beamed at her. 'Not at all, Colleen. I'm always glad to see folk come together. I just don't want anything holding up the chief and Detective Atkins. Seems to me they're doing God's work here too.'

'True.' Colleen turned to Barbara. 'I'm sorry if we've distracted you. Perhaps you could come and visit the church before you leave. We'd love to have you.'

Barbara nodded but felt less inclined to smile back. 'Well, thank you. Maybe I'll do that, ma'am.'

On a cold day in hell, she couldn't help thinking.

Colleen turned and walked away, seeming to glide across the mushy snow. Grace followed, a silent, cold shadow.

'Fucking bitch,' Rita muttered.

Barbara shot her a look of surprise. 'I got the impression you were friendly.'

'I'd jump into bed with Satan before that one.' Rita narrowed her eyes. 'Word to the wise. Keep her on your side but at arm's length.'

Barbara nodded. 'I hear you.'

Rita clapped her hands together. 'Good. Now, I've got some fresh coffee on to fuel those investigative minds. Shall we?'

'Be rude not to,' Nicholls said.

They walked up to the door of the town hall/police department. Rita unlocked it and stepped inside, followed by Nicholls. Barbara paused at the threshold. She felt a tingle run down her spine. *Eyes on her back.* We might have evolved to spend more time staring at our phones than our surroundings, but some of those primal instincts stuck around. She glanced behind her.

A figure dressed in black stood about halfway along the street. Too far away to make out more than a white blur beneath the heavy hood, but Barbara was pretty sure from the frame and posture it was a young male. She was also pretty sure he was staring right at her.

She remembered the kid Al had almost hit with his cab yesterday. Barbara still had the piece of glass in her pocket. Was it the same teenager? Similar clothing, but something told her no. This figure looked taller, broader. Barbara hesitated, wondering if she should approach him or not.

'Hey,' she called out in a friendly tone, taking a step towards him.

The figure didn't reply or move. Then, as she watched, he raised his hand, clenched into a fist. He held it at shoulder height and then struck his fist against his chest. Barbara's throat tightened. A Helsing salute. Representing a stake through the heart. A gesture of hate.

Like the tattoo.

'Hey!' she shouted, less friendly now.

But the word had barely left her mouth before the figure turned and bolted down the street, disappearing behind the general store. Barbara started to jog after him and then stopped, breathing heavily. Who the hell was she kidding? She was an overweight fifty-one-year-old in snow boots.

'*Dammit.*'

She stared down the empty street.

A Helsing salute. A hate tattoo.

Kids will be kids.

And that was the problem.

Let kids be kids and they'll burn the whole damn world down.

10

They sat around Nicholls's desk. Rita plonked three steaming mugs of coffee down and perched on the edge.

'You might be mistaken,' Nicholls said.

Barbara raised an eyebrow. 'I know a Helsing salute when I see one.'

'Can you describe the figure?' Rita asked.

'Dressed all in black. Hood up.'

'Could be any of the local teens.'

'I know.' Barbara bit back the frustration.

'Look –' Nicholls started to say.

Barbara interrupted. 'If you're going to tell me that all kids do shitty things to rebel, or emotions are running high, I think I've got that, thank you.'

He held his hands up. 'Okay. But as you saw from that little display just now, people *are* feeling this one hard. And with Colleen Grey stirring the pot, it will only get worse.'

Barbara considered. 'What's the story with the Reverend?'

'Reverend,' Rita snorted. 'Like hell. That one is baptised in snake oil.'

'She came to town a few years ago,' Nicholls said. 'With that assistant of hers, Grace. Asked for permission to turn a ruined shack on the edge of town into a church.'

'I couldn't really say no,' Rita said. 'Lot of folks in town were keen for a church.'

Barbara nodded. 'Seen a lot of so-called priests turning

up in colony towns. Most just collect their donations and disappear.'

'Well, I had my doubts, but she's stuck around,' Nicholls said.

'Like a bad smell,' Rita added. 'And not all of us are happy with what she's preaching.'

'Which is?'

'Oh, the usual. God will protect the worthy. The spawns of Satan will burn in hell. You know the drill.'

'That I do,' Barbara said wearily. 'Although she doesn't look like a typical fundamentalist.'

'No, she's an odd one, for sure. Cool as a long drink of milk but, make no mistake, that milk is sour.'

A good description, Barbara thought.

Rita sipped her coffee. 'Going back to the boy you saw, you might want to have a word with the school. He should be in class. Kurt Mowlam teaches tenth and eleventh grade. Only 'bout a dozen kids. He'll know who's missing.'

'You should be a detective, Rita.'

'Except,' Nicholls interjected, 'about half the kids are at home this week. Compassionate leave, after what happened to Marcus.'

'And *that* is why I'm not a detective.' Rita chortled. 'Now, while you real cops get on with things, I gotta make some house calls.'

She swigged the rest of her coffee, slid off the desk and headed for the door. As she pulled on her hat, she turned:

'You want me to pick you up some cookies while I'm out, Pete?'

'You need to ask?' Nicholls replied.

Another raspy chuckle and Rita was gone, in a blur of crimson and knitted bobbles.

'She's quite something,' Barbara said to Nicholls.

'She is. Certainly helped this townie settle in when I first arrived.'

'I'm surprised there's enough work here for a full-time mayor.'

'There isn't, and Rita isn't full-time. It's not an official position. More honorary. She fits it in around caring for her mother. She's pretty ill.'

'I'm sorry to hear that.'

He nodded. 'Rita is good with people. Sorts out a lot of minor stuff so I don't have to.'

'I wish I had that talent.'

'Me too.'

They regarded each other with slightly more warmth.

'So,' Nicholls said. 'You want to discuss the phone footage?'

'That I do, sir.'

She opened up her laptop. Nicholls slipped on an ancient pair of glasses, held together on one side with sticky tape. Another one who ate a lot of meals for one, Barbara thought. No one to nag him to *get those damn glasses fixed.*

She pressed play. When the video reached the shot with Marcus's coat in the background, she paused.

'You see, here,' she pointed. 'Hanging on the wall.'

Nicholls frowned, peering at the screen.

'It could be anything.'

'Well, if you think that, you need new glasses more than I thought. It's a coat. Marcus's coat.'

Nicholls continued to stare at the screen. And then he

sighed. A sigh that Barbara recognized. A reluctant admission that she was right, but he was damned if he was going to say it.

'Why would he take his coat off?'

'It was new. He didn't want to get it dirty lying on the ground.'

'That's a presumption.'

'Can you think of any other reason?'

'Even if you're right, it doesn't change anything. We still have a video that shows him being killed . . . by a vampyr.'

'No. We have footage *staged* to make it look as if he is being killed by a vampyr.'

'The boy is dead, Detective. There's no faking that.'

'I know. But this indicates it wasn't a random killing. The fact that Marcus hung his coat up proves he was complicit.'

'In his own murder?'

'Maybe he didn't think he was going to die?'

Nicholls slipped off his glasses, looking thoughtful. 'You think this is a turning gone wrong. Like Todd Danes?'

Barbara considered. She had studied the Danes file. There were certainly similarities. The boys were about the same age. Both killings had taken place at a secluded spot in the woods. But . . . that niggle again.

'I don't know,' Barbara said. 'What I do know is that we have footage that is partly staged. We have a dead boy with a Helsing tattoo and a live one giving a Helsing salute. You don't have to be Hercule Poirot to surmise that there could be something more going on here.'

'Hercule who?'

Barbara shook her head. 'Never mind. There's something else.' She reached into her pocket and took out the crucifix made out of incisors. 'Someone left this in the bathroom next to my room last night.'

Nicholls stared at the makeshift crucifix. His face darkened.

'Wrote me a message, too.' Barbara opened her phone and brought up the photo of the writing on the mirror.

Nicholls read it aloud: '*The sun will be turned into darkness. And the moon into blood.*' He glanced at her. 'Sounds biblical.'

'Doesn't it just?'

'You see anyone hanging around?'

'If I had, I'd be talking to them instead of you.'

She waited, watching as the realization settled on Nicholls's face. He might want her to call this and authorize a cull. He might have gotten used to a quiet life here in Deadhart, but beneath it, he was still a cop.

'Okay,' he said. 'What d'you want to do, Detective?'

'I need to talk to Stephen and Jacob . . . but first I want to look at the crime scene.' She paused. 'I want to see where Marcus died.'

Patience. It was something the girl had learned.

Time moved differently for her. Hours shrunk to minutes, weeks to days, years to weeks. The longer she lived, the more time compressed. A fact of her physiology. If time moved for her as it did for others, she would surely go insane.

Despite this, some days she felt the weight of her existence.

Patience was a necessary tool for survival.

As was the small plastic knife she kept hidden in her mattress.

Her Captor had worn many faces over the years. But she had grown to realize that this one would be the last.

And without her Captor, what would become of her?

She walked over to the window and pulled up the pink blind. While she couldn't see out through the black glass, she knew that an old iron drainpipe ran down the wall outside. She heard the water trickling through it every time there was rainfall or a thaw. She could tell, even without seeing it, that the pipe leaked a little. Not much. But enough, over time, to have penetrated the wall around the window frame, seeping through the cracks in the mortar and brick, making the interior wall soft and damp.

Using the plastic knife, she had started to scrape away at the plaster around the bars. Just a tiny bit every day. Fragments, crumbs, scooping it out and then loosely packing it back, pulling the blind so that her Captor wouldn't notice.

The process was painstaking. It had taken months, years, decades. But finally, the bars were beginning to loosen. Just a little. Not enough to remove them. Not yet. But soon. Once that happened, she would break the glass and escape.

She took out the plastic knife and began to dig away.

The murmuring in her mind increased. The tingling in her bones itched.

She was hungry. So hungry.

Often, during her captivity, she had craved the release of death.

But the purpose of all living things is to exist.

And to feed.

11

Tucker couldn't sleep. Normally, he would crash around dawn and wake at some point in the afternoon. Today, dawn had snuck up on him, casting a silvery light around the small cabin, where he still sat in his worn armchair, next to the cold embers of last night's fire.

After Athelinda had left, he had come inside and locked the door. Then he had turned on all the lights, lit the fire and sat, sinking bourbon straight from the bottle and mulling over their conversation:

'Why have you come back?'

'This is our home.'

'It's been twenty-five years.'

'The blink of an eye.'

He had sighed heavily. 'How is Merilyn?'

'Dying. But most of her died when she lost her family.'

'I'm sorry.'

'You fucking should be.'

'It wasn't –'

'Your fault. No, never is. Typical human. Sometimes, I think I should have left you in the forest.'

'Maybe you should.'

A smile. 'No, I think I like you better like this.'

'What do you want from me, Athelinda?'

'Talk to the town. Tell them we didn't kill the boy.'

70

The boy. Marcus Anderson. Tucker might be a semi-recluse out here in the woods, but he still had his sources. He had heard about the killing. It was tragic. But it wasn't any of his business. Not any more.

'They won't listen to me,' he said.

'Make them. This is a warning. We won't run this time. They come for us, *any* of us, we'll kill them in their beds. All of them. The mothers, the kids, the babies.'

She had glared at him with those slanted amber eyes, fierce as a wolf's, cold as death.

'You do that, you'll sign a death warrant for every other colony in the country. Play nice.'

She reached forward and picked up his drink. Smiling, she raised it to her lips.

Then she bit down hard, crunching on the glass. She spat the bloody shards out on to the deck.

'I'm not playing, Tucker.'

And then she was gone, like a gust of something foul.

Tucker stared into the fire's dead embers. *Make them.*

Yeah, right. To most of the townsfolk, he was an embarrassment. A pathetic recluse. A shameful failure who had failed to bring the killer of a young boy to justice. No one cared about Jensen Tucker. And those that did only cared that he wasn't dead yet. They'd be packing the church at his funeral. Just so they could spit on his grave.

He picked up the bottle of bourbon and then realized it was empty. He walked into the kitchen. Another bottle sat beside the cooker. The good stuff. He pulled the stopper out of the bottle and poured a small glass. He felt the heat in his stomach. An addict about to get their fix. He glanced out of the window.

Something grey hung on a tree at the edge of his clearing, next to the carcass of the slaughtered pig.

Tucker frowned. It looked like a jacket.

He debated with himself and then, reluctantly, pushed the glass away and strode back into the living room. He shoved the front door open, jogged down the porch steps and crossed to the tree.

He looked around. Who had left this here? Athelinda? Someone else?

He unhooked the jacket from the branch. New from the look of it. Except for a few rust-coloured stains around the collar. He felt his throat constrict.

A new, grey jacket with blood on it.

Instinctively, he found himself checking the pockets. His hand closed over something. Small, metallic and circular.

He pulled it out . . . and felt all the breath leave his body. *'Goddammit.'*

12

'The cabin's about ten minutes out of town and a short hike through the woods.'

Barbara wondered what Nicholls's definition of a 'short hike' was and decided she didn't want to know. She gazed out of the truck's window as they cruised along Main Street. Past Harty Snacks Café, past the general store with its self-loving Santa, past Dead Cool Clothing, Hart's Hardware and Deadhart Surgery. That reminded her . . .

'I still need to talk to Dr Dalton,' she said.

'Doc only works out of the surgery a couple of days a week,' Nicholls told her. 'Other than that, he sees patients at his house, up near Deep Hollow Lake.'

'Right. The lake formed in a deep hollow by any chance?'

He managed a small smile. 'Folks here do like to call a spade a spade.'

A larger, more modern, single-storey building drew into view on their right.

'Deadhart School,' Nicholls said. 'Elementary on one side. The other part is the high school.'

'That work out?'

'Has so far.'

Barbara could see a few younger children outside the school, playing tag. Too young to understand that dark clouds were gathering. Too young to realize that life was finite. Necessarily so. At eight you wanted to live for ever. At eighty you were glad that everything had its time.

After the school, the dregs of the town fell away. Buildings became sparser. A sign on their right pointed up a side road: 'Garrett's Tours – explore the beauty of Denali National Park with trusted, knowledgeable guides. Hiking, snowmobiles, wilderness camps, Colony tours.'

'Stephen's parents live up there and run their tour company,' Nicholls said.

'What about Jacob and his father?'

'They live on the other side of town.'

Said in a terser, more dismissive tone. *The other side.* A curl of distaste.

They were almost out of buildings when the cross drew into view. At least seven foot tall, planted firmly in the ground at the side of the road. Behind it, a short dirt track led to a modest-looking wooden building. A sign hung from the cross.

CHURCH OF THE HOLY CROSS.

'Nice,' Barbara murmured. 'Literal, right?'

'Colleen wanted to make sure people didn't miss the place.'

'I can see that.' Barbara peered closer. Her stomach lurched.

'Could you stop the truck a second?'

Reluctantly, Nicholls pulled to a halt. Barbara hopped out and walked over to the cross. From a distance it looked like it was constructed from two large, solid pieces of wood. Up close, Barbara could see that it was actually made up of numerous small bundles of wood bound together. Used stakes. Their sharp ends stained russet with dried blood.

A small sign at the bottom of the cross read:

This cross has been constructed with the tools of God and the weapons of His holy war. We will persevere.

'They're old,' Nicholls said as he joined her. 'Not illegal.'

Barbara rolled her eyes. 'A lot of things aren't illegal. Doesn't make them right.'

Nicholls stared at her. 'Come with me. I want you to see something.'

Barbara followed him down the dirt track, past the church. A large clearing had been created here between the straggly birch trees. At the entrance, a rough wooden board hung between two posts: DEADHART CEMETERY. Barbara could see a haphazard array of headstones and other markers poking up through the snow. Spirit Houses, crosses. At the far end of the clearing, a group of four men tended a roaring fire.

Barbara frowned. 'What are they doing?'

'Warming the earth,' Nicholls said. 'For Marcus's grave.'

'His body still needs to be sent to Anchorage for autopsy.'

'This time of year, it can take days, even weeks, to dig deep enough. The earth is as hard as granite. Everyone in the town will help. They'll take it in shifts, using pickaxes and drills. If they don't, Marcus's parents will have to wait till the spring thaw to bury him. Their only child. Murdered, and still not laid to rest.'

'I'm sorry.'

Nicholls nodded, face grim. 'So, maybe you don't get to be the judge of what's *right* around here.'

He turned and strode back towards the truck. One of the men threw another log on to the fire. The flames leapt and crackled. Barbara sighed – *well done keeping your only ally on side* – and walked slowly after him.

They drove off again in silence.

'Cabin' was something of a generous description for the heap of rotted wood that lurched lopsidedly among the dark spruces.

Nicholls shook his head. 'Never understood why kids like to hang around places like this.'

'You don't have kids yourself?'

'Nope. You?'

'No, but I remember being one.'

As a teenager, Barbara and her best friend had made dens in the forest near the river. Constructed of fallen branches and twigs, covered in moss and dead leaves. They were basic and flimsy. But they were *theirs*. Being a kid was tough. Being a teen was even tougher. You're told you're almost an adult but with none of the power that adults have. You're still helpless, still trapped in between. Teens needed escape. Places like this. A barely held together structure of rotten, falling-down wood. But it belonged to *them*.

'It's just us here, Babs. They can't touch us.'

She pushed open the creaky door, which was barely hanging on by two loose hinges.

The cabin was dark inside, lit by a few shards of wintry light slipping in through the many gaps in the wood and a larger hole in the roof. There was no real furniture apart from a few upturned crates. Melted candles were dotted around the place, along with crushed beer cans and the stubs of cigarettes and joints. Just what she would expect. About the only thing missing were a few discarded condoms.

'We searched it thoroughly before,' Nicholls said, defensively.

'I'm sure you did, sir,' Barbara replied. 'I'm not really looking for anything you've missed.'

Not entirely true. Barbara hoped there might be *something* Nicholls had missed or at least not registered. Fresh eyes often found fresh evidence.

She reached into her pocket and took out her flashlight. She flicked it on and scanned the floor. Easy to spot where Marcus had died. Despite most of the blood having been removed, there was still a large dark stain. She moved around the cabin, shining the flashlight around the corners and over the walls. On the right-hand side of the ram-shackle building, she spied a rusty nail sticking out of the splintered wood. She walked over and looked more closely. Something grey and wispy was caught on it. A thread. This was where the coat had been hung.

'You see this?' She turned to Nicholls.

He walked over and squinted at the thread. 'Just about,' he said.

Barbara extracted a plastic bag from her backpack and slipped the thread inside. Not that she had the boy's coat to compare it to, but still, you had to be like a magpie in this job. Pick up the things that caught your eye and hope-fully use them to feather your nest of evidence.

She looked back around the room, trying to picture what could have happened here. The boys had met up as usual. Text messages confirmed it. They had hung out, smoked a little weed, drunk a little beer. Nothing out of

77

the ordinary. At some point they had left, Marcus had come back for his phone – or maybe to rendezvous with someone else – and that was when he had been killed.

'What are you thinking?' Nicholls asked.

She wasn't sure. Something about this scenario just wasn't sitting right somehow, and she wasn't sure why.

'Let's run through it again,' she said. 'The boys came up here at what time?'

'Around seven, seven thirty.'

'How long would you say it takes to walk here from town?'

'Around half an hour, forty minutes maybe.'

'The timestamp on the video was 9.18 p.m. Stephen and Jacob said they last saw Marcus around 9 p.m., when they were halfway home, and he realized he'd left his phone in the cabin and went back for it. Yes?'

'Ye-es.' Said more cautiously as Nicholls saw where she was going with this.

'What time did Stephen's parents say he got home?'

'Around 10 p.m.'

'Why did it take so long? Must have only been a twenty-minute walk.'

'Maybe the boys waited for Marcus.'

'You told me that they didn't wait. *Boys don't stick together like girls.*'

Nicholls shook his head and touched his moustache again. Barbara noticed he did that when he was feeling uncomfortable. He should have caught this himself. Or maybe he did and just didn't want to think about it too much.

'It might mean nothing,' he said eventually.

'And it might mean everything.'

Barbara looked around the cabin again, letting it soak in, breathing in the smell: stale beer and weed, the cloying aroma of spruce. Beneath it all, the faint irony tang of blood. Death had come here, she thought. And it had been hungry. Ravenous. And there was something else too. Anger. Fear. Hatred.

Her head whipped around. A noise from outside. A flurry of birds taking flight.

'You hear that?'

'What?'

Barbara crossed the cabin quickly, yanking open the door and almost pulling it off its hinges. She was just in time to see a slight, blonde girl turn and disappear between the trees. Barbara hurried down the cabin's steps, slowing as she reached the edge of the woods. Easy to get lost in woods like these, if you didn't know the area. She walked a little way into the trees' embrace, conscious of keeping the cabin in sight behind her. She stared around. The girl was probably long gone . . .

And then she saw her. Standing a short distance away, half shrouded in the gloom of the thick spruce. She was dressed in what looked like an assortment of animal skins and her white-blonde hair hung over her shoulders in two long pigtails. Barbara didn't believe in ghosts, but for a moment, she looked just like . . .

Mercy.

The girl stepped forward and Barbara realized her damn foolishness. Not Mercy. How could it be? This girl was much younger, for a start. And her skin was pale. Mercy's skin had been dark, in striking contrast to her hair.

79

And when they drowned her for the fifth or sixth time, it floated like silvery seaweed in the river.

Barbara swallowed. 'You okay, sweetheart? You lost?'

She asked the question even though she was pretty sure the girl wasn't lost. Or a little girl.

'Who's Mercy?' the girl asked.

Ice slithered down Barbara's spine. She hadn't said the name out loud. She forced a smile, and the effort made her cheeks hurt. 'Just an old friend. What's your name?'

'You don't need to know, old woman.' The girl cocked her head slightly to one side. 'You a cop?'

'A detective.'

The girl nodded. 'Then you go tell that fuckwit chief that the Colony didn't kill the boy.'

Barbara flinched a little at the swearword. She was sure the girl had meant her to.

'You from the Colony?' she asked steadily.

The girl smiled, revealing sharp, gold incisors. Her natural incisors must have been broken, or removed, at some point.

'You catch on fast,' she said.

'You know about the murder?'

'I make it my business to know what goes on in the *human* settlement.' She spat out the word 'human' as though it tasted bad.

'Then maybe you could tell me who *did* kill the boy?'

The girl's amber eyes appraised her. 'Look closer to home.'

'Deadhart?'

'Ask 'em about the Bone House.'

'The Bone House?'

80

'You heard me. And keep the fuck away from the Colony.'

Before Barbara could ask anything else, the girl was gone, melting into the woods, like she had simply dissolved.

This time Barbara didn't try to follow. She traipsed back to the cabin, feeling unnerved. *Mercy.* Why had she thought of her? That memory had been buried a long time ago. But as the saying went – *Bad memories are harder to bury than a vampyr.*

Nicholls stood outside the cabin, looking worried and annoyed.

'Where the hell did you go?'

'There was someone outside. I followed them into the woods.'

'Well, that was a foolish thing to do.'

Barbara ignored him. 'It was a girl. Young, blonde. I think she was from the Colony.'

She saw something in Nicholls's face. A tiny twitch.

'You know her?'

'The leader of the Colony is a blonde girl called Athelinda. Centuries old but turned when she was a child.'

Barbara felt a chill grip her stomach. There was a reason why turning children had long ago been outlawed by the colonies. A turned child would never mature. Their physical development would simply stop. But their mind would continue to grow, to absorb experiences, gain knowledge. A centuries-old mind forever trapped in the body of a child. Most went slowly mad. Those who managed to maintain their sanity did so at a cost.

'I've heard she's dangerous,' Nicholls continued. 'Plenty of stories about hikers who disappeared in the mountains over the years.'

'Plenty of stories about Bigfoot, too . . .'

He gave her a look. 'If she's down here, this close to town, it means trouble.'

'She said the Colony didn't kill the boy.'

'Well, I guess she would.'

'She also said something about looking closer to home, and "the Bone House"?'

He frowned. 'No idea. But I wouldn't put too much store in anything she has to say. Most folk say she's insane.' And then, more crisply: 'Are we done here?'

'I guess so. For now.'

'Then we should get moving.' He glanced around. 'It'll be dark soon.'

He walked away. Barbara followed, still frowning. *The Bone House*. There was something there, she thought. Nicholls's denial was too quick. He knew what it was, but he didn't want to tell her. Which only made her more curious.

Still, she agreed with him about one thing. Athelinda was dangerous. In fact, there was nothing *more* dangerous than a child with power . . . and a few centuries' worth of resentment.

13

Beau hadn't been expecting the knock at the door.

But he had been waiting for it.

Like a lot of things, it wasn't a case of *if* but *when*.

He put down his mug, rose from his chair and walked down the hall.

For a moment he paused, composing himself. Then, with a sense of resignation, he unlocked the door and pulled it open.

The man outside was compact, and well dressed. His silver hair was neatly styled, and he sported a small goatee beard. He didn't really fit in in Deadhart. Never had. But he was a good doctor. He'd been kind to Patricia when she was ill, and for that Beau was always grateful.

'Dr Dalton,' Beau said. 'To what do I owe the home visit?'

'Oh, you know I like to check in on my favourite patients.'

A lie. Dalton hadn't checked in on Beau since Patricia died.

He was here for a reason. And Beau was pretty sure he knew what. You didn't take your dog to the vet for their final visit. You had them put down at home.

'Come on through,' he said, holding out his arm for Dalton to step inside.

He shut the door and led Dalton down to the living room.

'Well, well!' Dalton stopped and stared at the mounted heads on the wall. Two mature males. One adolescent.

Beau smiled. 'You always admired my trophies.'

'I did. I'm pleased to see them back up on the wall where they belong.'

Patricia had made Beau keep them in his work shed. Said they 'gave her the creeps'.

Dalton walked up to the trophies, reached out and stroked the cheek of the young male.

'Handsome devil.'

Beau supposed he was. Jet-black hair, slanted green eyes, alabaster skin. But 'devil' was the right word.

'There was a time when every hunter's lodge would have a dozen of these mounted on the walls,' Beau said. 'We were proud of who we were. And it kept the colonies in their place. They knew what would happen if they stepped out of bounds. Now –' He shook his head in disgust. 'If we kill them, we're the criminals. What kind of crap is that?'

'True,' Doc Dalton said. 'Those were easier times, Beau.' He was still staring at the heads. 'They ever talk to you?'

Beau turned sharply. 'What?'

'Some folks believe vampyrs can still communicate, even after they're dead. Like the colonies have some kind of hive mind?'

'You hear that, old man? A hive mind. Maybe you're not losing yours after all.'

'Pile of baloney,' Beau said, tone sharper than he meant it to be.

Dalton chuckled. 'That's what I think. Dead is dead, right?' He looked back at the heads. 'You know, if you ever want to sell them . . .'

'I've told you before, they're not for sale.'

'Some people would pay big bucks for heads like these.'

84

'I said no.'

'Okay. But if you change your mind . . .'

'I won't.'

Beau walked away from the trophies, indicating their conversation was over. 'Now, you have something to tell me?'

'Shall we sit?'

'Do I need to?'

Dalton smiled. Beau didn't find it comforting. It was the smile he used to put on when he gave Patricia bad news.

'I think we'd be more comfortable,' he said.

Reluctantly, Beau settled in his worn armchair. Dalton took the other one.

'So, how have you been, Beau?'

'Fine.'

'Except for the voices, right? You didn't mention those to the Doc?'

Beau brushed at his ear like he was batting at a troublesome insect. The Doc was preoccupied taking some papers out of his briefcase. He settled them on his lap and smiled again.

'I got your results back from the MRI and the other tests.'

'Okay.'

Beau straightened a little in his chair.

'I know you've been worried about going down the same path as Patricia. Like I told you, I couldn't see any real indicators. Being a bit forgetful and misplacing things is just something that happens as we get older. And headaches and dizziness can have lots of causes.'

'You told me all this,' Beau snapped.

'Okay. Well, the tests don't show any indicators for dementia or Alzheimer's.'

Beau felt the relief course through him. 'Thank God.'

'Yes.' Dalton nodded. 'That's the good news.'

'The good news?' Beau felt something stir in the pit of his stomach. He didn't like the look on the Doc's face. 'Is there bad news?'

Dalton sighed. 'I'm afraid the MRI picked up something else.'

14

'So, where to next?' Nicholls asked as they climbed back into the truck.

'Well,' Barbara said, just as her stomach rumbled, long and loud.

Nicholls gave her a look. 'How 'bout we grab a bite to eat?' He checked his watch. 'It's after three thirty.'

And almost totally dark, Barbara thought, staring out of the window. 'Sounds like a plan,' she said.

They trundled down the bumpy track back towards town, past the Church of the Holy Cross and Deadhart School. It had started to snow, and the wipers squeaked as they mushed the large flakes across the screen. Nicholls pulled up outside the police department.

'Harty Snacks serves decent burgers and sandwiches,' he said.

'Carbs are always good by me.'

They strolled across the road. Fairy lights adorned the windows of the café. A bright sign shaped like a heart hung above the door. As they drew closer, Barbara could see the heart was pierced by a stake. She sighed.

'You don't get to be the judge of what's right around here.'

Despite the darkness and bitter chill, a couple of tables and chairs had been arranged, somewhat optimistically, under heaters outside.

'People sit out in these temperatures?' Barbara asked, her breath fogging in front of her face.

'Only tourists,' Nicholls replied, pushing open the door.

A cheery bell rang as they entered. Inside, it was warm and cozy. Half a dozen mismatched tables and chairs jostled for space. A serving counter ran along one side with a display case full of bagels and muffins. The café smelt (confusingly) of fried bread, fish and some unidentifiable cooked meat.

A few other patrons sat sipping hot drinks and munching on baked goods. A middle-aged man wearing glasses. Two older, grey-haired women, and a mother with a young daughter. All heads surreptitiously swivelled as Barbara and Nicholls walked in. Nicholls nodded pleasantly. Barbara smiled. Only the small child grinned back. Then she turned to her mother and said loudly: 'Is that the vampyr supersizer, Mommy.'

'Shhhh,' the woman hushed. And then added: 'It's *sympathizer*, sweetheart.'

Great. Barbara turned to the counter. A young woman with blonde hair in a messy bun stood behind it. She offered Barbara a pleasant smile but addressed herself to Nicholls:

'Afternoon, Chief. You here for some muffins to take back to the office?'

'Actually, Kitty,' Nicholls said, 'we're running a little late for lunch today so maybe a burger and coffee.'

He glanced at Barbara. She wasn't really hungry any more, but she looked up at the menu on the wall.

- Reindeer sausage and eggs
- Reindeer dog
- Reindeer pancakes
- Wild boar, bison and reindeer burger

Santa would have real trouble finding a guide for his sleigh out here, Barbara thought.

'And what would you like?' Kitty asked.

'Erm, you got anything without reindeer?'

'Fry bread or a salmon burrito?'

'I'll take the burrito, thanks, and a strong coffee with milk, please.'

Kitty jotted down the orders and poured their coffees. The sound of running water made Barbara realize she needed to empty her bladder.

'Could I use your restroom?' she asked.

'Straight down, at the back.'

'Thanks.'

Barbara walked through the café, feeling eyes crawling over her. She pushed open the door to the Ladies. It was small. Just a single toilet and sink. But it looked pretty clean, except for some graffiti on the walls. She locked the door behind her and struggled out of her thick clothes to use the toilet.

She studied the graffiti. The usual mix of scrawled names, cartoon drawings . . . and there it was again, the Helsing symbol.

Barbara flushed, re-dressed and walked to the sink to wash her hands. A few stickers had been stuck on the wall around the mirror. *Al's Cabs*, *Talkeetna Air Taxis*, *Garretts Tours*, and a newer-looking one: *Be Damned Tattooists, Anchorage*. Interesting. Barbara dried her hands on a paper towel, then took a quick picture of the sticker.

She emerged from the restroom to find that Nicholls had sat down with the coffees at a table near the counter. As she made her way over, she almost fell over the foot of the middle-aged man with glasses, catching her balance just in time.

'Watch where you're going,' he snarled.

Barbara bit back a retort and walked up to Nicholls. 'Let's get some fresh air.'

Nicholls raised an eyebrow. 'O-kay.'

They picked up their coffees, exited the café and sat down on the seats closest to the heater.

'You don't mind the cold?' Nicholls asked.

Barbara shivered. 'I'd rather endure the chill out here than in there.'

'Try not to take it personally,' he said. 'It's not you. It's the situation.'

'Yessir. And I'm the one causing the situation.'

She gazed out across Main Street. Christmas lights twinkled in the darkness; snow glistened on rooftops. She could see the white tips of the Denali mountains in the distance, illuminated by a shy sliver of moon, and hear the call of moose and the wind rustling in the spruce. A reminder that whatever small space humans carved out upon this planet, nature, in all its callous ferocity, was never far away. She lifted her coffee to her lips and then paused.

A figure was walking down the middle of the road. A man. Broad and tall. Over six and a half foot, at a guess. As he drew closer, Barbara could see he was dressed in a long oilskin, cowboy hat and carrying a backpack.

For some reason, she felt her stomach tighten and the hairs on her neck shiver.

Beside her, Nicholls muttered: 'What the hell?'

A few other people out on the street stopped and stared as the man passed.

Nicholls shoved his chair back and stepped out into the road. Barbara noticed his hand hover near his gun.

'Can I help you?'

The man raised his head. Thick beard, black skin, dark eyes.

'Chief Nicholls.' The man smiled, flashing surprisingly white teeth in the worn face. 'Good to see you.' His voice was low and warm.

Nicholls didn't return the smile. 'What are you doing here?'

The man ignored him and glanced at Barbara. 'I'm guessing this is Detective Atkins from the DFVA.' He tipped his hat. 'Ma'am.'

Barbara rose. 'Pleasure to meet you, sir. Although you have me at a disadvantage – I don't think I caught your name?'

'Jensen Tucker, ma'am.'

Her eyebrows shot up. The former chief. Now, a recluse living in the woods. But here he was, large as life and twice as big.

'What are you doing back in town, Tucker?' Nicholls asked, tone still unfriendly.

'I needed to talk to you.'

'What about?'

'The boys' murder.'

'You mean Marcus Anderson?'

'I mean . . . both of them.'

15

Tucker looked uncomfortable inside the police department. Barbara got the impression that it was a while since he had seen civilization – if you could call Deadhart civilization. Or maybe he was uneasy being back in his old office, with another man wearing his badge.

She found herself studying the man again. He had taken his hat off, revealing long grey dreadlocks, tied loosely back. He must be in his early sixties by now and, despite the heavy beard and creases around his eyes, he was wearing it well. Isolation must suit him.

After his appearance in the street, Nicholls and Barbara had taken their lunch to go and carried it with them across the road. Rita was out, so Barbara pulled her chair over for Tucker. Nicholls sat down at his desk and started silently devouring his burger, seemingly intent upon giving Tucker the shortest shrift he could manage.

Barbara pushed her own paper-wrapped burrito to one side. Tucker watched her hungrily.

'Would you like some?' she said. 'It's only going to waste otherwise.'

'No,' Tucker shook his head. 'It's fine.'

Yet his eyes said different. Barbara glanced at Nicholls, who was still ignoring the older man. She sighed.

'So,' she said to Tucker. 'You wanted to talk to us. And,

I'm sure Chief Nicholls will agree, we're eager for any information that can help right now.'

Nicholls grunted and swallowed the remains of his burger. He made a show of wiping his lips prissily with a napkin.

Tucker shifted in his chair. He was too big for it. He was too big for most places, Barbara guessed. Outside, his height made him formidable. Inside, it made him hunched and awkward, like a giant in Lilliput.

'I have to show you this,' he said.

He reached down to the backpack on the floor by his chair. He unzipped it and pulled something out, which he laid on the desk. Barbara felt her heart jolt. A grey jacket. North Face. Russet stains all around the neck and front.

'Where did you get that?' she asked.

'I found it hanging on a tree outside my cabin this morning.'

She met Nicholls's eyes. Now he was paying attention.

'Marcus's jacket,' he said.

Tucker nodded. 'That's what I thought.'

'How d'you know about Marcus?' Nicholls asked.

'I keep my ear to the ground.'

Nicholls rolled his eyes. 'Rita.'

'We exchange the odd message.'

'Any idea who left the jacket?' Barbara asked, eager to keep Tucker on track.

He hesitated. 'I didn't see.'

That wasn't what Barbara had asked, but she let it slide.

'Any idea *why* they left it for you?' Nicholls asked.

'I think it's a message.'

93

'What sort of message?'

A hesitation, and then Tucker said, 'I found something else, inside the pocket.'

He reached into the coat pocket and drew out a small metallic object. He placed it on the desk.

A ring. Silver, inscribed with symbols that Barbara recognized. Vampyric.

She picked the ring up and turned it over in the light. 'This is a "becoming" ring.'

'A what?' Nicholls asked.

'It's given to colony children when they reach puberty. That's when the ageing process begins to slow. The ring is to signify the transition to becoming "immortal". It's engraved with their name and the date.'

'And?' Nicholls questioned.

'You read the file on Todd Danes's murder?' Tucker said.

'Yes.' Gruffly. Defensively.

Tucker glanced at Barbara. She held his gaze. 'Todd Danes was having a relationship with a young Colony member, Aaron Berkoff,' she said. 'According to Aaron, Todd wanted to be turned so they could be together. They agreed to meet in the woods to perform the turning. But something went wrong, and Todd bled out.'

Tucker nodded. 'Aaron made one of these rings to give to Todd, on his turning.' He paused. 'We never found it.'

'How can we be sure it's the same ring?' Nicholls asked.

Barbara showed him the ring, running her finger over the crude engraving.

'See here. This is the name "Todd" in vampyric . . . and this is the date.' She glanced at Tucker. 'You said you thought it was a message?'

He nodded. 'It always bothered me that we never found the ring – and Aaron swore Todd was alive when he left him.'

'So why did Aaron plead to manslaughter?' Nicholls asked.

Tucker's dark eyes flashed. 'Because I promised him that no one would touch the rest of the Colony and he would have a fair trial.' He shook his head. 'But that wasn't how it played out.'

No, Barbara thought. According to witnesses, Aaron's father and uncle tried to break Aaron out of his cell. A group of the town's men hunted the trio down and killed them. An unauthorized cull. But no one had been prosecuted. Tucker had quietly resigned, and the Colony had fled. End of story. Until now.

Barbara considered. 'Are you suggesting someone *else* killed Todd? And *they* took the ring?'

'I think . . . it's possible.'

'And if the same person left the ring in Marcus's coat pocket' – Barbara felt something run through her like a current – 'then it's possible that the same person killed him, too.'

Nicholls broke in. 'We're getting way ahead of ourselves. We don't know how this ring got into Marcus's coat pocket. For all we know, Aaron could have taken it back after he killed Todd. He could have given it to someone else in the Colony. Maybe Marcus simply found it in the woods.'

Tucker nodded slowly. 'Also possible.'

Damned with faint agreement, Barbara thought.

'Okay,' she said. 'But bearing in mind this new evidence,

95

I think we should go over both cases again and look for any similarities, even if it's just to rule out the possibility that this is the same perpetrator.' She looked back at Tucker. 'Mr Tucker, you were chief here when Todd Danes was killed. It might help us if –'

Nicholls cut her off. 'No. Absolutely not. We cannot have him privy to sensitive information during this inquiry.'

Barbara bristled. 'He could offer us valuable insight.'

Nicholls rolled his eyes. 'And he could screw up this case like he screwed up last time.'

Tucker rose. Barbara tensed, wondering if he was about to launch himself across the desk and punch the smaller man. Instead, he picked up his hat and glanced at Barbara. 'Good to meet you, Detective Atkins. Good luck with the case.'

'Thank you, sir,' Barbara said. 'And what should we do if we need to contact you again?'

'I doubt that will be necessary,' Nicholls said.

'But if it is?' Barbara persisted.

Tucker regarded her sombrely. 'If you need me, there's an ancient dead spruce, past the final turn out of town. Can't miss it. Walk one hundred yards north into the woods till you reach a small clearing. There's a fallen log there. Leave your message in the hollow of the log and it'll reach me.'

Barbara raised an eyebrow. 'Really? Will the termites deliver it to you, sir?'

Tucker kept a straight face just long enough. Then he pulled a battered cellphone out of his coat. 'You can get me on this . . . if the wind is blowing in the right direction.'

He leaned over the desk and scribbled a number on a corner of Nicholls's jotter.

Barbara tore the page off and pocketed it. 'Much appreciated.'

The big man turned and walked slowly out of the room. There was an awkwardness to his motions, Barbara thought. Like he lived with some pain deep in his bones. She remembered reading that he had been shot attempting to thwart Aaron's jailbreak, but the report hadn't been specific about his injuries. Come to think of it, the whole report had been frustratingly vague.

'He's an enigmatic character,' she remarked to Nicholls, keeping her voice casual.

'That he is,' Nicholls replied. 'Survives mostly by hunting. Keeps a few goats and pigs. Comes into town once every few months for a grocery order. But always after dark. Folks are happier *not* to see him. He's a bad memory.' He scratched at his chin, looking at the ring again. 'You really think the same perp could have killed Todd and Marcus?'

'I don't know,' Barbara said honestly. 'Twenty-five years is a long time for a killer to wait.'

'Or the blink of an eye when you're Colony,' Nicholls pointed out.

'*Or* maybe the killer left town and only just returned. Maybe they haven't waited at all. They've just been satisfying the need elsewhere.'

She looked at him meaningfully.

'You mean Nathan Bell?' he said.

'He was one of Todd's friends.'

'He was only a kid back then.'

'So was Aaron Berkoff.'

'You're still forgetting something – the video. I can tell you, that's not Nathan in the video. The figure is too small.'

The *damn* video. There was still something about it that Barbara was missing.

Why did Marcus film his own death? And if he expected to die, why worry about getting his jacket dirty? The answer was there, but tantalizingly out of reach.

Nicholls shook his head. 'Marcus was bled dry. If he was killed by another human, where's the blood? Nowhere near enough at the scene.'

This was also true. Barbara felt frustration bubble. 'Okay, I hear you. But there's a lot here that just doesn't add up.'

'And I guess that means you won't sign off this case till it does.'

'I wouldn't be doing my job otherwise, sir.'

A deep sigh. 'So what's the plan?'

'I'd like to talk to Stephen and Jacob . . . and Nathan.'

'Okay. Let's make those house calls tomorrow. It's been a long day.'

That it had. Hard to believe it was just over twenty-four hours since she had arrived.

Nicholls looked thoughtful. 'I still say there's a good chance Marcus just found this ring in the woods and put it in his own pocket.'

'So why did someone leave the coat for Tucker to find?' Barbara picked up the small piece of circular metal. 'I don't believe in coincidence. Tucker's right. The ring is a message.'

'From the killer?'

She nodded. 'And if this *is* the same killer . . .' She turned the ring over in her fingers, so it glinted in the light. 'They want us to know it.'

She dozed fitfully. Night and day meant very little to her down here, so sleep was a random thing, taken whenever she grew weary. And she was weary, for once.

The bar was looser than she had expected. It had only taken a little more excavating and then a large lump of plaster had given way and suddenly it was free at the bottom. A few more hours' work and she would be able to remove it completely.

The achievement had elated her, but it meant she had worked for longer than usual, scraping away more plaster than she normally dared. But the tantalizing idea of freedom had spurred her on. She had to force herself to stop, meticulously patting the plaster back into place and pulling the blind. Nothing more could be risked for now. And impatience could make her reckless.

Once she was done, she took herself into the bathroom and washed her hands thoroughly, removing every trace of dirt and plaster. She hid the plastic knife back in her mattress. Her top was a little dusty, but she brushed off as much as she could and turned off some of the lights. Hopefully her Captor wouldn't notice. Then, she curled up on the bed. A nap before her Captor came with food. Her Captor normally brought at least one meal a day. Normally. Sometimes there were aberrations. A day or two missed. She never complained. It didn't do to upset her Captor. Her Captor loved her. To complain would be ungrateful and there might be consequences. Like losing books or entertainment, or worse.

Once, her Captor didn't come to feed her for a longer time. She had wondered if something had happened to them. Had they been hurt?

Or perhaps died? She didn't believe they would just leave her. She had paced the room for hours, trying to quell her panic, and ignore her hunger. In between, she had worked more feverishly on the window, even though she knew she would be unlikely to make her escape before hunger and weakness took her.

Eventually, as she lay in bed, stomach convulsing with agonizing pangs, mouth dry, she had heard the familiar sound of a key turning in the lock above her and the slow tread of footsteps down the cellar stairs. Her Captor was back.

'Hello, darling.'

She jumped. Not a dream or a memory. Real.

Her Captor stood at the bottom of the stairs holding her meal.

She sat up, blinking, momentarily disorientated.

'Did I wake you?' her Captor asked, face creasing in concern. 'I'm sorry.'

'No. It's fine,' she said, sitting up.

'Are you hungry? I can come back.'

'No. I mean, yes, I'm hungry.'

And she was. Her stomach growled in anticipation.

Her Captor lay the tray down on the end of the bed. A small jug half full of rich, red liquid and a glass.

'I'm sorry it's not much,' her Captor said. 'The delivery is late. I just need you to be patient.'

Patient. Oh yes, the girl thought. She was good at that.

She nodded, opening her mouth to reply when her Captor's attention suddenly shifted, face creasing into a frown. The girl followed her Captor's gaze.

On the floor, near the window, lay a small piece of plaster. She must have missed it when she tidied up earlier. Her Captor walked towards the debris.

The girl tensed, mind whirring. If her Captor found out that she had been planning to escape, there would be consequences, and her chance would be gone for ever. She couldn't let that happen. Her eyes flicked to the stairs at the far end of the room. The door was open at the top. She could see a spill of light. Could she make it, if she ran? She was fast, but was she fast enough? Her Captor always made sure they had the means to debilitate her. And what if she reached the upper floor only to find the doors locked?

She needed to make a decision. But time spent here, captive, had left her unused to making choices; impotent, frightened, complicit in her imprisonment.

Her Captor neared the window and bent down. The girl half rose from the bed . . . and then, from above them, came a thump, thump at the front door.

Her Captor looked up. 'The delivery. I have to go.'

'Okay.'

A smile. 'I love you.'

'I know.'

The girl waited until she heard the basement door shut and the key turn. Then she leapt from the bed and ran over to the piece of plaster. Tiny. No more than a large crumb. But it could have ended everything. She debated for a few seconds and then she hurried to the bathroom and flushed it down the toilet. There. Gone.

She collapsed back on the bed. Her stomach rumbled. She poured herself a glass and gulped it down, wrinkling her nose. It was sustenance, but it was rough and poor. She yearned for the taste of something real, something richer.

She pushed the jug away.

Then she rolled up her sleeve. The skin here was shiny. Healed many times. And each, she promised herself, would be her last.

But not today.

She bent her face and placed her mouth over the soft flesh. Then she bit down hard and let the sweet warm fluid fill her mouth.

16

The Roadhouse Grill was even quieter this evening. No one propped up the bar and only a couple of tables were occupied. That suited Barbara just fine. She was tired and she needed some space to think.

The ring that Tucker had found was preying on her mind. *Could* the same individual be responsible for both boys' murders? And if so, did it change anything? The long gap and the nature of Marcus's killing (and that damn video) still all pointed to someone from the Colony.

She sighed and reached for her beer. Part of her felt she needed a clear head to try and work through all of this. Part of her craved the taste of something cold and wheaty to relax the knots in her shoulders and mind.

We all have our vices. Her mom's had been food. Cooking was a way to suppress her anxieties and placate her husband. When the home-made meat loaf and apple pie could no longer suppress his rage and discontent, she began to eat instead of cook: ice cream from the tub, whole boxes of cookies, raw dough and jelly. Debilitated by her own weight, she was unable to see how food had become her jailer rather than comforter.

Her dad's jailer had been bourbon and bigotry. Usually mixed together with a dash of violence for good measure. A small, sinewy man, the yin to her mother's yang, he burned his energy in fury and hatred. Jews, blacks, whores, leftist liberal scum, homos and, of course, vampyrs. In her father's eyes, they were all the source of his poverty, ill health, lack of money and discontent. And of course, he managed to wrap it all up in a righteous religious zeal that justified his bile.

Barbara recognized the symbols of hate – Klan hoods, swastikas, Helsing tattoos, vampyr teeth, stakes – because she had grown up around them. Indoctrinated from an early age about the enemy and how good, white, God-fearing families like theirs had to stand up against those who wanted to take away their land, their livelihoods, their very souls. Maybe she had even believed it when she was young.

And then she had met Mercy.

'Can I get you something?'

She started. Mayflower stood by her table. She wore a Soundgarden sweatshirt tonight and her hair had changed colour, from purple to blood red.

'Sorry,' Barbara said. 'Miles away.'

'Yeah.' The girl raised a cynical eyebrow. 'Wish I was.'

Barbara smiled sympathetically. 'Working here not your life's ambition?'

Mayflower rolled her eyes. 'When I was a little girl, I used to say, "Mommy, when I grow up, I want to work in a shit bar that stores bodies in the freezer. Just like every princess."'

Barbara chuckled, despite herself. 'I guess you're not waiting on Prince Charming either.'

'Damn right.'

'Well, if you care what a middle-aged cop has to say, I grew up in a town like this. My mom didn't want me to leave. Thought joining the police was a betrayal. But I got away.'

'And yet,' Mayflower spread her arms. 'Here you are.'

She had a point, Barbara thought. 'Well, sometimes life gives you lemons. Sometimes a crock of shit.'

Mayflower laughed. It completely changed her some-what sullen face into something open and beautiful. The gift of youth. And the folly.

'So, what can I get you?' she asked.

Barbara realized she was hungry. She hadn't eaten her burrito. And then she thought about Marcus lying in the deep freeze. 'You have anything that doesn't come out of the freezer – and isn't reindeer?'

'Chicken sandwich?'

'That would be great.'

Mayflower nodded. 'Anything else to drink?'

Barbara hesitated and then caved, 'Well, maybe one more beer.'

'Okay.'

Barbara waited for the girl to go, but Mayflower hov-ered. 'Mom had me clean off that writing on the mirror upstairs. It seemed pretty . . . biblical.'

'Yeah. Any idea who might have done it?'

Mayflower shook her head. 'No, but I've told Mom before about drunks wandering up there. They get lost, think it's the public restroom.'

Barbara nodded. She was pretty sure the writing and cross weren't the work of a confused drunk. 'When I was here before, you told me to watch out for Reverend Grey?'

Mayflower's face clouded. 'She acts all smiles and holy light, but that's not who she is.'

'How do you know?'

'I just know a faker when I see one.'

'What about Grace?'

'That creep who hangs around with her?'

'Yeah, her.'

'She's a real crazy.'

'In what way?'

Mayflower smiled thinly. 'Never says a word unless it's some religious quote, like she swallowed the whole damn Bible. Once told me I was going to hell for wearing a frigging Iron Maiden T-shirt.'

It was Barbara's turn to raise an eyebrow. 'Iron Maiden? Thought they'd be a bit before your time.'

'Good music died after the nineties.'

Well, that explained the sweatshirts.

'I used to say that about the eighties,' Barbara said. 'Although the nineties gave us better hair.'

'They say perms are coming back.'

'They say that about Elvis too.'

The girl smiled again.

'*Mayflower*, you done yacking over there? We got other customers waiting, you know!' The shout came from Carly leaning over the bar. Barbara couldn't see any other customers, certainly none waiting, but she got the gist.

Mayflower sighed. 'I'll get you that beer,' she said, and slouched away.

Barbara watched her go. As she did, she spied a new figure entering the Grill. A young man in a black parka with a duffel bag slung over his shoulder. He pushed back his heavy hood and raised a hand in greeting to Carly, who actually cracked a smile in return.

Barbara wasn't surprised. The man was a looker. Tousled dark hair, a hint of stubble and mournful brown eyes. Puppy-dog eyes. Put her in mind of that old actor, the one who was mighty handsome before all the plastic surgery.

She watched as he walked across the bar and joined an older man sitting at a table. Smartly dressed, silver hair, goatee. The pair spoke for a couple of minutes and then the older man suddenly rose, looking annoyed. He picked up his jacket and strode swiftly across the bar. The younger man sat back in his chair and ran his hands through his hair.

Interesting. Mayflower walked up to Barbara's table.

'Here you go.' She put the beer down.

'Thanks. Do you know the man over there?'

She half glanced back. 'Oh, that's Kurt Mowlam – he teaches at the school.'

Kurt Mowlam. Barbara remembered Rita mentioning his name.

Mayflower gave Barbara a look. 'Most women notice him.'

'I bet they do. And the man who just left?'

'Oh, that's Dr Dalton.' She grinned. 'You prefer a silver fox?'

'My interest is purely professional.'

'Right.'

She strolled off. Barbara debated with herself for a moment and then she stood, clutching her beer. She plastered a bright grin on her face and walked over to Mowlam's table. 'Evening, sir. Kurt Mowlam, right?'

Mowlam turned. 'Oh, hi, Detective . . .' He floundered, offering an apologetic smile.

'*Atkins*, sir,' Barbara filled in for him.

'Of course. I've heard about you. A forensic vampyr anthropologist. Sounds exciting.' His voice had a lazy drawl that matched his lazy, sloping eyes. He held out a hand. Barbara shook it.

'Mind if I join you?'

He glanced at the duffel bag. 'I have to mark some essays and prep for my lessons . . .'

'I wondered if I could talk to you about Marcus? I'll try to keep it quick.'

'Of course.' He acquiesced. 'Anything I can do to help.'

She pulled out the chair and sat down. 'Thanks.'

Mayflower returned with a black coffee, which she set down in front of Mowlam.

'Thanks, May.'

She nodded and walked off briskly. Seemed at least one person was immune to Mowlam's looks.

'I saw you talking to Dr Dalton,' Barbara said.

'Yeah, he's my landlord.'

'Having a disagreement about the rent?'

He added some sugar to his coffee and stirred it. 'No, just some repairs that need doing. You know landlords. Never want to put their hands in their pockets.'

'Oh, I've got that T-shirt.'

He laughed. 'Right?'

'How long have you been here in Deadhart?' Barbara asked.

'Almost two years.'

'What brought you here?'

A small shrug. 'Alaska sounded different. Mountains, glaciers, bears . . . vampyrs.'

'Where were you before?'

'Here and there. I've travelled a lot.'

'Teaching?'

'Not always. I like to mix things up.'

Barbara waited, but he didn't elaborate. 'What do you teach?'

'Well, English and history are my main subjects but, here, I cover a bit of everything.'

She nodded. 'Did you know Marcus and his friends well?'

'It's a small class, mixed grade, only twelve kids, so I know all the pupils pretty well. And the boys came to my after-school book club.'

'Really? I didn't think teenage boys were big readers.'

'Well, I've been trying to change that. Boys, especially in more rural areas, get left behind with literacy. Often because the study material is a little dry, shall we say?'

'So, what books do your group study?'

'We've read *Lolita, American Psycho, Dracula.*'

Barbara stared at him. 'Ever thought of trying something lighter, like *Mein Kampf*?'

He chuckled. 'You don't approve?'

'They wouldn't be on my reading list.' She offered a cool smile. 'What did your group make of *Dracula*?'

'It provoked a good discussion about historic myths of vampyrs versus what we know now. Or, at least, what we think we know.'

Barbara reached for her beer. 'It's a popular book with the Helsing League. You aware of any anti-vampyr feeling among the kids?'

'You get anti-vampyr feeling in all colony towns. Kind of gets passed down through the generations.'

'I guess. What was your impression of the three boys?'

He sat back and crossed his legs. 'Stephen is a bright kid, when he can be bothered. Jacob – quiet, reserved. Can't say he was always regular with his attendance. But there are home issues . . .'

'So I've heard.'

'Marcus – never going to be top of the class, but a trier. If he had any issues, it was that he could be a little easily led.'

Barbara considered this. 'Did you know that Marcus had a Helsing tattoo?'

Mowlam shook his head. 'No.'

'You don't seem shocked though?'

'Like I said, he was easily led. The type of kid that never says no to a dare.'

'You think he got a Helsing tattoo for a dare?'

'I don't know *why* he got it. I'm just telling you my impression of Marcus.'

'You got any tattoos, Mr Mowlam?'

'Most people do these days.'

'Ever heard of Be Damned Tattooists?'

'Afraid not. I got mine when I lived in New Orleans. You should visit. Big colony there.' He reached for his coffee and took a sip.

Barbara didn't like his tone. She got the feeling Mowlam was playing with her.

'And what are your feelings about colonies, sir?'

'I'm agnostic. I don't agree with culls, but people have a right to live safely. It's naive to pretend that vampyrs aren't dangerous. They're killers. It's in their nature, like a bear or a wolf.'

'They're not animals.'

'No, they're worse because they look like us. I don't bear them any ill will, but seems to me that vampyrs and humans will never co-exist together. It has to be one or the other. We should let nature take its course.'

'You mean hunting?'

'I mean survival of the fittest.' He regarded her curiously. 'I get the feeling you don't agree?'

'Not my place to agree or disagree, but the law says otherwise.'

He smiled, but there was nothing pleasant about it. 'And how many dead kids will it take for the law to change its mind?'

'You want your chicken sandwich here?'

Barbara turned. Mayflower stood by the table holding her plate of food.

'No.' She smiled back at Mowlam. 'I think I should let Mr Mowlam get on with his marking.'

Mowlam raised his coffee. 'Goodbye, Detective.'

'Goodbye. And thanks for your time, sir.'

Barbara took the plate from Mayflower and walked back to her table, feeling uneasy. Everything Mowlam had said was perfectly reasonable, but it was that easy-going plausibility that bothered her. He was a teacher. Persuasive, charming, good-looking. Catnip to impressionable teens.

Barbara took a swig of beer. The son of a bitch had got to her too.

'How many dead kids will it take for the law to change its mind?'

She picked up her sandwich . . . and paused.

That was it. Of course.

It explained the video, the jacket, the inconsistencies in timings.

She wiped her fingers on her napkin and grabbed her phone.

'Hello?' Nicholls sounded weary at the other end.

'I think I know what the boys were doing that night.'

17

Athelinda moved silently through the old mining settlement, eyes scanning the darkness.

The huge refinery loomed behind her. To her right were the cottages and bunkhouses where the rest of the Colony lived. Some had fallen into disrepair in their absence, but they would fix them, as they had before.

Ahead, a long track ran between the wooden buildings. Athelinda could see the old schoolhouse and the lodge (previously the home of the mine's managers, now her own abode). Further along was the factory where Colony members made clothing and shoes out of animal skins and old human clothes. Past this was the dairy, now used as an indoor barn and slaughterhouse. The land behind had been fenced into a grazing area for pigs and goats.

At the peak of the Deadhart Mining Corporation's operation, in the early 1900s, several hundred men had lived and worked here in the settlement. The town of Deadhart had expanded to service the mines, exporting ore and importing supplies via the river. Later, a spur had been built off the Alaskan railroad.

The human expansion had come at a cost to the Colony. While they had lived side by side with the local Dghelay Teht'ana population for almost two centuries, the incomers saw them as a threat. The Colony found themselves driven from the mountains into the Denali wilderness. The men had greater numbers and more sophisticated weapons. When the Colony tried to defend their land, they were hunted and slaughtered. Or worse.

However, everything has its time. By the early 1930s the copper had run out and the mine closed its gates. The buildings were abandoned and left to rot. That was when the Colony moved in, claiming the mining settlement as their own.

And they *had* been settled here. Until the boy. Until humans once again forced them from their home.

But now they were back. And this time they would not run.

The street was quiet tonight. Snow coated the ground. A few children played in a small makeshift playground, mothers chatting nearby. School had finished for the evening. Lessons started in the late afternoon during the winter, three days a week. Basic literacy, maths and vampyric history as well as cooking, crafts and other practical skills. There was little else to teach of use and sometimes Athelinda wondered why they persevered at all. The children would never grow up to have jobs or further their education. All of that was forbidden to them. They had so many years to live and yet so little of substance to fill their long lives.

Athelinda lingered near the playground, watching the children. Two girls and a boy, maybe four or five years old, playing on the tyre swings and slide. Athelinda paused, something tugging inside her. A distant memory. Playing with other children like this, but not in darkness; with blue skies above and the chitter of the morning birds filling the air. Wind rushed through her hair, laughter rang in her ears. And later, tucked into bed, a melodic female voice sang:

'*Rock-a-bye baby, on the treetop. When the wind blows, the cradle will rock.*'

For a moment the pang of yearning was so strong Athelinda felt faint. She reached out and grasped the wooden fence that bordered the playground. She closed her eyes, breathed deeply. Flashbacks. To before. She hadn't had one in centuries.

'Are you okay?'

She opened her eyes. One of the little girls, slight with dark hair, hovered on the other side of the fence. She looked at Athelinda curiously.

'You look sick. Are you going to puke? My mommy says that you go green when you puke.'

Athelinda studied the child: only a few inches shorter than she was, dressed in a faded green dress and long animal-skin jacket. At a glance, they could have been sisters or playmates, except for the eyes. The girl's were still open and innocent, free from guile. Athelinda tried to recall her name. *Gretchen*.

'I'm not going to puke,' she said.

'Good. I hate puking.'

Athelinda nodded towards the other children. 'Are those your friends?'

'Henry is my brother.' Gretchen pulled a face on the word 'brother'. 'Emily is my friend.'

'That's nice. Do you know who I am?'

Gretchen nodded. 'You're Miss Athelinda. You're in charge here, and Mom says you are hundreds of years old. Older than my grandma.'

'That's true.'

'You don't look old.'

'No.'

Gretchen considered then asked, 'D'you want to play?'

Before she could reply, one of the women called out:

'Gretchen, we need to go home now.'

Gretchen's face crumpled. 'Aw, Mom.'

'Now!'

The girl still hesitated.

'You should go,' Athelinda said.

'I don't want to.'

Athelinda leaned forward. 'Didn't your mother tell you? I like to eat little children.'

Gretchen's eyes widened. Then she turned and ran back towards the woman, who pulled her close, shooting Athelinda an uneasy look. It was a look Athelinda was familiar with. A mixture of apprehension, distaste and fear. Most of the Colony regarded her in the same way. Athelinda didn't blame them. They *should* be scared of her. She was a fucking monster.

Hundreds of years in this form had made her so. Her mind and body forced to endure more than it was ever intended to. Things that would have driven many mad. Sometimes she wondered if she *was* insane. Her head jammed so full of living that it felt like it might just explode. Perhaps then she would finally find some peace.

But not tonight. Tonight, she still had work to do.

The final building on her left was the settlement's recreation hall. A place for gathering, dancing to music, playing cards, telling stories. Tonight, she had requested a meeting to discuss the situation with the dead human boy.

Keeping everyone informed was paramount to keeping the Colony running smoothly. Yet still, it was with a heavy heart that Athelinda pushed the door open.

Around fifty people were seated in rows facing a small stage upon which stood Athelinda's ceremonial seat. She hesitated to call it a throne because they did not operate a system of privilege or unelected monarchy in the colonies. Leadership was granted by age, wisdom and a vote by colony members. But the chair was old, significant, and only Athelinda was permitted to sit upon it. So perhaps that was just semantics.

She climbed the steps and took her position, gazing out at the rows of enquiring faces. Most of whom she had known for several centuries.

She nodded in greeting. 'Welcome, kindred.'

The crowd murmured the greeting back.

'Thank you for coming,' she continued. 'I've called this meeting –'

'Did you speak with them?' a voice interrupted from the back.

Cain. As usual. A dour, contentious man who was prone to outbursts of temper. His wife was a downtrodden, nervous woman, his children cowed before they had even reached maturity. Athelinda disliked him. She knew the feeling was mutual. Cain resented being ruled by someone he still saw as a child. Ridiculous. She had a good two hundred years on him, if not more. But Cain was limited in both intellect and imagination. Occasionally, she wished she could be rid of him once and for all. But it was strictly forbidden for a vampyr to kill another vampyr. Unlike humans, they respected that rule.

Athelinda nodded. 'Yes. And I warned them of the consequences should they threaten the Colony.'

'And you expect them to listen?'

'No. I expect them to be fucking *warned*.'

'We shouldn't have come back,' another voice said.

Athelinda's head snapped around. 'This is our home.'

'We can find another settlement.'

She slammed her hand down on the polished arm of the chair. 'No. Not again.' She flashed an angry glance around the room. 'Have you forgotten why we came? For Merilyn. We stay. And we protect what is ours.'

'How?' This from one of the younger Colony members. Jonah. 'Seems like we're just waiting around for them to kill us.'

Murmurs of agreement from his friends beside him.

'We're waiting to be proven innocent,' Athelinda said steadily.

'They'll use the kid's death as an excuse to attack us.'

'So what do you suggest?'

'Attack them first. Take them while they are sleeping.'

Athelinda rolled her eyes. 'And then what? How will you fight against the soldiers that come? The UV grenades that flay the skin from your face. Do you think you can pick up your limbs and put yourself back together after a missile strike?'

He scowled. 'So we just do nothing? We let them treat us like animals they can murder at will?'

'We do not attack first,' Athelinda said, more firmly.

'Maybe we should.' Cain again. 'Maybe it's time for a Gathering.'

The Gathering – the last mythical battle between humans

and vampyrs. The victors gathered the souls of the fallen. Many vampyrs, especially the young, romanticized the idea. Probably because they had never actually had to fight for their survival.

Athelinda stood. 'Ever killed a human? Ever killed anything other than a goat or a pig?'

Cain stared at her sullenly but didn't reply.

Athelinda nodded. 'I have. More than you could imagine. I've feasted on their corpses. Some days I dream of doing it again. But I don't. Because killing *them* only endangers *us*. I won't put the Colony at risk because you have a hard-on for human flesh. Now, are there any more questions, or are we done?'

A hand rose in the crowd. Gwyneth, a graceful, quiet woman with two young daughters.

'Yes?' Athelinda said now.

'Will this affect the supplies?'

A good question.

'Right now, I don't know,' she said carefully. 'However, we should operate on the assumption that they will be delayed, or perhaps suspended for a time.'

Unhappier murmurs. Athelinda could feel their questions crowding her head. Uncertainty, fear ... and hunger.

'We can survive without the supplies,' she said firmly.

True. But what was survival if everything pleasurable had been stripped from it? Athelinda had long ago realized that the mind, human or vampyr, was not designed to endure long periods of absolute reality. It was why we dreamed, of course. But also, why we made up stories, read books, watched plays and films. It was also why humans drank and took drugs. For vampyrs, there were other stimulants that eased the long nights of the soul.

'And I think we'd all like to know – how *is* Merilyn?' This from Gwyneth again.

Merilyn. Athelinda felt the knot in her stomach tighten. She fought back the lump rising in her throat. Merilyn was the oldest member of the Colony and the last of her kin. Merilyn's husband had passed fifty years ago, and her children and only grandson were now also dead. Athelinda bit back hard on this thought because the anger and grief it conjured in her would be too much, and she could not let the mask of composure drop.

'She is dying.' She cleared her throat. 'It won't be long now.'

No more hands or questions. The mood was sombre.

She inclined her head. 'If that's all, I shall wish you goodnight.'

Athelinda made her way out of the hall. She had no desire to stay and socialize. Instead, she walked back up the street to her lodgings. She pushed open the door. Candles glowed within. A fire had been lit in the hearth. More for cheer than warmth.

Two moth-eaten velvet armchairs had been arranged around the fire. A handsome young man with a silky curtain of blond hair sat, reading, in one of them. He glanced up as Athelinda entered.

'You're home?'

'You're observant, Michael.'

He rose and took Athelinda's jacket, hanging it on a stand near the door. Athelinda sat down in the other armchair and took her pipe out of her pocket. She filled it with tobacco and lit it. Pungent smoke rose into the air.

'How are you?' Michael asked.

'Fucking tired.' She glanced at him. 'You weren't at the meeting.'

'No.'

'Why?'

He said tersely, 'You know how I feel.'

'The same as your friend Jonah?'

He didn't reply. Instead, he knelt and pulled out a small footstool from beneath her chair then lifted her feet on to it. He took off her boots and socks.

'Do you think Tucker will deliver the message?' He began to massage her feet, working out the tension.

'Yes. He still feels guilty.'

'He should.'

Athelinda would never admit it, but she had some sympathy for Tucker. It was the only reason he wasn't dead.

'There's another detective,' she said. 'A woman.'

Michael looked up. 'A problem?'

'I don't know.'

The woman looked harmless. Fat, dull, stupid. But Athelinda knew better than anyone that looks could be deceptive. She had sensed something more about her. It was hard to pinpoint.

'I told her to ask about the Bone House.'

'Are you sure you're right about this?'

'No. That's why I want your help. I want you to go back to that shithole bar.'

He frowned. 'I thought you didn't like –'

'I know what I said.' She cut him off sharply. 'And I know you've been visiting anyway.'

He looked up at her, startled. 'How?'

'You think you can hide your cravings from me?' She shook her head. 'You're my son, Michael.'

Athelinda reached forward and stroked his silky hair. She still loved the feel of it, trailing through her fingers; remembered how she would caress his soft head for hours while he lay beside her in bed. Born over ninety years ago, he had torn her apart on his entry into the world. She would never bear another child. He was all she had. Precious. Infuriating. And half-human.

'I understand,' she whispered. 'It's in your blood. That's why I allow you to file your teeth, to dress like them –'

'*Allow* me?' He shook her off and stood. 'I'm an adult.'

She snorted. 'You're not even a century old.'

'I'm old enough to understand that nothing will ever change if we don't challenge it. Why should we be forced to hide away, to live like savages?'

'The only change is you'll be dead.'

'And this' – he gestured out towards the settlement – 'this is living? We can't leave or work. We don't have electricity or internet –'

'We don't need those things.'

'It's not about need. It's about being part of civilization, about having rights. Fuck – I can't even go and get a job flipping burgers at a diner.'

She stared at him sadly. 'I understand. You want what they have. But what they have isn't so great, believe me. And they will never accept you, Michael. You have Colony in your blood too.'

'Yeah, don't I know it.'

The bitterness in his voice filled her with a familiar ache. He walked to the door and grabbed his coat.

'Where are you going?'

'To do what you asked.' Mockingly: 'Don't I always do what my dear mother tells me?'

'You're fucking supposed to.'

'Did you?'

She blew out a thick cloud of smoke. 'I killed my mother, ripped out her throat and drank her blood.'

He smiled, a hint of cruelty in his beauty. 'Don't give me ideas.'

The lodge shook as the door slammed shut behind him.

18

'You really think the boys *faked* that video to incite a cull?'

Last night, on the phone, Nicholls had been disbelieving and dismissive, but Barbara sensed he'd had some time to sleep on it. This morning he seemed in a more reflective mood.

She nodded. 'Yes, sir. I do. Or at least, to stir up trouble with the Colony. We presumed Marcus filmed his own death. But we never actually *see* that. Why? Because the whole thing is a set-up. One of the other boys pretends to be a vampyr. They film what looks like an attack. Maybe Marcus lets himself get roughed up a little. Then they go tell people there's a dangerous vampyr on the loose and the town immediately starts calling for a cull.'

'But Marcus ended up dead.'

'Yes, sir. But I think that happened later. Maybe Marcus really did leave his phone. Maybe the plan was for him to stay at the cabin a while and follow later. But at some point, after Jacob and Stephen left, he was attacked and killed.'

'It still seems like a hell of a coincidence.'

'It does. But it also explains a lot of the inconsistencies. The jacket, the timings, the tattoo. I'm also willing to bet if we dig into that phone, we'll find deleted versions of the video they didn't use.'

Nicholls rubbed at his moustache. 'You think the boys came up with this on their own?'

'That I don't know.'

'If you're right, we have no physical description of Marcus's attacker and no real time of death.'

'No, sir.'

Nicholls sighed heavily. 'Well, let's see what Stephen has to say for himself.'

Stephen Garrett's house was a large, double-storey wooden property. Next door was a storeroom and a large work shed. A polished but ageing truck sat outside along with a trail bike and a snowmobile that looked like it was being refurbished. Smoke puffed from a metal chimney on the roof and melted into the lightening sky.

Nicholls pulled up outside the property and they climbed out of the car. Almost as if he had been waiting for his cue, a tall, good-looking man with long sandy hair tied back in a ponytail emerged from the store. He wore a battered flying jacket, jeans, hiking boots and a wide smile.

'Hey, Pete. How's it going?'

'Hey, Dan. Not so bad.' Nicholls strode forward and the pair shook hands.

Pete, not Chief or sir, Barbara noted. But then it was a small town. People knew people. Hell, most people were *related* to people.

She saw Dan's eyes fall on her. The smile faltered a little around the edges.

'This is Detective Barbara Atkins,' Nicholls introduced.

Dan nodded. 'The vampyr detective.'

'That's me.' Barbara held out a hand. 'Nice to meet you, sir.'

Dan hesitated only momentarily before shaking it, but the hesitation was there.

'Likewise.'

'We wondered if Stephen was around?' Nicholls asked, keeping his tone casual.

Dan's eyes flicked between them. 'He's up in his room. Why? Didn't he give you a statement?'

'That he did,' Nicholls said. 'But Detective Atkins here would just like to go over a few things with him herself.'

Barbara forced a smile. 'My job is to dot the i's and cross the t's, sir.'

Dan nodded. 'Okay. Follow me.'

He led them into a large open-plan living area. It was bright and homey. Big, comfortable sofas, a widescreen TV, bean bags and a Shaker-style kitchen.

'Jess is just out visiting a friend,' Dan said. 'She won't be too happy to find you here, so if you can keep it brief. She'll be back in about half an hour.'

'Not a problem,' Nicholls said.

'We'll do our best, sir,' Barbara said. 'You have a lovely home, by the way.'

Dan nodded again. 'Thanks. I'll get Stephen.'

Barbara and Nicholls stood awkwardly in the living room. Barbara looked around. Family pictures decorated the walls. A sturdy cross hung over the fireplace. She walked over and looked at the photos. A large black-and-white wedding photo of Dan and (she presumed) Jess. They made a handsome couple. Both tall and rangy. Jess had long, curly blonde hair and enviable cheekbones. Most of the other pictures were of Stephen. A Disney-perfect kid who had grown up into a sturdy teenager with athletic good looks. Nothing out of the ordinary. A wholesome American family. For some reason, that immediately made her suspicious.

The stairs creaked and she turned. Dan walked down, a teenage boy slouching behind him. Stephen. He wore a sweatshirt and baggy jeans, blond hair tousled. Barbara felt her skin prickle with instant dislike. Still, she attempted a small smile.

'Hi, Stephen.'

Stephen glanced at Barbara but addressed himself to Nicholls. 'Dad said you wanted to talk to me again.'

'That's right. This is Detective Atkins.'

'I told the chief what happened.'

'I know you did,' Barbara replied. 'But there's a few points I need to clarify.'

'Best to do what they say,' Dan said.

Stephen gave a heavy sigh and threw himself down in a leather armchair.

Barbara and Nicholls lowered themselves on to the sofa, Dan perched on a higher occasional chair. Stephen slouched further into the armchair, radiating sullen teenage 'don't care' attitude. It was a little odd, Barbara thought. He had just lost a friend. He was off school on compassionate leave. Yet he didn't seem upset, or grief-stricken. Just put out.

On the other hand, people reacted to death in different ways. Especially sudden, violent death. It wasn't something you could ever prepare for. She wasn't going to hold his behaviour against him. Not right now, anyway.

'So,' she said. 'I've read your statement, Stephen, but I'd just like you to talk me through that night again.'

'Seriously?'

She smiled. 'Seriously.'

Another sigh. 'We agreed to meet up at the cabin like normal.'

Barbara nodded. 'What time?'

'Around sevenish.'

'And when you got to the cabin what did you do?'

'Drank beer, smoked a few joints.'

'That all?'

'Yeah.'

'You left at nine?'

He wasn't about to be caught out. 'No, earlier. It was around nine when Marcus realized he'd left his phone, and we were halfway home by then.'

'And when Marcus left, you and Jacob walked back home?'

'Yeah.'

'How long did that take?'

A shrug. 'For me, about fifteen, twenty minutes. Jacob had to walk further.'

'And your parents said you were back home by 10 p.m.?'

'That's right,' Dan said.

Barbara nodded. 'So, what were you doing?'

'What?'

'Well, if you left Marcus at 9 p.m. and it took you twenty minutes to walk home, you should have been back by nine thirty at the latest. But your dad here says you got back around ten, so what were you doing?'

'I dunno,' Stephen said now. 'Maybe we waited for Marcus for a bit. Maybe he left later. I mean, I'm not sure about the exact times.'

127

'Why are you asking all this?' Dan interrupted, sounding annoyed now. 'The boys didn't do anything wrong.'

'No one is saying they did,' Nicholls said calmly. 'But Detective Atkins has to ask, okay?'

'Not really,' Dan muttered.

'How do you feel about the Colony, Stephen?' Barbara asked.

'They're fucking animals.'

'You don't like them?'

He snorted. 'I don't like evil, undead things walking around. It's sick, man.'

'Ever think about joining any anti-vampyr groups?'

'No.'

'Ever give a Helsing salute?'

It was a wild guess, but she saw him flinch.

'Don't know what you're talking about,' he said.

Sure, she thought.

'What about Marcus and Jacob? They feel the same?'

'They didn't exactly love them.'

'You know Marcus had a Helsing tattoo?'

'No.' Immediate and defensive.

'You got any tattoos, Stephen?'

'*No.*'

'Cos sometimes kids get them together.'

'I'm scared of needles.'

Dan interrupted: 'I don't see what this has to do with anything. Kids get tattoos all the time.'

'Marcus was fifteen, sir.'

'That's right. And now he's *dead*. Killed by a vampyr.'

'Why don't we go back to the night Marcus died?'

Barbara said, not wanting to lose momentum. 'Marcus was wearing a jacket?'

'Yeah.' Stephen nodded. 'It was new.'

'And I bet it was cold that night.'

'Well, yeah. It's always fuck—' He caught himself. 'It's always cold here.'

'Okay. But in the video, Marcus isn't wearing his jacket. In fact, you can see it hung up on the wall.'

Stephen swallowed. The first tell, she thought.

'Any idea why that would be?' Barbara pressed. 'Because it seems a little odd, if Marcus was surprised and attacked by a vampyr, that he would have time to take his jacket off and hang it up?'

'Maybe he took it off first?'

'You just said it was freezing.'

Stephen remained silent. Dan was frowning.

'Here's what I think happened,' Barbara continued. 'I think Marcus *knew* he would be lying on the floor, and he took his jacket off so he wouldn't get it dirty. But *why*?'

'I *don't know*,' Stephen said, but he sounded rattled.

'I think you do,' Barbara said. 'You see, I think the whole thing was faked. I think you went to the cabin specifically to make that video. To make it look like Marcus was attacked but escaped. And then use it to incite a cull.'

Stephen's lip curled. He leaned forward. 'Prove it.'

And then a voice from behind them growled: 'What the *hell* is going on here?'

Barbara turned. A woman stood in the doorway. Lean, even in a thick jacket and jeans. Her curly blonde hair was yanked back into an untidy ponytail and her face was cut through with angry lines.

Dan stood. 'They were just going –'

Nicholls got to his feet. 'Good to see you again, Jess.'

The woman folded her arms. 'Can't say likewise.'

Nicholls gestured to Barbara. 'This is –'

'I know who *she* is, and I told you, I got nothing to say to her. Stephen has been through enough. He doesn't need you harassing him.'

Nicholls held out his hands in a placatory gesture. 'We're just here to make sure all the facts –'

Jess barked out a hollow laugh. 'The *facts*? The facts are this – a kid is dead, killed by a vampyr. Just like before. Just like in Ohio last year. Just like in Texas the year before that. And it will keep on happening until we deal with them once and for all.' She paused and shook her head. 'But why am I wasting my breath?' She scowled at Barbara. 'She's not here to help us. She's here to find excuses not to authorize a cull. Don't think we don't know it.'

'That's not true, ma'am,' Barbara said. 'I want to see the perpetrator of this crime brought to justice as much as you do.'

Jess took a step towards Barbara. 'You don't get it, do you? It doesn't matter which one of them did it. They're all the same. We need to wipe them from the face of the earth.'

Barbara kept her voice pleasant. 'Well, whether you like it or not, colonies are protected under the law and an unauthorized cull will land you in jail.'

'What I would *like* is for you to leave.'

Nicholls nodded at Dan, who was sitting in his seat,

looking uncomfortable. 'Thank you for your time, and Stephen's too.'

Stephen smirked at them from the armchair. 'See ya.'

Barbara rose. 'By the way, Stephen, we've sent Marcus's phone to Tech. Be interesting to see what they pull from the deleted files.' She paused. 'I'm guessing you didn't get the video right on the first attempt.'

The smirk dropped like a stone. Barbara walked to the door with Nicholls. She turned to Jess. 'Could I use your bathroom before I go?'

Jess raised an eyebrow. 'This the part where you use that as an excuse to sneak around our house upstairs?'

'No, ma'am. I've just got a bladder like a sieve.'

'Well, in that case, plenty of woods on the way back into town. Watch out for things that bite.' She moved to close the door on them.

'Wait!' Stephen suddenly stood up.

Gotcha, Barbara thought.

He glared at them resentfully. 'It wasn't our idea, okay? The Doc said he'd pay us five hundred dollars each to set the Colony up.'

19

Nicholls guided the truck carefully along the road. Snow was piled at the side, and it was icy in places but the 4x4 held its grip.

'There are only a couple of houses out this way,' he said. 'The Bell house is up there.' He gestured to a narrow track that disappeared into forest. 'Doc Dalton lives at the far end of the road, near the lake.'

As they rounded a bend, a property drew into view on their left. Large, chic and modern. Single-storey, with sliding glass doors, a wide deck and views out over the water.

'Nice,' Barbara said.

'Yeah, the Doc did well for himself here,' Nicholls said, with only a trace of bitterness.

Barbara hadn't seen where Nicholls lived, but she imagined that his salary didn't stretch to much, even in Deadhart.

'He built it himself?' Barbara asked as they climbed out of the truck.

'I think some developer did that for him. He used to live in town, close to Main Street. Rents that house out now to Kurt Mowlam.'

Barbara nodded, staring back at the house. 'I guess being a doctor pays well.'

'I heard he had an inheritance. At least, that's what he said.'

'You don't believe him.'

Nicholls sighed. 'Don't get me wrong, Dalton is a good doctor. Everyone in town will tell you so. Rita always says how he goes the extra mile for her mom. Whereas some would just brush you off, he's real thorough, checks everything, takes blood, the whole lot.'

'I sense a "but"?'

'He's an odd one. It's kind of vague how he ended up here, and he's always seemed a little flashy to me.'

'I guess if being flashy was a crime, Dolly Parton would be a criminal.'

'True.'

'Of course, inciting a cull' – she looked at him – 'that's a different matter.'

They walked up the wooden steps at the side of the deck. Lights glowed within the open-plan living space. Barbara could see comfortable modern sofas, arty-looking lamps, a sleek modern kitchen. All very European. And also, somehow out of place here in Deadhart, which was determinedly Alaskan. She could imagine how such a place might be viewed as 'flashy'. Still, Barbara imagined the Doc could live with that. As they reached the deck, she could see that the glass doors were open, just a little.

'People tend to leave their doors open here?' she asked Nicholls.

He frowned. 'Not in winter.'

She reached out a hand and pulled the handle. The door slid wider.

'Hello? Dr Dalton?'

Cautiously, she stepped inside. Nicholls followed, hand on his gun.

They stared around the room. A large log stove at the far end still glowed with the remnants of a fire, but the chill from the open door was palpable. Near the stove, a pile of folders had been stacked on a small table next to an armchair. Barbara walked over. The files had names and addresses on the front. She picked one up and flicked through it. Medical files.

'Looks like the Doc was just doing some work,' Nicholls remarked.

Seemed so, Barbara thought. But where was he now?

'Hello,' she called again. 'Dr Dalton?'

Still no reply. And no other sounds. No doors opening or closing. No footsteps, or music or television. Not even a shower or a toilet flushing. She didn't like it. You got a sense for these things after a time. You knew when empty was just empty, someone having stepped out of a room or about to return. And you knew when empty was full of foreboding.

'Let's check the rest of the house,' she said.

They moved through the living area into a wide hallway. More doors led off it on both sides. Barbara pushed one to her left. A modern, sleek bathroom. Nicholls tried a door on their right. A master bedroom. They proceeded along the corridor. A guest bedroom, and the final door. Nicholls pushed it open.

Barbara's heart sank.

'Shit!' Nicholls muttered.

Doc Dalton didn't look so flashy now.

He hung from a light fitting in the middle of the home office. A chair lay on its side near his dangling feet, only a few inches from the ground. But that was all it took,

Barbara thought. It wasn't pretty. It didn't smell too great either.

Nicholls looked like he was thinking the same.

'Shit,' he said again, in a wearier tone.

'Yeah,' Barbara said. Exactly. They both walked further into the room.

'Guess we should try to cut him down,' Nicholls said.

They could, Barbara thought, but it would be pointless. Dalton's face was already mottled dark red. He was beyond resuscitation. She touched his hand. Stone cold. He'd probably been hanging here for several hours.

'We should take some pictures first,' she said. 'And then we'd better get on the phone to the coroner in Anchorage.'

Nicholls nodded. 'Okay.'

Barbara took her phone out. 'Any sign of a note?'

Nicholls walked around to the desk. It was bare apart from a new MacBook Air, which Barbara found odd. Most home offices were messy. Papers left out; pens scattered. Maybe the doctor was a neat freak, but it still felt wrong somehow.

'No note that I can see,' Nicholls said.

'Anything on the laptop?'

Nicholls opened it and tapped the trackpad. 'Nope, and it needs a password.'

Of course. And this was not the movies, where an inspired guess or insane intuition would gain them access.

Barbara circled, taking photos. Dr Dalton was dressed in jeans, a shirt and shiny loafers. Dressed for work. But if he hanged himself last night or in the early hours, she would have expected him to be wearing night clothes or at least loungewear. And why had the door been ajar . . .

135

Her thoughts were interrupted by a thud from the bedroom next door. She glanced at Nicholls and they both sprinted for the hallway.

A thin figure in black ran back down the corridor.

Shit. Nicholls was ahead of her and gaining on the figure. They ran into the living room, Barbara panting behind. *Damn boots and jacket,* and she really needed to wear a sports bra for this type of thing.

The intruder sprinted on to the deck, Nicholls right on his tail. The chief grabbed for his jacket, fingers snagging the fabric. The intruder twisted, trying to get away, but he lost his footing and tumbled down the wooden steps, taking Nicholls with him. They both hit the ground hard, but the intruder managed to roll and break his fall. Nicholls landed more awkwardly; leg twisted beneath him. Barbara heard him yell in pain.

She pounded down the steps, stopping to check on him. 'Sir, are you –'

'Forget me,' he hissed through clenched teeth. 'Get the suspect.'

The suspect was already struggling to his feet. Barbara couldn't run fast, but she could tackle. She threw herself at him bodily, grabbing him around the waist and bringing him down. She heard an 'oomph' as the breath whooshed out of him. That was what a diet of bagels and burgers did for you, she thought. She pinned the intruder face down on the snowy ground, grabbing his arms and pulling out her handcuffs.

'You are under arrest for breaking and entering and assaulting a police officer.'

She rolled him over.

'I'm sorry,' he cried. 'I'm sorry. I didn't mean to. Don't shoot me.'

Damn. It was the same kid from the day she arrived. The one Al had almost hit with his cab.

'No one is going to shoot you,' Barbara said. 'What's your name?'

He stared at her with wide, panicked eyes. 'Jacob Bell.'

20

The chopper rose into the darkening sky, whisking snow into the air in a mini blizzard. It would transport Nicholls and the Doc's body to Anchorage Hospital. Marcus's body would have to remain here, in case Barbara needed to examine it again.

'You're damn lucky we made it at all,' the paramedic had told her. 'Another hour, with the dark and the storm coming in, we couldn't have flown.'

Yeah, lucky old her, she thought as she watched the chopper disappear into the distance. With Nicholls out of action, she was on her own. And while that had never really bothered her before, here, she was *really* alone. No other town for miles, no back-up, no support, and if she got cut off by the weather, no escape.

She trudged to the truck, where Jacob was sitting, handcuffed, in the back. She had managed to find the keys to lock up the Doc's house, which should preserve the scene. But what she wouldn't have given for a CSI or even another officer right now.

She settled herself into the driver's seat, grateful at least for the respite from the cold. Her eyes met Jacob's in the rear-view mirror.

'I didn't kill the Doc,' he said. 'He was . . . like that when I got there.'

'Good to know,' Barbara said. 'But we need to go back

to the police department to take a statement. And I need to call your dad.'

'He's not home.'

'You know where he is?'

A shrug.

'Well, let's try him.'

Grudgingly, Jacob gave her a cellphone number. 'He won't answer,' he muttered.

Barbara called it anyway. The phone went to voicemail.

'Mr Bell. This is Detective Barbara Atkins. I currently have your son, Jacob, in custody. Could you call me when you get this message?' She ended the call. 'You got anyone else I can call for you?' she asked Jacob.

Another shrug.

'Okay.' She turned on the engine. 'Well, you'd better think on the way to the police department. I can interview you without a parent or a lawyer present, but you might want someone in your corner.'

They drove in silence back down the main trunk road into town. It wasn't until the twinkling lights of Main Street drew into view that Jacob suddenly blurted out: 'Steve's mom. You could try her.'

Jess Garrett. Oh good, Barbara thought. Just what she needed.

She parked the car and picked up her phone again. Jacob recited the number.

Jess answered on the second ring, sounding out of breath and impatient.

'Yes?'

'Mrs Garrett, it's Detective Atkins,'

'What do you want now? Stephen's told you all he knows –'

'Mrs Garrett, I have Jacob Bell in custody.'

'Jacob? What for?'

'Chief Nicholls and I apprehended him at Dr Dalton's house up by the lake.'

'You're saying he broke in?'

'I'm not saying anything.'

'Well, what about the Doc?'

'Dr Dalton is dead.'

'*Dead?* Oh God.'

'Jacob has requested that an appropriate adult be present during the interview, and I can't get hold of his dad.'

Jess made a snorting noise. 'You won't. I saw his pick-up outside the Lame Horse.'

'The what?'

'A bar out on the AK-3.'

'Right. Well, maybe I should call them.'

'Don't waste your time. He won't be in any state to drive home.' Another flustered sigh. 'Okay. Well, sure. I guess I can be there. Where's Chief Nicholls?'

'I'm afraid he's in Anchorage Hospital with a broken leg sustained while apprehending the suspect.'

'Shit.' There was a long pause. 'Is Jacob in a lot of trouble?'

'Yes, ma'am,' Barbara said. 'I'm afraid he is.'

They settled in the office, cups of coffee in front of them. Barbara had offered Jacob some coffee, milk or water, but he had declined.

As he sat beside Jess, Barbara was struck by the difference between him and Stephen. While Jess's son radiated casual good looks, Jacob was thin-faced and scrawny, with pinched features and dark shadows beneath his eyes. He looked underfed and somehow beaten down. She thought again about his dad, Nathan. *You can't choose your parents.* Yeah, she knew all about that.

Barbara had located a tape recorder with what seemed to be a working cassette inside it in one of Nicholls's numerous desk drawers. She would record on her Dictaphone as well, but sometimes it was nice to have a hard-copy back-up. Retro. She set both on the table in front of her and pressed record.

'Okay,' she said. 'Interview with Jacob Bell. Date: November 15th. Time: 3.29 p.m. Present: Detective Barbara Atkins, Jacob Bell and appropriate adult Mrs Jess Garrett. You have declined a legal representative, is that right, Jacob?'

He nodded.

'For the record, please,' Barbara instructed.

'Yes, ma'am.'

'Are you sure about that, Jacob?' Jess asked. 'I know someone you could call in Anchorage.'

'It's okay, ma'am,' Jacob said. 'I don't need a lawyer.'

Jess looked back at Barbara. 'Just for the *record*,' she said, 'if you try to put words in Jacob's mouth or bully him into signing anything –'

'I can assure you,' Barbara interrupted. 'I'm not in the habit of doing either of those things, but thank you for your input.'

'Fine.' Jess folded her arms.

'O-kay,' Barbara said. 'Jacob, could you start by telling us what you were doing at the residence of Dr Dalton, at approximately eleven thirty this morning?'

141

Jess turned to Jacob. 'You don't have to say anything.'

Barbara bit back her irritation. 'Ma'am, we *know* Jacob was in the house. He knocked Chief Nicholls over and broke his leg, so we just need to establish what he was doing there.'

Jacob fixed Barbara with his dark eyes. 'I wasn't there stealing.'

'So, what *were* you doing there, Jacob?'

He let out a shaky breath. 'I was there to collect the supplies and take them to the drop-off point. I do it for the Doc every week. And he pays me.'

Barbara frowned. 'Supplies? You mean drugs?'

He shook his head. 'No. Blood.'

'Dr Dalton was dealing in illicit human blood?'

'Yeah.'

Barbara sat back in her chair. The colonies didn't rely upon human blood for nutrition, and hadn't for centuries. Animal blood had been deemed an acceptable alternative, a necessary adjustment to keep the peace between the two species. But still, the craving for many remained. And wherever there is a desire, there are people who will find a way to make money from it.

Selling human blood to the colonies had become a thriving illicit trade. Unscrupulous dealers would source it from the vulnerable who needed cash. Others stole from hospital blood banks. Doctors were not immune to accepting cash for high-quality human blood.

Barbara had worked one case where a pimp kept half a dozen young women chained in a basement to be used for feeding. By the time the department raided the building all but one of the women was dead. Barbara had never forgotten their emaciated bodies, blue from blood loss and covered in bite marks.

Prostitution of a different kind. And, just like paying for sex, in most states it was illegal. For good reason. Once some vampyrs had a taste for human blood they wanted more. And if they couldn't afford to buy it, they might just decide to take it.

'You know where he got it from?' she asked Jacob.

'Someone in Anchorage. He would travel up there every week.'

Barbara suddenly remembered something else Nicholls had told her: *'Rita said he was very thorough. Always took blood.'*

I bet he did, she thought.

'So,' she said, 'Dr Dalton would bring the blood back and then what?'

'I'd go and collect it, leave it at a drop-off point in the woods. There'd be cash, jewellery or gold waiting and I'd take that back to the Doc and he'd give me my cut.'

'When was your last supply run?'

'Monday.'

That explained something else. When Jacob ran in front of the cab he must have been running from the Doc's house. Carrying the supplies. No wonder he had looked scared. Scared he would get caught.

'You almost got yourself run over by my cab that day.'

Jacob's eyes widened. 'That was you!'

Barbara thrust her hand in her pocket and pulled out the shard of glass. She held it up between her finger and thumb. 'I found this and some blood on the ground.'

He nodded. 'I smashed a vial. The Doc was pissed. It wasn't a scheduled run. Doc said we needed to do an extra one and it had to be soon, so I was kind of panicked about being caught.'

'You know if the blood was for one particular person, or the Colony in general?'

A shrug. 'I don't know.'

'How much blood did you take up there?'

'Depended. Sometimes I took small amounts in vials, sometimes larger amounts in bags.'

Barbara considered. If the Doc was blood dealing, it might make sense of his death. Maybe he thought he would be exposed and couldn't face going to jail. Or maybe someone wanted to keep him quiet?

'Why don't you talk us through what happened today, Jacob?' she said.

'I got there as usual to pick up,' Jacob said. 'But something felt kind of off. Normally, the Doc leaves the stuff in a key safe outside so I can pick it up anytime. But the safe was empty and when I went up on the deck, I could see that the door was open.'

'So, you went inside?'

'I went to look for him and . . .' He paused, swallowed.

'You found him?' she prompted.

'He was just hanging there and . . . shit, it was horrible, and I just wanted to get out, but then I heard a car and . . . I was scared of getting caught, so I hid under a bed . . . and when I got my chance, I ran.'

The sequence of events made sense. But there were other questions.

'You didn't see anyone else?'

Jacob shook his head.

'Nothing out of the ordinary?'

'I don't think so . . .' He broke off. His eyes filled with tears. 'Shit, this is such a mess. It wasn't supposed to be like this.'

'What wasn't, Jacob?'

'Just . . . everything.'

Barbara leaned forward. 'Does the blood-dealing have anything to do with Dalton paying you boys to fake the video of Marcus being attacked?'

Jacob stared at her in shock. Then he threw a panicked glance at Jess.

'I already know,' Jess said wearily. 'Stephen talked. And what you boys did was damn stupid.' She gave Barbara a sharper look. 'But Marcus didn't deserve to die for it.'

Barbara kept her focus on Jacob. 'It's you in the video, isn't it?'

He nodded slowly. 'Yeah.'

'The fangs?'

'Just fake ones from a shop.'

That explained the bit of pink plastic. It must have broken off the fake teeth.

'I was supposed to scrape his neck up a bit, make it look like he'd been attacked but managed to escape. Me and Stephen would leave, and Marcus would stay behind and follow later.'

'So he never went back for his phone?'

'No.'

'When did you realize something was wrong?'

Jacob swallowed. 'We expected the police to come round after Marcus got home and told his mom and dad, but they didn't. The next morning Marcus's mom called, asking if anyone knew where he was. That was when we knew something was up.'

All of this tallied with what Stephen had said. But it was good to corroborate their stories. Check for inconsistencies.

'Why didn't you come forward then?'

'I'm sorry. It was stupid. We should have said something, but we were scared.'

Jess scowled at Barbara. 'Can't you see he's cut up about this?'

'A boy is dead, and Jacob and Stephen have seriously hampered a police investigation –'

'What does it matter? A *vampyr* killed Marcus, whatever else happened.'

'Inciting a cull is a criminal offence.'

Jess rolled her eyes. Barbara turned back to Jacob. 'How did you get involved with Dr Dalton?'

He cleared his throat. 'Through Marcus.'

'*Marcus?*'

'He bought drugs from the Doc. Everyone in town knows the Doc is the guy to go to for weed.'

The Doc really was a man of many talents, Barbara thought. And, although marijuana wasn't illegal in Alaska, selling it to minors was.

'So why didn't Marcus do the blood-running? Why get you involved?'

'He did it for a bit. But he'd almost got caught by his folks a couple of times. That's why he wanted to make the video. Seemed like easy money.'

No such thing as easy money, Barbara thought. A damn shame Marcus wasn't alive to learn that lesson. She glanced at Jess, who was sitting, arms still folded, face grim. Barbara guessed she was wondering if Stephen knew about all of

146

this. How deep in was he? How many more secrets was her son keeping from her?

'Have you any idea why Dr Dalton wanted to incite a cull?' she asked Jacob.

'No. He never said.'

The more Barbara thought about it, the less sense it made. Why would Dalton want a cull when he was selling blood to the Colony? He'd be cutting off his own cash flow.

The pieces didn't fit together. And then there was the ring that Tucker had found. How did that tie up with what Jacob had told her about Dalton and Marcus?

'Are we done here?' Jess asked. 'Are you going to charge Jacob?'

Barbara looked at Jacob. Was she going to charge him? He hadn't actually broken into Dalton's, and the incident with Nicholls was really an accident. But then, running blood was an offence and the boys had also lied and obstructed a murder investigation.

'For now, I'm going to release Jacob under investigation.' Barbara spoke into the tape recorder: 'Interview terminated at 4.23 p.m.' She clicked it off.

'So I can go home?' Jacob asked.

Barbara sighed. 'Jacob, you're a minor. Without knowing when or if your dad is coming home, I can't just let you go.'

'It's fine,' Jess said. 'Jacob can stay with us tonight. It's not the first time.'

'Thank you, Mrs Garrett.'

Jess turned to Barbara, and she braced herself, half expecting another diatribe.

'Could I have a word, in private?'

'Of course.'

They stepped outside into the corridor. Barbara pulled the door to.

'I owe you an apology, Detective,' Jess said.

'You do?'

'The boys lied. I was wrong about that.'

'Well, thank you.'

'But don't think it changes anything. Marcus is still dead, killed by a vampyr. We still need a cull.'

'Ma'am, I can only authorize a cull if the whole colony poses a threat.'

'So, we're just supposed to sit around, waiting for another attack?' Jess barked out a humourless laugh. 'You have any idea what it's like living in a colony town?'

'Yes, ma'am. I grew up in one.'

The woman faltered, the wind momentarily taken out of her sails. Then she sneered. 'And I suppose you're going to tell me you all lived peacefully, in harmony?'

Mercy. Silver hair floating in the water. Her dad's voice: 'You know what I hate more than liars . . . fucking vampyrs.'

Barbara kept her voice steady. 'No. I'm not going to tell you that.'

'Then *help* us. When the Colony fled after Todd's murder, it was like a shadow lifted. Things were good. Now they're back, another kid is dead and it's here again – the darkness. The fear. Why should we have to live like that? Why should *they* be protected?'

'It's the law, ma'am,' Barbara said, but her words sounded hollow.

Jess's face tightened. 'Yeah, well, look around. You *are* the law now. So, if I was you, I'd ask myself where my loyalties lie. Before it's too late.'

'I've warned you about doing this to yourself.'

The girl blinked blearily.

'What?'

Her Captor knelt beside her on the floor.

'You passed out. Blood loss.'

She realized her Captor was winding a white bandage around her wrist. They looked disappointed. 'You were lucky I came back down to check on you when I did.'

The girl swallowed. 'I'm sorry.'

Her Captor smiled sadly and raised a hand to stroke her face. 'It's okay. I know you're hungry and, I promise, I will sort something out. You just have to be patient.'

The girl smiled in return even as she felt like saying: I've been patient for years. I'm not sure how much longer I can hold on.

It would never be safe enough out there. She would never leave this place.

'I need the toilet,' she said, and stood up.

Something heavy clanked around her foot. She looked down. A thick manacle had been secured around her ankle. It was attached to a short chain that ran across the floor to a bolt drilled into the wall. No. Her Captor hadn't used the bolt and chain for decades.

She looked up in horror. 'Please.'

'I'm sorry,' her Captor said, rising. 'I've put a bucket here for you to use and you'll have to forego showers for a few days.'

'But why? I've been good.'

'Does this look good?'

Her Captor strode over to the window and yanked the blind up. They pulled at one of the bars and it came loose, damp plaster crumbling to the floor.

'Did you think I wouldn't find out?'

The girl bowed her head. 'I'm sorry. I just . . . it's been so long here.'

'Don't I look after you, provide for you, give you everything you need?'

'I need my freedom.'

Her Captor's lips pursed. 'The chain won't be for long. Just till I can get this window fixed.' Her Captor smiled, and the girl wondered — not for the first time — if everything her Captor did really was for her own good. She strained against the chain, but it was bolted in securely.

'I'll be back to empty your bucket later,' her Captor said, and disappeared up the stairs.

The girl sat down on the bed and put her head in her hands. She was angry, but she also felt lost, hopeless. The years seemed to be closing in and crushing her, burying her under the weight of time, of a life unlived.

And then she heard it.

'Hey.'

She looked up. The voice was back. In her head, but also real, out there. She could hear it faintly through the walls.

'Hello?'

'You're sad.'

'How do you know?'

'I can feel you.' A pause. 'Can you feel me too?'

And she could. She could feel energy, hunger and something else.

'How?'

'We're the same. Me and you.'

150

She shook her head. 'No, I don't think so.'

'I know what you are. And I know they're afraid of you. That's why they keep you locked up. Humans are always afraid of what they can't understand.'

'It's to protect me.'

'From what?'

A pause. She couldn't answer.

'How long have you been here?'

She swallowed. Normally she tried not to remember. Because thinking about time was like opening a dam. It would pour out in a relentless torrent of days, months, years and decades.

'A long while,' she said.

'Years, decades . . . longer?'

She nodded, and he seemed to know she had confirmed the latter.

'Don't you hate them?'

'Sometimes.' It felt good to say it. 'Yes, I suppose I do.'

'Then let me help you.'

'How?'

'I can get you out.'

'I'm chained up. They found out I was trying to get out of the window. It's going to be fixed up.'

'When?'

'I don't know. Soon.'

'Okay, then we'll have to find another way.'

'Why do you even want to help me?'

'Because you're one of us. Now listen.'

The girl listened. At the end, she smiled.

'And we'll make them pay?'

'We will.'

21

Only a few lights were on along Main Street. The sky had darkened, and snow gusted down in thick flakes. Wind rattled shutters and shook the gaudy decorations. Harty Snacks had taken in the chairs and heaters. The town felt like it was battening down, Barbara thought. Going into hibernation.

She pushed open the door of the café. The place was empty except for the same blonde-haired girl behind the counter – Kitty – who was engrossed in her phone.

'Hi there,' Barbara said.

'Oh.' The girl hastily slid the phone into her pocket. 'Hi. What can I get you?'

'Coffee, and –' Barbara glanced at the menu. Still reindeer-heavy. 'Some fry bread, please.'

'Sure thing.' The girl turned to the coffee machine. She glanced back over her shoulder at Barbara. 'Saw a helicopter landing earlier. Looked like the air ambulance?'

'Really?' Barbara smiled. 'Well, I hope whoever they picked up is okay.'

The girl continued to look at her and then said, 'Yeah. Well, they're lucky. Nothing will be flying out of here for a few days.'

Great, Barbara thought. She took her coffee and bread and settled in a far corner, away from any other customers that might come in. A lot to unpack from today. And a lot to do tomorrow. First thing in the morning she would head back to Dalton's. Any evidence would need to be sent back to Anchorage, along with the other samples she had collected. Cab and then air taxi was probably the fastest. If either of them was running.

The mould she had taken of Marcus's bite wound would be run through a 3D scanner, and any unusual identifying marks logged. It would also be compared to bite wounds from other cases. Unfortunately, it was too long ago for moulds to have been taken in the Danes case, but it might throw something up. Ideally, Barbara would take bite samples from every member of the Colony, but she had a feeling they might not be forthcoming on that. The colonies had learned not to trust humans. To minimize contact. To protect their own.

That's why it was unusual that the girl vampyr, Athelinda, had approached them near the hunting shack. *'Ask 'em about the Bone House.'* Barbara had run a quick Google search, but nothing relating to the Bone House in Deadhart had come up, which only made her more curious.

She took a sip of coffee. The door to the café swung open again. A familiar figure in a bright crimson snowsuit walked in. Rita. Barbara's stomach sank. She liked Rita, but she wasn't really in the mood for cheery conversation right now.

'Hey there!' Rita grinned. 'I was looking for you.' She lowered her voice. 'I heard about the Doc and Pete.'

Barbara glanced across the counter. Kitty stood with her back to them, tapping on her phone.

'How d'you hear?' Barbara asked.

Rita pulled out a chair and sat down. 'Pete called me

from the hospital. He told me about the video the boys filmed too.'

Barbara bit back her annoyance. Nicholls shouldn't be divulging information to anyone without running it past her. But then, she guessed Rita was his friend as well as the mayor.

'How is he?' she asked.

'They were about to wheel him into the OR. Metal pins and plates. Nasty break.'

'Damn.'

'To be honest, an enforced rest will probably do him good. It's not an easy ride here. The wages are low, and the work is tough. You get asked to do everything, from breaking up brawls to chasing off bears. Plus, blowtorching the lock on your front door every night because it's frozen solid soon stops being a novelty.'

Barbara nodded, wondering again how Nicholls ended up here. 'I can imagine. How do *you* cope?'

'Well, I'm Deadhart born and bred.' Rita chuckled. 'This is my normal.'

'Never thought of moving?'

'Maybe, when I was younger.' Something flickered across her face, and then it was gone. 'Anyway, what did Jacob have to say for himself?'

'Well, turns out the Doc was selling blood to the Colony. Jacob was running it for him. And he paid the boys to fake the video.'

'The Doc?' Rita's eyes widened. 'Well, I'll be damned.'

'Any idea why?'

'No.'

'Did you know the Doc was selling marijuana, too?'

'Well, it isn't illegal here.'

'He was selling to minors.'

Rita sighed. 'Oh. That I didn't know.'

Barbara wondered if she was being honest. It struck her that there wasn't much Rita didn't know about in this town. Which reminded her . . .

'Rita, have you ever heard of a place called the Bone House?'

Rita frowned. 'Well, that *is* a blast from the past.'

'So, you do know it?'

'I know *of* it,' she said cautiously. 'But that place was razed to the ground years ago.'

'What was it?'

'A brothel. For the men who worked in the mine. It was out by the cemetery, hence the name.'

'And that's it?'

'Not exactly.' A longer pause. 'It was a vampyr brothel.'

A vampyr brothel.

They were mostly a thing of the past, like freak shows. But occasionally the department would bust a new set-up. They were strictly illegal, not least because of the type of clientele they attracted. Vampyrs healed quickly. They could be abused in as many sick ways that you could think of and still recover. And then there were the men who wanted children who weren't *really* children.

Barbara swallowed down the sour taste in her mouth. 'And I'm guessing the vampyrs in the brothel weren't there by choice.'

'It's not something that the town is proud of,' Rita said quickly. 'You won't find it in any official history books. But like I said, it was a long time ago. Why are you asking about it, anyway?'

'It came up in conversation.'

Rita nodded, her face serious for once. 'A word to the wise, Barbara: there is such a thing as *too* much information.'

Barbara raised an eyebrow.

'What I mean is,' Rita continued, 'you're here to do a job. To determine whether Marcus was killed by a vampyr and if you should authorize a cull. Don't get distracted.'

Barbara cleared her throat. 'Well, I certainly won't drag anything up that isn't necessary to the investigation.'

Rita nodded. 'I knew you'd understand.'

Did you? Barbara thought.

Rita stood up. 'I should skedaddle. No rest for the wicked.' And then she paused. 'You know, you should come round for dinner tomorrow. Can't have you eating alone all the time.'

'That would be great,' Barbara said.

'I'm not the world's best cook, but I make a pretty mean reindeer pie.'

Barbara forced a smile. 'Sounds good.'

'And anything else you need, you let me know. Think of me as your wing woman.' Rita gave a salute. Then she adjusted her snow suit and sashayed out of the café.

Barbara gazed after her thoughtfully. Rita was only trying to do her best for the town, but Barbara knew when she was being warned off. Rita's duty was to Deadhart, not to a *cheechako* like Barbara, whatever she might say.

I'd ask myself where my loyalties lie.

Which put Barbara in something of a predicament. She

156

was now the only police officer in a town that didn't like her and didn't want her here. If Chief Nicholls was having surgery on his leg, he could be out of action for weeks. Barbara needed back-up. Someone she could trust, some-one who knew the town but wasn't tied to it. Someone who understood police investigations. And, just maybe, someone who understood the Colony.

She reached into her pocket and pulled out the scrap of paper she'd ripped off Nicholls's jotter. She stared at it for a moment.

Then she picked up her phone.

22

Beau poured a large whiskey and sat down in his worn arm-chair, facing his trophies. The hair was fake but realistic, the embalming a skilful job. Still, even the best taxidermist could never get the eyes right. Eyes are the windows to the soul, so they say.

Beau lifted his drink. 'But what if you ain't got no soul?'

The glass eyes gazed blankly back at him.

'How would you know, old man?'

'Oh, I know. I know you are spawns of Satan. You walk in darkness, and it is the right of every God-fearing citizen to send you back to darkness for eternity.'

'You know nothing. You wear your ignorance as righteousness. But your zealotry has poisoned you.'

Beau rose and walked towards the trophies. 'The only poison on this earth is your kind. I did what was right, to protect my family, to protect this town.'

'Are you sure, old man? Or are you protecting something else?'

'You won't trap me with your riddles. I'm a hunter and I hunt vermin.'

'Then why do we haunt you? Why are you talking to us still?'

Beau rubbed at his eyes. 'The hell I know.'

He threw back his drink. He wasn't crazy. The Doc had told him that:

'You have a mass on your brain, Beau. Only a biopsy can tell whether it's benign or not. I can arrange that for you.'

Dalton had left him a leaflet, listing symptoms to look out for. Headaches, blurred vision, dizziness, mood swings, hallucinations.

'You hear that?' Beau said to the trophies. 'You're not real. You're just a mass. A tumour. 'Bout sums you up.'

That's what the Colony had always been. A cancer growing on the town. Spreading, poisoning and killing. And the only way to deal with cancer was to cut it out. The whole damn lot. It didn't matter which of those bloodsuckers had killed the Anderson boy; they all needed to pay. Should have done it last time. And they *would* have done if that fool, Tucker, hadn't got in the way.

This time they needed to finish what they started.

Beau stood and walked back into the kitchen to pour another drink. He didn't bother to put the light on, even though it was almost dark outside, but as he reached for the bottle the kitchen was suddenly lit up, bright as day. The security lights. Beau had strung them up on some trees years ago, and then, after bears and moose kept setting them off (and you sure as hell didn't need a security light to tell you when a moose was in your yard) he'd unplugged them.

When the Colony returned, he'd plugged them back in.

Beau turned and squinted out of the window, hoping to see some critter scurrying away into the shadows.

His heart constricted.

A woman stood in his back yard.

His wife.

Patricia.

She wore a pretty blue dress and white sandals on her feet. Her favourite dress and shoes. He'd picked them out

159

especially for her to be buried in. And then added a cream cardigan because he didn't want her to be cold.

She must be freezing out there, he thought, and then bit back a hoarse laugh.

Freezing. She's dead, you old fool.

But she looked so real.

Her hair hung over her shoulders in silver waves. Like it used to, until it became too much for Beau to wash and brush. She got upset, like a child, when the shampoo got in her eyes, and cold when it lay damp on her back, and she cried when he tried to get the knots out. They had both cried when he cut it. Afterwards, she would reach up to her head, and stare at him in fright. *'Where's my hair, Beau? What happened to my hair?'*

Beau watched as she walked towards the cabin. Upright and graceful like he remembered her, not hunched and uncertain like she had become. Her sandals left faint foot-prints in the snow. Real. Too real.

He wanted to back away, but the sight of her held him transfixed. Even though he knew it must be a lie, it was such a beautiful lie. Some are. And sometimes the truth is ugly. Like how, towards the end, on the bad days, when he was exhausted and bruised from her attacking him, he had felt pleasure at her distress.

'Beau?' She smiled through the window. 'It's me.'

He shook his head. 'It can't be.'

'Let me in, Beau. Please. I'm cold.'

'No.'

'Beau. I'm your wife.'

'You're not real.'

'Of course I am.'

160

'No. You're dead.'

'How can you say that? I'm here. See.' She raised one pale hand and placed it against the window. 'Let me in. We can be together again.'

He shook his head, tears burning behind his eyes. 'I can't. It's not right.'

'Don't you love me?'

Grief clogged his throat. 'Of course I love you. I love you more than anything. I miss you every day.'

Her smile drew into a sneer. 'Did you love me when you visited that whore in Anchorage? Did you love me when you slapped me after too many beers? Did you love me when you left me lying in my own shit to go to the Roadhouse because it was all too much for your sad, pathetic ass to deal with? Did you love me then, Beau Grainger?'

He recoiled from the window, a cry choking him.

The sneer became a snarl. His wife's face twisted and re-formed. She began to shrink inside her clothes, and now he was looking at a child. A young girl of no more than nine or ten. Blonde hair, amber eyes, sharp gold teeth. *Her*. He clutched at his chest.

The girl dragged her nails down the window, leaving thin white scars in the glass.

'How do you like me now?'

'Get away from here.'

'What? You don't like the truth?'

Beau turned and yanked open a kitchen drawer, fumbling inside. He found the old cross and held it aloft.

She laughed. 'You really think that works? You really think that after all these years I'm not immune to your superstitious bullshit?'

He continued to hold the cross up with trembling hands. 'What do you want?'

'You know what I want.' She thudded her fist against the window and a spider's-web crack spread out across the glass. 'I want them back, old man.'

'Go to hell!'

Beau turned and staggered back into the living room, slamming the door shut behind him. He leaned against the wall, struggling to get his breath. *He needed his damn crossbow.* And now he could hear something – a strange rustling, fluttering noise. Coming from his trophies. *No,* coming from *behind* the trophies. The chimney stack. Like the sound a bird made when it was falling down towards the grate. But this was louder. Far louder. Like a whole flock of birds.

The realization struck just as the room billowed with smoke and the bats burst out of the fireplace.

23

Tucker stared at himself in the mirror. His face looked odd and unbalanced.

Taking the heavy beard off had left the area beneath his nose looking strangely soft and pale, like baby skin, or a corpse left in the water for too long. In stark contrast, the skin above looked even more weathered and lined. Like tanned leather. The discrepancy wasn't helped by the numerous bits of tissue paper stuck to his chin where it was bleeding from more than a dozen tiny razor nicks. Death by a thousand cuts, he thought grimly.

He was out of practice at shaving. Hell, he was out of practice at a lot of things. He wondered why he was even doing this. When Detective Atkins called, he had told her there was no way he was coming back to town as a temporary deputy. He had retired. He had nothing to offer. He couldn't help her. He had messed up before. He didn't intend to mess up again.

And yet he found himself thinking about the case. The ring. The jacket. Who had left them? What message were they trying to send? Could the same killer be responsible for two murders, twenty-five years apart?

Aaron had been adamant that Todd was alive when he left him all those years ago. But all the evidence had suggested he was lying or mistaken. They had DNA, they had the boy's own confession that he had been with Todd that night. Tucker had been under pressure to charge Aaron with murder and request a cull.

'You were the last one to see him alive. You admit you had engaged in underage turning.'

'We loved each other. I wouldn't kill him.'

'Maybe you didn't intend to kill him.'

'I didn't do it.'

'You didn't mean *to do it.'*

'I'm not going to lie.'

'I don't want you to lie. I want you to think of the Colony, Aaron. I want you to think of going to trial and the possibility of a full cull if you're found guilty of murder . . .'

Tucker had seen the boy's face falter. People think it must be hard to persuade someone to change their story. That police officers must have to intimidate and torture people out of the truth. The fact was, it didn't take much to make someone doubt themself. Their recollection, their own actions. In a small police cell, when you're tired, alone and scared, you start to doubt everything.

Aaron had admitted to manslaughter. A turning gone wrong. The courts would be more sympathetic, Tucker had told him. He would stand a far higher chance of getting a custodial sentence rather than the death sentence ('stun, stake and decapitate,' as some officers – the assholes – called it). Most importantly, a manslaughter charge meant that there would be no need to enforce a colony cull.

The boy had signed the confession with a shaking hand.

Tucker had told himself he did it with Aaron's and the Colony's best interests at heart. To save them. But was that true? Had he, subconsciously, wanted a vampyr to be responsible because to accept anything else would mean he had missed something?

It's not that hard to convince yourself of a lie, either.

And now another boy was dead. Another cull looming. What if Tucker had got it wrong back then? What if the real killer was still out there?

'Fuck it.'

He needed a drink. He chucked the razor into the sink, walked into the kitchen and pulled open the fridge. There was no food or soda inside. Just several bottles lined up on the shelves. He reached for one, took it out and pulled out the stopper. Saliva flooded his mouth. He lifted the bottle to his lips, feeling the usual mixture of desire and disgust.

'Sometimes, I think I should have left you in the forest.'

'Maybe you should.'

'No, I think I like you better like this.'

Tucker closed his eyes and tipped up the bottle.

24

Barbara's dad had taken her to the river almost as soon as Barbara could walk. Maybe even before. One of her first memories was of sitting on a shallow area of the bank, sharp pebbles digging into her chubby legs as the cool water lapped at her toes.

Behind her, Dad readied his line with bait, the pungent smell of one of his home-rolled cigarettes drifting across the air. Barbara kicked and splashed with her feet.

'You watch them little piggies, Babs,' her dad had chuckled. 'Or the fish might just come and bite 'em off!'

Barbara had shrieked and snatched her toes out of the shallow water, tears blooming in her eyes.

Her dad had laughed harder as he cast his line into the river. 'Aw, don't be a baby, Babs. They'll spit 'em back out.'

It had been a joke, but as she would learn, like all her dad's jokes, it was laced with malice.

Barbara hadn't dipped her toes in the river for a long while after that.

When she was older, she would watch as her dad reeled in fish and then killed them swiftly, whacking their heads on a flat stone. At home her mom would gut them for stews and pickle the flesh. They ate a lot of fish in the summer. For years after she left home, Barbara couldn't stomach the sight or smell of fish.

Her dad had tried to teach her to hold the line, wait for

a bite, but Barbara had never been patient enough and even when she caught a fish, she had felt bad for it, flapping wide-eyed on the end of the line. Gasping for breath, snatched cruelly out of its natural home. Once, she had thrown a fish straight back in and her dad had stormed over, eyes blazing.

'What in hell did you do that for, you damn stupid child?'

'I didn't want to kill it,' she had mumbled.

His face had darkened. 'You better get used to killing, Babs. Ain't no one gonna wipe your ass your whole life. We're fighting for our survival here, and this family don't carry no passengers.'

Then he had backhanded her across the face.

Barbara never fished again with her dad. But as she grew older, she often went down to the river alone to read or swim, or just to escape the stultifying atmosphere of home, a slowly simmering cauldron of tension. Her mom, trudging heavily from sofa to stove and then collapsing back on to her armchair to lose herself in soaps. Her dad, sitting wired at the kitchen table, throwing back beers and bourbon.

At some point there would be an argument, always the same – about money, dad's shit life, her mom's weight, Barbara. 'What the hell's wrong with you,' she once heard him shout at her mom, 'that you can't carry me a boy? Hey? What kind of woman can't give her husband a son?'

Things would be smashed, maybe there would be a slap or a punch, from either of them. Violence was as natural as breathing in her family. Her dad was wiry, but her mom outweighed him, two to one. Finally, her dad would storm off to 'the lodge', where he would throw back drinks with his 'hunting' buddies and let off about stuff they couldn't in other places, like 'them damn negroes, whore bitches' or 'those fucking blood-sucking spawns of Satan'. He spent more and more time there, especially after he was laid off from the post office.

'Is it like a secret club?' Barbara once asked her mom.

Her mom had rolled her eyes. 'Something like that, hun.'

Sometimes, her dad would go away for days on hunting trips. Those were always calmer times in their household, and when he came back, he would seem happier, like something inside him had been released, at least for a while. It was only later – too late – that Barbara would start to wonder what her dad actually hunted on these trips. He never brought anything home to eat, nor any trophies to hang on the walls, like the deer heads in the living room or the hog's head which snarled over the toilet in the bathroom.

'Gotta keep something for the lodge,' he would say with a wink. 'Maybe one day, when you're older, I'll show you.'

Barbara didn't really want to see. She liked the times her dad was away (and always felt a little guilty that she did). Her dad frowned on 'wasted time', unless it was his own. So, if Barbara wasn't at school, her job was helping around the house: cleaning, sewing, 'women's stuff'; stuff her mom was too big to do any more. When he was away, she would waste as much time as she liked. On hot summer days, she would hike through the woods and swim in the river or take her books and just hang out in a shady spot on the bank. Most of the kids at her school would take inflatables and swim further up, nearer the town. Barbara's family lived a couple of miles out, close to the woods and the mountains.

Barbara didn't mind. She didn't really have any close friends at school. She wasn't unpopular. Just invisible. And in truth, Barbara kind of liked it that way. Just like she liked the solitude here. The water was clearer and cooler. Barbara could float on her back and stare up at the sky, only the sound of buzzing bees and the circling eagles for company.

Until, one day, someone else came.

Barbara's first reaction when she saw the girl sitting at the side of the water, in the shadows of the trees, was annoyance. This was her space. Her *private* space. And then curiosity took over. The girl was around her own age, fourteen or fifteen. Her skin was dark, but her hair was silvery white and it fell in a jumble of dreadlocks almost all the way down to her waist. For a moment, sitting there, legs curled beneath her, Barbara thought she looked just like a mermaid.

And then she had smiled, revealing the sharp glint of her incisors.

Mercy.

Barbara blinked her eyes open. The name lingered on her lips, mumbled into the hard pillow. She rubbed at her face, wiping away the cobwebs of the dream. But the strands clung on. The image of Mercy's smile, the buzz of the bees. And then Barbara realized that the buzzing was coming from the room. The bedside table. Her phone.

Shit. She reached for it. Six twenty a.m. Caller – Decker. Great.

169

She fumbled the phone to her ear. 'Hello, sir?'

'Atkins. You got an update for me?'

'Well, sir. Right now, it is 6.20 a.m. here. I've just woken up and I have a very full bladder.'

A pause and a heavy sigh. 'About the case?'

She fought back a yawn. 'It's proving a little more complicated than I anticipated.'

'Complicated. How?'

'Well, turns out the video evidence is fake. A local doctor, Dalton, paid the three boys to fake the video showing Marcus being attacked in order to incite a cull.'

'You got this doctor in custody?'

'He's on his way to Anchorage morgue, sir. Suicide.'

'*What?* What does Chief Nicholls say?'

'Chief Nicholls is in hospital with a broken leg.'

A long silence.

'And when were you going to call and tell me about this?'

'You just beat me to it, sir. But you can rest assured it will all be going in my report.'

She could picture him pacing, rubbing his bald head, itching for one of the cigarettes that he had given up five years ago.

'So, what are you saying? You don't think this is Colony? You think it's a human homicide?'

'I'm not sure, sir.'

A rattled sigh. 'Atkins. I know you like to do a thorough job, but we cannot be seen to be weak on culling right now.'

'Making sure the right person is brought to justice is not being weak.'

'People need to have faith in the system.'

'Sir, the best way for everyone to have faith in the system is if I investigate the case thoroughly and follow the rules. Culls are only supposed to be a final . . .' She caught herself before she uttered the word *solution*. 'They're only supposed to be a last resort – when a colony won't hand over a perpetrator or when the colony as a whole represents a threat to the human population.'

She heard him tut. 'I can read the statute book too, Atkins, but you and I both know that the public don't see it that way. They see that we're toothless. Afraid to go up against the colonies. You know how close the VPA is to being repealed? If we don't deal with this decisively, I guarantee it will be another weapon for the Helsing League.'

Decisively. She bristled.

'Sir, I am here to do a job, and I will do it to the best of my ability. Now if you'll excuse me, I really need to pee.'

She ended the call, and then turned the phone on to silent. Not what she needed right now. She flicked on the bedside lamp and swung her legs out of bed. The room felt colder than ever, and the chill of the wooden floor permeated through her thick socks. *Okay.* She hoisted the blanket up over her shoulders. Plan of action. Brave the shower, dress and get her ass over to the police department to make an early start. She counted to three, threw the blanket off and scampered for the bathroom.

Twenty minutes later, she was stepping out into the dark and cold. A blast of icy wind snatched her hood from her head and almost knocked her off her feet. Snow coated the road and parked cars. It had fallen heavily in the night and, from the look of the bulbous black sky, there was plenty more where that had come from.

She clomped through the fresh snow (already halfway up her shins) over to the police department and fumbled Nicholls's keys out of her pocket. She inserted one into the lock and pushed open the door. There was a light on in the office. She walked inside.

A strange man sat in front of her desk. Huge with roughly cropped hair, a badly shaven face and dressed in a heavy jacket, threadbare shirt and jeans.

'*Tucker?*'

He inclined his newly shorn head. 'Yes, ma'am.'

'What are you doing here?'

'Accepting the role of deputy.'

25

'You said you weren't coming back.'

'I say a lot of things.'

'You kept your keys?'

'I guess I forgot to hand them in.'

Barbara regarded Tucker thoughtfully. The removal of the beard and dreadlocks had taken the edge off his 'wild man of the woods' appearance, and he'd obviously made an effort in a clean shirt and jeans. But the sheer mass of the man made him seem like a bear in captivity.

'Look,' Tucker said. 'If you've changed your mind, I understand. Hell, I'm not even sure if I should be here. So just say the word and I'll disappear again.'

'Let me tell you where I'm at, sir.' Barbara pulled out her chair and sat down. 'Right now, I'm up shit creek without a paddle. So, frankly, I'll take any help I can get.'

A low laugh. 'So, you want to get me up to speed?'

She filled him in on the events of the last forty-eight hours as concisely as she could. Tucker pulled out a battered notebook and jotted things down in a loopy scrawl. When she had finally finished, he deadpanned: 'That all?'

Barbara smiled. 'Anything leap out at you? Anything that might tie this case to Todd Danes's murder?'

'Aside from the ring?'

'Yeah.'

He sat back and considered. 'Not really. The blood-dealing – that's an odd one.'

'You know Dr Dalton?'

'No. He must have moved here after I left town.' He scratched at his chin. 'Seems odd to me that this Doc would want a Colony cull when he's making money selling blood to them.'

'Cutting off his nose to spite his face,' Barbara said.

'Yeah. I thought that too. And it might have nothing to do with Marcus Anderson's death.'

'No. But when something stinks there's usually shit nearby.'

Barbara's turn to laugh. 'Yessir.' She studied him. 'Tell me about the Colony. Some background.'

'Well, it's always been an uneasy coexistence. Colony was here first. Had a settlement up in the mountains. When the mine moved in, they were displaced, hunted, captured.'

'Yeah, I've seen some of the trophies in the Roadhouse Grill.'

Tucker sighed. 'A lot of folk here have views I don't agree with. But it takes time for attitudes to change. Generations. And it takes both sides wanting to change. The Colony aren't the Waltons.'

'I understand that, sir.'

'*But* I was working on it. Visited the Colony with clothes, medicines – even vampyrs get sick sometimes. Eventually got Athelinda to talk to me.'

'I met her. Out in the woods.'

'She's centuries old, dangerous and maybe a little crazy. And she has no love for humans.'

174

'Yet she talked to you?'

'Don't mistake self-preservation for friendship or cooperation. If she thought slaughtering every soul in Deadhart would help the Colony, she'd do that too.' He paused. 'I thought I was getting somewhere. But then Todd was killed, and everything went to hell.'

'You still think Aaron did it?'

He shook his head slowly. 'I don't know. That's why I'm here.'

'What about the men who hunted down Aaron and his family?'

'Only Beau Grainger left now, and he must be pushing eighty.' Tucker met her eyes. 'They thought they were doing the right thing.'

'Report says you were shot in the break-out.'

'An accident. And I mended.'

'You seem pretty forgiving.'

His face tensed. 'Every town has a tipping point. Todd was dead, people were angry, scared. Thought their kid was going to be next. They're trusting you to protect them. To make the right call.' He shook his head. 'I made the wrong call.'

Barbara decided to change tack. 'What do you know about Nathan Bell?'

'What do you want to know?'

'He was Todd Danes's friend, right?'

'One of them. Odd kid. Came to live with his grandparents in that big old house after his parents died.'

'So Nathan didn't grow up in Deadhart?'

'No. Arrived out of the blue one day. Most folk didn't even know Helen and Greg had a grandson.'

Barbara tapped her chin with her pen thoughtfully. 'When did Nathan arrive in Deadhart?'

Tucker's forehead creased. 'Summer of '98. I'd been here three years.'

'So a year before Todd was killed.'

About the same amount of time Nathan had been back in Deadhart now. And another boy was dead. Those co-incidences were stacking up.

'I know what you're thinking, Detective,' Tucker said. 'But Nathan had an alibi. He was home all night with his grandparents when Todd was killed.'

And relatives never lied for their loved ones.

'Were you surprised to hear he was back in town?'

'A little. Aside from Todd, he never had many friends here. Also, Nathan knew that Todd had been meeting Aaron. A lot of people blamed him for not saying anything.'

'Maybe he's back because he wants to make amends.'

'Maybe.'

'You don't sound convinced.'

'In towns like Deadhart, there are generally two kinds of people – those who never leave and those who never come back. I always figured Nathan for the latter.'

He had a point. Barbara sure as hell never intended to go back to the town where she grew up. But now she was curious about something else.

'Mind me asking, sir, how come *you* never left Deadhart?'

'I'm here for good, or bad.'

'But you're not a native?'

'No. I moved from Boston in '95.'

'Seems an odd choice for a young officer to make.'

He hesitated and then said, 'My wife was murdered.'

Barbara felt his words like a blow. 'I'm so sorry.'

'Thank you.'

She waited. Sometimes people wanted to talk about it. Sometimes the pain was too much.

'She was a teacher,' Tucker said eventually. 'There was this pupil, had a crush on her. She laughed it off. Said it happened sometimes, it would pass. This kid looked harmless. Skinny, blond, glasses. I even felt sorry for him. Then, one night, as she was walking to her car after class, he came up behind her and shot her in the head. Raped her while she lay dying.' He swallowed. 'I couldn't do my job any longer. I kept thinking, *I missed it. I didn't see that this kid was really a monster.* I was about to quit the force when the job in Deadhart came up. It seemed as far away from my old life as possible, so I applied.'

'Good enough reason.'

'It wasn't the only one.' He stared at her. 'Here, I figured, I'd *know* the monsters.'

Barbara nodded. 'And how's that working out for you?'

He gave her a rueful smile. 'I've spent twenty-five years living in a hut in the woods. How d'you think?'

Barbara reached into a drawer, pulled out a holster, gun and badge and pushed them across the desk. 'I think we should get to work.'

26

Jess dropped by to take her dad for breakfast once a week. A routine that had started after her mom had died.

Jess had never been particularly close to her dad, growing up. He was a hard man to get close to. A man bred in tradition. Emotion was weakness; discipline built character. Jess knew, or at least suspected, that he loved her and her brothers. They always had enough to eat, plenty of presents at Christmas, and he only ever raised his hand to any of them when they really deserved it. But she couldn't recall him ever saying he loved them.

When her mom's illness really started to take hold, she saw a different side to him. A softer, kinder side. He did everything for Mom, and although Jess tried to help, she had Stephen and the business to look after. Even when the doctor said Mom needed to go into a care home, her dad refused. It was his duty to care for his wife. In sickness and in health. Till death do us part. Her dad took duty and God seriously. And when God finally took her mom, Dad was by her side, holding her hand. It was the only time Jess had ever seen him cry.

After Mom – and Jess tended to divide her relationship with her dad into those two parts: before Mom and after – she made the effort to visit him more often. To make sure he was eating right. To bring him groceries, do his washing. He was still fit for his age and would regularly go out hunting with his buddies or to sink beers at the Roadhouse Grill, but Jess would make sure his small house was clean, the milk for his coffee wasn't a week out of date and there was always a home-cooked meal in the freezer. Women's work, but as the only daughter, and the only child who had remained in Deadhart, it was her duty.

The breakfast ritual had started as a way to get him out of the house, one that didn't involve shooting things or propping up the bar with his cronies. Jess would pick him up, they'd drive down to the Grill or sometimes Harty Snacks (although her dad still regarded that place as a bit new-fangled, even though it had been in business for over a decade now).

They would drink coffee, eat fry bread and reindeer sausage and chat about this and that: the town, the *goddamn* Colony and what could be done about them (Jess had encouraged her dad to come to the church, but Beau didn't care for the new female preacher). He liked to hear about Stephen. Beau was proud of his grandson, even though Jess sometimes worried that the boy was three quarters attitude and a quarter sullen defiance.

They talked, too, about the business. Her dad had put a sizable chunk of money into Dan's touring and adventure firm. He'd done okay from his own business, running a truck repair shop in town till he retired (and a bigger one in Talkeetna took the trade).

So far, Dad hadn't seen his investment recouped. The business had started okay, but in recent years there had been a decline. Dan had been quick to reassure Beau that it was only a temporary blip and had even shown him accounts and projections to back this up. What Jess could not tell her dad was that the figures were bullshit. The business had been leaking money like a slow puncture for a long time. And it was only getting worse.

Dan had wanted to trade on Deadhart's status as a colony town. To attract more than the occasional group of goths. The plan was to take groups hiking up in the mountains to visit the old settlement. Deserted, but largely intact. They could camp out there overnight, enjoy 'the real Colony experience', which Dan planned to charge a premium for.

But before Dan could really get his plans off the ground, there had been the incident with the wolves. A pack had taken up residence in one of the deserted buildings and a hiker had been attacked. He had survived, but staying overnight was deemed too risky and the company's insurance wouldn't cover it.

After that the Colony tours idea had started to die off. They still got the usual hiking and mountain-climbing business; the national park was a draw for many. But there were other, more touristy towns that could offer the same things. Places with big lodges and hotels, gift shops and brewpubs. Deadhart couldn't compete.

And then, around a year ago, the Colony had returned. Their protected status meant that the tours couldn't venture within a half-mile of the settlement lest they 'affect the natural habitat of the Colony'. Even the air taxis were restricted from flying over. That was bad enough, but now, with Marcus's murder, trade would be hit even harder. It seemed callous to think of such a thing, but dead children were bad for business.

Dan had tried to reassure Jess. It would be okay; just a

rough patch. Once a cull was authorized and the Colony dealt with, they could start up the tours to the settlement. They just had to sit tight. He had a lot of new ideas to drive more business.

In a way she admired his optimism. Dan always believed that things would work out. It was one of the things she loved about him. That and the fact he was hard-working, kind and a great dad to Stephen. Ultimately, she guessed that was why she forgave the dodgy accounting and his other indiscretions.

She pulled up outside her dad's home. It was a modest building. Wood cladding, two bedrooms upstairs, a small living room, kitchen and another bedroom downstairs. Growing up here, with five of them, it had been tight. Now that it was just Dad, the place seemed too big.

She was a little early today. Dan was out, picking up some supplies from Talkeetna. The weather was worsening, and they might be cut off for a day or two. Stephen was downstairs in the den with Jacob. She kind of hoped that Jacob would be gone when she returned. Not that he was any bother. He was an inoffensive kid. And she certainly felt sorry for him, with that sad excuse of a father. But he was an odd choice of friend for Stephen. Marcus and Stephen had been friends since kindergarten; they'd grown up together. She didn't understand how they had become best buds with Jacob Bell.

Still, she guessed right now that Stephen and Jacob needed to lean on each other. It was a terrible thing they'd been through. Every time she thought about poor Marcus, her heart constricted, and the same thought tore through her mind. *It could have been Stephen.* Her boy. Her only boy.

She and Dan hadn't found having kids easy and she'd been in her thirties before that magic double line had appeared and the pregnancy had held, unlike the others, that had all failed before ten weeks. But this time, she'd carried to term and delivered a beautiful healthy baby boy.

As soon as they could, they started trying again. Jess knew the best time to conceive was right after giving birth. But it was to no avail. Five years down the line, they still hadn't been able to give Stephen a brother or sister. After another two, they stopped really trying. The sex dwindled. Dan began to spend more time trekking, hunting and night fishing.

Jess had told herself it didn't matter. She was lucky to have Stephen. Lucky to have a child at all. And yet, she worried. More than she should. She never understood how other parents could be so carefree, so *careless*, with their children, while she spent every waking hour terrified that something might happen to Stephen; that he might be taken from her. He was so wanted and so precious and so *singular*.

If she lost him, what would she be left with? Nothing. It wasn't the same if you had more children. That was the cold, hard truth. Immense as the pain might be, you could keep going because you had other children to look after. And perhaps more importantly, you were still a parent. What were you when your only child was taken from you? An *ex*-parent? A *former* parent?

The thought often plagued her and, while she knew it was crazy, part of her felt a heavy premonition that however hard she held on to Stephen, he would be lost to her. So, she clung on harder. *Coddled him, spoilt him*. That was what Dan often said. But he didn't understand. It wasn't the same for men. Never could be. Until you had carried a child and then delivered it into the world, you could never quite know the fear of losing that child. If something ever happened to Dan, she would be sad, sure. But it wouldn't end her life. Stephen *was* her life. Without him she had no reason to exist.

She parked the truck up outside her dad's house. Unchanged since Mom died. His battered truck was parked to the side, snow had been cleared from the path. Everything looked just like it always did, and yet . . . for some reason, a sliver of ice shimmied down her spine. What the hell was that? Nothing. There was nothing here out of the ordinary. But still, the vague uneasiness remained. She climbed out of the truck, clomped up the path and knocked on the front door.

She stuffed her gloved hands in her pockets and shuffled her boots on the compacted snow. Her dad usually came to the door on the first knock, often as he heard the truck draw up. She raised her fist and knocked again. Still nothing. She frowned then reached out and tried the door handle. Locked. Okay. She *was* early. Perhaps her dad was in the kitchen with the radio turned up. His hearing wasn't so great.

She turned and crunched through the deeper snow around to the back of the house. Her anxiety amplified. The door to the kitchen was hanging open, the lock bust. Shit. She stepped inside, pulling the door closed behind her. It didn't feel any warmer in the house, which meant the door had been open a while.

'Dad?'

She waited. No response. She looked around the kitchen. An empty whiskey tumbler sat by the sink, the bottle nearby. She walked out of the kitchen and down the short hall.

'Dad? Are you here? Is everything okay?'

The words died in her throat as she reached the door to the living room. It looked like a bomb had hit. Soot smeared the walls, logs and charred embers were scattered over the floor. A chair was overturned, cushions scattered and a lamp smashed. The whole room stank of smoke.

What the hell had happened here? Jess scanned the room, heart pounding. Then she turned and charged up the stairs, more panicked than ever.

'Dad. *Dad!*'

She flung open doors. Bedrooms, empty. Bathroom, empty. Nothing up here appeared to have been disturbed. She ran back down the stairs and paused in the hallway. She could hear a noise coming from the living room: a flapping, scraping noise.

She walked cautiously forward. The scraping sound came again. It sounded like something dragging itself across the floor, and it was coming from behind the upturned armchair. Jess hesitated. It might be an injured animal, maybe a rat or a squirrel. Cornered animals could turn nasty, and she didn't want to worry about a rabies bite. She knew Dad kept his guns in a cupboard in the corner of the living room. She stepped over the shattered lamp and pulled the cupboard door open. A handgun and a hunting rifle hung in the rack. Where his crossbow should be there was an empty space. Jess grabbed the handgun.

She walked back over to the armchair and peered behind

it. A bat lay on the floor. One wing was torn, and it was trying to pull itself across the floor with the other one. Bats weren't common in Alaska, although some roosted in attics, caves and even chimneys. But this bat looked bigger than the small native browns.

Jess stretched out one boot and flipped it over. It raised its head and hissed at her, fangs bared. She recoiled. *Fuck.* A vampyr bat. What the hell was *that* doing in here? The bat flapped its good wing frenziedly, squealing in panic. Jess stared at it with a mixture of revulsion and pity. Then she raised the gun and shot it, obliterating its head and most of its body.

She turned and walked out into the snowy yard. Dad's house backed out on to open land and then forest, stretching as far as the eye could see. Before she and her brothers could read or tell the time, their parents had taught them how to use a compass, make a shelter and avoid a bear attack if they ever got lost. Survival skills. And Dad was a survivor too. *He had taken his crossbow.* Had he been going after someone – or some*thing*? Jess looked down. Footsteps in the snow led away from the house towards the trees. She hadn't noticed them before because she had been focused on the open back door. And there was something else. She crouched down. Red splotches. Blood.

She straightened and gazed out towards the forest. A mass of black sandwiched between the dark grey of the sky and white of the snow.

She tucked the handgun into the belt of her jeans. And then she followed the footsteps.

27

Barbara guided the police truck back up the road towards Doc Dalton's. She gripped the wheel tightly. She didn't drive a lot, and she wasn't used to driving in snowstorms. At the turn-off for the Bell house she stopped, remembering what Al had said.

'If a storm rolls in, the air taxi won't run . . . and the trunk road gets impassable pretty quickly . . . you might find yourself stuck here a while.'

This might be the last day they could drive out this way.

'How d'you feel about paying Nathan Bell a visit before we head up to the Doc's?' she asked Tucker.

'Could be interesting.'

'Okay.'

She turned on to the rough track. The snow was even thicker here, and the tyres fought to get a grip. The engine revved hard but ploughed on. As they rounded a bend, the trees thinned out, and a property drew into view.

The house was built of wood and slate. Two storeys, high eaves. The wood was aged and dark, ivy and fungus making a home between the gaping boards. A ramshackle-looking porch ran around the exterior, misshapen and tilted down at one end, the balustrade broken in places. For some reason an old chair sat atop the porch roof, and a large pair of broken deer antlers had been fixed above the front door. Outside, the forest leaned in on every side, close enough to whisper in the windows and scratch spindly twigs against the glass.

If Barbara had been forced to describe it in one word, *Psycho* would have been the one that sprung immediately to mind.

Tucker squinted up at the house. 'Never liked this place.'

'I can see why.'

'Belonged to Nathan's grandparents. When they left, it was rented out as a guest house for a while.'

'People *paid* to stay here?'

'Not your idea of a vacation?'

'I'd think twice about taking a shower, that's for sure.'

They climbed out of the truck and crunched through the snow. A rusted and dented old Dodge pick-up was parked outside. Barbara realized now why the building seemed so gloomy. It was devoid of the fairy lights and Christmas decorations that adorned the rest of the buildings in Deadhart.

They climbed the porch steps. The wood creaked and sagged but held their weight, for now. All the curtains in the house were drawn. Not even a glimmer of light from within. Tucker raised his hand and knocked twice on the door. They waited. Nothing. Tucker raised his fist and knocked again. Still no signs of movement from inside.

'Let's check out the back,' Barbara said.

They walked round to the back of the house. If anything, it was in a greater state of disrepair than the front. Obviously, no one ever used the back door, as drifts of snow had piled up high in front of it. Old furniture had been discarded in the yard, along with a child's bike. Again, all the windows were shielded by thick curtains.

'Mr Bell certainly likes his privacy,' Barbara said.

'Yeah, but from whom?' Tucker said, looking around. 'Nothing out here but moose and bears.'

They returned to the front of the house and climbed back up the rickety steps. Barbara hammered on the door a few more times. Still no response. She looked around in frustration. 'Guess there's nothing more here we can –'

Tucker reached out and twisted the front door handle. It clicked open. He glanced at Barbara. 'We should check everything is okay, right? Especially with a killer around?'

Barbara looked back at the open door. There was no real evidence that anything was wrong here. Nathan was probably just sleeping off a hangover. But then, she thought about the Doc.

'Okay,' she said.

They walked inside. The hallway was dark, and it smelt. Barbara wrinkled her nose. Stale alcohol and cigarettes, but something else, less definable. The smell of a house shut up for a long time. Damp, mould, disuse. And it felt cold. Barbara couldn't see any heaters in the hall. Her breath was puffing out in plumes.

'I'd say it smelt like something died in here, but it doesn't feel like this place is even lived in,' Tucker said.

The big man had an uncanny ability to read her mind, Barbara thought. She pulled out her flashlight and shone it in front of them. Three doors led off the narrow hall and a stairway to their left ascended into darkness.

'Mr Bell?' Barbara called out. 'Police!'

Nothing but the dead, cold silence and the smell.

'Okay,' she said. 'Let's check out downstairs first.'

Tucker nodded tersely and Barbara eased open the

living-room door to their right. It stuck and scraped across the wooden floor.

A sagging sofa and a battered leather armchair slouched around a coffee table littered with empty cans and an overflowing ashtray. The fireplace was dead and cold. A large flatscreen TV dominated the space. Barbara had been in her fair share of low-income homes, and one thing they all had in common was a massive television. She didn't judge. When your life sucked so much you had to sit on packing crates and cook on a camping stove, the bigger your escape from reality needed to be.

'Whoah!' Tucker said, staring at the TV. 'That is *big*.' He walked over and peered around the back. 'And where's the rest of it?'

'Twenty-five years of technological advances. TVs get bigger, phones get smaller and everything gets thinner . . . apart from the people using them.'

He shook his head. 'Well, I'll be damned.'

They walked back into the hall and entered the next room along. The dining room. Or at least, that was probably its original purpose. Now, it was crammed full of stacked furniture, plastic crates and boxes, an old oak table barely visible beneath the detritus.

'Looks like a house clearance in here,' Tucker said.

Barbara shone the flashlight around. The boxes and crates were packed with dishes, ornaments and cutlery. Larger boxes were full of old paintings.

'Maybe that's what it is,' she said. 'Maybe Nathan came back to sell off his family's stuff.' She picked up a heavy silver spoon. 'Could be worth quite a lot.'

'So why is he still here a year later?' Tucker asked.

'Good question.'

For which she had no answer.

They backed out and proceeded down to the kitchen. It was large and old-fashioned, lined with dark cabinets. Barbara pulled one open. No food inside, but something shiny and black scuttled behind a joint in the wood. She shut it again hastily. To her left a dented, scorched range tilted against one wall and, in front of her, a cracked Belfast sink was full of dirty dishes and empty shot glasses.

'I guess we'd better check –'

She broke off. A noise. A creak from the hall. Tucker's eyes met hers. Barbara turned and walked to the kitchen door. She stopped. Shit.

Nathan Bell stood at the bottom of the stairs. He was dressed in a stained T-shirt and jeans. He looked pissed off. And he was holding a shotgun.

'Who the fuck are you and what the hell are you doing in my house?'

28

She should have brought a flashlight, Jess thought. The forest was dark, and her phone light didn't penetrate far into the pockets of gloom between the trees. Only a little daylight trickled down between the thick spruce.

She had already tripped over coiled bundles of tree roots and almost fallen flat on her face twice. At this rate, if she busted an ankle or a leg, they'd be sending out a search party for her as well. Maybe this had been a bad idea. Maybe she should go back and get the police involved. But that would mean asking the new detective, Atkins, for help. And what use would an out-of-towner like her be? On the other hand, her dad was seventy-nine. What if he was hurt or injured? He wouldn't survive long out here in the cold.

If he was still alive.

She shoved that thought to one side.

'Dad! *Dad* – are you out here?'

A flock of birds took flight from the trees up ahead, stirred by her voice. She jumped and then shook herself. Her nerves were rattling like dead men's bones. Jess knew this forest well, but she also knew how it could trick you, how the landmarks you gave yourself could change, how the darkness messed with your sense of direction. The forest wanted you to get lost. It wanted to keep you within its silent, breathless embrace.

'DAD!' she called again, pushing through a stubborn clump of undergrowth. Just a little further and then she would turn back. Summon help. It would do her dad no good if . . . she paused. She thought she had heard something. A voice. Up ahead. She moved forward quickly but carefully, trying to pinpoint the direction. Somewhere to the left. She was so intent on tracking the sound she almost walked straight into a large tree trunk and scraped her head on a low-hanging branch.

'Shit.' She rubbed at her head and her fingers came away streaked with blood and dirt. She wiped them on her coat. Then the voice came again. *Dad*, talking in a low tone:

'I know you're out there . . . and I know what you want. But you're not having them.'

Jess cut the phone light and felt her way forward. As her eyes adjusted to the gloom, she could see a little more. Ahead, there was a clearing. A familiar white-haired figure stood in the middle, clad in a thick jacket but no gloves or hat.

'They deserved what they got,' she heard him say. 'He killed that boy.'

Who was he talking to? She couldn't see anyone else there.

Her dad raised his crossbow, pointing it at an unseen foe. 'You stay away from Deadhart. You hear me?'

'Dad?' Jess said.

Beau spun round; crossbow raised.

'Don't fire!' Jess cried. 'It's me.'

For a moment her father stared at her like she was a stranger.

'Jess?'

'Yes.'

He kept the crossbow raised. 'I won't let you trick me again. You hear?'

Jess stepped out into the clearing. 'Dad, what's going on?'

'It's really you?'

She frowned. 'Of *course* it is. What are you doing out here? Who are you talking to?'

He glanced back into the trees. '*Her*. She's out there somewhere.'

'Who, Dad?'

'The girl. The vampyr.'

'A vampyr?'

Jess flicked her phone light back on, aiming it into the trees around them.

'She must have gone, Dad. And you shouldn't have come out here on your own.'

He glared at her. 'She came to my house last night. Disguised herself as your mother. I almost let her in, but she revealed herself.' He turned and spat on the ground. 'And then she sent bats, Jess. To scare me.'

Jess thought about the bat she had shot, feeling uneasy. There were stories about vampyrs taking the form of bats. But everyone knew they were just folklore. Vampyrs might be Satan's spawn, but they were still flesh and blood. More likely the bats had been nesting in the chimney. Her dad had always been dismissive of such superstitious stuff. But recently, Jess hated to admit, he hadn't seemed his usual self. He had been distracted, irritable, drinking more than he should.

'It's morning now, Dad,' she said. 'What have you been doing all night? The living room, it's trashed . . .'

193

For a moment, he looked confused. Then he shook his head. 'I couldn't sleep so I came back out here looking for her.'

'Well, we should get you home,' she said. 'And then call that detective. She needs to know about this. A vampyr trying to get into your house. That's a violation of the law. They're not supposed to encroach upon towns.'

But her dad wasn't listening. His eyes searched the trees around them. 'She wants revenge, Jess. That's what this is all about.'

'Revenge? For what happened with the Danes boy?'

'Not just that.'

'Then what?'

Her dad's lips pursed. He looked suddenly old. His eyes had grown vacant, misty, like he was dwelling in another time, somewhere she wasn't a part of. Jess had seen it happen before, when he was talking about Mom. Her dad's mind was usually sharp, but occasionally, it slipped – from now to then. She shivered. It was freezing out. And her dad wasn't dressed for it.

'Okay,' she said more firmly. 'Let's talk at the house. You need to warm up.'

She took her dad's arm. She felt him stiffen, and then, reluctantly, he allowed himself to be led back through the woods. They pushed through the undergrowth in silence, Jess praying that she was heading in the right direction. After what was probably a few minutes but felt much longer, the trees started to thin – *Thank you, Lord* – and she could see her dad's house. They crossed the yard, she pushed open the back door and they stepped into the kitchen.

'I'll make us some coffee,' Jess said. 'And then —' She paused. There was blood on her dad's collar. She remembered the drops outside. 'Dad, did you hurt yourself?'

He raised a hand to his neck. 'I'm fine. Just a scrape from a branch.'

'You sure? I could —'

'I said *I'm fine.*' He pushed past her and walked down the hall and into the living room.

Jess followed him. 'You need to sit down and rest.'

'Rest?' He turned and stared at her. '*They* won't rest. They won't ever be done tormenting us.' He pointed to the heads on the wall. 'She took him, Jess. She took the boy.'

Jess glanced at the trophies. She had never really liked them. Not that she had a problem with anyone killing those fuckers, but she'd never felt comfortable sharing a home with them either. Mom had made Dad keep them in his workshop out back. The only thing Dad had changed about the house after she died was to bring the heads back in and mount them above the fireplace. Now, Jess noticed, one was missing. The boy. Aaron.

'You know why I keep 'em there,' her dad said. 'A reminder that they're animals. They'll always be animals.'

'I know. You told me, Dad.'

'It's always going to be us and them, Jess. We won't ever be safe; our *children* won't ever be safe here till every last one of them is dead.'

'I agree with you, Dad. And once we've warmed up, we're going to drive into town and report this. A vampyr broke into your house and stole from you. That's a crime.'

'No!' He glared at her. 'We don't report it, not while that new detective is here. She'll just want to take the rest of my trophies. We can't count on the law. We need to take care of this ourselves. Just like we did before.'

Jess sighed. Dad was probably right. That new detective didn't care about Deadhart. All she cared about was ticking her little boxes. Asking her stupid questions. She wasn't on their side.

'Okay, Dad. Leave it with me.' She turned. 'I'll make that coffee.'

She walked into the kitchen and filled the kettle, setting it to boil. Then she got out her phone. *We can't count on the law, Jess.* No. Dealing with vampyrs shouldn't be a matter for the law. It was a matter for God and His disciples.

She pulled up a number and waited while it rang.

'Hello?'

'Reverend? It's Jess Garrett.'

29

Barbara raised her hands slowly. 'Sir, we're police. I'm Detective Atkins.'

'Police?' Nathan squinted at her. Tucker stood a little further back in the shadows.

'Yes, sir.'

'How did you get in?'

'Your door was open, sir.' Barbara offered a friendly smile even as her heart hammered. 'We were concerned.'

Nathan's eyes fell on Tucker. 'What about him?'

Tucker took a step forward. 'It's Jensen Tucker.'

'Tucker?'

Tucker nodded. 'Former Chief Tucker. Been a long time, I know.'

Nathan blinked rapidly and licked his lips. He looked like he was trying to work out a difficult sum in his head or drag back a memory obscured by time and alcohol. Then, slowly, he lowered the gun. 'Chief Tucker. I'm sorry. I . . . I didn't recognize you.'

'Well, I'm sure we've both changed.'

'Yeah, sure.'

Barbara offered another sympathetic smile, heart beginning to resume a more normal beat. 'I'm really sorry about intruding like this, sir.'

Nathan nodded again. 'You should be. Most people here shoot first and ask questions later.'

'I appreciate your restraint, sir.'

He regarded her suspiciously from beneath his lank hair. 'You're not here because of an open door.'

'No, sir. We wanted to talk to you.'

''Bout Jacob?'

'And other things.'

Something in his face shifted. 'What things?'

'Why don't we take a seat in the living room and have a chat?' Tucker said in his low, easy tone.

Nathan's eyes flicked to him. The momentary aggression he'd displayed when he confronted them with the gun had evaporated. He looked confused and scared.

'Okay.'

Barbara cleared her throat. 'And perhaps leave the gun out here, sir.'

Barbara and Nathan sat on the sofa and Tucker squeezed uncomfortably on to the armchair.

Nathan hadn't offered any drinks and Barbara wasn't sure she would have accepted anyway, after seeing the state of the kitchen. He placed his phone on the coffee table alongside a crumpled pack of Marlboro Lights and a battered silver Zippo.

'You mind if I smoke?' he asked.

Barbara did mind, but if it helped to relax him then it might help him talk.

'You go ahead, sir.' She smiled and pushed the ashtray closer.

He was already reaching for the pack. As he did, Barbara noticed his knuckles. Each had a rough black square tattooed on it. Like he had tried to crudely cover up some old tattoos underneath.

Nathan caught her looking. 'Never got a tattoo you regretted?'

'No, sir, can't say I have. Mind me asking what it was?'

Nathan flicked open the Zippo and lit a cigarette. 'Yeah, I do.'

Tucker stared at him. 'When d'you take up smoking?' he asked.

'Can't really say.' He squinted at Tucker through a cloud of smoke.

'So,' Barbara said, 'did you get my message about Jacob?'

Nathan nodded. 'Got himself in to some trouble up at the Doc's yesterday.'

'That's right, sir. I'm sure you'll be relieved to know that he is not being charged with anything and is currently staying at his friend Stephen's.'

Nathan scowled. 'Boys will be boys. And word is that the Doc didn't only dish out prescription drugs, if you know what I mean. That's probably why Jacob was up there. Lot of kids get their dope from the Doc.'

Seemed the Doc's drug-dealing was pretty well known. Barbara wondered again about Rita's plausible deniability.

'Well, the Doc also had a side line supplying blood to the Colony,' she said. 'And Jacob was his mule. You know anything about that?'

Nathan dragged harder on his cigarette. 'No.'

'Never wonder where he went at night?'

'He's fifteen. They get to that age, you can't keep 'em in.' He gestured around the room. 'You think he wants to be stuck here, staring at the TV? He wants to be out with his friends . . . hell, it's not as if there's much for kids to do in a dump like this. Not much for anyone to do.'

'Dalton also paid the boys to fake the video of the vampyr attack. I guess you didn't know about that either?'

'No, and it seems like you should be talking to the Doc, not me.'

'He's dead.'

'*What?*'

'We think it's suicide,' Barbara said. 'But we can't rule anything out at this stage.'

'Where were *you* the night before last, Mr Bell?' Tucker asked.

He shifted uneasily. 'Here, watching TV.'

'And last night?'

'Up at the Lame Horse. It's a bar on –'

'I know where it is,' Tucker said curtly.

'And where were you the night Marcus Anderson was murdered?' Barbara pressed.

Nathan seemed to start a little. 'Why d'you want to know that?'

'Just answer the question, please.'

'I guess I was probably at the Lame Horse again.'

'You don't sound sure.'

'No, I'm pretty sure I was.' He looked at Barbara. 'You can call 'em and check.'

She glanced at Tucker, who gave a small incline of his head. 'We'll do that, sir.'

'Is that it?' he asked.

'Not entirely,' Tucker said. 'We'd like to talk to you about Todd.'

'Todd?' Another hard drag on the cigarette. 'Why do you want to talk about Todd?'

Barbara noticed how he answered a question with a question. Stalling, buying time.

'Well, sir,' she said. 'It was the last Colony killing in Deadhart, and it could be relevant.'

'Thought you caught the vampyr that done it?' He aimed the question at Tucker.

Barbara saw Tucker flinch a little. 'I thought that too,' he said.

Nathan reached forward and stubbed out his cigarette. 'I told you everything I could before. It was a long time ago.'

Tucker looked at him. 'I guess this must feel like history repeating?'

'What d'you mean?'

'I mean, you were friends with Todd, and he was killed. You come back. Your son is friends with Marcus and now Marcus is dead.'

Nathan glared at him. 'You accusing me of something?'

Tucker shook his head. 'Just making an observation.'

'Yeah, well, maybe you should be observing that those bloodsuckers are back, and another kid is dead. Maybe they're looking for revenge?'

'As I said,' Barbara cut in, 'we're examining all angles at the moment.'

Nathan snorted. 'Well, you can go "examine" elsewhere. I've nothing more to say to you.'

Barbara glanced at Tucker. They couldn't do any more. They had nothing but supposition and guesswork.

'If that's what you want, sir.' Barbara stood and nodded

at Tucker to do the same. He clambered out of the chair with some difficulty.

'If you change your mind, Mr Bell . . .'

'I won't.'

'Okay then. We'll see ourselves out.'

'Yeah. You let yourselves in, right?'

They walked out of the front door and back into the freezing air. It was actually a relief after the stale, smoky atmosphere in the house.

Barbara coughed and patted her chest. 'One of those homes where you want to wipe your boots when you leave.' She glanced at Tucker. 'You got Nathan's hackles up.'

Tucker looked thoughtful. 'He's lying about something.'

'You said he was never a suspect.'

'Doesn't mean I was never suspicious.'

They both looked back at the house. A curtain twitched in the living room then dropped closed again.

'Nathan didn't used to smoke,' Tucker said.

'He was fifteen. Maybe he took it up later.'

'Maybe, but something doesn't feel right.'

Barbara nodded. 'Agreed. But we can't arrest folk because things don't feel right.'

She wished she could. The idea of a Jacob living here with a dad like Nathan gnawed at her gut. A little too close to home.

'I'm curious about those tattoos,' she said.

'Ex-offenders often have knuckle tattoos,' Tucker said. 'Maybe Nathan spent some time in jail?'

'Well, we can check on that.' Barbara pulled a dirty shot glass out of her pocket.

Tucker frowned. 'Where d'you get that?'

'Picked it up in the kitchen. Must have forgotten to put it down. I'll bag it and we can check Nathan's prints. See what comes up.'

He raised an eyebrow. 'So, you're not all by the book, Detective Atkins.'

She smiled. 'Sometimes, I read between the lines.'

They walked over to the truck. The windscreen was coated in snow. Tucker started to wipe it off with his coat sleeves.

'You know the truck has a heated windscreen?' Barbara said.

He stared at her in wonder and dusted the snow off his jacket. 'Man, modern tech.'

Barbara pulled open the driver's door, then paused. A slight, dark-clothed figure walked along the track towards them. *Jacob.*

She raised a hand. 'Hi.'

He frowned. 'What are you doing here?'

'Just having a little chat with your dad.'

'Why?' His voice rose in panic. 'I've told you everything.'

'It's okay,' Tucker said. 'We're not here to get you in trouble.'

Jacob's eyes flicked to the big man.

'This is Deputy Tucker,' Barbara introduced. 'He's helping out.'

Jacob swallowed. 'Right.'

'You walk all the way from Stephen's house?' Barbara asked.

'Yeah, I didn't want to cause his mom any more hassle.'

'You stay there a lot?'

He shrugged and shuffled his boots in the snow. The boy seemed more on edge than ever this morning.

'Is everything okay?' Barbara asked more softly.

He looked at her. 'What d'you mean?'

'I mean, if there are problems at home, there are people you can talk to.'

She saw Jacob's eyes shift, from her to the house. She turned. Nathan Bell had appeared in the doorway. He stood there, watching them and smoking.

'I need to go,' Jacob said, and started to walk away.

'Jacob –'

'I'm fine, *okay*. Just leave us alone.'

He put his head down and hurried towards the house. Barbara watched him run up the steps and disappear inside. Nathan shut the door behind them.

'Dammit.' She climbed into the truck.

'Nervous kid,' Tucker said.

'Yeah.'

'What d'you want to do?'

There was nothing she *could* do. And that was the problem.

'Okay,' she said, trying to get her mind back to the job at hand. 'Let's head on up to the Doc's. See if we can find anything else up there.'

She started the engine and gave the Bell house a final look.

History repeating.

She sighed. She sure as hell hoped not.

30

Athelinda hurried across the settlement. Snow fell heavily around her. The main street was deserted. Most of the Colony were inside at this time of day, sleeping. The place she was visiting was on the outskirts of the settlement. Here, the buildings straggled out. Most of this area had fallen into dereliction, sliding down the mountainside towards the river. A small stream cut through. Only a couple of lopsided houses and one other, bigger building remained.

It was here they took those like Merilyn. Larger than some of the other dwellings, it offered space and privacy. It also meant that the rest of the Colony didn't have to confront what was happening inside. An old sign, half faded, still read: *Hospital.*

Athelinda reached the door and, with a heavy heart, raised a fist and knocked three times. After a moment, the door eased open. A young red-haired woman peered out. Henny. She was a nurse here in the Colony. Not formally qualified, of course. That avenue was closed to her, as any form of employment or education was to all colony members. But Henny had a passion for biology and medicine, and she had taught herself through stolen and donated medical textbooks.

The Colony was allowed to claim basic medical supplies – antibiotics, painkillers – so long as they registered each year with a medical facility nearby. That was how Athelinda had made contact with Dalton. The doctor had been useful in more ways than one. Henny did the best she could with the rudimentary tools they had available, but it was blood – human blood – that had kept Merilyn from deteriorating for so long.

'Miss Athelinda.' Henny bobbed her head. 'Thank you for coming.'

'Can I come in?'

'Of course.' Henny held the door open wider and Athelinda stepped inside.

'How is she?' Athelinda asked. A pointless question. She would not be here if things were well.

Henny's lip trembled and she shook her head. 'Not good, miss. That's why I called for you.'

Athelinda nodded. 'Let me see.'

Henny led her through the main ward. A hole in the ceiling let in small flurries of snow. A couple of candles set on tables provided a vague, flickering illumination. Beds still ran down either side of the ward, the mattresses mouldy and water-logged. Abandoned medical trollies had been pushed to one side. They reached a door on the right. A private room. Henny nodded and Athelinda pushed the door open.

The stench hit her first. Ripe, rich and sickening. The smell of rot and decay. It felt stuffy and warm, despite the fact that a window was open and the temperatures out-side had dipped below freezing. The room was febrile with putridity.

Merilyn lay on the bed, plastic sheeting beneath her to soak up the bodily fluids that seeped from her loose and cracked skin. In places it had broken down completely, revealing the blackening flesh beneath. Her scalp had shifted on her skull, giving the impression of a badly fitting wig, and her eyes had gone, just deflated yellow sacs. Merilyn had been this way for almost five years.

And there was the irony. The unspeakable horror that even the elders of the Colony rarely spoke of. A fate they tried to keep from the youngsters for as long as possible.

There is no such thing as immortality. Death visited us all eventually. The only difference was when he came and how long he lingered.

When you lived for centuries, you died for decades.

Athelinda sat down on a chair beside the rotting woman. She wasn't sure if Merilyn could hear her, or if the woman was aware of anything other than her own agony, but Athelinda gently held her wet, disintegrating hand.

While the lives of humans seemed frustratingly short, there was something to be said for brevity when it came to death. Yet, as fleeting as human lives were, still they held power over the colonies.

Athelinda remembered an older vampyr once saying to her: *The tree has lived here for two hundred years. The man only a few decades. But the man has an axe. And the tree cannot run.*

And now man had more than axes. They had powerful, automatic crossbows, they had UV guns that could flay the skin from a vampyr in one burst. They had armies and tanks and helicopters. Technology that had been denied to the colonies.

Of course, vampyrs had genetic traits that gave them an advantage over humans. Strength, speed, less fragility of the body. They could attack the town in the dead of night and kill many. But, despite her threats to Tucker, Athelinda knew it would by a pyrrhic victory. An attack would only result in retribution. The Colony would be hunted down, obliterated.

'But I promised you justice, Merilyn,' she said. 'I won't renege on that promise.'

Not tonight, dear Athelinda. Tonight is for mercy and release.

Athelinda sighed and stroked the putrefying flesh of Merilyn's arm. She was not that old by vampyr standards. Barely five centuries. But grief had sucked the life from her. First her husband, killed by hunters when her children were still young. Her daughter-in-law had died during childbirth. Then her sons and her only grandson. Murdered by Beau Grainger and his cronies. Human scum. And still he denied Merilyn her kin. She would never see them all returned to her now. It was too late. But Athelinda could offer her some small solace.

'I brought him to you, Merilyn. I couldn't bring the others, but I have your grandson.'

She reached into the sack and placed Aaron's head on the pillow beside Merilyn, so she could hear him. Then she picked up Merilyn's hand and laid it upon his skull. Athelinda watched as her fingers gently traced the shape of his face. Together, at last.

Athelinda stood and walked to a medical table by the wall. Rusted surgical instruments lay on top. On the shelf beneath, other older instruments: a sharp wooden stake and a mallet. Athelinda picked them up.

It was strictly forbidden for a vampyr to kill another vampyr. To do so would see a vampyr branded and ostracized from their colony. That was why no one spoke of what took place here. Leadership came with its own heavy burdens.

Athelinda placed the tip of the stake above Merilyn's chest.

'Forgive me, old friend.'

She raised the mallet and drove the stake deep into Merilyn's heart. The woman's chest gave with a sickening squelch. Blood and bodily fluids spurted hotly into Athelinda's face. Merilyn bucked once, briefly, and then released a final, foul breath. Her body settled, seeming to somehow deflate as the life flickered out.

She was gone.

Athelinda took a moment. Her throat swelled with grief and tears burned behind her eyes. She composed herself and walked from the room. Henny waited outside. A good girl. A good nurse. And discreet.

'Is it done?' she asked.

'It is.' Athelinda handed her the bloodied stake. 'Put this on the pyre with her body. We'll light it at sunset. Let it be known.'

'And what shall I tell the Colony?'

Athelinda wiped some of the blood from her face. 'Tell them she died quietly in her sleep. Like the others.'

She walked briskly back through the hospital and pushed open the door, eager for the fresh bite of the winter air. Outside, she paused. A figure stood in the street, wrapped in furs, blond hair blowing in the wind. *Michael.*

Athelinda stared at her son. 'What the fuck are you doing here?'

'I followed you.'

'Why?'

'I wanted to see . . . Merilyn is dead, isn't she?'

She hesitated and then nodded. 'Yes. We'll light the pyre at sunset.'

'She never saw justice for her kin.'

Athelinda's eyes flashed. 'Don't fucking lecture me, Michael. Not when you fraternize with the very humans you'd have me kill. Or is your plan to fuck them all to death?'

He glared at her. 'Why did we come back here, if not for revenge?'

'Because this is our home. We belong here.'

He shook his head. 'This will be our grave if we don't do something.' He paused. 'Some of the Colony want to take matters into their own hands. They won't wait much longer.'

Athelinda clenched her fists. 'Fucking idiots. They think I'm waiting because I'm afraid?'

'Why else?'

She walked up to him. She was barely half his height, but she still saw him flinch. 'A storm is coming. It will cut off the town. No help. No reinforcements. They'll be on their own. Scared, angry, vulnerable.'

'That's when you plan to attack them.'

'No . . . that's when I want *them* to attack us.'

'I don't understand.'

'No, you don't.'

She began to walk around him, circling. 'Colonies are protected, Michael. By their own human laws. If we attack the town, we sign our own death warrant. But if they come for us, here . . . well, we have no choice but to defend ourselves. It's our right. Morally and legally.'

She stopped and watched her son's face as the realization sank in. But then he frowned. 'What if they don't attack? What if they're too weak?'

Athelinda smiled. 'Sometimes, the best way to make a wolf hungry . . . is to feed it.'

31

Tucker stood on the wooden decking of Dalton's house. The still lake offered a dark, inverted image of trees and sky. In the distance, the mountains rose jaggedly, white tips disappearing into clouds. The snow had eased momentarily, but the wind still cut like a million icy knives.

'Guess blood money can buy you a mighty nice view.'

Barbara nodded. 'Although it helps if you're alive to enjoy it.'

She turned, unlocked the patio doors and slid one open. The living room looked the same as when she had left it, as far as she could tell. They stepped inside. Tucker started to move forward, and Barbara put out a hand to stop him.

'What?' he asked.

She fished in her bag and pulled out latex gloves. She handed Tucker a pair.

'Right now, we're our own CSI.'

He frowned. 'CSI?'

'Forensics.'

'Sorry, a bit rusty.'

'S'okay.' She hoped. Barbara needed help with the case, not an added liability.

Tucker snapped on the gloves They were too small, but they just about did the job. 'So, this is how you found it?' he asked, looking around.

'Yessir. Although when we first arrived, that stove was still warm.'

The files were still stacked on the table next to the chair. Tucker walked over and picked one up. 'Patient files?'

'Yeah. I thought he must have been reading them,' Barbara said.

But why stop partway through and kill himself? Now, in context, it seemed a little odd. She walked towards the stove and grabbed a poker. She crouched down, opened the door and prodded at the crumbly black wood. And then she saw it. A flash of something silver. She reached in and picked it up, blowing black ash off her fingers. A staple. She regarded it thoughtfully. 'I don't think he was reading the files.' She glanced back at Tucker. 'I think he was burning them.'

She rose. Tucker flicked through a folder. Each had a name written on the front in marker and was filled with notes. Some were thicker than others. It seemed a slightly archaic way to retain patient information . . . *unless* you wanted to be sure you could dispose of it thoroughly at short notice. The best IT whizz in the world couldn't retrieve a file from ash.

'I think I know why,' Tucker said.

He handed her a folder. Barbara looked at the papers inside. Fairly mundane patient information.

'Keep going,' Tucker said.

Barbara flipped past the first few pages.

'Damn,' she cursed.

The contents of the folder abruptly changed. Now, she was looking at printed photographs of vampyr artefacts. Some innocuous like items of clothing and jewellery.

Others, sickening images of body parts, amputated limbs, hands, teeth, heads, internal organs.

Names and contact numbers were listed. Notes had been made, transcripts of conversations.

'Client has requested that the teeth be adolescent. Undamaged. They have also put in a request for hair and a vampyr finger.

Note: this client is concerned with aesthetic and age. Artefacts must be in prime condition or they will be rejected. Photographs and examples necessary. Specialist interest – pre-pubescent specimens. Will pay a high premium for a perfect, intact head.'

Barbara felt her stomach roll. An image flashed in her mind.

Heads. At least a dozen of them. Men, women, children.

'This is the only place vampyrs "hang" around here.'

She closed the folder. 'The Doc was dealing in illegal vampyr artefacts,' she said. 'He was playing both sides – sourcing human blood for the Colony and vampyr artefacts for human collectors.'

'Looks that way.'

Although he obviously wasn't getting them from the Colony here. He must have been sourcing from further afield. But that *certainly* explained the new house. Successful dealers could make a lot of money from their trade.

She replaced the sheets of paper. 'Let's take a look at the other files.'

They methodically examined the remaining folders. Each contained similar paperwork. Probably a dozen in total. Plus, those that had already been burnt.

'I can see why the Doc was keen to get rid of these,' Tucker said.

Barbara considered. 'And if you were one of his clients, you'd be even keener.'

She tapped her chin thoughtfully. It made sense that the Doc might want to get rid of evidence of his trading, especially with the police asking questions. But why kill himself? And why stop halfway through?

As if reading her mind (again), Tucker said slowly, 'Seem a bit strange to you that the Doc didn't finish the job?'

They looked at each other.

'Maybe he decided that it wasn't worth clearing up the evidence if he was going to kill himself.'

'Or someone decided to clear up *all* the evidence here, including the Doc.'

Barbara sighed. 'No signs of struggle. No break-in. Let's take another look at the office.'

They walked through the house to the office at the back. It was darker here, and Barbara flicked on a light. They stared around the room. The chair remained tipped over on the floor. But nothing else was out of place.

'Neat,' Tucker remarked.

'Isn't it just?' she said.

She looked at the chair. Then she knelt and took a small fingerprinting kit out of her bag. Tucker stood at the desk, frowning down at Dalton's MacBook Air.

'Looks like someone flattened the Doc's computer with a steamroller.'

Barbara moved over to stand next to him. She dusted the keys and trackpad.

'Needs a password,' she said.

'Any ideas?'

'If it isn't "password" or a favourite pet I'm all out.'

Tucker hit some keys while Barbara opened drawers in the desk. None were locked and most were empty. One contained some envelopes and sheets of A4 paper. Another, a notebook that looked brand new. The bottom one contained nothing but some paper clips and a stapler. Barbara shut them all again. She was struck by the empty desk. Her own desk usually looked like a bomb had hit it, followed by some kind of apocalyptic event.

Tucker tutted at another failed password attempt.

'What did you try?' Barbara asked.

'Deadhart.' He shrugged. 'You never know.'

Barbara put her hands on her hips and stared around the office. The bookcase was the only place that was untidy. Crammed with medical journals, crime fiction and a number of non-fiction and anthropological books about vampyrs. Prior to what she had seen in the Doc's files, Barbara would have put this down to a healthy medical interest. Now, it seemed far more sinister. And there was something else. Something missing from this picture.

'I haven't seen the Doc's phone anywhere. Have you?'

Tucker shook his head. 'No. Unless it's so thin I've missed it.'

'You check the living area again. I'll search the bedroom.'

The bedroom was also neat and functional. Barbara looked in the drawers in the bedside table and then investigated the wardrobe. She rifled through the clothes, patting down pockets, noting that all the brands were designer and the loafers lined up beneath were expensive-looking leather. Finally, in the very last outdoor jacket, she found a bulge of something heavier in one pocket. A wallet.

Wallet, but no phone. She turned as Tucker walked back from the living room. He shook his head. 'No sign.'

'I guess he could have disposed of it,' Barbara mused.

'What about Jacob?' Tucker asked. 'Perhaps he took the phone?'

'And not the wallet?'

'Wallet was hidden. You checked inside for cash and cards?'

She flipped the wallet open. No bills, but the credit cards were still there. Barbara slipped them out. As she did, a couple of business cards fluttered to the floor. She picked them up,

Revere and Ransom, the header read on the first, in fancy gold-and-blue writing. *Real Estate Agents, Ontario.*

Interesting. Maybe the Doc was in the market for a move. She looked at the second card. White with a black Gothic-style print: *Be Damned Tattooists.* That name again.

Barbara showed the card to Tucker. 'I saw a sticker for this same tattoo shop in the toilets at Harty Snacks Café. And Marcus Anderson had a Helsing tattoo.'

'The Doc look the sort to have tattoos?'

She thought about the smart, silver-haired man. 'Not really.'

Tucker rubbed at his chin, looking thoughtful. In contrast to Nicholls's impatient efficiency, there was a steadiness to him. Not slow, just measured.

'Anything else strike you as odd about this place?' he said.

Barbara looked around the bedroom. Sterile, she thought. 'Well, it's all too damn neat.'

'Exactly,' he said. 'The Doc was dealing in vampyr artefacts. Where are they?'

It was a good point. They'd searched the house. 'You think someone took them?'

'*Or* the Doc stored his stock somewhere else. Keeps his hands and his home clean. A second property or a storage unit maybe?'

Barbara considered, and then something came to her.

'He rents out his old house to Marcus's teacher, Kurt Mowlam,' she said. 'And I saw Mowlam and Dalton arguing in the Roadhouse Grill the other night.' She smiled at Tucker. 'You are not so rusty after all, sir.'

He tapped his head. 'Just getting those cogs moving again.'

She slipped the cards back into the Doc's wallet. 'Okay. Let's take what we have here back to the police department. We'll make some phone calls and –'

Her phone buzzed. She rolled her eyes and pulled it out of her pocket. 'Hello?'

'Barbara, it's Rita.'

'Hi, Rita.'

For once, there was no preamble. 'Marcus's parents are back. They're ready to talk to you.'

Her Captor was happy today.

The girl could tell even before she heard the tread of their footsteps on the stairs. Lighter, relaxed. Not heavy and fierce.

She had heard her Captor singing and smelt the aroma of freshly baked cookies. The girl liked the smell, even if she couldn't eat them. Her Captor often seemed to forget this, because they entered carrying a plate, along with the girl's usual jug of sustenance.

'Hello, dear. How are you?'

'I'm fine.'

She wasn't fine. The heavy manacle had rubbed at her ankle and chafed the skin. But she didn't want to complain and spoil her Captor's mood.

Her Captor knew her though. They glanced at the manacle.

'We'll need to get some antiseptic on that. But don't worry. It won't be for much longer.'

The girl felt her spirits lift.

'You'll unchain me?'

'Soon.'

Soon, the girl thought. She had heard that often enough.

'I just have to put something in place first.'

'What thing?'

Her Captor sat on the bed beside her. They smelt of dried sweat and baking. 'Sweetheart, I just want to keep you safe. You know that?'

'Yes.'

'And I realized, well, that window, it was just temptation. Taunting you. It was cruel.'

'Okay.'

Her Captor sighed. 'So, I'm going to stop being cruel. I've ordered some bricks and cement and I'm going to take out that old window and brick it up. It's for the best.'

For the best.

Her Captor kissed her quickly on the head and stood. 'Now you enjoy your snacks.'

For the best.

Her Captor walked from the room and back up the stairs.

For the best.

The girl looked at the cookies and the jug of red liquid.

For the best.

She wanted to scream and throw them at the walls, but that would only incur her Captor's wrath.

She took several deep breaths and from the depths of her mind she tried to summon up a call. To put out a thought to the other side of the wall. To the outside. To him.

'I need you. Come soon. There isn't much time. Help me. HELP ME!'

32

Grief was a cancer. You could spot the grieving like you could spot those in the throes of a terminal illness. The light had been lost from their eyes, their skin was dry and sallow, their cheeks hollowed and even their movements seemed laboured.

People often talked about the stages of grief – denial, pain, acceptance. But few mentioned the fourth – terminal. Those for whom there would never be any recovery. Barbara remembered one grieving mother telling her: *'I'm already with my little girl. This heap of flesh and bones just hasn't caught up yet.'*

Janice Anderson looked like she was half gone from this world already. She was a slight woman with brown hair in a straggly ponytail. It didn't seem like it had been washed in a while and her shirt was missing a button. Barbara got the impression that staying upright and breathing were taking everything she had. In comparison, her husband, Ed, was stiff and tense. Like he was using every muscle to hold in the scream.

Barbara could feel her own heart growing heavier, just by being in the house. It was a modest home just off Main Street. Barbara imagined that 'before', it had been a cosy, cluttered place, scattered with the detritus of a teenage boy. Sneakers discarded on the floor, coats slung over chairs, an ever-multiplying pile of dishes and dirty mugs beside the sink.

Some of those things were still here. She had noticed a boy's sweater hanging in the hall and shoes lined up by the door. But the kitchen was clean, and the house felt cold. Barbara knew this was probably because Janice and Ed had been away, stopping with Janice's parents, but she had a feeling it might never feel warm again.

'Thank you for seeing me,' Barbara said. 'I'm so sorry for your loss.'

Janice gazed at her blankly. Ed cleared his throat. 'Thank you.'

'I'd just like to ask you a few questions about Marcus, if that's okay?'

Ed looked at her from under hooded eyes. Patchy grey stubble covered his chin and cheeks. 'Rita told us the video isn't real. The boys faked it.'

'Yes, sir.'

'Why?'

'Someone paid them, sir. We don't know why.'

'But . . . Marcus is still dead. Killed by a vampyr, right?'

Barbara hesitated. 'Right now, it looks that way,' she said.

This time Janice spoke. Slowly, like someone gradually coming out of a trance. 'I remember when Todd Danes was killed. I was *angry* that people here wanted to kill an entire colony for the sins of one individual. I told my parents it was barbaric . . .' She paused. 'But it's different, isn't it? When it's your own son, your only child.' She took a trembling breath. Her husband reached for her hand. 'So, can you promise me, whoever is responsible, you'll make sure they pay?'

Barbara knew she shouldn't promise. Too easily given. Too easily broken.

She swallowed. 'I promise I will do everything in my power to make that happen.'

Janice stared at her and, finally, she gave a small nod. 'What do you want to know?'

'Tell me about Marcus. Tell me about your son.'

The woman's face softened, and Barbara could almost see a little life trickle back into her eyes. 'He was a good boy. I guess all parents say that. I had him late, and he was two weeks late arriving. That became a bit of a joke with Marcus. How he was never in a rush. He was placid, unhurried. Like, he was a little slow on the walking front, but once he got there, he ran everywhere. We used to say: "He'll get there in the end and then he'll make up for lost time . . ."' She paused, perhaps realizing that there would be no more time to make up for Marcus.

She reached for a glass of water on the table, took a sip.

'Marcus grew up here in Deadhart?' Barbara asked.

'That's right. We took over the general store from my parents when they retired.'

'When did Marcus become friends with Stephen and Jacob?'

'Stephen and Marcus grew up together. And they stayed close, even though they were pretty different kids.'

'How so?'

'Well, Stephen was always the leader – you know, the one who would shout the loudest, call the shots. Marcus was quieter. He'd kind of go along.'

Which matched up with what Kurt Mowlam had said about Marcus being easily led.

'And what about Jacob?' Barbara asked.

222

Janice's face clouded. 'If I'm honest, we weren't crazy about the friendship.'

'Why?'

She hesitated, and Ed jumped in:

'It's not Jacob. It's his dad, Nathan. He's not exactly popular around here.'

'Because of what happened with Todd Danes?'

'He *knew* Todd was meeting that vampyr and he didn't tell anyone.'

'People blamed him,' Barbara said.

She didn't like Nathan Bell, but she was starting to feel some sympathy for him. Here, he would always be a reminder of something terrible that had happened. For-ever associated with his friend's death. And people wanted a scapegoat. Someone to pin something on.

Barbara paused, giving them both a moment, and then asked: 'Did Marcus ever talk about the Colony?'

'Just the usual stuff,' Ed said. 'I mean, teens, they're all interested in the Colony – morbid curiosity and all that.'

'We always told him to be careful,' Janice said.

Her voice caught again, and Barbara's heart contracted. You could tell them, give them all the warnings, but you couldn't protect kids from themselves. Barbara was glad she didn't have children. She didn't think she could handle the terror that such unconditional love brought. *'Like trying to guide a balloon through the world without puncturing it,'* Susan had said to her once. Hell, Barbara couldn't even keep a relationship afloat, too scared that love only brought loss.

'Forgive me for asking this,' she continued, 'but did Marcus have an interest in any anti-vampyr groups?'

Ed sighed. 'One time we caught the boys watching some anti-vampyr stuff online.'

'What sort of stuff?'

'Bad stuff – beheadings.'

Barbara felt her stomach tighten.

'Marcus said it was just curiosity,' Janice said. 'It's so damn easy to find this stuff. He lost his internet privileges for a while and promised he wouldn't look up anything like that again.'

Barbara took a breath. 'Marcus had a Helsing tattoo, on his shoulder? Did you know about that?'

They just stared at her.

'A tattoo?'

'Yes. Any idea where he could have got it?'

'No.'

'The boys ever go over to Anchorage?'

Ed nodded slowly. 'Sometimes. One of us would drive them to Talkeetna to catch the train. Janice has a sister in Anchorage. They'd stop with her a couple of nights, then get the train back.'

'I don't see what this has to do with anything,' Janice said, hostility creeping in. 'So what if Marcus had a tattoo? How does any of this help you catch his killer?'

'Any information about who Marcus was associating with could help us find the perpetrator,' Barbara said steadily.

'And what if it doesn't?' Ed said. 'Will you authorize a cull then? Because if it can't be one, then it might as well be all of them.' His voice caught. 'No one else should have to go through this.'

Barbara felt a hard knot in her gut. What would it take?

She knew what Decker would say: *All this other crap is a distraction, Atkins. Either a vampyr killed the kid or they didn't. If the Colony are protecting someone, then we are within guidelines to authorize a cull.*

Reluctantly, she said, 'I'm not ruling anything out, sir.'

'Thank you, Detective.'

She nodded. 'Would you mind if I took a look around Marcus's room?'

It looked like most teenage boys' rooms. A mess. The aroma of hormones and sweaty socks still hung in the air. But that was fading. Already time was gathering up the remnants of Marcus's existence and packing them away. Dirty mugs and a couple of plates with dried food on them sat on a computer desk alongside a monitor and keyboard. An old PlayStation and Xbox sat on the floor underneath. Dust had started to gather on the consoles and controllers.

Barbara scanned the rest of the room. The bed was hastily made, duvet thrown across the squashed pillows. It was black and red with the name of some band scrawled across it. Core or Hate or Vomit. It was hard to read the florid Gothic writing.

A battered chest of drawers stood next to the bed and a wardrobe was crammed into the opposite corner, lop-sided, one door hanging off. It was obvious that the Andersons weren't exactly rolling in money. Was that why Marcus had agreed to fake the video?

She opened the wardrobe. Sweatshirts and shirts hung up haphazardly, jeans folded up beneath and trainers thrown in on top. She shut the door again and moved to the chest of drawers. Underwear, socks, more T-shirts. Nothing hidden or stuffed inside.

She felt like she was missing something. Or maybe there was nothing *to* miss. She walked back towards the door. The floorboards creaked. She looked down. In her experience, people rarely hid stuff underneath floorboards in real life. There wasn't much room, and you usually needed a tool to get the damn things back up. Not to mention the splinters. Still, sometimes a cliché was a cliché for a reason.

She crouched down, eyes scanning the scarred and uneven floor. Did one of the boards look a little looser than the others? She felt around with her fingers. Definite movement. She reached into her pocket and pulled out her keyring. She wedged one of the keys down the side and, hey presto, the board lifted up. She pulled it free, flicked on her phone torch and peered inside.

The first thing she spotted was a large wad of bound cash. Barbara took it out. She guessed this was the money the Doc had paid Marcus. She stuck her hand back in the hole in the floor and scrabbled around, hoping she wouldn't feel the flutter of spider legs over her fingers. She didn't. They closed around a large plastic bag. Barbara pulled it out. The bag was full of weed and another, smaller bag of white powder.

'*He bought drugs from the Doc.*'

She tucked the bag into her pocket, replaced the floorboard and stood up. A creak from outside the room. Barbara turned. Ed stood in the doorway.

'I'm just about done here, sir.'

He walked inside and looked around. 'Janice won't clear

anything away. Nothing. Like she thinks he's still going to come back.'

Barbara felt the lump rise in her throat. And then Ed suddenly gripped her arm. She jumped.

His eyes were hollow with desperation. 'He won't, will he? Marcus won't come back?'

She stared at him, the chill freezing her spine to its core. *He won't come back.* Not as one of them. A vampyr. Undead.

'No,' she said softly. 'He won't come back, sir. I'm certain of that.'

33

Barbara waded back through the snow, feeling drained and despondent. Grief had a way of rubbing off on you. She was almost at the police department when she spotted a familiar figure striding down the street towards her. Her heart sank.

Colleen Grey. Just what she needed right now. As always, the Reverend was dressed as though for a Victorian funeral. Long, flowing dress and a black, hooded overcoat, dusted with snow. Barbara shivered just looking at her.

She forced a smile. 'Evening, Reverend.'

Colleen pushed back her hood and smiled widely in return. 'Good evening, Detective. I hope you've had a fruitful day?'

'Well, ma'am, sometimes you move an inch, sometimes a mile, but as long as you're covering ground, that's what's important.'

'I heard Marcus's parents are back.'

'Yes, ma'am. I've just been to visit them.'

'I imagine that must have been difficult, especially with no news to bring them.'

Barbara bit hard on her tongue. 'Did you want something in particular?' she asked. 'It's just, I can't feel my toes out here.'

'I had a worrying call from a member of my congregation earlier. Jess Garrett.'

'I'm sorry to hear that,' Barbara said.

'Jess claims the child vampyr, Athelinda, was at her father's house last night. She threatened him.'

'Well, Mrs Garrett should have reported the incident.'

A tight smile. 'Not everyone trusts you here, Detective. Some suspect your motives.'

'My *motives*? My motives are to find a killer.'

'I wondered if you might join us at church tomorrow morning. I thought you could address the congregation. It would be an opportunity for you to allay some of their concerns and answer questions.'

Barbara reined back her irritation. It wasn't Colleen's place to call a town meeting. That was down to Rita. However, it wasn't a bad idea.

'I'd be happy to. I'm actually having dinner with the mayor tonight, so as long as it's okay with her.'

'Good. We'll see you at 10 a.m.' Colleen pulled up her hood. 'Send my regards to Rita and her mother.'

Barbara watched her walk away, feeling unnerved and aggravated in equal measure. The damn woman set her teeth on edge, like biting on tin foil or hearing nails scrape against a chalkboard.

She turned down the road, towards the police department, and fumbled the keys out of her pocket. She inserted them in the lock and pushed open the door.

Tucker sat at Nicholls's desk, a pile of papers spread out before him. As Barbara entered, he turned and stuffed something back inside his jacket pocket. Barbara couldn't be sure, but it looked suspiciously like a flask.

Their eyes met. *Damn it.*

Barbara debated with herself. Tucker didn't seem drunk.

She hadn't smelt alcohol when she walked in, and she had a nose for that type of thing. Growing up, she could tell you what her dad had been drinking just by entering the room. Beer meant a fast, furious blow-out, whiskey meant the rage would grow more gradually and often end in melancholy. Home-brewed moonshine and you got the hell out of Dodge.

'Something wrong?' Tucker asked her.

Maybe she was mistaken. Maybe it was just water. Barbara decided to give him the benefit of the doubt. She didn't have much choice. She needed him.

'No, just desperate for a coffee.' She smiled. 'Can I get you one?'

'No, I'm good, thanks.'

She nodded. 'What are you doing?'

'Just going over my notes from the Danes case.'

'Anything leaping out at you?'

'Not really.'

'Right.'

She walked over and peered down at his desk. There were photographs in the file: the crime scene, Todd's body and one of Todd and Nathan together that she didn't recall seeing before. Perhaps she had flicked past it, more intent on studying the details of the murder. You could be guilty of that as a cop. Too intent on death to take notice of the living. She hadn't registered how similar in appearance Todd was to Marcus. Skinny, blond, a wide, easy-going smile. It was slightly eerie.

Nathan was different. He looked away from the camera. His hair fell over his face. She could feel his discomfort at being photographed. She stared at him, trying to see the man in the boy. Certainly, they shared an odd awkwardness.

But she still felt like she was missing something. She put the photo down.

'How did it go with Marcus's parents?' Tucker asked.

'Pretty terrible. Did you speak to the tattooists?'

'Yeah.' He sat back in the chair. It creaked worryingly. 'I said I was looking to get a tattoo. Apparently, *Be Damned Tattooists* shut three years ago. But a couple of the tattooists take on custom work.'

'Like a Helsing symbol?'

'I asked about that. The guy got cagey. Asked me to leave my name and number. Said he'd pass it on and, if the tattooist is interested in the job, he'll get back to me.'

'Okay.'

Of course, they could just be leading themselves on a wild-goose chase. The tattooists could have nothing to do with the Doc's death. The Doc's death could have nothing to do with Marcus. But why did Dalton have the card in his wallet? She didn't like the coincidence.

'What about the Doc's realtors?' she asked.

'Spoke to a nice lady called Tammy. Got the feeling my call livened up her day. Seems the Doc was planning on retiring to Ontario. Been over a couple of times to look at some nice lakeside properties.'

'How nice?'

'Around the three million mark.'

Barbara whistled through her teeth. 'Doesn't sound like a man about to kill himself.'

'Nope. Sounds like a man expecting a big payday.'

'But where from?'

Their eyes met, the answer striking them both at once. Barbara got there first.

'A cull,' she said, the idea so obvious it felt like a slap in the face. 'A whole colony cull. *That's* why the Doc paid the boys to fake the video.'

Tucker nodded. 'A lot of dead vampyrs. A lot of valuable artefacts.'

It made perfect sense. Despite their protected status, colony culls were still poorly regulated affairs. The bodies were supposed to be cremated afterwards, but many went missing. People took souvenirs, including the police meant to safeguard the bodies. Barbara had once caught a young cop with a penis in his lunchbox. And that wasn't a euphemism.

A cull of this size could be the Doc's big payday. His retirement fund.

'Let's say that was the Doc's plan,' Barbara said. 'Was Marcus's murder part of it?'

'Maybe the Doc thought an attack wasn't enough.'

'You think he set Marcus up?'

'It's possible.'

She tapped her chin. 'But the killing still has all the hallmarks of a vampyr killing. Why would a vampyr want to see their own colony culled?'

'Perhaps we're looking at this wrong,' Tucker said. 'What if this vampyr, this killer, isn't one of the Colony?'

Barbara frowned. 'An outlier?'

It was rare, but some vampyrs did live apart from colonies, usually because they had been cast out. And usually, they didn't last too long. Isolated from their colony, a vampyr was vulnerable. They often got into trouble searching for food or fell prey to illegal hunters.

Vampyrs might once have been regarded as fearsome

monsters, but those days were long gone. UV flares for self-defence were readily available online and many homes had UV security lights. UV guns, grenades and 'light bombs' were supposed to be restricted to law enforcement, but some still found their way on to the black market. Living as an outlier was dangerous. Only the most damaged and desperate vampyrs chose that life.

Barbara mulled Tucker's suggestion over. 'Okay, but I keep coming back to the ring. Why would the perpetrator want us to *know* they killed both boys?'

'Killers often like to boast about their crimes.'

'Human killers, usually.'

'You think this is a human killer now?'

'No. But . . . maybe the motive is more human.' Her mind was whirring. 'Most vampyr attacks are opportunistic, driven by hunger and need. Often there are minor attacks first, where the victim survives. There's usually an escalation. But there's none of that here.'

Tucker nodded thoughtfully. Barbara continued, a theory forming in her mind.

'We've worked on the assumption that this is the same – a vampyr driven by the desire for blood. But what if our perpetrator is simply driven by the desire to kill? The blood is a bonus. The pleasure is in the murder itself. And in getting away with it.'

Tucker's face creased. 'Like a serial killer?'

'Possibly. And why do serial killers usually send messages to the police?'

'To taunt them.'

Barbara nodded, a coldness seeping into her gut. 'And to let them know they're not done yet.'

34

The chapel was dimly lit. Cold crept between gaps in the wooden frame and the floor was dirt and sawdust. Makeshift pews were arranged in front of an altar, behind which hung a large, white cross.

It was a functional space. Still, Colleen had tried to make the best of the raw materials that God had provided. To create a warm and relaxing ambience for worship. Choral songs played softly and the scent of incense drifted up towards the rafters. A pastor should do all they could to welcome people, both the faithful and those who weren't yet part of the flock.

A willing Christian was always better than one who felt obliged or forced to convert to the path of righteousness. After all, the duty was hers. To lead sinners from temptation. To show them the light, as she had been shown the light. To take those, even the ones some would call irredeemable, and convert them to God's care. That was her mission.

She had shed her coat and sat with her head bowed, enjoying this time of contemplation. The cold didn't bother her. Never had. She felt herself insulated in God's love. Warmed from within by her own sense of purpose.

The boy's murder was a tragedy. But perhaps it was a necessary sacrifice. God had his reasons. He wanted the people of Deadhart to see the evil that shadowed them.

You could not live side by side with Satan. You could not compromise with the Devil. Evil, in all its forms, must be banished. She had learned that at a young age. The Devil wore many faces.

Prayers and protests were not enough. Christians were soldiers. They needed to fight for their way of life. Just as Colleen had fought to become who she was today. To escape her background. To change her destiny. She was a patient woman, and she had waited a long time for this moment. She smiled to herself, aglow with conviction and belief.

'Reverend?'

She turned. The girl – Grace – stood behind her. Colleen composed her face into a smile.

'How are you, child?'

'Better now I've rested, Reverend.'

Colleen frowned and stood up. 'You still look a little pale.'

'I'm okay.' Grace rubbed at her arms beneath the thick smock.

'How are they healing?' Colleen asked.

'Just itchy.'

'Let me look.'

Reluctantly, the girl let Colleen unbutton her cuffs and roll up the sleeves. Angry welts criss-crossed both arms. Along the line of the veins, at least a dozen old bruises and puncture wounds.

Before Colleen had rescued Grace, she had been a sinner, condemned to damnation. Colleen had freed her, in the same way she herself had been emancipated. But conversion to the side of the Lord did not come without sacrifice. Colleen rose and wrapped her arms around the girl. She felt frail. Skin and bones.

'You are doing so well, Grace. Your devotion will be rewarded. Why don't you go and make a start on dinner? We cannot fight the good fight on empty bellies.'

She smiled at the girl as she walked back across the chapel. A door at the rear led to private quarters where the pair shared a small bedroom, bathroom and kitchen.

Colleen was just about to follow her when the front door to the chapel swung open. A flurry of snow and a blast of icy wind blew in, along with a figure in a thick, hooded jacket.

Grace turned. 'Oh, good evening, Mr Mowlam.'

The teacher smiled charmingly. 'Evening, Grace. You look very . . . serene.'

A faint flush spread up Grace's cheeks.

'Grace,' Colleen snapped. 'Could you give us a moment?'

Grace nodded, bowed her head and disappeared into their quarters.

Mowlam watched her go. 'Pretty girl. A little pale.' He turned to Colleen. 'Hope living with you isn't taking too much out of her?'

Colleen gripped the pew in front of her tightly. 'Why are you here?'

Mowlam sauntered towards her. 'You hear about the Doc?'

'Yes.' The town grapevine had spread the news of Dr Dalton's suicide. 'A tragedy. I wish he had come to me before taking his own life. Maybe I could have helped.'

'Oh, I think we both know that the Doc was beyond help.'

Mowlam regarded her with a glint in his eye. He was a handsome man, but Colleen knew trouble when she met it.

'Is that supposed to mean something?' she asked.

'Well, it would be pretty convenient for some people

236

around here if the Doc wasn't able to talk to that new detective.'

'Inconvenience isn't a reason for murder.'

He shrugged. 'Depends. I mean, everyone has secrets. Even those who claim to be holier than thou.'

She kept her voice steady. 'None of us are without sin, Mr Mowlam. As the Good Lord said, "I have not come to call the righteous, but sinners to repentance."'

'And do you think your congregation would be forgiving of your sins, *Reverend*?' He soaked the word 'Reverend' in sarcasm. 'Perhaps we should tell them?'

Colleen swallowed. 'I don't have the cash, okay? It will take some time.'

Mowlam sighed. 'I want to help you out, Reverend. You and I are on the same side, despite – well, despite what I know.'

He rose and walked closer. Colleen could smell cigarettes, sweet aftershave and malevolence. She fought the urge to recoil. Behind the handsome face, the soulful eyes, there was danger here. She could feel it in her bones.

'So maybe, instead of cash, you can do something else for me.'

Her skin crawled. 'What?'

Mowlam smiled. 'Oh, don't worry. You're a little on the old side, but your young friend . . .' He glanced towards the back of the church.

Colleen raised a hand. 'Don't you –'

The church windows exploded inwards in an avalanche of glass. Colleen shrieked. They both fell to their knees, covering their heads as the razor-sharp slivers rained down. Snow and wind squalled through the broken panes.

'What the hell?' Mowlam cowered under a pew. Some glass had nicked his eyebrow and blood trickled down his cheek.

Colleen forced herself to look away. She could hear something. From above them. Scrabbling sounds, as if a creature was running or crawling over the roof. Almost immediately they were followed by another sound. This time from the front door. Thumping and scratching. Like someone was desperate to get in.

And now Colleen could hear the voices. In her head.

'Let us in. Let us in. Open the door.'

Colleen stared at the front door. She could almost see the wood buckling. She stood. Mowlam grabbed her ankle.

'No.'

She yanked her leg away and strode down the aisle.

'Are you fucking kidding me?' he shouted. 'You're going to get us killed, you stupid bitch.'

Let us in. Let us in.

No, she thought. They won't harm me.

She paused for a moment, composing herself. Then she pulled the door wide open.

The voices abruptly stopped. No one stood outside. But at the end of the path, she could see flames reaching high into the night sky. The cross was on fire. A short distance away, a disembowelled pig lay on the ground, guts steaming in the freezing night air.

Its blood had been used to scrawl a message in the snow: 'WE ARE GATHERING.'

35

Rita beamed. 'I hope you're hungry, because I've cooked enough here to feed the five thousand.'

'Oh, I'm always hungry,' Barbara replied. 'My mom used to say I'd eat a damn horse if I could.'

Of course, her mom stopped cooking meals when Barbara was about ten. After that everything came out of a box or a can and, eventually, even that stopped when her mom took to the sofa, but that probably wasn't one to throw into light conversation.

Barbara followed Rita into a living/dining room. Like her host, it was bright and cheery. Lots of indigenous tapestries and pictures adorned the walls. The colour scheme was corals and warm, earthy tones. A fire blazed in the hearth and a small round table in one corner had been set for dinner.

'Your home is so welcoming,' Barbara said.

'Thanks. I like to think it's small but perfectly formed, like me.' A chortle. 'We're all on one level. Two beds. Mom gets the bigger one because that's kind of her living room, too.'

'How is she? Chief Nicholls mentioned she's not well.'

'Stage-four ovarian cancer. We're coping. But she's eighty-four. She sleeps a lot. She had her dinner early, so she'll watch a little TV – if you hear any noise, that's her watching her favourite crime shows.'

Barbara smiled. 'Good choice.'

'Oh, she'd bend your ear about your job if I gave her a chance, but I figure you'd like to get home at some point this week! Anyway, dinner will be in about half an hour. Can I get you a drink? Beer, wine, whiskey?'

'A beer would be good,' Barbara said.

It must be hard, she thought, being a carer, especially for a parent. A lot of people struggled with the role reversal, seeing the person they had always relied on rendered so helpless. Many resented it. And it was tough the other way too. *'I just hate having to be so damn grateful all the time,'* the elderly relative of a friend had once told her. *'I wiped his ass till he was ten years old and now he expects me to kiss it just for going to the grocery store for me.'*

Rita bustled back into the kitchen. 'So, I hear Tucker is back?' she called out.

As Barbara suspected, not much here got past Rita.

'Yeah, with Nicholls out of action, I needed some help.'

Rita emerged back into the room with two cans of beer. 'Right. Well, it can't hurt, I guess.'

But something in her voice said otherwise. She handed a beer to Barbara. It was ice cold. Barbara took a swig. Damn good.

'How is Nicholls doing?'

'Out of surgery and going out of his mind already. I reckon they'll have to chain him to the hospital bed to stop him trying to escape.'

'You tell him about Tucker?'

'It came up.'

'I got the impression Nicholls didn't like him.'

Rita popped open her own beer. 'Nicholls is straight

down the line. He likes order, rules. Tucker resigned in disgrace. In Pete's opinion, he shouldn't be anywhere near an investigation. And twenty-five years is a long time away from duty.'

'Did no one visit Tucker in all that time?'

'Anyone who went near got warned off with a crossbow. After a while, most folk stopped trying.'

'Except you?'

'I don't give up so easy.' Rita's face grew more serious. 'But a word to the wise – Tucker has spent a quarter of a century hiding from the world. I'm not saying the chief's right, but you don't come back from that without some damage.'

Barbara thought about the flask again. Then pushed the thought away.

'Something wrong?' Rita asked.

'No.' She shook her head. 'Oh, I meant to say, I bumped into the good pastor on the way here.'

Rita perched on the arm of the sofa. Her feet, in large fluffy slippers, barely touched the floor.

'And what did she want?'

'She wants me to talk to the congregation tomorrow morning, answer questions people have.'

Rita nodded slowly. 'You up for that?'

'Well, there's only so much I can share, but I know the town is hurting and people want answers.'

Or perhaps what they really wanted was to be told something was happening. That someone was *doing* something. That they were being listened to.

'If you're happy to do it, I'll be there for support,' Rita said.

'Well, hopefully no one will turn up with their pitchfork.'

Rita grinned. 'We keep those for summer. It's burning torches this time of year!' The grin faded a little. 'While we're talking work, you asked about the Bone House.'

Barbara raised an eyebrow. 'I thought that was history.'

A sigh. 'Look, I don't know how it's relevant and, like I said, it's not something folk here like to talk about, *but* I dug out some old photos of the town. You might find some of the Bone House in there.'

'Thanks, Rita.'

'Sure. You can take a look after dinner, while you rest before dessert.'

'I'll need to rest?'

'Oh, trust me – you'll need to rest!'

36

Tucker hadn't meant to end up in the Roadhouse Grill. But then, there were a lot of things in life he hadn't meant to do.

He shouldn't really be drinking. It didn't have the same effect it used to, and it upset his guts. But old habits die hard.

The Grill was pretty empty. Still, Tucker felt the atmosphere shift, tension cut through the air as he walked in. Faces turned at his approach.

Carly stood behind the bar. Older, thinner (if possible), but the scowl was just the same.

'Tucker. Well, to what do we owe the displeasure?'

'I'm helping out while Chief Nicholls is in hospital.'

'That detective must be really desperate.'

He smiled pleasantly. 'I guess so. A double bourbon, please.'

The scowl deepened. Tucker was sure the thought of not serving him crossed Carly's mind, but she obviously needed the customers. She poured bourbon into a shot glass and slammed it on the bar in front of him. No ice.

'Thanks.' He pulled some crumpled bills out of his pocket.

'That'll be six dollars.'

His eyebrows shot up. He pulled out some more notes. Carly snatched them and crossed to the till.

'Keep the change,' Tucker said.

'Wow. I'll buy a penthouse.'

He sighed and walked to a table in a far corner. He felt people's eyes move with him. He deliberately kept his own averted. He was a big man, but he avoided confrontation. Tried never to be the one to start the fight. As a black male, that was something you learned from an early age. Don't provoke. Don't give them a reason to pull a knife or a gun. Don't give them an excuse to claim it was self-defence. If the police stop you, do what they say, never turn your back or walk away. They say drop, you drop. Survival. Self-preservation. Yeah, he knew all about that. Just like the Colony did.

He sat down with his drink and took a sip. It burned his throat and his guts ached. But it still felt good. There was a lot to mull over. Dalton trying to instigate a Colony cull to profit from the carnage. That made sense. But was Barbara right about Marcus's killer? Tucker had never heard of a vampyr serial killer, but he supposed it was possible. Humans killed for kicks, so why not a vampyr? And it explained the connection to Todd.

He let his mind drift back. He could still picture Todd Danes with his scruffy blond hair and freckles. A slight, quiet kid, something of a misfit in Deadhart. He had a younger sister, and his parents ran a motorhome park over in Talkeetna. After Todd died, people talked like they all knew him, like he was one of their own. The truth was that Todd was bullied at school and didn't have many friends aside from Nathan.

His family left town a few months after his death. Tucker didn't blame them. Deadhart hadn't been kind to

Todd when he was alive. Little wonder they couldn't stomach the place now he was dead.

Aaron was also something of an outcast. A curious kid, he was drawn to the human world. A lot of younger colony members were. They craved the comforts and technology that the colonies didn't have. They wanted more. What kid doesn't? Just like Todd wanted more than Deadhart had to offer. Unsurprising, in a way, that the pair found each other. And friendship – love – shouldn't be wrong. It wasn't so long ago that interracial relationships were illegal, and still, in some places, you could expect to attract stares and comments.

It took time for things to change. Yes, Todd and Aaron were minors, and Tucker would have advised Todd to wait before he took a momentous decision like a turning. But ultimately, kids will always push boundaries.

Tucker often wondered if the anger directed towards Aaron was partly because the town couldn't accept that two boys, a human and a vampyr, could be in a relationship. Todd's desire to be turned was a rejection of everything they stood for. A rejection of humanity. Of course, it didn't change the fact that the relationship got Todd killed. But was it Aaron's fault, or did Tucker get it wrong? And had another kid paid the price for his mistake?

He reached for his drink.

'Tucker?'

He looked up and felt his heart still.

'Jess?'

The last time Tucker had seen Jess Garrett she had still been Jess Grainger. Twenty-two years old, with a head of wild blonde curls and an attitude. She had her father's temper and piercing blue eyes, and her late mother's intelligence and fine bone structure. A winning combination.

Back then, he had expected her to leave Deadhart and move to the city. Some people just seem too big for small towns. Instead, she had stayed and married Dan, an out-of-towner who had turned up one summer to start an adventure business and then stuck around.

Maybe it was her mother, already showing the first signs of dementia, that held her back. Maybe it was love. Or convenience. Tucker had only ever met Dan briefly. He was one of those laid-back, outdoorsy types. Easy-going, good-looking in a careless way. Unchallenging. He could see why that might have appealed to Jess. The opposite of her dad. Still, he was surprised the pair had lasted.

She folded her arms, regarding him with a mixture of appraisal and hostility. 'So, you're back? Long time, Tucker. Lot of people thought you were dead.'

'Thought, or hoped?'

A thin smile. 'Guess they'll have to put the bunting away again.'

'You don't seem surprised to see me.'

'No. Ever since the Colony crawled back, I've been expecting you to do the same.'

'Nice to know I've been missed.'

'You haven't.'

'And I was thinking you came to see me especially.'

'I was passing. Saw you walk in here.'

He wasn't sure he believed her. Not that he was flattering himself, but there was history here.

As if confirming his suspicions, she said: 'You going to see Dad?'

'I don't think so,' Tucker said tightly.

'He's getting old, Tucker. He's not the man you knew.'

'Well, that makes two of us.'

'You know he always respected you. Thought of you as a friend.'

'Your dad shot me and left me for dead.'

'You gave him no choice. You let that vampyr loose from jail.'

His hand tightened around the glass. 'Because you told me your dad and his lynch mob were planning to storm the police department and take justice into their own hands. It was my job to protect a minor.'

'And my dad was protecting Deadhart.'

'You set me up, Jess.'

Her face softened. 'And I'm sorry.'

'Yeah.' Tucker nodded at the seat opposite. 'Why don't you sit down?'

She hesitated then pulled out a chair. 'What are you really doing here, Tucker?'

'Detective Atkins asked me for help.'

'That's it? She doesn't look the type to charm a man out of a quarter of a century hiding in the woods.'

'I was never one for a pretty face.'

'You were once.' She smiled sadly. 'But you told me I was too young.'

'You were. I was closer to forty than twenty.'

That wasn't the only reason, of course. Beau would have never said it to his face, but there was no way he would have let his daughter date a black man.

'And what about now?' she asked.

'Now you're married, and I'm too old.'

She gave a short, bitter laugh. 'Yeah, guess we're both screwed.'

'Jess –'

She waved a hand. 'Forget it. It's just been a day.' She gave him a harder look. 'That freak from hell was at my dad's house last night.'

'Athelinda?'

'She threatened him, Tucker. And it's not the first time she's been seen hanging around.'

'Beau report it?'

'No – and you know why.'

'Yeah, I do. Perhaps that's why she was there.'

'I might have guessed you'd defend her.'

'Your dad killed three of her colony and kept their heads as sick trophies. You ever think she might find that upsetting?'

Jess rolled her eyes. 'Don't give me that. The woke brigade can try to paint vampyrs as harmless, persecuted victims, but we both know they're killers. It's in them. We spend thousands of dollars on campaigns encouraging us not to be afraid of colonies. To respect them. It's garbage. We *should* be afraid. For ourselves, for our children.'

Tucker nodded towards the crucifix around her neck. 'That what your church tells you?'

Her hand fluttered to the crucifix and then dropped. 'Reverend Grey has been good for Deadhart. If it wasn't for her and Rita, you'd have a lot more angry people to deal with. They're the ones that have kept everyone calm.

Told them to trust the police to do their job. But if you betray that trust . . .'

'What?'

'God has his own army.'

'Sounds like a threat.'

'You know what they called the last battle between vampyrs and humans? The Gathering. A battle for people's very souls.'

It was Tucker's turn to roll his eyes. 'I thought you were smarter than that, Jess.'

Her face darkened. 'There will be a Gathering, Tucker. Maybe here, maybe somewhere else. And you won't be able to stop it.'

He studied her, wondering what happened to that bright, vibrant young woman with ambition and plans. She wore cut-off denims and tiny tank tops in summer back then. She talked about books and British rock music, not religion and vampyrs. Not a damn crucifix in sight.

A figure walked up to their table. A slim young girl with red hair and a pretty face wearing a Nirvana T-shirt and ripped jeans.

'Can I, erm, get you anything?' she asked.

Jess turned. 'Mayflower. How are you?'

'Okay.' The girl shuffled a little awkwardly.

Jess offered a cool smile. 'You dyed your hair again.'

'Yeah, I wanted a change.'

'Yeah, well, we all want a change sometimes. But most of us go back to our roots in the end.'

They stared at each other, then Mayflower nodded. 'Let me know if you want to order anything later.'

She turned and walked away.

Tucker frowned. 'Anything I should know?'

'Nothing worth knowing.'

He didn't push it. That never worked with Jess.

'How's Stephen?' he asked.

'Okay, considering his best friend is dead and those damn spawn are still alive.'

'I'm truly sorry about what happened to Marcus. But if the boys hadn't faked that video . . .'

'What? You're saying it's their fault?'

'No. I'm saying it muddies the water, Jess. Atkins, she's a good detective –'

A snort. 'Says you.'

'I'm *saying* she will investigate every angle, tie up every loose end before she even considers a cull. Hiding stuff, making it harder for her, is just going to slow things down.'

'Whose side are you on this time, Tucker?'

He sighed. 'I'm not on anyone's side. I just want to find Marcus's killer. And if you want a cull then you need to put Atkins in a position where she *has* to authorize one. Where there's no wriggle room, no doubt.'

He waited. There was no point appealing to Jess's sense of compassion when it came to the Colony. You had to appeal to her hatred. And he had a feeling, a hunch, that she knew something.

She seemed to debate with herself. Then she shook her head. 'Fine. The detective mentioned a tattoo Marcus had?'

'A Helsing tattoo.'

'Where did he have it?'

Tucker frowned. 'On his shoulder, I think.'

She nodded. 'It was new.'

'How do you know?'

'Because Marcus slept over about a month ago. Boys, they wander in and out of the kitchen all the time, often just in shorts . . . he didn't have the tattoo then. And the last time the boys got the train to Anchorage was at the beginning of September.'

'You sure?'

'Yep. I drove them to the station. They stopped over with Marcus's aunt. His dad picked them up.'

'Marcus could have gone on his own after that.'

'His dad's truck was out of action and the train didn't run in October because of a rockfall. Everyone was complaining about it.' She folded her arms. 'Marcus must have got the tattoo from someone here, in Deadhart.'

37

Despite Barbara thinking she couldn't stomach reindeer, she managed a serving and a half of Rita's pie with vegetables. And two more beers.

Over dinner, Rita entertained with crazy stories about growing up in Deadhart: trying to shoo a young bear out of the grocery store, and the time a whole family of moose blocked off Main Street. Fun tales of living in the wilderness that Barbara suspected she had honed for visitors. Barbara didn't mind. She was happy to roll with it for now.

In return, she offered an edited version of her own life story. Not lies, just omissions. Like Rita's stories about Deadhart, it was a well-worn tale. Reality with the hard edges rubbed off. She didn't mention her dad or Mercy and she glanced over her relationship with Susan. Which was less than Susan deserved. But talking about her ex still hurt. Love and loss. You can't have one without the other, she thought.

Rita started to gather the plates. Instinctively, Barbara stood. 'Here, let me help.'

'No, you sit.'

'I insist.'

'Okay, well, we can do it together.'

They carried their plates into the kitchen and Rita stacked them in the dishwasher. Distantly, Barbara heard a cry.

'What was that?'

Rita sighed. 'Mom.' She wiped her hands on a dish towel. 'I'll just check she's okay. You all right to finish here?'

'Loading a dishwasher I can manage.'

Rita bustled out of the kitchen and Barbara finished loading the dirty dishes. Once they were in, she straightened. She needed the bathroom but didn't want to disturb Rita and her mother. She walked into the hallway. There was a door on her right. She tried it. The door opened.

'Whoah – stop!'

Barbara jumped. Rita stood at the end of the hall, looking alarmed.

'Sorry, I was just looking for the bathroom,' Barbara said.

'A lot of people do the same. But that's the cellar. No light, and the steps are lethal.'

'Oh, right.'

Rita smiled. 'Bathroom's this way. Much safer.'

Barbara shut the door and followed her. 'Thanks.'

The bathroom was tiny and cramped, made more so by the number of mobility aids crammed in there. Seats for the toilet, handles and hoists for the bath. For all Rita's cheery demeanour, these spoke of a far tougher life here with her mother. Barbara wondered about costs, too. Cancer treatment was expensive.

She washed her hands quickly and joined Rita back in the living room. The mayor had produced a small cardboard box from somewhere.

'I'll make some coffee while you take a look.'

'Thanks.'

Barbara took a seat back on the sofa while Rita moved around in the kitchen. The box was battered and dusty. It smelt a bit damp too. She opened it up.

'There's a lot of boring stuff up front,' Rita called from the kitchen. 'Council records. Censuses. But if you dig down, you should find plenty of old pictures of the town and the mine.'

Barbara started to sift through the documents. 'This all belong to your family?'

'A mix. As mayor, I inherited the town records. Well, those that hadn't got lost or eaten by mould. Mom had a lot of old pictures that I guess got handed down over generations. I couldn't tell you half the folk in them.' She walked in with two coffees. 'The Bone House would have been around the 1920s, so any photos are probably towards the bottom of the box.'

Barbara dug down, pulling out papers. The order was fairly random, and a lot of the documents were barely legible. Literacy was not high among the early Alaskan settlers. Plus, the writing had faded with age and run with water damage. Typically, she had left her glasses in the office. Barbara held up some loose census papers. In 1901, the population had been just eighty-nine people. Beneath the papers, a flyer proudly declared: 'Deadhart Mine Opening – Celebrations to take place at the newly established Roadhouse Grill!'

Further down, photographs showed some kind of town event. Independence Day, perhaps. People smiling and dancing. Kids running around. She flicked through a few more. The opening of the police department: stern-looking men with moustaches standing proudly outside. Another photo showed a row of kids in a formal pose. 'Deadhart School. 1945,' a note on the back said.

It was easy to see how the tiny settlement here had grown with the advent of the mine. Earlier photos showed only a few scattered houses, and more Indigenous faces. In later photographs, the buildings became bigger, more clustered, the faces almost exclusively white.

The good old white settler, Barbara thought. Crashes the party, steals all the booze, kicks out the owners and then trashes the house.

Barbara picked up another photograph. Something tingled at the back of her neck.

A sturdy wooden building, basic, not much more than a large barn. A scraggy-looking woman, wearing too much make-up and an obvious wig, stood outside with two other hard-faced young females. In contrast to the more utilitarian clothing of the other townsfolk, their frocks were fancy and garish. A young boy squatted in the corner of the shot; face covered in dirt.

'This is it,' she muttered. 'The Bone House.'

Rita peered at the photo. 'Ah, yeah. I thought there might be a picture somewhere. I think those were the – what do you call them? – *madams*.'

Barbara frowned. 'You said the Bone House was out near the cemetery?'

'That's right.'

'Is there nothing left of it at all?'

'No, and it's been built on since then.'

'So, what's there now?'

'The Church of the Holy Cross.'

Barbara stared at her. *Holy fudge*. The Reverend had built her house of worship on the bones of dead vampyrs. She felt a shiver of distaste.

'Does the Reverend know?'

'Nope. And I don't see any purpose in telling her.'

Barbara laid the picture down, and then another caught her eye. The same building but, this time, a group of three young men stood outside. Miners, from the look of them. They clutched beers and cigarettes, smiling drunkenly. One stood out. Taller than the rest. Blond-haired, a cocky edge to his grin. He was familiar somehow.

'Why do I feel like I recognize this man?' Barbara held the photo out to Rita.

Rita glanced at it and her face tensed. 'Well, you might have seen his photo up in the Grill. He was a foreman at the mine. Built one of the first houses in the town. Kind of a founding father.'

'And he was a visitor to the Bone House?'

Rita's voice hardened. '*A lot* of miners visited the Bone House. Doesn't mean anything.'

'What was his name?' she asked.

'Joseph Grainger.'

'Grainger? As in *Beau* Grainger?'

'Joseph was his grandfather.'

A phone chimed. Rita's.

''Scuse me,' she said, and bustled away to get it.

Barbara studied the old photo. Despite the man's good looks, she felt an instant dislike. There was an arrogance to his posture, a hard glint in those eyes. She put the photo down just as Rita hurried back in. Her face was grim, and Barbara's stomach immediately sank.

'Bad news?'

'There's been an incident at the church.'

'What sort of incident?'

'An attack – by the Colony.'

38

The night air stank of acrid smoke. It rose up from the charred cross. The wood was old and mostly dry, so it had gone up like tinder. The remains were half the height of the original cross, a truncated stump. Barbara tried hard not to feel some satisfaction at the sight. She didn't succeed.

She walked past and stared down at the disembowelled pig and the writing in the snow. The letters were already starting to blur and disappear beneath the fresh flakes falling from the sky, but the sentiment was clear.

A warning. A threat.

'Well, this is a freaking shitshow,' Rita muttered from beside her.

'Yeah.'

They walked into the church, where Reverend Grey sat with Grace. Mowlam stood nearby. Shattered glass covered the floor. Snow drifted in through the gaping windows.

'Detective, Rita,' Colleen said. 'Thank you for coming.'

'Got here as fast as we could,' Rita said. 'We're just glad you're okay.'

'Yeah, well, we might not have been,' Mowlam said, looking at Barbara.

She turned pointedly to Colleen. 'Can you tell me what happened?'

'Mr Mowlam and I were in the church –'

'What was Mr Mowlam doing here?'

'I came by to tell the Reverend about Dr Dalton's death,' Mowlam said. 'I thought she should know.'

'And how did *you* know?'

'It's a small town. Hard to keep secrets.' He smiled smugly, and Barbara had an overwhelming desire to punch him in the mouth.

'And where was Grace?'

Colleen put a protective arm around the girl's shoulders. 'She was in the back,' she said.

'Okay. So, you were all in the church, and then what?'

'Someone smashed the windows,' Colleen said. 'Threw rocks at them. Then there were noises on the roof and hammering at the door.'

'What did you do?'

'I opened the door to confront whoever it was.'

'Wasn't that a little risky? You didn't think to call the police first?'

'I had faith that God would protect me,' Colleen replied.

He didn't protect Marcus, Barbara thought.

'Okay, and that's when you saw the pig and the writing . . . and the burning cross?'

'Yes.'

'But you didn't see anyone from the Colony?'

'No.'

'Did you see anyone at all?'

'I'm afraid not.'

'What about the folk preparing the ground in the cemetery?'

'They've had to break because of the weather.'

'No other witnesses?'

'No.'

'So, we don't know for sure that the Colony is responsible?'

'Seriously, who else could it be?' Mowlam said.

'I'm just establishing all the facts.'

'The fact is,' Mowlam continued, 'a young boy is dead and now the Colony are threatening the rest of the town. I'm pretty sure that warrants a cull.'

'I thought you were agnostic, Mr Mowlam?'

'I'm also realistic.'

Barbara regarded him steadily. 'I still need solid evidence that the Colony did this.'

'For God's sake.' He looked at Rita, who had so far – and unusually – remained silent. 'And do you agree, Mayor?'

'I think we should let Detective Atkins do her job.' But she didn't sound quite so sure.

Barbara looked at Colleen and Grace. 'Are you okay to stay here tonight? Or do you need some alternative accommodation?'

'Demons do not scare the righteous,' Colleen said.

'So, I'll take that as a no?'

'I'll call Jared at the hardware store, get him to come over and board up those broken windows,' Rita said.

Which meant another person would know. There would be no containing this. And that could cause real problems.

'Thank you, Rita,' Colleen replied. 'It would be good to have the church weatherproof for the meeting tomorrow.'

'You still want to hold the meeting here?' Barbara asked.

'I think it's more important than ever.' Colleen smiled. 'We need to come together, as Christians, to face down this abomination. To fight the good fight against the devil's disciples.'

Before Barbara could reply, Rita cut in: 'The Reverend is right.'

Barbara stared at her in surprise. 'Really?'

'We should warn people in case of an attack.'

'If the Colony wanted to attack, they could have done it tonight,' Barbara pointed out.

Rita sighed. 'I have a duty to protect the town.'

'And the last thing we want to do is spread panic. Scared people do stupid things.'

She paused. A truck engine growled. Headlights illuminated the road and a large 4x4 pulled up. The lights cut and a figure climbed out. Jess Garrett. Barbara's heart plummeted even further.

'Is everything okay here, Reverend?' Jess asked.

Colleen nodded. 'Just a little Colony trouble.'

Jess took in the burnt cross, the words in the snow. Her face turned to thunder. She marched up to Barbara. 'This enough evidence for you, Detective? Written in blood.'

Barbara kept her voice even. 'Right now, we all need to stay calm –'

'*Calm?*' Jess shook her head. 'You don't get it, do you? Look around. Another snowfall tonight and we'll be completely cut off. We are on our own. Because *you* dragged your feet over a cull.' She paused. 'If the Colony attack, you'll have the blood of the whole damn town on your hands. I hope you can live with that.'

39

Barbara had grown up living with the taste of fear and blood. A backhander, a punch, a kick, a lick of the belt.

Anything could provoke it. The wrong word, the wrong clothes, the time of day, the number of beers or spirits. Sometimes, trying to avoid the beating was pointless. You just had to minimize the damage.

This particular morning, Barbara had cooked her dad's eggs wrong.

'These are like fucking rubber, Babs.'

The eggs and plate had hit the wall and her dad's hand had whipped her head almost off her shoulders. While he yanked a beer out of the fridge, Barbara had escaped the house and run down to the river. Her nose stung, but she didn't think it was broken. Dad had used an open hand rather than his fist.

She was kneeling by the water, splashing her face, trying to wash away the blood dripping from her nostrils, when she heard the girl's voice:

'Are you okay?'

She turned.

Her again. The mermaid. Long, silvery-white dreadlocks; burnished dark skin. Eyes as green as the fields. So different from Barbara, with her pale, blotchy skin and lank, brown hair.

'I-I'm fine,' she stuttered. 'Just a nosebleed.'

The girl nodded. 'I saw you the other day. I'm Mercy.'

'Erm . . . Barbara. I live over there.' She gestured towards the fields.

The girl smiled. 'I'm from the Hoka Colony, over in the Bluff.'

Barbara had stared at her in shock. The Bluff was a heavily wooded mountainous region that ringed the town. Everyone knew that vampyrs lived out there, but Barbara had never seen any of them before.

'But you don't look like a vampyr,' she said.

Mercy had giggled. 'What? You expect me to be all pasty white? Or to float around like a bat?'

'No, I-I don't know.'

Barbara had been flummoxed. And embarrassed to admit that she kind of *had* expected that. All she really knew about the Hoka Colony was what the school taught and what her dad said, although she was now at an age where she realized that a lot of stuff her dad said – about blacks and whores and Jews – was cruel, a lie and offensive. So, she guessed that might be true of vampyrs too.

'Why don't you have bigger . . .' She gestured awkwardly to her mouth, not wanting to say 'fangs'.

'Oh, right, well, I'm only fifteen so the *fangs* don't come through fully for another year or so.' Mercy grinned more widely, showing off her elongated incisors. 'They're getting there, though.'

Barbara flushed. 'Right.'

Mercy sat down next to her. 'You come here a lot?'

'Yeah, it's like my special place.'

Mercy glanced up at the grey-blue sky. 'It's nice.'

'What are you doing here?' Barbara asked. 'I mean, aren't you supposed to sleep in the daylight?'

'You never sneaked out of your room at night when you're not supposed to?'

'No.'

Mercy laughed. 'Well, I'm good as long as I keep to the shade under the trees. I'm not going to burst into flames.' She jumped up. 'Let's go for a swim.'

'A swim?'

'What? You think vampyrs can't swim either? I can swim like a fish.'

Mercy yanked her dress over her head, revealing small, pert breasts and slightly too-small panties. She wasn't shy or coy about her body like Barbara. She ran down the bank and splashed into the shallows of the river. After a moment, Barbara pulled off her T-shirt and shorts, revealing her tired old bra and knickers beneath, and followed her. The water was chilly in the shade of the trees, so she floated just outside, in the warmer water.

That was how they would always swim afterwards. Mercy in the shadows and Barbara in the sunlight, floating on their backs, fingers almost touching.

'So, what do they tell you about us?' Mercy asked.

'I'm not sure I want to say.'

'Go on.'

'That you're demons, damned. And we can ward you off with a cross, or garlic.'

Mercy snorted. 'Good luck with that.'

'Oh, and you can only come into a house if you're invited.'

Mercy seemed to consider. 'Never tested it, but it sounds like crap.'

Barbara giggled. 'Is all of it wrong?'

'Mostly. Anything else?'

'*Goddam, evil, blood-sucking spawns of Satan.*'

'My dad,' Barbara said, 'he says a lot of bad stuff. He hates vampyrs. He thinks you're an abomination.'

'There's a lot of vampyrs hate humans too. I'd be in trouble if my folks found out I was here.'

'What would they do?'

'Oh, probably stop me from coming again. Put me to work skinning the pigs for a while. What about your dad?'

The reply came to her, so sudden and involuntary, Barbara didn't even think before articulating it:

'He'd kill you.'

Summer couldn't last. Perhaps that added to the intensity of their relationship. A feeling that, right from the start, it was finite. Their moments were secret, snatched and special. Stolen in dappled shade. Lying together in the rough grass. Talking, giggling, kissing.

But secrets are hard to keep in a small town. One day, Barbara arrived home, hair still damp from the river, clothes dishevelled, and she knew.

Someone had seen them.

Her dad stood outside the front door in just his trousers and vest, taut as trip wire, face a mask of barely contained rage. His battered old truck was parked just outside. Barbara's heart had started to pound, but she tried to act casually.

'Hi, Dad. Shall I get your dinner on?'

'Where you been, Babs?'

'Down by the river.'

'Doing what?'

'Swimming, reading. You know.'

'I don't. That's why I'm asking.'

'Okay.'

'You there on your own?'

She hesitated. Admit to meeting Mercy but deny she was Colony? Or deny meeting anyone at all? But then, her dad wouldn't be asking if he didn't think he already knew the answer.

'No,' she said eventually. 'I bumped into another girl down there. We just hung out for a bit.'

Her dad nodded and took a step forward. 'That so? What's she called, this other girl.'

'Mercy.'

'Where's she from?'

'I don't know. I think she said her family were travellers . . . I didn't say before because, well, she's black.'

She paused, tasting the panic in her throat, hoping it would be enough to convince him. Who had seen them? How much had they seen? What could they possibly know?

He took another step towards her.

'Well, I'm disappointed, Babs. You know how I feel about *blacks*.'

'I'm sorry, Dad.'

'But you know what I hate worse? Liars!'

His hand shot out and slammed into the side of her face, knocking her to the floor. She landed on her knees on the dusty, parched grass.

He stood over her. She could smell alcohol and sweat.

'And you know what I hate more than liars?'

He booted her hard in the side. Her kidneys erupted into fire and Barbara retched, feeling like she might throw up.

'Fucking *vampyrs*.'

'She's not a –'

265

Another boot to the spine. She howled and curled into a ball.

'You were *seen*, Babs. Frank's daughter saw you. Frank knows all those vampyr scum, and *she's* one of them.'

'I didn't –'

'Don't. Lie. To. Me.' Each word punctuated by another kick. Barbara screamed and tried to cover her head.

'You stupid little bitch. She ain't your friend. She's preying on you. Corrupting you. Did she touch you, Babs? Bite you?'

'No.'

'Get up.' He hauled her to her feet. 'Take your clothes off.'

'NO!'

He slapped her hard around the face again. Blood exploded from her lip.

'*Do it!*'

Slowly, she shed her shirt and shorts.

'Everything.'

She slipped off her damp bathing costume. She wrapped her arms over her breasts and crossed her legs to hide her lady parts, shame overtaking the pain. Her dad walked around her in a slow circle, staring at her body, lifting her hair to check her neck. She shuddered at his touch. Eventually, he spat on the floor.

'Get dressed. And then get in the truck.'

She couldn't refuse. She hastily pulled her clothes back on and then climbed into the truck. Her dad climbed into the driver's seat and started the engine.

'We're going for a drive.'

The truck bumped and juddered down the track. Every jolt sent paroxysms of pain through Barbara's battered

266

body. For a moment, she thought her dad was driving her into town, but then he turned off down another, even narrower, track that cut and weaved through the heavy forest. Finally, when it seemed like the track had petered out entirely and they were just bumping along scrubland between the trees, the forest opened out into a clearing. A large wooden cabin stood in the centre. The lodge.

Her dad stopped his truck outside. Then he jumped out, walked around and yanked open her door.

'Get out.'

She half climbed, half tumbled out, clutching her sore ribs. Her dad grabbed her arm and dragged her over to the lodge. He took a heavy key out of his pocket.

'Dad, please?'

'Shut your mouth.'

He fumbled the key into the lock.

'This is our town. A good, Christian town. The Colony, they're feral, creatures of Satan. They got no place on this earth.'

'I get it. Can we just go home?'

He grabbed her face, squeezing. 'You need to understand.' Then he pushed open the door and shoved her into the darkened room. 'This is the only place vampyrs "hang" around here.'

He flicked on a light. Barbara turned.

The room was sparsely furnished with battered couches and chairs, careworn rugs thrown over the floor. A makeshift bar had been set up in one corner and a scarred table was scattered with cards. A place for men to meet, drink, gamble . . . and admire their trophies.

They were mounted on every wall. Heads. At least a

dozen. Men, women, children. They gazed down with dead, glassy eyes. Fair-haired, dark, auburn. Faces frozen in anguish. Teeth protruding in paralysed snarls.

'No,' Barbara muttered. 'No!'

'It's where they belong, Babs. They're animals – and we hunt them like animals.' Her dad smiled a thin, cruel smile. 'But don't worry. They won't bite.'

He slammed the door shut. Barbara heard the key turn on the other side. Horror rose in her throat. She threw herself at the rough wood.

'Let me out! Don't leave me here!'

Her dad's laughter sounded through the door. 'You love 'em so much, you get to spend the whole night with 'em, Babs. And tomorrow, I'm going to pay your little friend a visit.'

She heard his footsteps crunch away and the splutter of the old truck engine disappearing into the distance. She screamed. She kicked and hammered at the door. But it was no good. The wood was sturdy and strong, and there was no one to hear her cries.

Barbara turned and looked back around the lodge. Windows that were too small and too high to reach. No other door. She was trapped.

Just her and the trophies.

The multitude of vacant eyes stared back.

And that was when she noticed it.

On the far wall, amid the snarling decapitated heads, was an empty wooden mount.

'Tomorrow, I'm going to pay your little friend a visit.'

Mercy.

40

Barbara's eyes shot open. She wasn't sure what had woken her. The room was dark and silent. Just the sound of her own breathing. And yet, something felt off.

She reached for her phone and glanced at the time: 3.30 a.m. The Grill had been shut when she got back from the church. After a quick wash, she'd collapsed into the embrace of the sagging mattress and fallen straight asleep.

Now, she felt wide awake. She stretched out her fingers and felt for the bedside lamp. She clicked it on. Nothing happened. Damn. A blown bulb maybe? Then she realized what was wrong. The room was too dark.

Normally, the glow of the Christmas lights provided illumination through the thin curtains. But tonight, there was nothing. It must be a power cut. Unsurprising. In the town she grew up in power cuts were a regular occurrence, especially in winter, the grid as unreliable and cranky as the people who lived there. The power would probably come back on at some point and . . . something thudded downstairs. The sound of a heavy item falling. *Shit*. Barbara sat up.

Carly and her family lived a couple of houses further down the street. Other than that, it was just her and anyone else who might be staying here. Barbara debated with herself. She had Carly's number, but then, what was Carly going to do if there was an intruder in the place? Call the police. And Barbara *was* the police.

She yanked a jumper on over her pyjamas, slipped her feet into her snow boots and reluctantly picked up her gun and holster from the bedside table. Her bag was on the floor at the end of the bed, alongside Rita's box of photos. Rita had agreed to let Barbara take them to look over again. Barbara rummaged inside the bag and pulled out a flashlight. She flicked it on, the beam blinding her as it hit the mirror opposite.

'Crap.'

She blinked to clear the red stars in her eyes and pointed the flashlight around the room. All looked as she expected. But from downstairs she heard more thuds. Someone was moving about.

Barbara walked over to the door, unlocked it and stepped outside. The corridor felt even cooler than her room. She shivered a little as she padded along to the top of the stairs and shone her flashlight down the narrow staircase. Carefully, she descended. Treads that didn't seem to make a sound in daylight groaned under her weight. Finally, she reached the bottom. She took a breath and pushed open the door to the bar.

One hand on her gun, she swept the room with her flashlight, left and right. The booths and tables looked empty; chairs stacked on top, but it was hard to see beneath. Keeping her eyes on the room, she reached for the lights to her left, flicking the switches just in case. Still out. Damn. She turned towards the bar. Nope, no one hiding there ready to jump out. That only left the kitchen. Barbara swapped the flashlight into her left hand and pulled out her gun. Moving forward, she pushed open the door to the back of the restaurant with her shoulder.

She swung the flashlight around, hoping to catch an intruder by surprise. The kitchen wasn't that big. Chrome ovens and grills lined either side. Utensils hung from hooks. A pan lay on the floor. Knocked there? She walked forward, gun held at her side. It was cold in here. Really cold.

And now she could see why.

The freezer door hung open.

It must have its own generator.

Her heart thudded in her throat. She shone the flashlight into the freezer, telling herself that the shaking in her hands was only the sub-zero temperatures. She could see Marcus's body lying on the steel table. *Of course. What had she expected?* But she couldn't deny the momentary shudder of relief.

It was short-lived. Someone had been in here. The freezer had been disturbed. Hunks of meat lay on the floor and freezer bags full of . . . *what the hell?* Barbara walked inside, keeping the flashlight trained in front of her. She bent down to examine the bags more closely. Hearts, she thought. But they didn't look like animal hearts to her. They looked like . . .

Clunk.

She whirled round, flashlight jittering in her hand.

The freezer door had swung closed behind her.

'Shit!'

She jogged back to the door. Rattled the handle. Tugged at it. The damn thing wouldn't give. She tried to quell the panic. Most walk-in freezers had an emergency release fitted so they could be opened from the inside. It was a health-and-safety regulation. But then *this* was a place that stored dead bodies in its kitchen freezer. Health and safety

271

weren't exactly top priorities here. Barbara ran her flashlight over the thick metal but couldn't see any kind of release mechanism. Just scratched and dented steel. And suddenly she remembered Nicholls's words.

'The townsfolk wanted to keep the body somewhere more secure.'

More secure. Fuck and dammit. This wasn't just a place to store meat, it was a place to make sure the meat didn't get up and walk out. Okay, think. Maybe there was an alarm? She scanned the walls with her flashlight beam, fingers tingling with cold, but she couldn't see one.

What time was it? Maybe 4 a.m. by now. It would be at least another four or five hours before anyone came to look in here or heard her calling out. She was only wearing pyjamas, a sweater and boots. Would she make it that long? She had no idea. Certainly, without gloves to insulate her fingers, she was in danger of frostbite. Hypothermia could creep in gradually. Shit.

She started to pace, clapping her hands together. Try and keep warm. Try and keep calm. Did someone really intend for her to freeze to death in here? Maybe the door had swung shut on its own, although that was unlikely, as it was heavy and stiff. Maybe whoever shut it hadn't realized she was in here. Or that she couldn't get out. Maybe it was a prank and they were still out there, congratulating themselves on scaring the crap out of her.

Barbara turned back to the door, raised a fist and thumped on the freezing metal.

'HEY!! Is anyone out there? You've had your fun. Now, can you open the door?'

She waited. Nothing. She hammered on the door again.

'HELP! *Please*. I'm going to freeze in here. Just let me out!'

She pointed the flashlight around the small room, skimming over Marcus's body and trying to control the irrational feeling of jumpiness every time she did. He remained stiff and silent, cocooned in the black body bag.

She paused. The body bag. Designed to keep the body preserved. Could it also help her preserve much-needed warmth? The idea was hardly appealing. The last thing she wanted to do was wrap herself up like a corpse. But if she didn't, she might join Marcus in *becoming* a corpse.

Barbara walked towards his body. With numb fingers she fumbled with the zipper. It was stuck, frozen in the cold. She tugged and tugged, ripping one of her nails. Finally, she felt the zipper give. She yanked it down. Marcus's white, frozen face looked back at her, sunken eyeballs grey beneath his half-open lids.

Hadn't his eyes been fully closed before? Perhaps she was misremembering. Often, the eyes of the dead didn't stay closed. Morticians used special contact lenses with small spikes to keep them that way. She was probably just being stupid. Crazy. And yet, Barbara felt an overwhelming urge to be away from Marcus's body, and out of this freezing cell. She glanced back towards the door. Maybe she should try calling for help one more time. She backed away then turned and thumped on the door as hard as she could.

'HEY!!! HELP! LET ME OUT!'

Still nothing. She leaned against the metal. *This was hopeless. Futile. There was no one —*

A clunk from outside. The door suddenly swung open, dumping her in an undignified heap on to the floor.

'Ow. Shit.'

Barbara had never been more relieved to land flat on

her face. She lay there for a moment, shivering, disorientated. A pair of dainty feet drew into view, toenails painted black. She squinted up. Long, bare legs. A baggy sweatshirt. Tousled red hair.

'Mayflower?'

'Detective Atkins?' Mayflower stared down in concern.

Barbara struggled into a sitting position. 'W-what are you doing here? Did you lock me in?'

'No, ma'am.' The girl's eyes widened in horror. 'I thought I heard a noise – and then I came down and heard you calling.'

Barbara frowned, brain struggling to catch up. 'Came down. From where? What are you doing here?'

Mayflower looked awkward. From the bar, the sound of a chair clattering to the floor. Someone else was here.

'It's –' Mayflower started to say, but Barbara was already on her feet and pushing past her.

'Stop!' she shouted, bursting out of the kitchen door, hand reaching for her gun.

A tall figure sprinted towards the exit.

'I said stop, or I'll shoot.' And to prove her point, she fired a shot into the ceiling.

A light exploded, showering down glass. The figure ducked and stumbled into a table, crashing over it and landing on the floor.

Barbara walked over, gun still raised. 'Stay where you are.'

The figure slowly turned over, holding his hands up.

Barbara pointed the flashlight at his face.

'I can explain,' Dan Garrett said.

41

The voices followed him. Before, Beau only used to hear them occasionally. Now, they were with him constantly. Whispering in his ear. Even in his sleep. He got up, moved from room to room, but they refused to abate.

'Leave me alone,' he muttered, and they chuckled softly. *'We can't. We're part of you, old man.'*

He shook his head. 'I won't listen to your devil tongues.'

Beau was not a fanciful man. He believed in right and wrong. Good and evil. But in reality, he had never been a regular churchgoer. He called himself a Christian, but he hadn't worshipped enough. Since Patricia died, he didn't regularly say grace, he drank a little too much, he had let his devotion falter.

Truth be told, he wasn't fond of that new preacher. Something about her. Well, maybe it was just that she was a woman and in Beau's opinion a woman had no place being a preacher. Maybe he needed to get over that and get back to church. Maybe now was as good a time as any for praying.

He knew he should have mentioned the Doc's news to Jess. But he didn't want to worry her. She had enough on her plate with the business and her boy and that useless husband of hers. Perhaps more selfishly, he didn't want to see the pity in her eyes. The fear. He didn't want her to look at him the way she had looked at her mother.

He walked downstairs to the kitchen. His throat felt

scratchy and dry. Beau turned on the tap and filled a glass with water, gulping it back quickly. Maybe too quickly. He felt it swirl in his stomach and then belched. A little of the water came back up and he spat over the sink, hanging there for a moment. He felt light-headed and dizzy.

'*You're sick, old man – and you're only going to get sicker as we get stronger.*'

'That isn't going to happen.'

But even as he said it, Beau felt the fear. The fear of becoming like Patricia. His mind slipping through his fingers like sand. The mass taking over.

'Damn you.'

He turned and walked back up to the bedroom. A picture of him and Patricia on their wedding day stood on the table beside the bed. Next to it, a framed photograph of their children. On the chest, an older photograph – his parents and grandparents with Beau and his sister. It was a rare picture of his grandfather. He usually hated being photographed because of his burns.

When Beau was a child, he had been told his grandfather had been badly injured in a fire at the mine. It was only later, when his father's tongue grew looser as death loomed closer, that he learned the truth.

Beau turned from the photograph and walked to the window. When Patricia was ill, he often used to stand here, the window wide open, freezing wind blasting his face, pretending he couldn't hear her cries of distress from downstairs.

He wiped condensation off the glass with his sleeve and looked out. His heart stalled. Three figures stood outside. Two men and a younger adolescent boy. They gazed up at him, skin white as the snow, eyes glowing, long animal-skin coats billowing in the wind. Not possible, he thought. Dead. You're all dead.

'Are we? Maybe we've been here all along. Waiting. Only now you can see us as well as hear us.'

Beau ducked back against the wall. His heart pounded and sweat crept from his hairline. Not real. It couldn't be. It couldn't. He waited, breathing heavily, trying to calm himself. Then, slowly, he edged forward and peered around the curtains.

A face hovered outside the window. Beau screamed. The man stared in, amber eyes glowing, teeth bared in a smile, one hand pressed against the glass.

'No, no, no.'

Vampyrs couldn't fly or float. It must be . . .

'In your mind, a hallucination?'

Beau moaned. Nausea overwhelmed him. He staggered across the hall and made it into the bathroom just in time to spew up a stream of water and bile. He hung over the toilet bowl and retched until his stomach ached.

After a while, he hit the flush and then, on unsteady legs, turned to the sink and splashed his face with water. He looked at himself in the mirror. White hair so thin he could see the pink of his scalp. Loose bags like deflated balloons beneath his eyes. His skin looked clammy and pale. Like he was coming down with something.

'What's happening to me?' he croaked. 'What in hell is happening to me?'

From somewhere inside his head, the darkness chuckled. And the voices whispered in his ear:

'You know.'

42

The power had come back on, and Mayflower had dressed and made them all coffee. She perched on a chair beside Dan, arms folded, a defiant look on her pale face.

'Okay,' Barbara said. 'Why don't you explain what you're doing here, although you can spare me the gruesome details.'

The pair exchanged glances.

'And don't try telling me it's not how it looks, either,' Barbara added.

Dan sighed. 'Okay, so Mayflower and me, we hook up here maybe once or twice a month and, well, we use one of the guest rooms.'

'Romantic.'

'It's not supposed to be romantic,' Mayflower said. 'It's sex.'

Barbara raised an eyebrow. 'And how does your wife feel about you *using* the rooms here?' she asked Dan.

He shifted uncomfortably. 'I tell her I'm going hunting or night fishing.'

'She buys that?'

He glared at her. 'To be honest, I don't think Jess cares where I am or what I'm doing. Half the time she's at that goddamn church with that crazy preacher, and when she is home, well, things between us have been sour for a long while now.'

'So why haven't you left?'

'It's complicated.'

'It's Stephen,' Mayflower broke in. 'Dan can't just walk out. He's a good father.'

Yeah, such a good father he was banging a girl not much older than his son.

'So, you arranged to meet here tonight?' Barbara continued.

Mayflower nodded. 'I finished shift at ten thirty. Dad got home about midnight after locking up. I waited till him and Mom were settled and then sneaked back out. Dan texted me and I let him in around the side.'

Barbara nodded. 'What time was this?'

'One thirty a.m.'

'When you arrived, everything was locked up?'

Mayflower nodded. 'Yes, ma'am.'

'No sign of anyone else about?'

'Nope.'

'Seems like a heck of a lot of sneaking around.'

Mayflower gave a small shrug. 'We don't really have anywhere else to go, 'cept the woods or Dan's car. And they're both freezing this time of year.'

Again, the romance.

Barbara sipped her coffee. 'You notice the power go off?'

'No.'

'But something disturbed you?'

'Yeah, I heard a noise downstairs. Banging, and someone shouting.'

'I guess that would have been me,' Barbara said with a thin smile. 'And that's when you came down and opened the freezer?'

'Yes, ma'am.'

Barbara glanced at Dan. 'And where were you, sir?'

'I was right behind her.'

'Funny. I thought you were trying to sneak out of the bar.'

He glared at her. 'I was trying to protect Mayflower.'

'Really?'

Mayflower laid a hand on his arm. 'We both agreed we'd keep this secret till Stephen turns sixteen.'

Dan gave a small nod but didn't say anything.

'Then we'll leave this shithole and set up someplace else, right?' Mayflower turned to Dan.

He managed a weak smile. 'Sure.'

Barbara eyed him cynically. If she had a dime for every time a man had spun a young girl *that* hackneyed line, she sure as heck wouldn't be freezing her ass off in Deadhart right now.

When the time is right. When the kids are grown. We'll leave and make a new life.

Few ever did. And those that actually managed to grow a backbone and leave soon came crawling back. The grass was never greener. Young girls grew older, sex became sparser, and babies are harder work at fifty than thirty.

Barbara had thought that Mayflower was too smart to fall for any of that baloney, but perhaps the cynical, world-weary facade was just that.

'Look,' Dan said now. 'You've asked your questions, Detective. We haven't committed a crime. It's after four thirty in the morning and I need to get home.'

For a moment, Barbara had a vindictive urge to make him stay. Or better still, to force him to come to the police department to make a statement and reveal his deception.

But what good would that do? The likelihood was that Mayflower would be the one who got hurt while Dan remained in his 'sour' marriage with Jess and a son who now saw his father for what he really was. And no child needed that. Sometimes, lies are the things that bind a family as much as love.

'Of course, sir – and thank you for your help. But I'd like your phone number in case I need to speak to you again.'

Dan got out his phone and Barbara put his number into hers. She smiled. 'Well, I think we're all done here. I'm sure you'll be keen to get back to your wife and son. Being the *good* father you are.'

Dan looked as if he was about to retort, but then seemed to think better of it.

'I'll let you out,' Mayflower said.

'It's fine. I can do it myself.'

He turned and stalked off towards the door. He opened it a crack, peered through and then slunk out.

'I can see why you fell for him,' Barbara said. 'A real Prince Charming.'

Mayflower gave her a look. 'Slim pickings around here, if you hadn't noticed.'

'Can't say I was looking,' Barbara said.

'You still need me, or can I go too?' Mayflower asked.

Barbara considered. 'Actually, I'd like you to look at something.'

The girl sighed. 'Fine.'

Barbara rose and walked back around the bar through the kitchen. 'You ever store stuff in the freezer for other people, aside from dead bodies?'

'Sometimes we've stored the odd deer carcass for one of the hunters.'

'Nothing else?'

'Not that I know of.'

'Okay.' Barbara pulled open the freezer door and then paused. She glanced over her shoulder. 'Not being funny, but you got something to prop this with?'

Mayflower walked back to the bar and came back with a heavy stool, which she used to wedge the door open.

'Shit!' she exclaimed as she took in the spilt bags, the blood and frosted organs. 'What the fuck?'

'Couldn't have said it better myself,' Barbara said grimly.

She walked across the freezer and picked up one of the bags. Two frozen organs nestled inside. 'You know what these are?'

Mayflower stared at her, wide-eyed. 'Hearts, and I'm guessing they ain't pig.'

'Nope. Looks to me like these are vampyr. And I'd say they're fresh.'

She looked around the freezer. When she was here with Nicholls, her focus had been on Marcus's body. She hadn't really paid much attention to the rest of the room. Now she looked around more carefully.

Mayflower rubbed at her arms and shivered. 'What are you looking for, anyway?'

'Not sure.' Barbara's eyes narrowed. She walked towards one of the stainless-steel storage units. Metal containers were stacked on the shelves. She pulled the lid off one. It was half full of Saran-wrapped meat. The meat looked like deer. She examined a couple more and wondered if her gut instinct about this was right. She reached to the back. There were two bigger containers here, both with lids on. She used both hands to pull one out. It didn't feel as heavy as the others, despite its size. She prised open the lid.

'Jesus Christ!'

She recoiled in revulsion, the container slipping from her fingers. It hit the floor with a clang and landed on its side.

Mayflower let out a scream. The contents of the container rolled across the floor, coming to rest at Barbara's feet.

She looked down.

The decapitated vampyr head stared lifelessly back at her.

43

'We didn't know what was in the containers. We was just doing the Doc a favour.'

Carly glared at Barbara, bony arms crossed over her chest.

Barbara met her gaze evenly. 'So, these aren't *your* containers?'

Carly glanced at her husband. 'No.'

'And you didn't think to ask why Doc Dalton wanted you to keep these containers in your freezer?'

'We thought it was something to do with his work.'

'And you never looked inside?'

'No.'

'What about the hearts? They were just bagged up on your shelves. You didn't think that was unusual?'

'Thought it was for research or something.'

'Human hearts?'

'Vampyrs ain't human,' her husband muttered.

Barbara glanced down at her notes. *Hal.*

'So, you *did* know they were vampyr hearts then, sir?'

'He ain't saying that,' Carly snapped. 'Look, we've told you all we know. And the Doc is dead, so I don't see what difference it makes.'

Barbara let out a sigh. The four of them sat around a table in front of the bar. Barbara still hadn't had a chance to change out of her pyjama bottoms or brush her hair.

After calling Carly, she had set about documenting the scene. She had taken photographs of the hearts and head and then replaced it in the container. It was male, late forties in appearance and, from the style of the hair and the piercings in the ears, not old enough to be antique. The second container held another head. Younger, female. Bleached-blonde hair shaved on one side. A girlfriend perhaps. Both had bad skin and teeth. Maybe the two had been outliers, living rough? Lone vampyrs were easier prey than those from established colonies. Barbara was pretty sure the victims weren't local, either. They had a city look about them.

'Whether you were aware of what was in the containers or not,' Barbara continued, 'possessing vampyr hearts or heads is a criminal offence.'

'Bullshit! You can't blame us for something we didn't know about.'

'Mom,' Mayflower said in a low tone.

'Don't you "Mom" me. You still ain't explained what you're doing here at five in the morning.'

'I told you, Mom. I couldn't sleep. I thought I'd come in and get started early – do some cleaning, y'know.'

Carly looked dubious. Barbara broke in: 'I'm afraid ignorance is no defence in the eyes of the law. Of course, if you have any more information that might help the investigation, ma'am, I'm sure I could take that into account?'

She smiled at Carly and Hal. Hal looked like he was about to speak, but Carly got in first: 'We've told you everything.'

'Okay . . . well, in that case, I'm afraid this area is now a crime scene. No one in or out. That means the Grill doesn't open until I've finished gathering evidence.'

'*What?* We need to run a business.'

'Not this morning, ma'am. Until further notice, the Grill is closed.'

Carly and Hal stared at her with undisguised hostility. Mayflower put a hand on her mom's arm. 'One morning isn't the end of the world, right?'

Carly snatched her arm away. 'You're not the one paying the bills.' She shoved her chair back and stood. 'C'mon, let's leave the detective here to get on.'

Hal and Mayflower both stood. Carly continued to glare at Barbara: 'I'd have thought you'd be more concerned with the dead fifteen-year-old in the freezer than those vampyr scum. If you ask me, you should be congratulating whoever killed those fuckers.'

'Well, I'll be sure to take your feedback into consideration, ma'am.'

The trio turned to go. Barbara cleared her throat loudly. 'Just one more thing.'

Carly turned.

'I'm going to need your keys,' Barbara said.

Carly shook her head but reluctantly took out a bundle of keys. She took two off and handed them to Barbara. Hal and Mayflower did the same.

'These all the keys?' Barbara queried.

'Yep,' Carly said.

Barbara wasn't sure she believed her, but it would have to do. Unless she could find signs of a break-in, someone out there must have another set of keys. Either that, or they had somehow managed to hide in here after closing.

'Thank you, ma'am. I'll let you know as soon as I'm done here.'

Carly responded with a snort and the trio let themselves out. At the door, Mayflower glanced back at Barbara and mouthed, 'Thank you.'

Barbara just nodded. It wasn't up to her to tell Mayflower's parents about her secret rendezvous and, as far as she could see, it wasn't relevant to the case. Although, right now, she wasn't entirely sure what *was* relevant to the case any more. Each new piece of information brought more questions.

There were only two things she felt sure of: Dr Dalton's death wasn't a suicide. And he wasn't working alone. Someone had wanted to get in here and remove the evidence. Someone who didn't care if they murdered a cop in the process.

But was the same individual responsible for the murders of both Marcus *and* Dalton?

Or was there more than one killer in Deadhart?

This morning, he had told her. It would happen this morning. The girl needed to be ready. Without a watch or a clock, she had no real idea of time, but he had told her to count, as best she could, the minutes and hours.

Now, she heard voices outside the low basement window. She strained against the extent of the chain.

'So, you want me to leave these bricks and cement right here?'

'Thank you. I have to say you're more helpful than the usual driver they send from the hardware store. Nice and early, too.'

'Well, I can't let you go lugging heavy building supplies around by yourself.'

'I'm used to it.'

'Are you sure you don't need someone to do this work for you? Don't seem like something a young lady like yourself should be doing.'

The girl had frowned. Young lady. *Her Captor was old. Why was he lying?*

'Thank you for your offer, but I'll be fine.'

'Okay.' A pause. 'Could I ask one favour?'

'What?'

'Could I use your bathroom? I got a load more deliveries to make and, well, I forgot to go before I left.'

A hesitation. Her Captor was suspicious of people. They rarely had visitors. They were isolated and self-sufficient, and it was, of course, all for her own good.

She heard her Captor reply: 'Of course. It's the least I could do.'

'Thank you.'

The voices faded. Going back around to the front of the house. This was where it would happen. Where the plan would succeed or fail.

'We're not going to hurt them,' her Rescuer had told her. 'We don't want to be hunted for murder. We just need to get the keys and get you out.'

She had wondered at which point they would 'make them pay' but didn't ask. Right now, she had to trust her Rescuer. He was her only chance of escape.

She sat on the bed. She realized she was holding her breath. She could hear floorboards creaking overhead, but the voices were too far away to make out. And then she heard a more distinctive sound: a scream. And a heavy thud. She tensed. More movement upstairs. Different from her Captor, lighter, faster. Then, finally, the sound of a key in a lock. The door to the basement opened with a familiar creak. Footsteps down the stairs.

She tensed. A figure rounded the corner.

For the first time in all these years, she looked upon a face other than her Captor's.

44

Snow had coated the town in a heavy drape of white. The Christmas lights glowed from within shrouds of ice and cars parked along the street had been reduced to white humps in the drifts. A few trucks and SUVs were managing to plough through the snow, but it was still falling heavily.

Barbara moved from the window and sat down at her desk.

'Guess Jess is right. The cavalry isn't going to be rolling in anytime soon.'

'No one's getting *out* of here anytime soon, either,' Tucker said.

Barbara rubbed at her eyes. 'And I've just shut down the only place in town to get a beer.'

'You sure know how to win friends and influence people.'

She gave him a look. 'You think Carly and Hal were telling the truth about not knowing about the heads?'

'Nope. In fact, I think if we request copies of their bank statements, we'll probably find some interesting payments going in from Doc Dalton.'

'I'll put a warrant for bank statements on my list.' She scribbled it down.

'What about our mystery tattooist? Could they be the Doc's accomplice?' Tucker said.

He had told her about his chat with Jess Garrett. Seemed

Jess was more forthcoming with Tucker than with Barbara, which made her wonder if there was some history there.

'It's a possibility,' she said. 'The question is, who is it?'

'Nathan has tattoos,' Tucker said. 'Plus, Jacob was running blood for the Doc.'

There was definitely *something* going on with Nathan Bell, but Barbara wasn't sure that was it.

'I keep coming back to Kurt Mowlam,' she said. 'He was arguing with Dalton the night the Doc was killed, and we still haven't checked his house out.' She tapped her pen against her chin. 'We'll talk to both of them again.' She made another note then glanced at Tucker. 'What do you think about the attack on the church?'

He shook his head. 'It doesn't make any sense to me. Why would Athelinda want to provoke the town when emotions are running so high? She's smarter than that.'

He was right. It didn't make sense. Unless provoking the town was the point.

'Perhaps she *wants* to push folk into going after the Colony.'

'Why?'

'Because if the Colony are attacked, they have a legal right to defend themselves. There was a case in Maine a couple of years back. Half a dozen men tried to set fire to a colony settlement. Two were killed. Authorization for a cull got turned down because the men had entered a protected settlement illegally with intent to harm.'

Tucker looked at her. 'And right now the town can't call for back-up. If anyone went in there . . . it would be a goddamn slaughter.'

Barbara's phone buzzed on the desk. She picked it up and glanced at the caller. Nicholls.

'I'd better take this.' She pressed answer. 'Hello, sir.'

'Atkins. How's it going?'

She was struck by the difference between his clipped, efficient tones and Tucker's slow drawl.

'We're making progress, sir. How are you?'

'Bored. I hear you shut down the Grill.'

Carly must have been on the phone pretty fast.

'That's right, sir. I found vampyr artefacts being stored in the freezer. It's a crime scene.'

A heavy sigh. 'Can't you find somewhere else to keep the evidence?'

'Well, that's my intention.'

'Good. And maybe use the meeting this morning to try and make some peace with people. With the attack on the church, they're going to be scared and angry.'

He knew about the attack, and the meeting too. *Rita*, she thought.

'I'll try my best.'

'Tell them what they want to hear.'

'And what would that be, sir?'

'That you're going to authorize a cull.'

She bristled. 'I'm not in a position to do that yet.'

'Hear me out. The storm will keep everything stalled for a few days. No one will be able to do anything till it clears. It buys you time. You can revoke the cull if you find out anything else. In the meantime, it keeps people on side.'

'What if the Colony find out?'

'Make sure they don't.'

'I'll give it some thought,' she said reluctantly.

'You do that. Now, excuse me while I go pee in a bottle.'

'Goodbye, sir.'

He ended the call.

Barbara looked up at Tucker. 'You hear that?'

'I got the gist.'

'What do you think?'

'I think I know far too much about the chief's toilet habits.'

'Aside from that.'

'It's not a bad idea. Like he says, it buys time. Might stop folk acting rashly, especially if what you suspect about Athelinda's motives is true.'

'Okay. Well, I'll consider it.' She glanced at the time, 'I guess I'd better be going. You coming?'

'I'm not sure my presence will help. I thought I might try and make it up to the Lame Horse. Check out Nathan's alibi.'

She frowned. 'Only one truck.'

'Damn.'

'Tucker can take mine.'

Barbara turned. She hadn't heard Rita walk in. The woman might be hard to miss (in a bright orange ensemble today) but she moved like a ninja.

'Thanks, Rita.'

Rita smiled. 'Least I can do for the new deputy. Even got fresh snow tyres on.' She fixed Tucker with her sharp, dark eyes. 'You sure you remember how to drive?'

'I was driving before you were born.'

She laughed. 'That's why I'm worried.'

She fished in her pocket and threw him the keys. Tucker caught them.

Barbara stood and grabbed her coat, suddenly feeling like an outsider again. 'Any last-minute words of advice?'

Tucker raised his eyebrows. 'You're asking me?'

'Good point.'

Rita looked at Barbara. 'You ready?'

The church was packed. Around a hundred people seated, with more standing. Not the whole town by any means, but certainly a lot of people.

The dead pig and writing had gone from outside, but the half-burnt cross remained. Inside, the glass had been cleared up, but the boarded-up windows meant the light was dim. Only a couple of bulbs in the ceiling provided illumination. It gave a gloomy, funereal feel to the scene. Which was perhaps appropriate.

A small wooden altar and lectern stood at one end of the church and, behind, on the wall, hung a large white cross. Three chairs had been arranged next to the altar. Colleen Grey stood by one, talking to Carly. No sign of Colleen's shadow, Grace. Barbara and Rita walked down the aisle towards them. As one, heads turned in their direction. The murmur of conversation subsided. No pitchforks, Barbara thought, but if looks could kill, she'd be flapping on the floor like a landed trout.

'Rita, Detective Atkins,' Colleen smiled warmly. 'Welcome to our gathering.'

Barbara was damn sure the choice of words was deliberate.

Carly gave Barbara a poisonous look. ''Bout the only place people can gather right now.'

Before Barbara could reply, she turned on her skinny heels and strode back to her seat.

'Thanks for doing this.' Colleen clasped Barbara's hand. 'The town appreciates it.'

'You're wel—' Barbara started to say, and then stopped. She stared at the cross. It was constructed of bones.

Colleen saw her looking. 'It's antique,' she said. 'Passed down from an old friend.'

'Of course,' Barbara said tightly. 'Shall we get on?'

Barbara and Rita took their seats as Colleen turned to address the crowd.

'Thank you for joining us here this morning, in this place of worship. The last few days have been hard for all of us in Deadhart. A child is dead, and a shadow has fallen over our town bringing sorrow, anger and fear.' She paused. 'Last night this church came under attack from the Colony . . .'

A ripple ran through the crowd. Great, Barbara thought. That'll help.

'But we are not cowed. Darkness always seeks to destroy light. And it will always fail. God will give us strength in our fight against evil.' Another pause. 'But many of you want to know how the authorities are going to help us in our battle. That is why I have asked Detective Atkins here this morning, to explain what she is doing to apprehend Marcus Anderson's killer and keep our town safe.'

Colleen stepped aside and gestured for Barbara to take her place. Fire them up with religious fervour and send out the sacrificial lamb. Barbara steeled herself and walked up to the lectern. She looked around. She couldn't see Marcus's parents, but she recognized Mowlam slouched carelessly on a chair near the front. Carly and Hal sat partway back, Carly still glaring at her with undisguised hostility. Barbara had expected Jess Garrett to be here, but maybe she had already said her piece. Other faces she had seen

295

around but couldn't put names to. They all regarded her with hard eyes and crossed arms.

'Thank you, Reverend Grey.' She cleared her throat. 'As some of you already know, I'm a detective with the Department of Forensic Vampyr Anthropology.'

'We don't care about your fancy title,' a voice called from the back.

'Fine by me, sir. It's certainly something of a mouthful.' She smiled. 'I'm here today to update you on the investigation and try to answer any questions you might have.'

'Where's Chief Nicholls?' asked an older man three rows back.

'He's in Anchorage Hospital with a broken leg.'

'I got a question,' another male voice called out from the left. She turned. Bearded, scrawny, mid-fifties. 'When are you going to authorize a cull so we can be rid of those damn vampyr scum for good? What are you waiting for?'

'I'm happy to explain what we are waiting for, sir. Culls are not authorized lightly. In recent years, only two full colony culls have been approved. In both those cases there had been numerous attacks and multiple fatalities.'

Disgruntled noises, hollow laughter.

'So we have to wait till another child is killed? That's what you're saying?' The bearded man looked at Barbara stonily.

'No, sir. Any loss of life is a tragedy.'

'What about the video?' A younger man at the back. 'We heard you got a video of the killer.'

Barbara hesitated and then said: 'Upon further investigation, I'm afraid the video was discounted as evidence.'

'Why?'

'I can't say at present.'

'But a vampyr still killed Marcus, right?'

'From my examination, yes. It is most likely that Marcus Anderson was killed by a vampyr.'

This time the murmur that ran around the crowd was louder, angrier. Barbara gripped the edges of the lectern.

'So, what else is there to know?' The bearded man from before. 'A vampyr killed that poor boy. We need a cull. To protect our kids.'

Barbara swallowed. 'My title may be different from a normal detective's, but my job is still the same. To find the perpetrator of the crime. The *individual* responsible.'

'We all know they won't give up one of their own, so you might as well just save yourself time and sign the order now.'

Murmurs of assent. She thought about Nicholls's advice. Tell them what they want to hear. But she had never been good at that.

'I don't see a murder investigation as a waste of time, sir,' she said firmly.

A woman with short grey hair stood. 'Since the Colony returned, a boy is dead and our church has been attacked. How much more proof do you need that the Colony is a danger to this town? We need to defend ourselves.'

'Ma'am, I understand how you feel –'

'Do you?' Carly stood. 'Seems to us, you care more about protecting *them* than you do about this town, or that poor dead boy.'

A few people clapped. Cries of, 'Hear, hear.'

'That's not true,' Barbara said. 'I'm here to find a killer and prevent any more loss of life.'

Mocking laughter. She ignored it.

'That means not panicking or acting rashly. Right now, I need everyone to stay calm and continue with normal security measures. Make sure homes are locked at night. If you have UV lights, use them. Don't let children out alone after dark –'

She broke off as the church door suddenly swung open and a blast of icy wind and snow blew in. A thin, slightly stooped figure entered. Beau Grainger. The man wore no coat, and his white hair was thick with snow. *He must be freezing*, Barbara thought. He walked slowly down the aisle like a jilted lover about to object to a wedding.

'Beau!' Rita stood. 'What are you doing here?'

He ignored her, staring at Barbara. He didn't look well, Barbara thought. His eyes were bloodshot, and his lips had a blueish tinge.

'Did I miss the meeting?'

Barbara smiled. 'No, sir. If you have a question . . .'

'Questions!' he snorted. 'It's too late for questions.'

He turned to the seated crowd.

'Look at you all, sitting here, like sacrificial lambs. What do you think the Colony is doing while you waste time talking? Why do you think they haven't run?'

People shifted awkwardly.

'You think they're up there waiting to be culled? No. They're planning their revenge. That's why she's back.'

'How do you know?' someone called out.

Beau grinned, a sickly leer. 'I hear them.' He tapped his skull. 'I hear what those damn vampyr scum are thinking.'

Uncertain looks. A couple of people at the back stood and moved towards the door. Barbara glanced at Rita, who gave a tiny headshake.

298

Beau stared around. 'I *hear* them,' he repeated, louder. 'And I saw them too. Outside my house.'

Barbara frowned. 'Sir, are you saying some of the Colony came to your home?'

He turned to her. 'They were there. Oh yeah. Aaron and his family. They came back. They're trying to scare me, punish me. They want me to think I'm losing my mind. But I know it was them.'

'All right!' Rita clapped her hands. 'I think it might be time to adjourn our meeting. Reverend?'

'Indeed.' Colleen rose gracefully. 'Thank you all for coming –'

'NO!' Beau shouted. 'We're not done here.'

But the mood had shifted. More people rose and shuffled towards the door, eyes cast down in embarrassment. Beau glared at them. '*Why won't you listen?*'

Rita walked up to him. 'Beau, maybe you should sit down a moment? You don't look so good.'

'I'm fine!'

But the older man was starting to shiver now. Barbara didn't like the pallor of his skin. Hypothermia could present with delusions. She stepped down from the altar.

'Sir, did you walk all the way here?'

'It's not far.'

'Maybe not in good weather, but it's minus five out there and that wind is like a knife. Here.' She took her coat off, wrapped it around Beau's shoulders and guided him to a spare seat.

She glanced back at Rita and Colleen. 'Someone should drive him home. He's at risk of hypothermia.'

Rita shook her head. 'I lent my truck to Tucker, remember?'

'And I'm afraid I don't have a vehicle at the moment,' Colleen said.

'Okay.' Barbara sighed. It wasn't like she was investigating a murder or anything. 'Well, if I take Beau back, can you get into town, Rita?'

'Sure. I can catch a lift with someone.'

Barbara smiled at Beau. 'Why don't I drive you home, sir, and make sure you're okay?'

'I don't need your help,' Beau grumbled.

'Sir, it's just a lift. Otherwise I could arrest you for disturbing the peace and take you to the cells instead.'

Beau looked like he was about to refuse. Then he seemed to sag. 'Fine.'

Barbara nodded. 'Okay.'

She felt a cool hand on her shoulder. She turned. Colleen smiled at her beatifically. 'Thank you for doing this, Barbara. You're a true good Samaritan.'

'Yeah, well, love thy enemy. Isn't that the motto of the story?' She fixed the Reverend with a hard look. 'Maybe a few people round here could try it sometime.'

45

The Lame Horse was an apt name.

Set back from the road, it was a faux hunting lodge inhabited by the type of clientele who looked as if a bar was the last place they should be while also looking like they had absolutely nowhere else to go (except maybe a twelve-step programme).

Tucker used to be a regular. Go figure.

The lodge was large yet gloomy. A bar took up most of one side, an (unlit) stone fireplace took up most of the other, and tables and chairs were cluttered around the rest of the room. Fringed lamps lent a dusty light to the place. Moose and reindeer antlers decorated the walls, alongside a few yellowed vampyr skulls. Incongruously, raggaeton music played a little too loud from a speaker somewhere. The whole place smelt of stale beer and fresh urine.

At just before lunch, it was almost entirely empty. Probably the weather, although even in Tucker's day it was never bustling. Aside from him, there was only one other person at the bar. A woman, smoking a cigarette and nursing a beer. She wore a sequinned black-and-white dress with cowboy boots and a tasselled waistcoat. Bright orange hair cascaded in curls down her back.

Tucker walked up. 'Buy a girl a drink?'

She turned. Up close, the hair was obviously a wig. Her face was creased with heavy lines, thick make-up caked into them. Crinkled eyes were thickly lined with kohl and painted with blue eyeshadow. Her lips, as always, were coated in bright red lipstick.

Twenty-five years ago, Tucker wouldn't have put Margot at a day under seventy. Now, she didn't look a day under ninety.

The lips drew into a smile, revealing yellowed teeth. 'Well, look what the devil dragged in. Jensen Tucker. I heard you were dead.'

Her voice when she spoke was the throaty rasp of a dedicated thirty-a-day nicotine addict.

'You shouldn't believe everything you hear,' Tucker said.

Margot stood, somewhat shakily, and embraced Tucker in a surprisingly hard hug. Her head barely reached his chest.

'You feel good.'

'Thanks.'

'You want to make an old lady feel good?'

'Maybe after a drink.'

She laughed, which then morphed into a hacking cough. She thumped her chest.

'Okay. Beer?'

Tucker took a stool. It creaked beneath his weight.

'Thanks.'

It was early and he was driving, but this wasn't the type of place where you ordered a spritzer. He waited, resting his arms on the bar. It felt sticky.

Margot walked behind the bar, grabbed a bottle of Bud out of the fridge and plonked it down in front of him. 'I'd say on the house, but this house needs every dollar it can get.'

'That's fine,' Tucker said, reaching for his wallet. 'How is business?'

'Booming, as you can see.'

'Thought that might be the weather.'

'Not much better most of the time. A lot of the old crowd got sober or cirrhosis. Folks have more choices. You know there's a brew pub opened up in Talkeetna?'

'Things change, I guess.'

'Yeah, and not always for the better.' She took the note he handed her and stuffed it into the till. No change. Then she took a drag on the cigarette. 'What are you doing here, Tucker?'

'You hear about the kid that was killed?'

'Yeah, I heard.'

'Well, I'm helping with the investigation.'

Her tattooed eyebrows raised.

'You're working as a cop again?'

'Temporarily.' Despite himself, he took a sip of beer.

'So, I'm guessing this isn't just a social visit?'

He smiled. 'Maybe I just missed your face.'

'This face? No.' She eyed him curiously. 'Mostly I don't like to lose regulars. But some . . . it's for the best.'

'Well, in that case, I guess this is business. Were you here the night before last?'

She stubbed out the cigarette. 'I'm here every night. Can only afford a couple of staff on the weekends.'

'So, you were here on Friday the 10th too?'

'Yup.'

Tucker held a twenty out. 'If you can answer a few questions, I got some more dollars.'

She plucked the twenty from Tucker's fingers. 'What d'you want to know?'

'I need to know if a man was in here two nights ago. Around forty. Dark hair, dishevelled.'

303

'Well, that's about fifty per cent of our clientele.'

Tucker wished he'd got a photo of Nathan. 'His name is Nathan, and he has tattoos – a black patch on each of his knuckles.'

Margot's grin faded. 'Oh yeah, I know him.'

'You sound like you'd rather you didn't.'

'Well, I know he was in here a couple of nights ago because he gave me twenty dollars to tell anyone who asked he was *definitely* in here on Friday, November the 10th.'

'Was he?'

'Nope.'

Tucker chuckled. 'Okay. So, you don't like him. Why?'

'He got overfamiliar with my staff a few times. Asked one of them if he wanted to go to his truck with him. Even offered him cash.'

Interesting. 'The staff member take it?'

'He's a nice boy. He politely declined.'

'That the last of it?'

'I had some words. Nathan backed off. Then he found himself a new friend. They'd sit and have a drink then disappear outside for a while. To his truck, I guess – and I don't think they were checking the oil.'

'This a regular hook-up?'

'Regularish. Maybe once a week over the last few months.'

'What did he look like, this hook-up?'

'Young, long blond hair, pretty.'

Tucker felt unease stir in his stomach. 'You got a name?'

Margot hesitated. Tucker sighed and reached back into his wallet. He produced another twenty. Pretty much all he had.

'This help?'

'It's not the money.'

'Then what?'

'What d'you need to know for?'

'Well, Nathan is a person of interest, you might say – his friend might be able to tell us more about him.'

'And that's all?'

'That's all.'

She seemed to consider. 'You know my story?'

Tucker did. Margot used to be called Martin. Long time ago. Before Tucker was a regular here. Tucker didn't care. As far as he was concerned, Margot was Margot. Everyone should be able to live their life comfortable in their own skin.

She lit a fresh cigarette. 'I was wearing dresses before anyone had a phobia about it. But I know what it's like to be discriminated against, spat on, attacked just for who I am.'

Tucker nodded. 'Well, that's something we got in common.'

'Yeah. So, I got sympathy with people who don't fit in.'

'I hear you. And I only want to talk to this guy. I don't care if he's gay or soliciting.'

'It's not that.'

'He's underage?'

Margot gave a short laugh.

Tucker frowned. 'Then what?'

'He used to come in here a long time ago –'

'When?'

'Must be almost thirty years, before you were a regular – and he looked exactly the same.'

'He's Colony?'

'His name is Michael.'

Michael. 'Dammit,' Tucker cursed.

'You know him?' Margot asked.

'Yeah.' Tucker sighed and reached for his beer. 'He's Athelinda's son.'

46

'You okay there, sir?' Barbara pulled off carefully down the snowy road. More snow than road now, she thought, gripping the wheel tightly.

'I know what you think,' Beau muttered.

'What's that, sir?'

'I'm crazy.'

'No, sir. I don't think that.'

'I saw them looking at me in there. You get old, and people look at you like you're pathetic, stupid.'

She guided the truck around a slight bend. 'Well, sir. You should try being a woman.'

She saw his lip twitch. A relaxing in the tight hostility of his face.

'My wife, Patricia. She had dementia,' he said.

'I'm sorry to hear that. Dementia is a cruel illness.'

'But this isn't *that*.'

Barbara nodded. 'What did you mean about *hearing* them? You mean the Colony?'

The guarded look returned.

'Sir,' Barbara said, 'I've studied colonies. One of the ways they communicate is through a kind of hive mind – telepathy, if you will. They've been known to use it to get into people's heads.'

Barbara didn't add that there were certain predilections for this: adolescence, illness, being half-turned and certain mental health conditions. Then there was the more fanciful myth that once you killed a vampyr, you carried them with you.

Beau shook his head. '*Damn* Colony. We should have got rid of them when we had the chance. Saved ourselves a lot of trouble, and Janice and Ed would still have their boy.'

'Sir, you and I might have different views about the Colony –'

'No "might" about it.'

'But we both want to see Marcus's killer brought to account. If there's anything you know about the town or its history that could help . . .'

'History is history for a reason.'

'But if we don't learn from it, we repeat it.'

'You get that out of a fortune cookie?'

'Saw it on a bumper sticker.'

He made a noise that might have been a grunt or a short chuckle. 'Over here,' he said, gesturing towards a turn-off in the road. Barbara pulled up outside a neat clapboard house. She left the engine running. She had a feeling there was more here. Something had happened, and Beau wanted to talk.

He sighed, then reached for the door and pushed it open.

'Guess you'll be wanting to come inside – make sure I don't drop down dead.'

The house was cold. Yet Beau didn't seem to notice. He walked straight into the kitchen at the end of the hall.

'You want coffee?'

It sounded more like an accusation than an invitation, but Barbara said, 'Yes, thank you, sir.'

'I've not got any milk.'

'Black is fine, sir.'

She followed him into the kitchen, noting the closed door to her left, presumably the living room. She guessed Beau didn't want her to feel too much at home. She waited while he picked up two mugs from the drainer and set the kettle to boil.

'So, Rita tells me your family has always lived in Deadhart?'

'My grandfather came here, like a lot of men, to work in the mine.' He spooned coffee into mugs, hand trembling slightly. 'Why are you interested in Deadhart's history?'

'I think there may be a connection to what's happening now.'

He poured hot water into the mugs, brought them over to the table.

'The connection is obvious. The Colony. They came back, and another kid is dead. That's all they bring. Death. Won't ever change. It's not right to ask good God-fearing people to live alongside them. Not without being able to defend ourselves.'

He sat down heavily on one of the hard wooden chairs.

'And you think attack is the best form of defence?' Barbara asked, pulling out the chair opposite.

'It's us or them,' he said. 'We took care of things before.'

'An unauthorized cull. You killed Aaron, his father and his uncle.'

'Tucker was letting a killer escape.'

'And what if you were wrong? What if Aaron didn't kill Todd Danes?'

Beau blinked at her. 'He confessed.'

309

'To protect the Colony.'

Beau's hand went to his head, rubbed at it. 'No. You confessed,' he muttered.

Barbara frowned. *You?* A slip of the tongue, or something else?

'What do you know about the Bone House, sir?' she asked, deciding to change tack.

She saw him start. 'Why are you asking about that place?'

'I'm interested.'

'If you know the name, you already know what it was.'

'A whorehouse, where men had sex with vampyrs. I understand your own grandfather was a visitor.'

The blue eyes flashed. 'Lots of men visited. It was a different time. Your type always act like vampyrs are the victims. Kids used to go missing from Deadhart all the while back then. Rita ever tell you about her mom's older sister? Six years old. Lost in the woods. Never found her body. But everyone knew it was the Colony.'

'No, Rita never told me,' she said, and wondered why.

'Well, I guess her mom don't like to talk about it.'

'Two wrongs don't make a right though.'

'No. And maybe that's why that vampyr girl hates us so much. Why she wants revenge.'

'Athelinda?'

He nodded. 'It ain't just about Aaron and his family. It's about that place – the Bone House. What they did to her there.'

'What they did . . .'

And suddenly the penny dropped. *Of course.* How had she missed it?

'*Athelinda* was kept at the Bone House?'

Beau nodded. 'When my grandfather had a little too much to drink, he'd talk about the Bone House – and a girl. "*A cascade of blonde curls, sweet as a cherub,*" he would say. "*But she was truly a devil.*"'

Barbara's throat felt dry. 'She was a child.'

'She's a vampyr, using innocence as a disguise.' He shifted in his seat, winced. 'So, now you see. This town. The Colony. There's no coming together. No making amends. There's too much hate on both sides.' He clutched at his head again, shivered.

Barbara frowned. 'Are you all right, Mr Grainger?'

'I'm fine.'

Barbara felt a twinge of guilt. She'd been questioning the old man too hard.

'Mr Grainger, it's cold in here. Maybe we should go into the living room, light a fire.'

'I said, I'm *fine.*'

'You're shivering.'

'I can get a sweater.'

'And I want to make sure you're okay.'

She walked down the hall.

'*No!* You can't go in there.'

A scrape as Beau pushed his chair back. Barbara shoved open the door to the living room and stopped.

'Shit.'

The room was small, cosy, but it looked like it had been disturbed. A lamp was broken, and ash smeared over the walls. It smelt of smoke. But that wasn't what caused Barbara to pause, ice snaking down her spine.

Above the fireplace, mounted on wooden stands, were two vampyr heads. Older males, with thick grey hair.

311

A third mount was empty. When Aaron and his family were killed, the heads had been taken. No one ever claimed responsibility.

'We hunted 'em fair and square,' Beau said from behind her.

Barbara turned. 'Really? Did they have weapons too, Mr Grainger?'

He gave her a withering look. 'They don't need weapons. The boy was a killer. We did what was necessary.'

'And displaying them like sick trophies, that was necessary too?'

He walked past her, up to the heads. He had stopped shivering. In here, he seemed to have regained some of his colour, his strength. 'You're not a hunter, Detective. There's a relationship between hunter and prey.' He raised a hand to touch the cheek of one of the men. 'Almost like a marriage. What you kill, you own . . . for better or worse.'

Barbara's stomach churned. 'Where's Aaron?' she asked, nodding at the empty mount.

'That child demon came here the other night, and she took him.'

Good for Athelinda, Barbara thought. She took her phone out and snapped a picture of the heads.

'You can't keep these,' she said to Beau. 'They need to be returned to the Colony.'

'I've kept them for twenty-five years –'

'And you have twenty-four hours to relinquish them voluntarily, or I'll be back with a warrant.'

He turned back to her. 'You don't understand –'

She cut him off. 'Oh, I do, sir. My dad was a hunter. He hunted because he needed to feel power over other creatures. But once you took away his weapons, he was a weak, bitter man.'

'Don't seem like any way to talk about your father.'

'He wasn't much of a father, or a man.'

'He still alive?'

'No. He killed himself when I was sixteen. Only time he shot anyone who deserved it.'

She slipped her phone back in her pocket. 'I'll give your daughter a call. Tell her to come check on you – and bring some packing boxes.'

47

Tucker's body felt tired. His skin and eyes itched. But his mind felt more alert than it had in a while. He had missed this – investigating, being a cop. He had been stagnating. Existing, but not really living. Now, it felt like he was being given a second chance.

He pulled up in a space outside the Grill. The street was quiet. Most people were indoors, sheltering from the weather or at the meeting in the church. He climbed out of the truck, bracing himself against the wind. Barbara had stuck crime-scene tape over the entrance to the Grill, but it had blown loose, or perhaps been pulled off?

Tucker wondered if he should just check everything was okay and no one was taking the opportunity to tamper with evidence. He walked up the steps to the front door. Straight away, he could see scratches around the lock. He tried the handle. Unlocked. He stepped inside and the hairs bristled on the back of his neck. A sense, even before he heard a noise or saw a shadow. *Someone was here.*

He closed the door quietly behind him and looked around. The light in the bar was dim, the air floating with specks of dust. But he could see the particles swirling, like it had been minutely disturbed. Not long ago. He stood still, listening, breathing in the scents of the room. Beer, sweat, food and another scent – human.

Upstairs, the floorboards faintly creaked. Tucker moved

across the bar as quietly as a six-foot-six, two-hundred-pound man could, and advanced up the narrow staircase behind the bar. The stairs groaned beneath his weight. It was pointless trying to be discreet.

He moved faster up the remaining stairs. Only one way out of here. He heard more movement in the bedroom to his left. He shouldered the door open, gun raised. A gust of icy wind made his eyes water. The room had been trashed and a message scrawled in red on the wall behind the bed:

Woe to those who call evil good and good evil, who put darkness for light and light for darkness.

A can of spray paint was discarded on the floor and a thin girl dressed in what looked like a turn-of-the-century frock coat and a long dress was perched at the open window, half inside and half outside the room.

Tucker pulled out his gun. 'Stop right there. Don't do it.'

The girl turned to look at him. Her thin, pale face was defiant. A flat look in her eyes. Tucker had seen that look before. In the eyes of the drugged, but also in the eyes of the converted.

'You won't shoot me,' she said.

'Maybe not, but where are you going to go? You jump, that snow out there won't break your fall.'

'The Lord will save me.'

Tucker shook his head. 'He might save you, but he sure as hell won't stop you breaking your ankles or legs.' He lowered the gun. 'Your choice.'

She glared at him. He waited, every muscle tense. If she

decided to jump, he didn't think he could reach her in time. She shifted on the windowsill. And then, reluctantly, she swung both legs back inside.

'Thank you,' Tucker said.

She snarled at him. 'Fuck you, pig.'

He advanced towards her, unhooking the cuffs from his belt. 'Your Lord teach you to use language like that?'

She held out her wrists and he got the distinct impression this was not her first time being handcuffed.

She smiled as he put the cuffs on. 'He will smite those who are unbelievers and followers of Satan's path.'

'Well, until then, I'm placing you under arrest for breaking and entering.' He snapped the handcuffs into place. 'Amen.'

48

Barbara's phone rang just as she pulled out on to the road.

'Hello.'

'It's Tucker –'

'Did you know?'

'Sorry? Know what?'

'That Beau Grainger kept the heads of Aaron and his family as trophies. Stuck up on the goddam fucking wall.'

A silence.

Barbara sighed. 'You did?'

'I wasn't in any position to take them from him.'

'*Jesus Christ*, Tucker. I thought you were different from the rest of this town, but you're just as bad.'

'I got shot trying to save Aaron's life. Back then, I might well have found my own head up there, too. I couldn't help them once they were dead.'

Barbara seethed, but she knew he was right. It wasn't his fault. She was angry and taking it out on him.

'I'm getting a warrant to have them repossessed and returned to the Colony,' she said.

'Good.'

'Why are you calling?'

'I have Grace, Reverend Grey's assistant, in custody.'

'What? Why?'

'I caught her trashing your room and leaving you a message from God on the wall.'

317

So, Grace was the mysterious message leaver. But was she acting alone, or on the orders of her guardian?

'She say *why*?'

'She's not saying anything right now.'

'Okay. I'll be there in five minutes.'

Barbara put down her phone and guided the truck carefully down Main Street. She could feel the truck's tyres having to work harder to push through. The windscreen wipers moved slush around the screen but didn't do much in the way of wiping. She squinted through a tiny patch of clear glass.

A small group of people stood in a huddle outside the café. Talking about this morning's meeting perhaps, or Beau's strange behaviour. Or maybe just seeking safety in numbers. Ultimately, humans were pack animals.

She pulled up outside the police department, climbed out of the vehicle and traipsed through the snow up to the door. She let herself in. Grace was sitting inside one of the small cells, head bowed, hands clasped in prayer. Tucker was in the office, just putting down the phone. Barbara shook snow out of her hair and looked at him questioningly. 'So?'

'I've taken fingerprints. She's declined legal representation – or at least she shook her head – which is just as well, seeing as the nearest lawyer lives in Anchorage.'

Barbara was impressed at his efficiency. 'She talking at all?' she asked.

'Only thing she has said is to ask for the Reverend Grey to be here.'

'Oh goody. I take it that's who you were calling?'

'Yup.'

Barbara let out a sigh of irritation through her teeth. 'Any idea how she got in?'

'Found this on her.'

He held up a lock-picking device.

Barbara raised an eyebrow. 'Wonder where she got that? Not what you'd expect from a disciple of God.'

She walked across the corridor to the cells. Tucker rose and followed her.

'Hello, Grace,' Barbara said.

The girl half raised her head but remained silent.

'I understand you've refused a lawyer.'

Silence.

'And you don't want to speak to us unless Reverend Grey is present?'

No reply.

Barbara nodded. 'Okay. Well, you're not a minor, so I'm afraid we can't let Reverend Grey sit in the interview with you.'

Grace suddenly looked up. 'I *am* a minor. I'm sixteen, not eighteen.'

'Sorry?'

'I'm sixteen, not eighteen.'

Barbara exchanged glances with Tucker. 'You can prove that?'

The girl turned away. 'I'm guessing you'll find out soon enough.'

Barbara motioned to Tucker to return to the other room.

'You said you took her prints. Did you put them in the system?'

He glanced at the desktop then back at her. 'I'm not so hot on the tech stuff.'

'I'll do it.' Barbara sat at the desk and scanned in the fingerprints that Tucker had taken. Some departments had new-fangled digital scanners, but somehow the DFVA seemed to be last on the list for new tech. She hit submit. Now they just had to wait.

'How long do you think it will take?' Tucker asked.

Barbara shrugged. 'Depends on the queue. Could be two hours or two days. I've still not had the latents back from Dalton's or the set from Nathan Bell's house, but that could just be because there are no matches.'

'You think she's in the system?'

'I don't know. Colleen said she had taken the girl under her wing. I'm wondering how they met.'

The front door buzzed.

'Guess we're about to find out,' Tucker said.

Barbara pressed the intercom. 'Police department.'

'It's Reverend Grey.'

Barbara glanced at Tucker then pressed enter.

The door opened and Colleen strode in. She didn't look quite as composed as she had earlier. The striking white hair was coming loose from its clasps and her face looked tense. Barbara was struck by how the woman could be anywhere from thirty to sixty.

'Thanks for coming, Reverend.'

'You have Grace in custody?'

'Yes, ma'am,' Tucker said. 'She was caught breaking into the Grill and vandalizing Detective Atkins's room. Would you know anything about that?'

Colleen's lips pursed. 'Of course not.'

Barbara continued: 'Right now, she is refusing to

cooperate unless you are present. She also states she is six-teen, not eighteen.'

To Barbara's satisfaction, the woman looked uncom-fortable, the sheen of serenity cracking.

'Cooperating now could help Grace in the long run, Reverend,' Barbara said. 'So how about you tell us the truth about how you met?'

Colleen smiled tightly. 'Her name is Rhiannon, she's sixteen years old and, when I found her, she was about to jump off a bridge. Does that help you, detectives?'

They sat at the desk, Tucker and Barbara facing Colleen and Grace/Rhiannon.

'So, shall we start at the beginning, as Julie Andrews likes to say?'

Colleen and Grace looked at her blankly.

'Okay.' Barbara smiled. 'Not *Sound of Music* fans. Rhian-non, can I call you that?'

'My name is Grace now.'

'Okay, but for the record, can you state your given name and your date of birth.'

Grace glanced at Colleen, who gave a faint nod. 'Rhian-non Davis, 11th June 2008.'

'Okay. You have requested that Reverend Colleen Grey be here as your appropriate adult, correct?'

'Yes.'

'Ms Grey, could you state that you consent to this?'

'I do.'

'You have also declined a lawyer.'

'Yes.'

'Right. First off, can you just explain how you two met and your relationship.'

'Is that necessary?' Colleen asked.

Barbara smiled. 'You are aware, Reverend Grey, that trafficking a minor across state lines is an offence?'

'I am, Detective, which is why I asked Grace's mother for permission, which she gladly gave.'

'And I presume you have that in writing?'

'I do. It's at the church. I would be happy to show it to you.'

Barbara mentally gritted her teeth. 'So, how did you end up travelling together?'

'Reverend Grey saved me,' Grace said flatly.

'Grace ran away from home at fourteen,' Colleen said. 'She was living on the streets. Using, drinking, stealing.'

So that explained how she was so adept at breaking and entering, Barbara thought.

'Satan had me in his grip,' Grace said. 'He convinced me to kill myself so he could take my soul.'

Barbara resisted the urge to roll her eyes.

'I was walking home from a church service,' Colleen continued, 'and I saw a young girl standing on the edge of a bridge. I talked to her for a while and managed to persuade her to climb down.'

'You saw the light?' Tucker asked Grace.

'I saw a different way, with God. I realized there was a gap in my life that had allowed Satan in. Reverend Grey showed me that I could fill it with the light of the Lord instead.'

And *that* was how they got you, Barbara thought. It was no surprise that drug addicts and alcoholics found God during their recovery. They had to replace one addiction with another.

'And now you live and work with the Reverend?'

'I help her with God's work, yes.'

'And is that what you were doing this morning in my hotel room? God's work?'

Grace's lips tightened.

Colleen cut in. 'This is my fault. Grace has been misguided.'

'Is that so, Grace?' Tucker asked.

She stared at him. 'Your sort don't understand.'

'My sort?'

'Those in league with devils.'

'Alrighty.' Barbara was starting to think she preferred it when the girl didn't speak. 'So, you admit to breaking into the Grill and vandalizing my room? Did you also break into the Grill on Monday night, and leave writing on the bathroom mirror and a choker with a cross made of vampyr teeth?'

Grace nodded once.

'For the record, the suspect has nodded.'

'Detective,' Colleen said, 'Grace thought she was helping me and our cause.'

'By trying to warn me off.'

'Grace is young, and passionate in her beliefs. I'm sure you did things that were impulsive and irrational when you were young?'

Barbara didn't meet her gaze. 'When I was sixteen, I was in full-time education, ma'am, which is where Grace should be.'

'Grace is educated in the way of God, Detective. There is no higher teaching.'

'Well, I'm sure that will look good on her CV.'

The two women glared at each other. Tucker cleared his throat.

'Perhaps we should stick to the charges at hand.'

'Of course,' Colleen said. 'I respect the law. And I don't want discord in Deadhart.'

Yeah, right, thought Barbara.

'I'll tell you where we're at,' she said. 'Grace, or Rhiannon, has confessed to breaking and entering, and vandalism.' She paused. 'But she is a minor. It's a first offence, in Deadhart at least. I'm going to give her a warning and release her back into your care, on the understanding that this doesn't happen again.'

Colleen nodded. 'Thank you. I appreciate your mercy.'

Barbara leaned forward and snapped the recorder off. 'It's not mercy. It's practicality. I've got enough to deal with right now without any more paperwork.'

Ten minutes later, Barbara and Tucker stood at the door and watched the pair walk back down the street. The wind was whipping up a frenzy and the clouds didn't seem to be running out of snow anytime soon. Yet Colleen and Grace swept through the drifts in their long coats and dresses, seemingly oblivious to the weather.

'Something not right with those two,' Tucker muttered.

'Yeah,' Barbara agreed. 'Maybe I need to get me some of that Godly glow . . .' She slammed the door shut. 'Or thermal underwear.'

They retreated to the relative warmth of the office.

'How did your meeting at the church go?' Tucker asked, easing his frame into a chair.

'Well, I'm still here to tell the tale,' Barbara said, plonking herself down at her desk.

'How come you ended up back at Beau's house?'

'I drove him home after he burst into the meeting. Didn't seem well. Claimed he could hear the Colony talking to him.'

Tucker frowned. 'That doesn't sound like Beau.'

'Yeah, well, maybe living with stuffed vampyr heads on your wall affects you after a while.' She gave him a look.

He sighed. 'Okay. Point taken.'

'Did you find out anything at the Lame Horse?'

'Nathan wasn't there on the night Marcus was killed. Even though he paid the bar's owner to say he was.'

'Really? So, either he's guilty or paranoid.'

She thought about the tattoos again. Prison tattoos. Maybe he'd done time and wasn't keen to do more.

'I also found out he's been hooking up with someone,' Tucker continued. 'A young male.'

'So, Nathan is gay or bi. Maybe that's why his marriage broke up.'

'Looks that way. That's not all. The male he was meeting, he's Colony.'

'Any idea who he is?'

Tucker hesitated. 'From the description, I think he's a vampyr named Michael . . . and he's Athelinda's son.'

'He's *what* now?' Barbara's eyebrows shot up. 'Athelinda has a son? But . . .'

Athelinda is a child, she was going to say. But of course she wasn't. She only *looked* like one. But still . . .

'Who's his father?' she asked.

'I don't know. But I do know that Michael is a halfling.'

'His father is *human*? I thought Athelinda hated humans.' She paused, something suddenly slotting into place in her head. 'The Bone House,' she muttered.

325

Tucker gave her an odd look. 'What's that place got to do with anything?'

'You know about it?'

'I've heard tales. It burned to the ground in the late twenties. Most of those inside died.'

'Did you know that Athelinda was kept there?'

She could see the shock in his eyes. 'No.'

'So, if her son is half-human, maybe that's where she got pregnant.'

Tucker nodded, trying to take this information in. 'Maybe. Damn.'

Barbara let out an irritated sigh. 'Problem is, everything I'm finding out just gives the Colony and Athelinda more reason to want to hurt Deadhart.'

'If Athelinda wanted to hurt Deadhart, she'd have done it before now,' Tucker said.

'You think Nathan knew he was meeting a vampyr?'

'No, I don't think so.'

'You think Athelinda knew her son was hooking up with a human?'

'Nothing happens in the Colony without her knowing about it. If Michael was meeting up with Nathan, you can bet there was a reason.'

'Maybe gathering information?' Barbara mused. 'Or maybe she has a specific interest in Nathan?'

'That I don't know.'

Barbara considered. There was something else that Beau had said:

'Kids used to go missing from Deadhart all the while back then.'

'Is it true that kids have gone missing from Deadhart before?'

326

'Not on my watch.'

'I'm talking a long time ago, maybe thirties, forties, or even earlier?'

He shifted in his seat. 'I heard stories. Mostly loose tongues in the Grill, talking about the good old days when they could hunt the Colony.'

'Beau mentioned Rita's aunt – said she disappeared when she was a little girl.'

'Look, it sounds harsh, but kids were often neglected in small towns like these back then. Left to run wild. Got killed by bears or lost in the woods. If a kid fell in the river or down a ravine – their body might never be found. Rita would tell you the same.'

Barbara nodded. 'But what if it *was* a vampyr? Maybe our killer has been killing for a lot longer than we realized?'

His face creased. 'I don't know. There've never been any murders like Todd or Marcus before.'

'That you know about.'

'True, but what about the long gap?'

Barbara considered. 'The reason most serial killers don't get caught earlier is because they move around. They count on someone not joining the dots. But often they have a favourite place. A killing spot they return to. That's usually what gets them.'

'Well, we know Nathan recently returned to Deadhart, and he was here when Todd was killed.'

He was right. But somehow Nathan didn't strike Barbara as a serial killer. Usually they were smart, organized, good at covering their tracks. Unless the aggressive-drunk act was a double-bluff. She thought about Mowlam again. The good looks. The easy charm. The feeling that his

327

persona was all snake oil. Something else lurking just beneath the slick surface.

'Kurt Mowlam is another recent arrival,' she said.

'But he'd only have been a kid back when Todd was killed. Barely in double figures.'

'Unless he's a vampyr?'

Tucker let out a long sigh.

'Okay . . . so who do you want to talk to first?'

49

Athelinda didn't remember being turned.

Occasionally, fragments of her human life would come back to her. Sunlight. A strange sensation of warmth, which she thought might be joy or love. Music sung in a soft, lilting voice.

Afterwards, there was darkness, violence and blood. Many turned children didn't survive for long. They were killed by their own families out of shame, or abandoned, left to fend for themselves. Athelinda had been lucky, in a way. After she had killed her mother – an act of impulse and unreason she still occasionally felt pain about – she had been found wandering the streets and taken in by a travelling freak show.

This was back in seventeenth-century England, where child vampyrs were still curiosities, especially beloved of aristocrats and royalty. She had been dressed all in black, placed in a coffin in a cage, and people would gasp in breathless terror as the pretty blonde child drank the blood of small animals.

But then the puritanical, religious movement began to grow. To be entertained by vampyrs was seen as evil and satanic. Vampyrs were seized and culled. Athelinda had only narrowly escaped with her life after some of the other performers took pity on her and smuggled her out.

She had found herself on a boat to another country. The journey lasted weeks. And then a sickness descended.

Most of the others on board didn't make it. Athelinda arrived with a ghost ship of corpses and made her escape before anyone found out that many had been drained of their blood.

The new country was vast, busy and full of human stench. The streets bustled with people, carts and horses. America. A place Athelinda had heard talked of, often in a state of wonder.

But Athelinda found nothing wondrous about its mass of filthy streets, the chorus of coarse voices or the vampyr heads displayed in shops. She walked by night till the buildings and bustle of bodies lay far behind her. Now she had her freedom, she wished to preserve it.

For a long while she travelled alone, keeping to the forests and wilderness on the edge of towns. She taught herself to build a basic shelter and to hunt to survive. Not just animals. Any creature who ventured into the wilderness was fair game for her.

She made her way further and further north, following the darkness and the cooler weather. Eventually, perhaps inevitably, she met other vampyrs. Initially distrustful, they had formed a loose alliance and began to travel together. To her surprise, Athelinda realized that she found comfort in others of her kind.

In the way that most colonies grew, they added more members, and Athelinda became an unofficial leader. She was one of the oldest. She was also fierce and brutal. Being turned so young, she had less humanity to ease the edges off her bloodthirst and fury. But she also learned that such desires needed to be controlled. Murdering humans was seen as barbaric among other vampyrs. It reinforced the view that they were beasts and monsters. More to the point, it was bad for the colonies. Dead humans attracted unwanted attention.

Athelinda learned to curb her desires. Mostly.

For a while, their colony was nomadic, traversing the country by horse and cart or boat, but like all creatures, the urge to put down roots, to create a more permanent home, grew. Somewhere they could build a community and be left alone. That was how they found themselves in the mountains here. Cold, dark and isolated, away from the human hunters. The local Dghelay Teht'ana population had accepted, or perhaps respected, them. The 'night walkers', they called them.

The Colony built their settlement from scratch. Cut trees, sawed wood. Relationships were formed, children and then grandchildren born. Athelinda mellowed. They had found a home where they could live, untroubled.

And they did, for almost two hundred years. But it couldn't last. Humans were like a plague. They infected everywhere. When huge copper reserves were found in the mountains, men and their machines followed. The Colony was driven from its settlement into the woods. But that wasn't enough for the humans. Next came the hunting parties. They raided on the brightest of days, when they knew the Colony was most vulnerable. They killed, tortured and captured those they thought they could make use of. Like Athelinda.

She found herself at the mercy of men's desires and depravities. Chained, in a child's bedroom. Pink ruffles and cuddly toys. They dressed her in a gingham frock with a lace petticoat that itched, and white ankle socks that made

331

her feet sweat. Her long blonde hair was tied up in two bunches.

'*Pretty as a picture,*' Bonnie, the toothless hag who ran the whorehouse, would cackle, blowing pungent cigar smoke into Athelinda's face.

'*Now you make nice with your daddies when they come.*'

Athelinda did not make nice. But she didn't fight either. Bonnie took pleasure in punishing those who stepped out of line. She would remove fingers, eyes and sometimes limbs for transgressions. Athelinda had heard that she once hung a girl from a pole outside for seven days straight, not quite letting her die. Eventually, she slit her open from throat to pubis and hooked out what was inside her with a hot poker. Punishment for getting pregnant.

Athelinda wasn't sure if it was true. She heard these stories from the servant boy who brought her sustenance and cleaned her wounds. The boy liked to talk, and she listened, storing the information. In her own way, she was fond of the boy and only occasionally considered killing him.

While most humans looked alike to her, she began to recognize the faces of her visitors. Some were more palatable than others. Rough, but bearable. But there was one who even Athelinda feared. Good-looking with a thick head of fair hair, sharp blue eyes and a tall, lean physique. His smile was easy, but his eyes were dead. Athelinda recognized evil when she saw it. She'd seen those desires reflected in her own eyes.

The first time he visited her, he brushed her hair and then choked her with his belt. The next visit, he brought a knife. Another time, he used flame. He always had a new torture, each more extreme than the last, in order to derive his pleasure. And each time he knew she would be waiting, for she would not die.

On the worst day, Bonnie had to call for a doctor. Through a fog of brutal pain and blood, Athelinda was vaguely aware of their conversation:

'Just put her down.'

'*No*, she makes me good money. Joseph pays well. We need to keep her.'

'Then it will take time. I can give her drugs, for the pain. But there's no guarantees. The scars should heal eventually . . . at least on the outside.'

Athelinda had spent weeks in a drug-induced fever dream. Screams, pain, visions, more pain. She had cried out for her heart to be pierced, for sweet release. But then, eventually, her body had begun to heal, the fog of pain had lifted.

The first face she was aware of was that of the servant boy.

'You're back,' he said.

She had struggled to speak. The boy handed her a glass of thick, viscous blood. She had drunk it greedily.

The boy regarded her curiously. 'The man, he hurt you badly.'

'Why do you care?'

He shrugged. 'If it was me, I'd want to kill him.'

'Maybe I will.'

'How? They've taken everything from you. Your teeth. Your fight. Your colony.'

She glared at the boy. 'You mock me?'

'No. I want to help you.'

'Then fuck off.'

333

He nodded. 'As you wish.'

He rose and walked to the door, closing it behind him.

Athelinda pushed herself up. Something lay on the table beside her bed. A box of matches, with a small scrap of paper underneath. She picked it up.

Just two words, scrawled in Vampyric: *Birnen heo.*

She frowned. How did a servant boy know Vampyric?

She looked after him curiously. Then she read the note again. A smile spread across her face.

Birnen heo.

Burn them.

50

Mowlam's house was small and shabby, the clapboard blistered and warped, the front door dirty and peeling with old paint. Snow had coated the windows, making it impossible to see inside.

'You sure this is it?' Barbara asked.

'This is the address.'

'Dalton sure did move up in the world.'

'In more ways than one.'

A rusty Toyota was parked outside. But the house looked empty. Felt empty. The windows were dark, despite the failing light. No noise of a generator or steam from a heating system.

Barbara stared at the house, something inside her thrumming. A feeling. A bad feeling. She knocked on the door, loudly. They waited. No response.

She reached out to knock again then changed her mind and tried the door handle. Unlocked. She glanced back at Tucker. 'Seems like people could save themselves a lot of money on locks around here.'

She pushed the door open. 'Mr Mowlam? Police. We'd like to talk to you.'

Silence. Barbara reached for a light switch and flicked it on. The house was pretty much a two up two down, with a staircase bisecting it.

Two doors led off the hall. Barbara pushed open the

one on the right. Two things struck her straight away. The overwhelming smell of weed and the fact that the room had been trashed. Sofa cushions slashed, drawers pulled out, contents scattered, lamps tipped over, coffee table smashed.

'Whoah!' Tucker walked in behind her.

'Yeah,' Barbara said.

'Someone was looking for something.'

'Maybe.'

Barbara wasn't so sure. Why tip the lamps and smash the coffee table? In Barbara's experience, when people searched for something, they didn't slash the sofa cushions and yank out drawers. That was just for the movies. Normally they were more methodical – and who the hell hid anything in sofa cushions? Searches tended to involve phones and computers. This looked more like someone wanted them to *think* the room had been trashed in a search.

'I'll check upstairs,' Tucker said.

'Okay.' And although Barbara didn't think the house was occupied, she added, 'Be careful.'

There was a small kitchen in an alcove off the living room. It was hard to tell if this had been disturbed as the space was already strewn with half-opened packets, mouldy cups, tins and dirty crockery. She looked around, wondering if she was brave enough to actually touch anything, just as Tucker emerged back downstairs.

'Find anything?' she asked.

'Nothing seems to be disturbed up there. Our friend, Mowlam, doesn't carry much baggage. Few sweatshirts and jeans in the wardrobe, toiletries in the bathroom. Found these in the bathroom cabinet.'

He held up two large baggies – one full of green weed, the other white powder.

'I'm guessing that isn't smelling salts and seaweed,' she said.

'Nope. Plus, there were some Oxycontin in there too. Maybe he has a bad back or . . .'

Or Mowlam is fond of his pharmaceuticals. Something else that linked him to the Doc.

'Okay,' she said, stepping over some broken glass. 'One room left down here. Let's see what else we've got.'

They crossed the hall. The bad feeling ratcheted up. Barbara placed a hand on the door handle and pushed it open. She flicked on the light.

'Shit!'

Bad. Bad. Bad. She took in the scene. The room was set up as some kind of studio. Inks and a tattooing gun sat on a table. Flash art adorned the walls: anti-vampyr, white-supremacist, Helsing symbols. These were mixed with brutal photographs of dead vampyrs, beheaded, eviscerated. Sturdy storage cases were stacked along one wall. A cabinet held a gruesome display of vampyr artefacts. A woman's hand, a heart preserved in a jar, a skull crafted out of vampyr teeth and another skull, which appeared to be prepubescent.

In the centre of the room was a large chair, similar to the type you sat in at the dentist's.

Kurt Mowlam reclined in the chair.

He'd been shot in the head and a stake had been driven through his heart.

'Taking a wild guess, I'd say we've found the Doc's accomplice,' Barbara said.

'Yeah,' Tucker replied. 'Shame someone else found him first.'

Barbara wondered how this had gone down. Although the living room was trashed, it didn't look like the scene of a struggle. The destruction had come later, after Mowlam was dead. It looked likely Mowlam had known his killer and let them in. They had walked into his studio and the killer had pulled a gun. Why? To shut him up. To send a message? The shot to the head would suggest the former – an execution. The stake through the heart suggested the latter. Hoisted by his own petard, she thought.

Tucker walked over to a small computer desk in one corner of the room.

'What you got?' Barbara asked.

He held up two phones. The screensaver on one looked like the cover of some kind of heavy-metal band. Mowlam's, she guessed. The other showed a beautiful portrait picture of the Doc's house and icy lake.

'Dalton's phone,' Barbara said.

'So, Mowlam was in the Doc's house that night.'

'*Or* his killer was –'

'Well, at least we know where Marcus got his tattoo.'

Barbara remembered Mowlam talking about the book club. A way to befriend the kids and influence young minds. Did Marcus stay behind some nights, talking a little longer? Was that how Mowlam had twisted his mind, maybe the other boys' too?

'I think Stephen knew about this,' she said.

'And Jacob?'

'Possibly. Probably.'

Tucker sighed. 'Okay.'

Barbara looked around the room again. The vampyr artefacts. The body left out on display. The Doc's phone in plain sight.

'Anything about this strike you as a bit too . . . convenient?'

'How d'you mean?'

'It's like someone *wanted* us to find all this,' she said. 'We got our accomplice and mystery tattooist. I'm willing to bet somewhere around here there's a key to the Grill.'

Tucker turned and picked up a key from the table. 'Like this one?'

She sighed heavily. 'We got the person who locked me in the freezer. It's all been laid out for us. Everything neatly tied up.'

'Yeah.' Tucker looked around. 'We've still got one big loose end, though.'

'What?'

He nodded to the body splayed on the tattooist's chair, brain matter and blood pooled thickly on the floor beneath.

'We haven't got a damn clue who killed Mowlam.'

51

They processed the scene as best they could. Numbering and photographing everything, bagging up evidence, dusting for possible prints and collating DNA. Not that Barbara had anywhere to send it while the weather kept transport grounded.

That just left Mowlam's body.

'He can't stay here,' Barbara said.

'So, where do we put him?'

They stared at the corpse. Barbara wished she could find some sympathy, some sorrow. But looking around this studio, at all the artefacts of hate, it was difficult. Sometimes, you really did reap what you sowed.

She sighed. 'He'll have to come back to the Grill.'

They used garbage bags to wrap Mowlam up. There wasn't much they could do about the stake sticking out of his chest, like he was some kind of human popsicle.

Tucker pulled the truck around the back of the house. They loaded the body into it and drove to the Grill. Darkness had descended and the street was deserted, but Barbara didn't want to take any chances. They drove down the side of the Grill and manhandled the corpse in through the fire escape. Once inside, Barbara opened the walk-in freezer, and they laid Mowlam on the floor beside the table where Marcus lay.

Barbara shook her head. 'Rate we're going, this place

will have more bodies than Anchorage morgue.' She slammed the freezer door shut again and they walked into the bar.

'I'm going to make a coffee.' She glanced at Tucker. 'Want one?'

'No, thanks.'

'Tea? Water? Bourbon?'

'I'm good.'

Barbara turned to the coffee machine, something niggling at the back of her mind.

'So, where do we go from here?' Tucker asked.

'Door to door. Mowlam's killer is still out there,' she said.

'Mowlam's murder looked like a message. The stake. Punished for his crimes.'

'Maybe.' She grabbed a mug and turned the machine on. 'Or maybe that was what it was *supposed* to look like. I still think this is connected to Marcus's murder.' She brought the coffee over to the bar and put it down heavily. 'When Todd Danes was killed, was there anyone else you considered as a suspect? Anyone at all?'

Tucker frowned. 'Not really. All the evidence pointed to Todd being killed by Aaron.' He looked down. 'But maybe I got that wrong.'

'You followed the evidence. And Aaron confessed.'

'Because I cut him a deal to save the Colony. Instead, I got three of them killed and let the real killer go free.'

Barbara studied him. 'What really happened that night?'

'I've told you.'

'With all due respect, you've told me less than a gnat's fart in a teaspoon. Seems to me you did nothing wrong, yet you've been living like a hermit for twenty-five years. Why?'

'I let the town down. I let Todd's parents down. I couldn't be around them any more.'

'So why not leave, move someplace else?'

He remained silent.

'What's kept you here, Tucker?'

'The weather?'

'Well, it sure isn't the food. I've not seen you eat a thing in forty-eight hours. Nor taken a drink of anything, not even water.'

He swallowed. 'I don't get very thirsty.'

'Right. So why do you carry a flask around with you?'

His jaw tensed. 'It's not alcohol, if that's what you're thinking.'

'That's not what I'm thinking. Not any more.' She picked up her coffee. 'You want to save us both time and tell me exactly when you got turned?'

52

25 years ago

Tucker glanced at the clock. It was an hour off. Had been since spring. He kept meaning to change it, but the truth was, he'd got used to the difference. In a couple of weeks, the clock would be right again. Most things caught up with you eventually.

The minute hand ticked over. Eleven minutes past nine. But really, past ten. Time was dragging this evening. His insides felt coiled up tight and his heart jittered. He was on his fourth cup of coffee and on edge.

Rita, the young woman who helped out in the office a few days a week, had left about an hour ago.

'You're sure you're okay here on your own?' she had asked, looking worried.

'I'll be fine,' he'd said. 'Just got to get through tonight and the Feds will be here in the morning to take Aaron away.'

'I guess, but you're in for a long night.'

He had smiled. 'I got a gallon of your coffee to keep me company. I can handle it.'

In fact, it was his third night sleeping in the police department, guarding the Colony kid. Except tonight there would be no sleeping. He had other plans.

'They'll be coming for him at midnight.'

That's what Jess had told him when she turned up this morning, looking nervous and ill at ease.

'Who's they?' Tucker had asked, even though he knew.

'My dad and some of his cronies. They plan to break him out and make him pay. They're not messing around. They want that kid.'

He stared at her. Just twenty-two and beautiful with those cheekbones and that mane of gold curls.

'Why are you telling me this? I thought you hated the Colony too.'

'You know why.'

He had shaken his head. 'What do you expect me to do, Jess?'

'Get that kid out of here. Because they won't let anyone, not even you, stand in their way.'

And then she had pulled up her hood and left.

Tucker glanced at the clock. Thirteen minutes past nine (ten).

'They'll be coming at midnight.'

He stood and walked across to the cells. Aaron was curled up on a blanket on the bed.

'Hey.'

The kid looked up at him with vivid green eyes. He was a pretty kid, with a shock of thick dark hair and delicate features. 'Elfin' was the word that came to mind.

'Are you ready?' Tucker asked.

The kid swallowed. 'Are you sure?'

Tucker nodded. His original plan had been to get the kid out of there before Beau and his cronies arrived. Drive to Talkeetna. Get an air taxi over to Anchorage. Then deposit him with the Feds.

344

'And then what?'

The question had come to him in his wife Laura's voice.

'What will happen to him then, Tucker? You really think they'll let him live?'

There would be a trial, of sorts, behind closed doors, with expert judges and doctors. A lot would depend on the judge. Some were more sympathetic to colony members than others. But there was more pressure these days to be tough. Most cases involving vampyrs never even made it to trial. The chances that a judge would rule in favour of incarceration for a vampyr guilty of killing a human, regardless of whether it was accidental or not, were slim. In fact, he couldn't think of a single occasion when it had happened, even with a minor. Despite his assurances (lies) to Aaron, he knew in his gut that the verdict would most likely be a humane kill.

'So, the kid dies either way.'

The only difference was that Beau and his cronies wouldn't stop with Aaron. They'd want to take the whole colony.

'Did you contact them?' he asked Aaron.

He frowned. 'I think so. I tried.' He motioned towards his head. 'It's easier when I'm closer.'

'But they understood? You all need to run. Tonight.'

Aaron nodded. 'They understood.'

'Okay.' Tucker walked back into the office and looked at the clock.

9.23 p.m. (10.23 p.m.). It would take about an hour and a half to hike up to the Colony settlement. Once Beau and his friends arrived here and realized what had happened, they would be on their tail fast. It didn't leave much time.

He thought about Laura. How he had wished he could kill the kid who took her life. But he knew what she would say:

'What good would it do? It won't bring me back. How does more death help?'

Tucker picked up his gun and stuck it in his holster. Then he grabbed his thick, black duffel and a spare one for Aaron. The boy looked up at him.

Tucker took his key and opened the door to the cell.

'Let's go.'

They left on foot and cut around the back of Main Street. Not many people were out and about. The wind was bitter and snow was flurrying down. The weather was good camouflage. No one saw faces in the cold. Just hunchbacks with their hoods up.

Town soon fell behind them. They kept to the side of the road. The tall spruce of the forest and the peaks of the Denali Mountains loomed on their left. Further on, Tucker knew there was a rough path that ran through the forest and then joined the old rail tracks up to the Colony settlement.

Aaron suddenly grabbed his arm. Tucker turned.

'What?'

The boy's eyes were wide. 'Something's coming.'

And now Tucker heard it: the low whine of engines. He looked up. Headlights rounded the corner and blinded him. He raised a hand. Beside him, he felt the boy wince. Two trucks crawled down the road towards them and pulled up, side by side, blocking their way. Shit. The lights flared and then dimmed. Four figures climbed out.

Josh Barnes, Cooper Flint, Tom Jenner . . . and Beau Grainger.

Tucker felt the betrayal like a sucker punch. Jess had set him up.

He stared at the men. Their faces were grim, and they all carried weapons: shotguns, crossbows and UV guns. Josh Barnes held a large axe.

Tucker focused on Beau. He tried to keep his voice calm. 'What are you doing here?'

'Maybe you should tell us what you're doing,' Beau said. 'Because it looks like you're trying to abscond with a killer.'

Tucker pushed Aaron slightly behind him. 'I got a warning some folks might attack the police department. It's my duty to protect the suspect.'

'I thought your duty was to protect the people of Deadhart?'

'The two aren't mutually exclusive.'

'Yeah they are,' Josh growled.

'I'm just taking him somewhere safe.'

'You're not taking him anywhere,' Beau said, raising his crossbow. 'Drop your weapon, Tucker.'

'I'm the chief of this town.'

'No. Right now you're a criminal, aiding and abetting a murderer. Drop your gun. Slowly.'

Tucker felt the anger burn, but he was outnumbered and out-armed. Slowly, he took out his weapon and threw it to the ground. Josh picked it up. He handed it to Beau.

Tucker shook his head. 'I'm not going to let you hurt him.'

Cooper raised his shotgun. 'You ain't got any choice.'

The shadow moved fast, from out of the trees. It launched itself at Cooper, taking him down hard. Cooper screamed.

Beau raised his crossbow but, in the dark, limbs flailing, it was impossible to get a clean shot. Just as fast, another shadow sped from the forest towards Tom Jenner. He raised the UV gun and let off a flare of light. The figure screamed and crumpled to the ground.

'Dad!' Aaron cried, darting forward.

Tucker grabbed his arm. 'NO. Run, Aaron! Get out of here. NOW.'

The boy hesitated for a second and then took off between the trees.

Tom started after him. Tucker grabbed a fallen branch and swung it at the man, knocking him to the ground. Before Tucker could swing again, Josh grabbed him from behind, ramming the handle of the wooden axe across his throat, choking him.

'You fucking Judas,' he hissed in Tucker's ear, spittle smelling of liquor.

Tucker grabbed at the axe, but Josh was strong. They staggered back and forth. Tucker felt his breath constricting. With one final effort he bucked forward and threw Josh over his head, releasing the chokehold. Josh landed heavily. Tucker grabbed the axe and smashed the handle into his skull, knocking him out.

He turned just in time to see Beau raise his crossbow and fire an arrow into the back of the figure on top of Cooper. The vampyr, older and grey-haired, collapsed to the side. Cooper sat up groggily. At the edge of the road, Aaron's father still writhed in the snow. Tucker knew he was probably beyond help – the UV gun had burned away most of his face – but he started to move towards him.

And then a voice said: 'Stay where you are, Tucker. And don't make me ask you twice.'

Tucker looked round, the axe still in his hand. Beau stood in the middle of the road, crossbow slung over his back, pointing Tucker's own gun at him.

Tucker shook his head. 'You've killed one of them. Isn't that enough?'

Beau stared at him. 'That creature murdered a kid, Tucker. One of our own.'

'He's just a kid, too.'

'No. He's one of *them*. Devils. And they need to be sent back to hell.'

Cooper struggled to his feet. He picked up his shotgun.

'I'm not letting you go after Aaron,' Tucker said, holding up the axe.

'You ain't got no choice,' Cooper growled.

'Don't get in the way, Tucker,' Beau pleaded, voice softening. 'Let us finish this.'

Cooper raised the shotgun. 'It's them or us. You need to choose a side.'

'Then I choose the side of the law.'

Tucker flung the axe at Cooper. Cooper ducked. Beau fired. Once, twice. The axe landed harmlessly in the snow. Heat exploded in Tucker's chest. The force knocked him backwards, and he hit the ground like a sack of cement. He lay there, chest burning, breath wheezing. *Fuck. So, this was what it felt like to be shot.*

A shadow fell over him. Beau's voice croaked: 'I'm sorry. I really am.'

Boots walked past. Tucker heard the sound of the axe whooshing through the air. A cry, a thud, and silence.

349

He blacked out. When he opened his eyes again, he was alone. And cold. He couldn't move. It occurred to him that the bullet may have severed his spinal cord. Not that it mattered. He wasn't getting up from this. Blood would be flooding his internal organs. He could already feel it in his throat, making every breath a labour. His hearing was muffled, and it seemed like he was staring down a tunnel. He was fading. Body shutting down.

A face drew into his blurred vision. A girl. Blonde hair. Familiar. In his semi-conscious state, mind deteriorating, for one delirious moment he thought she might be an angel. And then she spoke:

'You stupid fucker.'

Athelinda.

'I tried,' he wanted to say. 'I tried to save him.' The words wouldn't come. But in his head, he heard her voice:

'You screwed up.'

'I'm sorry.'

'You should be.'

She was so close. He could smell her. Bitter and dark. Like the grave.

'Are you here to watch me die?'

'No.'

She bent over him and, just before her mouth closed over his neck, he heard her whisper.

'You're already dead.'

53

Barbara took a sip of her coffee. It had cooled and tasted bitter.

'You're not fully turned?'

He shook his head. 'I was infected by Athelinda's bite. But I never drank her blood.'

'You're a halfling.'

The half-turned would crave blood and live a little longer than a normal human, but not to the extent of a full vampyr. They existed between worlds.

'What do you feed on?' Barbara asked.

'I keep some pigs and goats.'

'Does anyone else know?'

'No.'

'What about Beau? He shot you. He must have thought you were dead.'

'He might suspect, but he can't say anything. Not without admitting what he did.'

'He shot a cop,' Barbara said flatly. 'He should be in jail.'

'And I tried to break out a murder suspect. By rights, so should I.'

She nodded. 'Okay. Anything else I should know?'

'You mean, do I ever feel like ripping out someone's throat and drinking their blood?'

'I was thinking more like are you coping okay in the day-light? Is it affecting your concentration or energy? But the other stuff is great to know, too.'

He looked sheepish. 'I'm good, thanks.'

'Look,' Barbara said. 'As long as it doesn't affect your job, I don't care. But other people will.'

'Yeah, I know. It's illegal for vampyrs, even halflings, to work.'

Barbara caught the bitterness in his voice. 'I don't make the rules,' she said.

'Do you ever question them?'

'I used to. When I was younger.'

'What changed?'

She hesitated. She had never spoken to anyone about Mercy. But she guessed she owed Tucker some honesty back.

'When I was fifteen, I had a friend. She was Colony.'

'What happened to her?'

'She was murdered. By my dad and his friends.' Barbara swallowed. 'They found out we were meeting up and drowned her in the river. They made me watch.'

The door to the lodge swinging open, the morning sunlight almost blinding her. Her dad standing there, grinning. 'Change of plan, Babs. I want you to see this. All of it.'

'I didn't think vampyrs could be killed by drowning,' Tucker said.

'They can't. When the sixth or seventh time didn't kill her, they burned her alive.'

'Jesus,' Tucker murmured. 'That's horrific.'

Beautiful hair gone. Features nothing more than a formless mass of melted flesh. Trying to stand, brittle, blackened bones snapping beneath her as she staggered forwards and finally fell.

'Yeah,' Barbara said. 'After that, I guess I learned to stick to the rules. It was safer.'

'It wasn't your fault.'

She sighed. 'I knew what my dad was like, Tucker. I should have told Mercy to stay away, that being friends was just too dangerous. And I didn't.'

Because love was selfish. She'd loved Mercy, and that had gotten her killed.

'You had to live with your dad afterwards?' Tucker asked.

'Not for long. He shot himself the following summer.'

Tucker shook his head. 'Seems to me that devils really do walk among us . . . only they're not vampyr.'

Barbara swigged the dregs of the coffee, wishing it was something stronger. 'Well, at least those devils don't come back from a shotgun in the mouth.' She shoved the coffee cup away. 'Okay, if we're done with the soul-baring, shall we get back on track?'

'O-kay.'

'Who would want Mowlam dead?'

'Someone else involved in the artefact trade?'

'The only other people we know were involved with the Doc are the boys.'

'Marcus is dead.'

'Which leaves Stephen and Jacob,' she mused. 'And only one of them was there the night Doc Dalton was killed.'

'You think Jacob's a killer?'

'No . . . I don't know . . .' She raised her hands and let them drop helplessly. 'I think we're missing something,' she said. 'And I think it's time to talk to the Colony.'

'You mean Athelinda?'

'Seems she's more likely to talk to you than me.'

Tucker shifted uncomfortably. 'Just because I'm half-turned, doesn't mean I'm one of them.'

'Can you hear them? The telepathy?'

'No. They don't let you hear if they don't want you to.'

'Still, you know Athelinda better than anyone else here.'

'She hasn't got more time for me than any other human.'

'She saved you.'

'Athelinda didn't save me. She wanted to punish me.'

Barbara opened her mouth to reply as her phone pinged with a message. She picked it up and glanced at it.

'It's the prints I took off the glass at Nathan Bell's house,' she said.

Tucker leaned forward. 'He's in the system?'

She clicked on the attached file. 'Looks that way.'

The photograph was fairly recent. Unmistakably Nathan Bell. The same sallow face and sullen look. Tousled dark hair, longer in this picture.

Arrested for assault and disorderly conduct. And not the first arrest. There was a long list of previous convictions – theft, fraud, burglary.

That didn't surprise her.

What did surprise her was the name underneath the mugshot.

Mitch Roberts.

She stared at Tucker: 'He's not Nathan Bell.'

Her Rescuer was thin and gangly. Long, dark hair tied back. His teeth were yellowed with sharp incisors, one slightly cracked.

He was dressed in patched jeans and a dirty T-shirt, and he looked nothing like the girl had hoped for. Rescuers in books were always gallant and handsome. Not like this.

'What are you staring at?' he asked. 'C'mon. We haven't much time.'

He held out a key. She inserted it into the lock around her leg, releasing the manacle.

'Thank you,' she said.

He looked at her, frowning. 'You got any other clothes?'

She glanced down at her thin sundress. 'Well, I guess I have some other dresses.'

'They all like this?'

'Mostly.'

'Okay. We'll grab something from upstairs.'

Her Captor's clothes? But her Captor was an old lady. Before she could question him, he had grabbed her hand. His palm felt rough and calloused. 'C'mon. I knocked her out. But we need to drag her down here before she wakes up.'

'She's alive?'

'Yeah.' He pushed her towards the stairs. 'We don't want the police turning up and finding a dead body. We lock her down here. Hopefully, it's a while before she's found. We'll be long gone.'

They climbed the stairs and emerged into a small hallway. The girl

355

paused, suddenly feeling dizzy. The first time she had been upstairs, out of her basement room for . . . how long? The air tasted different. The light was so bright it made her squint.

'I'm gonna run up and get you something to wear.'

Her Rescuer disappeared up another staircase.

The girl took a few deep breaths and looked around. To her right she could see a kitchen. She walked forward and entered. Neat and tidy. Shiny chrome appliances, a small table with a chequered table-cloth. Everything in its place. The smell of baking in the air. She walked slowly through to the adjoining living room.

Her Captor lay on the floor, blood trickling from a head wound. A hammer lay nearby. The living room was bright and homely. Saggy floral sofas, an overflowing bookcase. A huge white cross hung above the fireplace and music played faintly on an old radio. A song she vaguely recognized. Something about a Mr Blue Sky.

'Here you go.'

She turned. Her Rescuer had returned. He handed her a pair of jeans and a jumper. They looked big and matronly. Of course. They were her Captor's clothes.

'These are grown-up's clothes,' she said. 'I can't wear these.'

He frowned again. And then something seemed to click. 'You have any mirrors down there?'

'No. Why would I?'

'You've been here a long time.'

'I know, but I'm not like her. You said I'm like you.'

'You're a vampyr. Time slows for us, but it doesn't stand still completely.'

He took her arm and led her back into the hall. A mirror hung on the wall beside the door. He nodded towards it.

'Go on. Don't believe the old wives' tales about having no reflection.'

The girl stared at herself in the mirror. A stranger looked back. Not a girl. A grown woman. Slender but tall. Ridiculous in the flimsy dress which barely reached halfway down her thighs. And her hair. She had always thought it was lightest blonde. But now she could see it wasn't blonde. It was white.

'Are you okay?' her Rescuer asked. 'I thought you knew.'

She reached out a hand and touched the woman — the old woman — in the cool glass. Then she turned and strode back into the living room.

She heard her Rescuer shout, 'NO.'

But it was too late. She picked up the hammer and smashed it into her Captor's head, again and again, until her skull was nothing but a mush of grey and white matter oozing into the floorboards.

The girl paused, breathless but filled with a sudden sense of invigoration.

'What the hell?' Her Rescuer strode over and glared down at the mess on the floor. 'You stupid bitch.'

He swung his arm and slapped her across her face. The girl reeled backwards, gasping in shock. Even her Captor had never struck her.

'You realize how much shit you've got us in. Fuck!' Her Rescuer glared at her. 'I only saved your ass cos we're short on female company. You'd better pay me back good for this.'

The girl stared at him, wide-eyed. 'I will. I promise.'

'Damn right you will.' He grabbed her hair. 'Me and my friends, we been apart from our colony a long time. We're hungry — and I mean real hungry.' He smiled, all ugly teeth and bad breath. 'We're gonna pump you so full of cum it'll ooze out your goddamn eyeballs.'

And the girl realized her mistake. This wasn't her Rescuer. This was just another Captor.

She raised the hammer and swung it into the side of his skull. He stumbled backwards. She swung the hammer a second time and a third, a fourth, savouring the ache in her arms, the soft squelch of his

357

disintegrating brain. Once her (former) Rescuer's head was simply a nasty, lumpy stain, she took a hefty kitchen knife, dug out his heart and stabbed it into tiny pieces; raw, wet morsels.

She wiped a bloodied hand across her mouth, relishing the irony tang, and smiled.

'Now, I'm okay.'

54

Barbara pulled up outside the Bell house, which looked gloomier and more dilapidated than ever.

'The pick-up's gone,' Tucker said.

Barbara cursed. 'Let's go check inside.'

They traipsed through the snow towards the falling-down porch. Barbara pulled out her gun. As an extra precaution, she had her UV gun tucked into a second holster. They still didn't know who, or what, they were dealing with here. They climbed the steps to the front door. Barbara could see it was ajar. She shoved it open.

'Police!'

Silence. The house was dark, cold, and Barbara could smell something. A familiar irony tang.

'Check the dining room and kitchen,' Barbara instructed Tucker. He nodded wordlessly and disappeared down the hall.

Barbara walked slowly forward and pushed open the door to the living room.

'Shit.'

Blood. Everywhere. The walls and furniture were spattered with red. Thick rivulets ran down the TV screen and a large stain had turned the faded rug in the middle of the floor black. Blood-soaked towels had been dumped on the sofa, as if someone had made a futile attempt to clean up.

Tucker walked back into the room and stared around. 'Damn. That's a lot of blood.'

'Let's check upstairs,' Barbara said tightly, trying to swallow down the bitter taste in her throat.

A quick check of Nathan's closet showed a clean sweep of empty hangers. Jacob's room was oddly bare for a teenage boy. No posters of rock bands on the walls. No PC or laptop. But his wardrobe was still full of clothes. Dread dug its claws into Barbara's gut.

'What are you thinking?' Tucker asked.

'Nothing good,' she said.

'Maybe Jacob was injured, and Nathan went to get help.'

'After packing up all his clothes?'

But then, if Nathan had killed Jacob, why not leave the body and flee?

'There's only one road out of Deadhart,' Tucker said. 'That's the AK-3 to Talkeetna.'

'And from there?'

'If Nathan makes it to Talkeetna, which is unlikely in this weather, it's still a long way to Anchorage, and that's if the road is passable.'

'But if he *does* make it, he could disappear pretty quickly.'

Barbara looked around. *Dammit*. She had known something was wrong here. She should have followed her gut.

'He can't be that far ahead of us,' she said. 'That blood looked fresh.'

'What d'you want to do?'

Barbara debated with herself. They should call the state police. Get them to be on the look-out. It was probably

360

foolish trying to catch up with Nathan in this weather. However, there might still be time to save Jacob.

'We go after them,' she said.

After easing a little, the snow was coming down heavier again and the wind had picked up. Barbara could hear the yowl over the engine and feel it rocking the vehicle as they pulled out on to the highway. She leaned forward, nose almost pressed to the glass. The windscreen wipers whirred noisily back and forth.

She had notified the state police before they left the Bell house. An APB was out so all the patrols in the area would be on alert for Nathan and Jacob.

Tucker was on the phone to Rita. 'That's right,' she heard him say. 'Yes, Jacob is missing too. We're heading out on the AK-3, but we need you to be on the look-out in case he's come back into town.' A pause. 'Okay, put the word out. But not too many words. A need-to-know basis.' He nodded. 'Yeah, I do know what you're like.'

He ended the call and turned to Barbara. 'Done.' He paused. 'Do you think Nathan is our killer?'

Barbara squinted into the white. 'I have no idea . . . about anything any more. Is Nathan Bell even Nathan Bell?'

'You think he's this Mitch Roberts?'

'If so, why pose as Nathan Bell? What does he get out of it?'

'A house,' Tucker said. 'And all the stuff inside. It looked like they were packing stuff up to sell, right?'

She thought about this. 'So, Roberts killed Nathan and took his identity . . . for that old wreck of a house and some family silver?'

Tucker shrugged. 'I've seen people killed for less.'

'And how does Jacob fit in?'

'Maybe he's just dragged along for the ride.'

Can't choose your parents, Barbara thought again.

'Let's just hope we can find him in time,' she said.

'Yeah.'

Tucker didn't ask 'in time' for what. They both knew. *The blood, all that blood.*

The truck crawled onwards. Barbara wanted to ram her foot down on the accelerator, but she didn't dare. The tyres' grip felt precarious, and the snow was settling on the windscreen faster than the wipers could shove it off. The truck's headlights barely cut through the misty sheet of white in front.

Tucker suddenly leaned forward and pointed. 'Up ahead. Look.'

Barbara squinted. His eyesight was better than hers, but now she could just make out a red shape ahead, off the road to their right. A truck, its back end in the air, bonnet smashed into a tree trunk.

'Dammit.'

She pulled the police truck over, stopped and stuck the hazards on. They climbed out and approached the truck. The brake lights glowed faintly. The back looked relatively unscathed. It was only when they reached the front of the vehicle that they could see the damage.

The impact had caused the entire hood to concertina, like a crumpled tin can. The windscreen was smashed out, blood smeared all over the jagged glass. Barbara peered inside. A mangled mess. The dash and steering wheel were rammed so hard into the seats that it was hard to see where

362

one ended and the other began. More slick trails of dark red were smeared over what was left of the interior. But the cab was empty.

Barbara turned. 'Let's look around.'

They trudged through the snow. A short distance away, Barbara spotted something black half buried in the white. She walked up to it. A backpack. Must have got thrown out of the cab. She unbuckled it clumsily with her gloved hands. Stuffed inside was a bundle of men's clothes. Nathan's, she thought. So, he'd been in the truck. Where was he now?

It was several metres before they saw the body. That happened sometimes in a crash. No seatbelt. High impact. A body could fly a long way. Sometimes not all of it at the same time. The figure lay face down in the snow, limbs flung out in a star shape. But the angles were all wrong. The arms crooked, palms facing up, knees twisted the wrong way. Blood formed a halo around the head.

Barbara waded through the drifts towards the body, Tucker close behind. She knelt down. You weren't supposed to move crash victims in case you caused more injuries, but Barbara could tell it was already too late here. She turned the body over.

Jacob. His head flopped sickeningly on his neck, which had been ripped open in a wide scarlet grin. His clothes were lacerated with broken glass, blood seeping from multiple wounds. His eyes stared blankly upwards, snowflakes landing and melting on the delicate corneas.

'Damn!' Barbara cursed. Then she turned away and screamed into the storm. 'Fuck and shit and screw your Gods to hell and back!'

She took a few deep breaths, the biting air scouring her throat.

'Feel better?' Tucker asked.

'No.'

'You couldn't have done anything. It was an accident.'

She turned on him. 'We were *there*. We were there in that damn house, and we knew something was wrong. We could have saved him.'

'You can't save them all,' he said thickly.

But that was a cop-out, Barbara thought. Just like her mom blinding herself to her dad's abuse with food and soaps. Just like the townsfolk who confided in her after his death that they had always worried for her, what with his drinking and temper, but they *didn't like to interfere*. Barbara had recognized the warning signs with Nathan and Jacob, and she had still walked away.

'*Shit*,' she cursed again, more wearily. Then she looked around. 'Where the hell is Nathan's body?'

'Maybe he was thrown further?'

She stood and they walked into the forest, torches scanning the snow. But there was no sign of another body.

Barbara glanced back towards the truck. 'He can't have been thrown further than this.'

'You think he got out?'

Barbara thought about the concertinaed cab. 'Not without severe injuries ... but I haven't seen any tracks or blood.'

'If he's out there, he won't last long,' Tucker said. 'Especially if he's injured. Either a bear or a wolf will get him, if he doesn't freeze to death first.'

He was probably right, Barbara thought. But what if

Nathan *had* somehow escaped the crash? What if he'd jumped clear before the truck hit the tree? The forest was deep and dense. He could already have a decent head start. And they had no idea which direction he would head in.

'We can't just let him get away,' she said, feeling frustration gnaw at her.

'We're not. But it would be crazy to try and search for him in this weather. He's already the walking dead.'

'Fine,' she said reluctantly. 'We'll head back into town with Jacob's body. I'll update the state police. As soon as the weather improves, I want a search party out there. We get him, dead or alive.'

They wrapped Jacob's body in an emergency foil blanket from the back of the truck and laid him gently inside. He seemed light, insubstantial. Barbara fought back the burning behind her eyes and climbed into the driver's seat.

She put the truck into gear and pulled off. They drove in silence, the only sound the heavy whirr of the wipers and the howl of the wind outside. Barbara clung to the steering wheel. Blood stained her gloves. She realized something was still bothering her.

'The blood in the house? Do we still think it's Jacob's?'

Tucker took a moment to reply. 'If he was injured or dead before the crash, I guess so.'

'So, either Nathan was driving to get help or to dispose of the body?'

'Looks that way.'

The twinkling lights of Deadhart came into view as they breasted the hill.

'Yeah, I suppose it does,' Barbara said. But it was there again. That niggle.

365

They drove back down Main Street. No lights glowed in the windows, only the omnipresent Christmas decorations, but Barbara couldn't be sure no one was watching. Once again, they pulled around the side of the Grill, and Tucker carried Jacob's body into the kitchen. Barbara flicked on the lights.

'Lay him down on the floor,' she said. 'I want to take another look at his injuries.'

Tucker did as she instructed. Barbara bent down and peeled back the foil blanket. She forced herself to look at Jacob's body again. In the harsh fluorescent light, the wounds looked even more brutal. She inspected his throat. Glass fragments from the shattered windscreen were embedded in the torn flesh. Larger slivers protruded from his body. Several limbs were broken. All typical with a car crash. Barbara couldn't see any injuries that looked deliberate. Certainly, none that would have generated the amount of blood they had observed in the house. The spatter on the walls and television – that spoke of a frenzied attack, multiple wounds, perhaps a severed artery. She wasn't seeing any of that on Jacob's body.

So, whose was the blood in the house? Nathan's? Was he the one who was injured? Had Jacob attacked him for some reason? But why? The sense of *wrongness* itched at the back of her skull.

'What are you thinking?' Tucker asked.

'I'm thinking that we have one crash victim, one missing person and a crime scene covered in a large amount of blood that doesn't appear to belong to either of them.'

There was something they weren't seeing. Again. A crucial piece of the puzzle. They both looked down at

Jacob. Barbara's heart clenched. He looked so young, so vulnerable.

'Okay,' she said wearily. 'Let's put him in the freezer with the others.'

And if that wasn't a depressing sentence, she didn't know what was. They carried Jacob's small body into the walk-in freezer and laid him down next to Mowlam. Marcus's body still lay on the steel table. Barbara felt anger and sorrow swell in her throat.

'You okay?' Tucker asked.

'Oh, yeah. Dandy. I got two dead kids lying in a damn walk-in refrigerator, not even the dignity of a burial. I got the town breathing down my neck for a cull. I've still got no idea who our killer is. Things could not be going more swimmingly.'

She slammed the freezer door shut.

'You're right.' Tucker pulled up his hood and walked towards the door.

Barbara stared after him. 'Where are you going?'

'To speak to Athelinda.'

'*Now?*'

'You said yourself, it's got to be done eventually. And she knows *something*.'

'Fine. Then I'm coming with you.'

'No humans are allowed in the settlement. I go alone.'

'You go alone. Really? I know it's been twenty-five years, but that macho crap was old back then.'

He sighed. 'It's not like that. You'd slow me down.'

'Because I'm a *woman*?'

'No, because you're overweight and unfit.' Before she could retort, he continued: 'Look, I'm the only one who knows the way to the settlement. And shouldn't one of us stay here, to keep an eye on the bodies?'

Barbara bristled. She was angry, but sometimes, you had to batten down your pride. He was right. It would make more sense for Tucker to go alone. And yes, someone should stay here. And yes, she should cut back on the carbs.

'Okay,' she said grudgingly. 'Keep your phone on. I want to be able to contact you.'

He nodded.

'And Tucker?'

'Yeah.'

'Try not to get yourself killed . . . again.'

55

Beau sat in his favourite armchair, the one Patricia had always nagged him to replace.

'We could get you a brand-new leather recliner,' she would say.

'I'm good as I am,' he would reply.

'It's old, worn and ugly,' she would say.

'So am I,' he would reply, and she would laugh. Every time.

And he *had* been good. For a long while. Coasting along like an old ship on familiar waters. But even familiar waters have darker depths. Bad things lurking below the surface, just waiting for a chance to drag you down.

Beau had always believed that what they did with the vampyr boy and his kin was right. It was justice. It was the order of things. Beau believed in the order of things. Good and bad. Right and wrong. Saints and sinners. Of course, most men were a combination of both, but God was a forgiving God.

Beau had grown up hunting vampyrs. Most men around these parts had. Vampyrs were the devil made flesh. Undead, soulless. Humans had a right to kill them. A duty, even. *Satan shall not walk this earth.* You owed it to God to call out evil, to chase it down, banish it. That was what his father and grandfather had taught him.

But his grandfather had also fraternized with vampyrs. Beau learned that as he grew older. He also learned that his grandfather was a cruel man when he wanted to be. Not to Beau. But he had seen the scars his grandmother bore on her face and arms.

'Clumsy on the stairs. Splashed cooking oil on my face. Burned myself on the oven.'

He once heard her say to his mother: *'It was better when he had the Bone House.'*

And his mother had replied: *'Better if he'd died in there.'*

Of course, Beau didn't know what they meant at the time. Later, he understood. And maybe that was the curse of growing up, the passing of youth and innocence. Understanding that the adults we once looked up to are flawed and imperfect and, sometimes, just plain rotten.

His father had followed in the family tradition. Beau had felt the lash of his heavy leather belt on more than a few occasions, some deserved, some not. And while beltings weren't uncommon for most kids growing up back then, Beau had never forgotten the look of pleasure in his father's eyes whenever an opportunity for a beating or punishment arose.

Beau liked to think he was a better man. But we all like to believe that we are different from our parents. The truth is that we can only fight our genes so much. Hadn't he, on occasion, been cruel to Patricia, even if he didn't raise his fists? Hadn't he enjoyed the thrill of hunting, of *killing*, a little too much?

Maybe that was the problem with old age. As your days grew shorter, your memory grew longer. It stretched away from you like a shadow in the dying sun, reaching further into the past.

'Or maybe you just see things more clearly, old man. Proximity to death makes honest men of us all.'

370

Beau reached for a tumbler of whiskey and took a sip. It dulled the whispers, but only a little. They rustled around inside his head, like dead leaves blowing in the breeze. He couldn't catch all that they said, just the odd phrase. Sometimes they talked to each other, sometimes directly to him. They taunted, chided, cajoled, bullied. They were growing, and eventually he knew they would drown out his own thoughts.

He looked at the heads above the fireplace. Their eyes swivelled to stare back at him. Bright and accusing.

'You did this to us, old man. How can you say you're not like your father?'

'Shut up,' he murmured, but his voice was weak.

He reached for the whiskey again, but his hand twitched and swiped the glass from the table, sending it crashing to the floor.

'Dammit!'

He stood wearily, bones creaking, to get a brush to sweep up the glass. A knock at the front door caused him to pause. He hesitated. The knock came again. He walked to the door and pulled it open a crack.

A trio of men stood outside. He'd known them all since they were kids. Jared, Hal, Frank. He pulled the door open wider. An icy blast of wind blew in.

'What are you doing here?' he asked.

'We're done waiting, Beau,' Jared said. 'We plan to attack, in the morning, first dawn.' He glanced at the others. 'We thought you might want to be there. Finish what you started?'

'Are you ready to finish it, old man? You really think you can beat us?'

No, Beau thought. But he could die trying.

56

Within the folds of the forest, the wind abated. The spruce provided cover from the snow, which fell more gently between the branches.

Tucker could still feel the chill of the descending night biting at his bones. The cold out here was stealthy like that. Minus five doesn't feel so different to minus twenty-five. But cold is insidious. It creeps. Before you know it, you're finding it harder to think. Your movements are getting sluggish. Your breathing erratic.

Tucker was used to it, but he knew he needed to keep his wits about him. He kept his hood pulled well over his head, his gaze ahead, footsteps regular. He clasped a flashlight in his gloved hands, but he didn't really need it. His eyes were well adjusted to the dark and he knew this route from memory, or maybe instinct.

About an hour into his trek the land started to rise and the trees thinned. Tucker could feel his calves aching as the incline steepened and, despite the cold, sweat trickled down his back, his breath coming in rasps. Eventually, he crested the ridge and paused.

The forest fell away before him, and the land opened up. Between Tucker and the settlement, undulating mounds of gravel and rock sprawled out (waste from the mine's excavations), the bleak hillocks dotted with sparse vegetation. To his right, a splintered and derelict railroad bridge ran over the shallow river below; all that was left of the old Deadhart spur that used to connect the mine to the Alaskan railroad.

The mining village had been a huge settlement in its heyday. Now, the half-derelict buildings loomed up out of the mountainside like the jagged ruins of some ancient mythical castle. Many had succumbed to the elements and collapsed, sliding slowly down the incline. But the main processing plant was still intact, rising up like a watch-tower, and the lower part of the settlement, the residential buildings of the town, were in good repair.

The front gate was illuminated by two huge flaming torches. More torches were dotted around the settle-ment. Tucker couldn't see from here, but he was sure there would be guards at the gates. The settlement was secure. Approach over the rock and gravel dunes and you could be seen a mile away. Around the back, the forest was dense. Easy to get lost. The only way in was over the rickety old railroad bridge. *If* the Colony decided to let you cross.

Tucker started to make his way down, around the side of the waste mounds, keeping to the scrub and shelter of the trees. The ground was rough and uneven, and there was another near-vertical climb to reach the railroad tracks. He scrambled up to the top. The bridge lay a couple of hundred yards ahead. A Russian-roulette course of splintered rotten sleepers and a twenty-foot drop to the stony riverbed.

He took a step forward. A low snarl stopped him. He turned. To his left, twin pairs of amber eyes glowed in the gloom. Another growl to his right. Sleek grey snouts twitched in the undergrowth. Wolves. They slunk from the cover of the trees, teeth bared, haunches raised, forming a loose circle around him, blocking the bridge and any escape route back into the woods.

Tucker swallowed, not daring to move a muscle. He could see the wolves' hot breath misting in the air, feel the barely contained aggression. But they didn't advance any further. They were waiting, he thought. For a command.

He licked his lips. 'Okay,' he called out. 'You made your point. Call your pets off.'

A pause, one that felt very long, standing there in the wolves' sights. Then, a tall blond man in jeans, a furred jacket and leather boots stepped out of the trees and stood between the great beasts.

'They're not pets. They're *guards.*' Michael stared at Tucker: 'And what the fuck are you doing here?'

'I need to talk to Athelinda.'

'Why?'

'I need her help.'

'Hasn't she helped you enough?'

Tucker swallowed. 'Another kid is dead. I think Athelinda knows something.'

Michael's eyes narrowed. 'Right now, it would be easier to kill you. It's tempting.' He moved closer. 'Kill you, let the townsfolk come, see who comes out on top.'

'Is that why you attacked the church? To provoke them into a battle?'

Michael spat on the ground. 'Maybe it's what we need. Maybe we're tired of living in fear. Our existence a favour granted by humans.'

'Listen to me, Michael,' Tucker said, more urgently. 'Whoever is doing this doesn't care about the Colony. They *let* Aaron and his kin die. They would happily see you all culled so they can carry on killing. Help me, and we can save Deadhart *and* the Colony.'

'Maybe I don't want to save Deadhart. Or any humans.'

'Really? You're half-human yourself. Don't you crave what our world offers? Isn't that why you hang out at the Lame Horse and pick up human companions?' Tucker paused. 'You know, I could have you arrested for soliciting.' He glanced at the wolves. 'Or we could just let sleeping dogs lie.'

'You're *threatening* me?'

'Bargaining.'

Michael remained silent, considering. His long blond hair gleamed, skin alabaster in the moonlight. Michael had his mother's beauty and callous cruelty. But Tucker didn't believe he had her killer instinct. At least, he hoped not.

Finally, Michael turned to the wolves and said something rapidly in Vampyric. Tucker picked out a little: *Ou gaest* ('You go.') As one, the pack turned and melted back into the woods.

He glanced back at Tucker. 'Follow me. Athelinda's expecting you. She smelt your stench a mile away.'

He walked forward and stepped on to the bridge, jumping lightly over several rotting sleepers. Tucker hesitated. The bridge seemed to sway slightly in the wind. Snow had coated the rotten wood, making it slimy and even more treacherous.

Michael waited, halfway across. 'You scared, Tucker?'

'Abso-fucking-lutely.'

He smiled. 'You're half-turned. You fall and crack your skull, you'll mend . . . probably.'

Tucker gritted his teeth and stepped out on to the bridge.

57

Barbara felt restless. She had made calls to Talkeetna and Anchorage. She had checked the weather reports – and it looked like the storm should have passed by tomorrow morning. She had even made a call to Decker.

'You think Nathan Bell is our killer?' he asked.

'I really don't know, sir.'

She heard him tut. 'Seems like there's a shitload you don't know right now. I could paper my house and have plenty spare to wipe my butt on with what you *don't* know.'

'Pleasing as that image is, sir, there's a lot here that doesn't make sense.'

A sigh so long she could hear the phlegm in it. 'This the long way of telling me you can't authorize a cull?'

'Yes, sir.'

A longer pause. 'Make sure you have all your ducks lined up on this one. You need to be certain beyond doubt that this isn't connected to the Colony. Understood?'

'Yes, sir. You know me. Plenty of ducks.'

'Don't be facetious.'

He ended the call. Barbara looked at the phone, a little nonplussed. Decker knew the word 'facetious'.

She laid the phone back on the table and took a sip of coffee, staring across at the bar and the distasteful decorations above. Amid the vampyr paraphernalia, a few old photos of the town had been hung haphazardly. They reminded Barbara that she hadn't taken another look at the photos Rita had given her. The box was still up in her room. And there wasn't much else she could do right now.

She traipsed upstairs, only remembering that her room had been trashed by Grace when she pushed open the door. She stared for a moment at the writing on the wall, the yanked-off bed covers, overturned chair and slashed mattress. Oh well, at least Grace hadn't tampered with the evidence.

Barbara grabbed the box and took it back down to the bar. Settling herself at a table, she opened it and began to sift through, thinking again about what Beau had said about kids disappearing. Not recorded as murders back then. Written off as accidents. She wondered if there might be something about the disappearances in here.

She shuffled through photos and pieces of paper. One fell to the floor. She picked it up. It was folded into a tight square, the creases so worn in the paper almost tore as she gently peeled it apart.

A newspaper clipping. Dated March 15th, 1953.

TOWN TURNS OUT IN SEARCH
FOR MISSING GIRL

The whole of Deadhart turned out this morning to help search for missing six-year-old Mary Dawson . . .

The little girl Beau had mentioned. Rita's aunt. The accompanying photo showed a plump-cheeked girl with chunky pigtails. Another photo showed a group of townspeople. The search party, she presumed. Barbara squinted at the picture.

Slightly to one side of the group stood a thin, dark-haired boy. She frowned. Something about him looked familiar. She rifled back through the pile of papers till she came to the pictures of the Bone House. The hard-faced madams glared back at her, but this time her eyes were drawn to the figure crouching in the corner. Skinny, legs like sticks in ragged shorts. She hadn't paid the boy much attention before. Now she held the photo up. It was old and faded. Dirt camouflaged his face. But . . . could it be the *same* boy?

A *thud, thud, thud* at the front door.

'Shit.' She jumped. Someone must be desperate for a drink.

And then a familiar voice called: 'Hey, Detective Atkins? You in there?'

Mayflower. Barbara walked over to the door, unlocked it and pulled it open. The wind almost blew her back off her feet.

'Mayflower? What are you doing here? Is it an emergency?'

The girl was bundled up in a big, black parka. She rolled her eyes. 'Kinda. My dad's all out of beer. Plus, Mom wants some steaks out the freezer.'

'They ever heard of a shop?'

'Yeah, but Mom says they've already paid for this stuff, so if they can't serve it to customers they might as well use it.'

Barbara sighed. 'Okay. Come on in before you freeze.'

'It's not so bad,' Mayflower said, stepping inside. 'It's usually colder in January.'

Barbara raised an eyebrow. 'Well, no offence, but I hope I won't be here to see that.'

'Yeah, wish I could say the same.'

The girl pushed her hood back and straight away Barbara could see her eyes were red and swollen.

'Are you okay?'

Mayflower's hand fluttered to her face. 'Yeah. Well, no. Dan dumped me.'

Of course, Barbara thought. Men like Dan were only ever faithful to an easy life.

'Sorry to hear that,' she said.

'But not surprised?'

'Well, "I told you so" never helped anyone a whole heap.'

'Right.'

Barbara considered. She didn't really have time to be a shoulder to cry on. Her shoulders were pretty heavy with other stuff, like the trio of corpses in the freezer. But sometimes, you had to put the living first.

'You want a coffee?' she asked.

'I guess.'

'Come and sit down. How d'you take it?'

'Black, no sugar, thanks.'

'Coming right up.'

Mayflower hovered near the booth where Barbara had been sitting.

'Mom and Dad are going apeshit that this place is still shut.'

'Yeah, well, sorry about that,' Barbara said, walking over to the coffee machine and turning it on. 'But till we can get the coroner over here I've got to preserve the evidence.' She caught herself, thinking that some of the evidence was people. People who, only days ago, had been as alive as she was.

The coffee machine gurgled. She stuck a mug under it.

'You know when that will be?' Mayflower asked.

'Well, if the storm clear ups, hopefully tomorrow afternoon.'

'Right.'

Barbara eyed her carefully. 'You really here for beer and steak, or did your mom send you over to quiz me?'

Mayflower shifted awkwardly. 'Bit of both. Mom's used to being the one who knows everything. It's driving her crazy not being the font of all gossip.'

Barbara smiled and brought the coffee over. 'Well, I'm afraid I can't share any information about an ongoing investigation.'

'Yeah, I thought that's what you'd say.' Mayflower accepted the coffee and sat down.

'Look,' Barbara said. 'I understand that people are worried, and angry, right now. But Deputy Tucker and I are doing all we can to solve this case, bring the killer to justice . . . and get out of your hair.'

Mayflower nodded. But she still seemed distracted. Something was wrong.

'Any other reason you're here?' Barbara asked, as casually as she could.

Mayflower looked down into her coffee. It was the first time Barbara had seen the girl uncertain, her armour of attitude lowered.

'Mom and Dad – they're traditional, right? Grown up in Deadhart, been here their whole lives, say grace before dinner, Second Amendment types.'

'I've known a few.'

'But they're not bad people. Mom can seem a bit harsh, but she works hard to keep this place afloat.'

'And your dad?'

'He used to have a problem with gambling, but he's stopped.'

Barbara nodded. 'That's good.'

'What I'm saying is . . .' A hesitation. 'When they said they didn't know about the stuff in the freezer . . . they were telling the truth.'

Barbara stared at the girl, feeling the sour taste of disappointment at the back of her throat. 'But you did?'

'Yeah.' Mayflower's cheeks flushed. 'Kurt Mowlam . . . before Dan, we had a bit of a thing.'

'Mowlam?'

'No need to sound so shocked.'

'No, it's just . . .'

He's lying dead in the freezer with a stake poking out of his chest.

'I guess he doesn't seem your type. Go on,' she said.

'A few months ago, Kurt asked if I could do him a favour. Not for free. There'd be some cash in it for me, too.'

'He asked you to store vampyr body parts in your deep freeze?'

'Yeah.'

'Did you know Mowlam was involved in illegal artefact trading?'

'Not when I first met him, but later I found out he was involved with the Helsing League. He showed me some of the stuff he collected.'

'Guess that made him even more exciting, right? Every girl loves a bad boy.'

Mayflower's eyes flashed. 'Actually, no. That's why I dumped him.'

'But you didn't inform the authorities?'

'In case you hadn't noticed, this is a small town. I didn't want to make trouble for myself.'

'You could have refused his request, though?'

The girl glared at her. 'Look, I'm not proud. But we needed the extra cash, okay? This place barely keeps going and, with Dad's debts, I just thought it would help.'

Barbara nodded. 'So, when your parents said the Doc asked them, they lied to protect you.'

'Yeah. They were pretty pissed.'

Barbara thought of something else. 'You gave Mowlam a key so he could sneak stuff in and out?'

Mayflower nodded. 'I didn't know he'd shut you in the freezer, okay?'

Barbara was willing to believe her.

'Why are you telling me now?' she asked.

'Because Mom said if all this comes out, if you charge them for keeping vampyr artefacts in the freezer, they'll lose this place, and I don't know what they'll do if that happens.'

Barbara sighed. She was angry with the girl. What May-flower had done was wrong, sickening. But she had done it to help her parents. Poor people didn't have as many options as those with a healthy cushion of wealth. As the saying goes, the road to hell is paved with good intentions. But sometimes, if you cut people a bit of slack, you could keep them from heading all the way down.

'Mowlam pay you in cash?' Barbara asked.

'Yeah.'

'Okay. Then the way I see it, your parents have denied knowing those heads and hearts were in the deep freeze. Without any evidence to the contrary, I shall have to take them at their word.' She gave Mayflower a keen look. 'This conversation never happened.'

Mayflower nodded gratefully. 'Thank you.'

'Now, you got anything else you want to spill?'

'Actually, well, I don't know if this is relevant . . .'

'*Everything* is relevant right now.'

'Okay. I heard Kurt had started visiting the church pretty regularly.'

Barbara sat back. 'You mean "visiting" as in partaking of prayer, or "visiting" as in . . .'

'Well, he isn't the religious type.'

Colleen was a striking woman. And Mowlam *had* been there the other night. But Barbara couldn't see Colleen trashing everything she had built here over some stubble and puppy-dog eyes.

'That's certainly interesting,' she said. 'Maybe I'll have another little chat with Reverend Grey.'

Mayflower nodded. 'What about Mowlam? Are you going to arrest him?'

'Well –' Barbara began, and broke off.

She'd heard a noise.

Thud, thud.

'Is that someone at the door?' Mayflower asked.

The noise came again:

Thud, thud.

Barbara shook her head. 'It's not coming from the front door.'

Thud, Thud.

'It's coming from the kitchen.'

They both slowly turned. The wind rattled the shutters.

And then, of course, the lights went out.

58

Athelinda took out her pipe and tobacco. Carefully, she packed the bowl and lit it. Tucker waited.

They were sat, just the two of them, in her living room. An honour, Tucker knew. Few were invited inside Athelinda's abode. It was modest and surprisingly homey. But then what had he expected? Cobwebs and coffins?

She blew out a cloud of smoke. 'You must be fucking desperate if you've hiked all the way up here to bother me.'

'I am.'

'So, what do you want?'

Tucker took the 'becoming' ring out and set it on the table.

'This is Aaron's, right? The one he was supposed to give to Todd.'

Athelinda picked the ring up. 'Where did you find this?'

'In the pocket of Marcus Anderson's bloodied jacket. Someone left it for me. I think they wanted me to know the killings are connected.'

Athelinda continued to study the ring. Then she muttered something in Vampyric under her breath and slipped it into her pocket.

'Go ahead. Ask your questions.'

'Tell me about the Bone House.'

She tapped a sharp, gold tooth with her finger. 'You want to know how they pulled out my incisors to stop me biting, or how every night the men would come? Some just wanted to rape a child. Some liked to do other things only a vampyr is good for.' She sucked on the pipe. 'One girl became a cripple. Stumps for arms and legs. Some of the men, they enjoyed that even more.'

Tucker swallowed. His throat felt like it had something stuck in it.

'I was in that place for over five years,' Athelinda continued. 'I've no fear of hell because I've already been there.'

'I'm sorry.'

Her eyes sparked. 'I don't need your fucking pity. I'm just telling you how it was.'

'Okay.' He nodded. 'You told Detective Atkins to ask about the Bone House. Why? What has the Bone House got to do with the murders?'

This time Athelinda took longer to reply. Pungent pipe smoke swirled in the air. Eventually, she said:

'There was a boy who worked at the Bone House. An orphan. He served the men drinks, cleaned the place, helped patch up the girls when they got hurt. He was the one who gave me the matches to burn it down.' She paused. 'I expected to die in the fire, but he rescued me. Later, I found out I was pregnant. The boy saved us both – me and Michael.'

'What happened to him?'

'For sixty years, I thought he was dead. And then one day, I saw him again. In Deadhart.'

'You recognized him all those years later?'

A thin smile. 'Different clothing. Different haircut. But he hadn't aged. Not a single day.'

Tucker let this sink in. 'He was a vampyr, like you?'

385

'Yes.'

'Who is he, Athelinda?'

'At the Bone House, he went by the name Isaac. When I saw him again, he had a different name —'

'What?'

'Nathan Bell.'

'Shit,' Tucker cursed.

All along, they had been right.

'You never spoke up,' he said to Athelinda. 'Not even when Todd was murdered.'

For once, a sliver of uncertainty crossed her face. 'Aaron confessed. And just because the boy was a vampyr, it didn't mean he was a killer. He was living as a human. I couldn't betray him.'

'But you suspected?'

'Yes. Then you fucked up Aaron's escape and we all had to run. I had other concerns. I forgot about him.'

'Until you returned this time — and saw him again.'

'When the other boy was killed, I knew.'

'That's why you told Detective Atkins about the Bone House.' He shook his head. 'Why not just tell her who he was?'

'Because I don't owe her anything. But I owe *him*. I wanted to believe I was wrong. I even sent Michael to hang out at that shithole lodge. To get information.'

That explained why Michael had been fraternizing with Nathan at the Lame Horse. Except . . . Tucker frowned. 'Nathan Bell is a grown man.'

Athelinda rolled her eyes. 'You still don't fucking get it?'

'Get what?'

'That's not Nathan Bell.' She leaned forward. 'Child

386

vampyrs who aren't part of a colony will often find a human companion to travel with. They'll pass them off as a relative – aunt, uncle, parent.'

It suddenly hit. Like a sucker punch.

Athelinda smiled. 'Now you get it.'

'*Jacob.*'

He wasn't Nathan Bell's son. Jacob *was* Nathan Bell. And Isaac. And who knew how many names and lives in between.

Which meant . . .

'Shit!' Tucker stood.

'What?'

'I need to get back. I have to warn Barbara. He's not dead.'

59

Barbara entered the kitchen cautiously, Mayflower behind her, flashlight held out in front.

Thud, thud.

Her uneasiness intensified. The noise was coming from the freezer.

'Shit. Is someone locked in there?' Mayflower asked.

Yeah, Barbara thought. But they were all supposed to be dead.

'I want you to go home, get your parents to call Rita,' she said to Mayflower. 'Tell her there is a situation at the Grill. I might need her help.'

'But –'

'Go!'

Mayflower looked like she wanted to argue but then thought better of it and hurried out of the kitchen.

Barbara turned back towards the freezer. She could hear the hum of the generator. No more thuds, except from her pounding heart. She drew her UV gun out of the holster, walked up to the door and pushed down on the sturdy handle.

The door swung open.

Marcus's body lay on the steel table, Mowlam lay next to it on the floor and, beside him, Jacob, wrapped in the silver foil blanket. One, two, three. So, who was knock, knock, knocking on the door?

Barbara walked into the freezer. She stared around and then walked up to Jacob's body. Her breath plumed out in front of her. She crouched down, knees creaking. Her phone vibrated in her pocket. Damn. She put the flashlight down and drew it out with tingling fingers. Tucker.

'Hey – where are you?'

'Almost . . . back . . . danger.'

His voice was breaking up.

'Tucker, I can't –'

'Listen – Jacob . . . killer . . . vampyr.'

'What?'

His voice cut through: 'Jacob is our killer. Jacob IS Nathan Bell.'

The line crackled and went dead. Barbara looked at her phone. Then she looked back at the body.

Jacob IS Nathan Bell.

She reached forward and carefully unwrapped the blanket from Jacob's head.

Marcus's frozen face stared up at her.

What the hell?

And that was when she heard the tear of a zip.

She turned. Jacob leapt from the body bag on the table and landed on the floor. His hair was frosted with ice, throat black with crusted blood.

'Jacob!'

His lips cracked in a smile and he darted for the door. *Shit.* Barbara pushed herself to her feet and ran after him. The kitchen was dark. She pointed her flashlight around. There weren't many places to hide in here, except behind the row of stoves.

'Jacob.' She took a couple of steps forward. 'Or should

I call you Nathan? Posing as your own son. Clever, I'll give you that.'

Silence.

'You want to tell my why you killed Marcus, and Todd?'

This time he spoke. 'Because I'm a killer. All vampyrs are.'

Ahead, to her right. She moved forward in that direction.

'If you're so proud of being a vampyr, why pretend to be human?'

'I did what I had to, to survive.'

'That why you hooked up with Mitch, pretended to be father and son?'

'We were useful to each other. I helped him scam people. He gave me cover.'

'So, why come back here?'

'Money. The house – and because there's no place like home –'

Two heavy pans hurtled in her direction. Barbara dodged, but one still skimmed her ear, knocking her into the stoves.

'Owww. Shit!'

She clutched at her ear. The door to the bar thudded open and a dark shadow scuttled out. He was so much quicker than her, and he had the advantage of seeing in the dark. Cursing again, Barbara stumbled after him, bursting through the door into the Grill. She couldn't let him get out of here. Once he did, he could disappear back into the forest. She needed to block his exit and take him down.

A chair scraped to her left. She spun the flashlight round but could only see more tables and chairs.

'Even if you get out of here, Jacob, you won't get far with the entire state police searching for you.'

A glimpse of movement ahead. Barbara raised the UV gun. Jacob was faster. He erupted from the darkness and barrelled into her, sending them both crashing to the floor. The gun flew from her hand. Jacob lunged for her throat. Barbara felt his hot breath, saw the glint of his teeth. She braced her arms against his chest, raised a knee and jammed it into his groin.

He cried out and his grip loosened. Barbara pulled away and scrabbled for the gun, but Jacob was on her again before she could reach it. He grabbed her head and smashed her skull into the hard floor. Pain and dizziness swamped her. She tried to push him off but could feel her consciousness fading.

'GET THE FUCK OFF HER!'

Something *whooshed* through the air. Jacob's head snapped sideways with a sickening crunch, and he fell backwards. Barbara squinted up at a huge, dark shadow which gradually solidified into Tucker, wielding a heavy barstool. He put it down and held out his hand. She reached for it, but before their fingers could touch there was an animal-like roar and Jacob reared up from the floor. He flew at Tucker, knocking the big man off balance. Tucker staggered a few paces and then toppled into a table stacked with chairs, Jacob falling on top of him.

'Shit!' Barbara pulled herself up. *The gun. Where was the damn UV gun?*

And then she saw it, lying a short distance away. She grabbed her weapon and stood up. Ahead of her she could hear crashing, grunts and heavy breathing. She advanced a few steps, pointing the flashlight around. The beam illuminated Tucker and Jacob wrestling on the floor amid broken chairs and an overturned table.

Barbara raised the gun in her other hand. Then hesitated. She needed to get a clear shot or the UV light might fry Tucker too. She trained the gun on the pair, finger poised.

'Dammit,' she muttered.

But for once fate was on her side. With a stuttering buzz the lights in the bar suddenly sprang back on. Jacob reeled back, shielding his eyes. Barbara pulled the trigger. The flare threw him across the room. Flesh sizzled. She smelt burning. She walked over to where Jacob lay, curled on the floor, by the window. Half his hair had been burnt away and the skin beneath was raw and blistered. His face was a charred mess.

As she approached, he opened his eyes.

Barbara kept the gun trained on him. 'It's over, Jacob.'

He pushed himself to his feet, reached up to his head and cracked it back into position.

Like the goddamn Terminator.

'It's never over,' he croaked.

The UV gun must have seared his vocal cords. His voice was hoarse and cracked. No longer that of a young boy, but something more ancient. Barbara thought about the faded photographs. The skinny boy who looked so familiar.

'You had a good run,' she said. 'You've been killing for what – a century?'

'I've been killing since before your grandparents were born.'

392

Barbara felt her finger itch on the trigger. 'Well, it's good that you're familiar with death. Because there's only one way this is going to end.'

'This ends when I decide it ends.'

'So you can go on killing, for kicks?'

'This is who I am. It's who every vampyr is. They've just forgotten – and they need reminding.'

'And that's what you're doing?'

His lips twisted. 'Every time I kill, it creates more hatred between humans and colonies.'

'You want a war?'

'A Gathering. Except this time, we win.'

'You've already lost.'

'You can't kill me.'

'Everything dies, Jacob. Everything has its time.'

'NO!' It came out as a ragged roar. '*You* die. Humans. You die and rot. Not me. I'm fucking immortal.'

He turned and leapt for the window. Barbara fired just as he crashed through in a hail of shattered glass. Snow gusted in through the broken panes.

'Fuck!' Barbara glanced back at Tucker, who was sitting up groggily, face a mask of blood, nose oddly off angle but mostly intact.

He stared up at her. 'Guh after him.'

Barbara didn't need to be told twice. She ran for the door, fumbled it open and burst outside. She squinted against the storm, trying to take in the scene.

Christmas lights illuminated the street. Jacob crouched on all fours in the snow, dripping blood. A short distance away, another slight figure stood, motionless: Athelinda. Clad in tattered animal furs and hiking boots, blonde hair blowing around her porcelain face. She held a large axe in her hands.

'Hello, Isaac,' she said.

Jacob looked up at her and laughed bitterly. 'Really? After everything they did to you?'

'This isn't about them.'

He stood, swaying in the wind. 'Then what?'

'Aaron and his kin are dead because of you.'

'No. Because of *them*.' He pointed back at Barbara. 'They're the ones who killed your kin.'

'You let the Colony take the blame for the boys. You used us.'

'I *saved* you.'

'And I'll always be in your debt.'

'Then fuck them.' He raised his arms. 'We could kill all of them. Right now.'

Athelinda smiled. 'Believe me, I've wanted to.'

Jacob took a step towards her. 'Then do it. You're a killer, Athelinda. Like me.'

They stared at each other. Barbara raised the gun.

'No.' Athelinda shook her head. 'I'm not like you. You are like *them*. This needs to end.'

Jacob sneered. 'Vampyrs don't kill vampyrs. It's forbidden. I know the rules.'

'You're no vampyr . . .' She lifted the axe. 'And here, I *make* the fucking rules.'

He lunged towards her. Then stopped, jerked upright like a marionette yanked by its strings. A steel arrowhead burst through his chest, piercing his heart from behind. Jacob looked down in shock. He clutched at the arrow, realization dawning. Something like a smile spread across his ruined features, and he crumpled gently to the snow.

Beau Grainger walked out of the shadows, holding a heavy metal crossbow. He looked down at Jacob and wiped a trembling hand across his mouth. 'Vampyr scum.'

Athelinda regarded him dispassionately. 'Is it my turn now, old man?'

Beau turned to her. He looked bad, Barbara thought. Face gaunt, dark shadows beneath his eyes. Like he was already the walking dead.

'They told me to come here,' he croaked. 'The voices in my head. They won't give me any peace.'

Athelinda nodded. 'You're dying. That's why you hear them – what you kill eventually becomes a part of you.'

'Make it stop.'

'I can't.'

He pointed the crossbow at her. 'Make it stop.'

She laughed. 'You think I fear death? I'm four hundred fucking years old. I welcome death.'

Beau made a strangled cry and flung the crossbow to one side. He dropped to his knees and bowed his head. 'You want revenge for your kin. Kill me.'

Athelinda looked down at the axe in her hands. She licked her lips, gold incisors glinting. Then she shook her head. 'You don't deserve my fucking mercy.'

She threw the axe to the ground. Beau grabbed it.

'Oh, shit.' Barbara started down the steps, but she was already too late.

Beau swung the blade back at himself, slicing deep into his own neck. Blood spurted. His head flopped backwards, tendons and muscles severed, throat gaping in a violent scarlet howl. For a few seconds, he remained kneeling, head lolling on his spine, eyes staring at the stormy sky. Then he collapsed sideways. Gurgling noises bubbled from his ravaged throat. His hands flapped limply around in the bloody snow.

Athelinda stared at him. 'You stupid old fuck.'

With a heavy sigh, she marched over, snatched up the axe and brought it down cleanly on Beau's neck with a soft, wet *schlop*. She bent and picked his head up by the hair.

'Wait,' Barbara shouted, stumbling into the street. 'What are you doing?'

'Taking him,' Athelinda said flatly. 'You can have him back when the rest of my kin are returned.'

Without waiting for a reply, she strode away down Main Street. Halfway along, she paused and stared at the sparkling Christmas lights, as if only just noticing them. For a moment, illuminated by twinkling stars and prancing reindeer, her face seemed aglow with a childish wonder.

Then she glanced back at Barbara: 'Your Santa is jerking off. You might want to do something about that.'

And as Barbara watched, she disappeared into the snowstorm, small boots leaving faint bloody marks in her wake.

60

48 hours later

The storm had passed. Outside, a pale sun made the snow glisten.

'So, I guess you're heading off then?' Rita said.

Barbara nodded. 'Al's on his way. He'll drive me to Talkeetna. Then I'm on the plane back to Anchorage.'

'You going to visit Nicholls?' Rita asked.

'I thought I'd drop in, take him some grapes.'

'He hates grapes.'

'Oh.'

'Take him some Saltwater Taffy. He loves Taffy.'

'Okay.' Barbara smiled. 'You going to be all right here?'

'I'm sure we'll do just fine with Tucker holding the fort.'

Barbara glanced at Tucker. His nose was bandaged, but his face didn't look too bad. Only she knew how much of a beating he had taken. Otherwise, well, questions might be asked.

'Maybe you could stick around?' she said. 'Nicholls needs a deputy.'

'I'll think about it. For now' – he picked up a large crate – 'I've got a delivery to make.'

They all looked at the crate. 'Athelinda will be happy to get them back,' Barbara said.

'And make sure you come back with Beau,' Rita said.

'Jess wants an open casket, and I'm having trouble putting her off.'

Barbara and Tucker exchanged looks. Then Barbara held out a hand.

'Good working with you.'

Tucker shook it. 'You too.'

'Maybe I'll catch you again sometime.'

He winked. 'You could try.'

She watched him walk out of the station. Then she turned back to Rita.

'Well, then . . .'

'I guess that's everything wrapped up,' Rita finished.

'Guess so.'

The state police had found Mitch Roberts's mutilated body covered in a tarp in the back of the pick-up. His throat had been ripped out. They figured that Jacob and Roberts must have had some kind of dispute. Roberts was a thief and a fraudster, not a killer. Maybe he got cold feet about the murders, so Jacob killed him and decided to flee, dumping the body on his way. However, instead he lost control of the truck in the snow and crashed.

All evidence seemed to point to Kurt Mowlam being responsible for the Doc's death, maybe to stop his involvement in the artefact dealing from getting out. The coroner had ruled out suicide and Mowlam hadn't been too careful about leaving trace evidence around the Doc's house.

As for who killed Mowlam? Barbara glanced across the hall to where Grace sat on a chair, just outside the cells. She was dressed in more regular teenage clothes – jeans and a sweatshirt – and a small backpack sat at her feet.

Colleen Grey had cut and run. Just upped and left in the

middle of the night, leaving only a note and Grace behind. The theory was that Colleen and Mowlam had been having an affair (Mayflower wasn't the only one who had noticed clandestine comings and goings). Mowlam had threatened to expose the affair and Colleen killed him.

Something about that still didn't sit quite right with Barbara. Colleen had seemed too composed for a crime of passion. But then, innocent people didn't usually do a midnight flit.

They had contacted Grace's mom, who hadn't signed anything saying her daughter could be taken out of state, but, more to the point, didn't care. Grace was going to stay with her grandparents, who had been out of their minds with worry ever since she ran away and were more than delighted to have her.

'She saying anything yet?' Barbara asked.

'Nope. Not a word.'

Barbara sighed. 'Well, it might take time.'

'Yeah, and all that time Colleen is making her way who knows where.'

There was an APB out on the Reverend, but Barbara had a gut feeling that Colleen Grey had already disappeared, if she had ever really existed. They couldn't find any official details for anyone with that name. No social security number, no previous employment, birth certificate, bank account. The woman was a ghost.

And there was something else.

'Don't suppose there's any news on the other artefacts?' she asked Rita.

'No.'

Somehow, in the midst of the carnage that followed

Jacob's and Beau's deaths, the vampyr body parts from the Grill had mysteriously gone missing. Mayflower swore she hadn't taken them and no one else had claimed responsibility.

'Guess that's going to remain a mystery,' Rita said.

'Guess so. Probably get a good price for them in certain markets.'

'Well, I wouldn't know about that.'

'No.' Barbara smiled. 'How's your mom?'

'Got her on some new meds.'

'That must cost a lot, even with insurance?'

'Yeah, well, we get by.'

'Really? I mean, you don't get paid for being the mayor. It's more of a title than a job. You must only get a small salary for helping at the police department. It's got to be tough.'

'Sometimes.'

'And you've got no other income.'

'Okay.' Rita's voice hardened. 'What are you really asking me?'

Barbara eyed her more keenly. 'You've lived here all your life. You know everyone in this town and everything that goes on. I find it hard to believe the Doc and Mowlam were trading illegal vampyr artefacts right under your nose. And the Doc's plan, to get a cull authorized and steal the bodies? Someone in authority would have to have been involved. Even if they didn't get their hands dirty.'

Rita stared at her. 'So, you think I was taking bribes? That is a mighty big accusation. You got any proof, Barbara?'

'Nope. And I'm sure if I came to your house and asked

to look in your basement, I wouldn't find anything illegal stored down there, would I?'

Rita swallowed. 'Of course not.'

'Good.' Barbara nodded. 'Do the drugs work?'

'For now, they're helping.'

'What happens when you need more?'

'I always keep a little something aside for a rainy day.'

'I bet you do.'

'We all done here now, Detective?'

'Yeah, I guess we are.'

Outside, a horn beeped. Barbara picked up her bag. She walked to the door and then paused.

'You know, I wouldn't hold on to those "rainy day" things for too long, Rita.'

'Why's that?'

'They might start to whisper.'

Barbara climbed into the back of the cab next to Grace. Al dumped their bags in the trunk and sat down in the driver's seat.

'I hear you caught the vampyr that killed those boys.'

'I had help – from the Colony.'

He shook his head. 'I guess they ain't all bad then.'

'No, sir.'

He shook his head. 'Next thing you know, one of 'em will want to be a police officer.' He chortled at the thought.

Barbara smiled. 'Now that would be crazy, right?'

'Oh yeah.'

Al started the engine and pulled away, big tyres making light work of the mushy snow.

Barbara turned to Grace. 'You all right?'

The girl folded her arms and looked out of the window. It was going to be a long journey. Al started to talk about the storm and cancelled flights. Barbara let his words wash over her. Then she reached into her pocket and pulled out the note that Colleen had left in the chapel. It had been addressed to 'Detective Atkins'.

Dear Barbara (if I may call you that)

I'm sorry I couldn't make your acquaintance for longer. But the time has come for me to leave. Quicker than I would have liked, but when God calls, his children must listen.

I have decided that it is better if I continue my journey alone. Grace has been a loyal companion, but now she must find her own path. I trust you will take care of her.

For now, I am leaving you this. You might think it odd, but for a long time before I found my true calling, this item was a symbol of hope for me. Something I clung to in the darkest of hours. Maybe, if you wish to know more, you should take a trip to a small town in Oregon called Madeline Springs. There's a house there, in the woods, where I lived, for a long time.

Yours,
Colleen Grey

'Guess she really was mad as a box of bats,' Rita had said when she'd read the note. 'And why in hell did she leave you *that thing*?'

'I have no idea,' Barbara had said, staring at the small plastic knife.

But Colleen was right. She would like to know more.

The girl had hitched across the states. No real aim but to get far away from the place she had been held captive for so long. She met other travellers along the way. Humans and vampyrs. Some she had befriended. Others she had killed. It was in her nature. Even though she longed for it not to be. She longed to be saved from herself. She longed . . . to be human.

Her time in captivity had not made her hate humans, or even fear them. Far from it. She had seen the alternative. While she was grateful to her Rescuer, she had also been repulsed by him. They were not the same. She knew nothing of vampyr ways. But all her TV watching and reading had educated her in the human world. That was where she wanted to live.

She had filed her teeth, forced herself to endure more and more hours of daylight and to sleep during the dark hours. She even managed to hold down small amounts of food without being ill. But it still wasn't enough.

And then she had met a priest. An inspiring man, God rest his soul. He had convinced her she could overcome her nature. With the love of God. God was all-forgiving. God could perform miracles. The devil had been an angel once. Why couldn't a devil become an angel? She just had to prove her faith.

This had become her mission. To show God she was worthy of redemption, of being released from her curse. She would cleanse the world of vampyrs and, in doing so, prove herself worthy of a miracle.

It was a role she had found she was uniquely suited to. She had certain gifts that meant she could entrance congregations. They listened to her, followed her, donated generously to her churches. She travelled the country, using new names, building new places of worship in colony towns, inspiring people to rise up against the demons in their midst. She had, indeed, found her calling. And of course, no one suspected that a preacher was actually a vampyr.

Of course, she still needed blood, but as long as it was pure human blood, only small amounts would suffice. That was why she always had a companion. Someone who could provide for her. And there had been plenty willing to do so along the way. Some she had let go, like Grace. Others had made the ultimate sacrifice. It was God's will. Their deaths served a higher purpose.

God always had a purpose. It was why he had guided her to Deadhart, even before the Colony returned. Although perhaps her own instincts had also played a part. Still, she had built a strong congregation there, and she felt aggrieved at having to leave. But too many questions were being asked.

It was unfortunate she had been forced to approach Dr Dalton for blood when Grace became ill for a while. Oh, she knew all about the Doc's blood dealing. A preacher gets to know the sins of their congregation. But then the teacher, Mowlam, had discovered her secret and started blackmailing her. Killing him had been necessary and, she had to admit, pleasurable. God's work was not always clean work. Sometimes you had to get your hands dirty.

Now, she was once again travelling, alone. She would find a new town, a new name and a new companion. She always did. There were always girls who needed to be rescued.

Epilogue

6 months later

A brisk knock at the door. Decker looked up. Edwards. He didn't like Edwards. He was young. And enthusiastic. And good-looking. All qualities that crawled right up Decker's butt crack. Even the way he knocked boiled Decker's piss.

'Yeah?' Decker snapped.

Edwards pushed open the door. 'Sir, I just took a call from Landon Police Department in Minnesota. Two kids went crazy in school this morning, killed their teacher and two other pupils.'

'So? Why are they calling us? We don't deal with active shooters, and it's Minnesota, for fuck's sake.'

'These kids didn't shoot anyone. They ripped out their victims' throats.'

Decker stared at him. 'They're Colony?'

'No. The two kids say they were held captive and turned against their will. They claim they couldn't help themselves.'

'What the *hell*?'

'There's something else.' Edwards produced an A4 photograph, which he laid on Decker's desk. 'This was written on the wall of one of the classrooms –'

Decker stared down at it. 'Jesus Christ!'

'I mean, it might not mean anything. It's not an uncommon –'

405

'Call Atkins,' he said.

'She's on leave.'

'Not any more she fucking isn't.'

Edwards nodded and exited. Decker picked the photograph up and studied it again.

Four words, scrawled in blood:

BARBARA – PRAY FOR MERCY

Acknowledgements

So, here we are again. Book number six. And for that alone; for the huge privilege of being able to make stuff up for a living, I am incredibly thankful.

Obviously, I owe a huge debt of gratitude to my brilliant agent, Madeleine Milburn. If she hadn't scooped my first manuscript from the slush pile, none of these books would have happened. Thanks to Hannah for the TV and the whole team for being superstars.

I am ever grateful to my editors, Max and Anne. Every time I pitch them a new idea – each one weirder than the last – they just say: 'Sounds great' and let me go for it. Their insight and experience - and nice ways of telling me something doesn't work – are invaluable. I'm not someone who gets it right first draft. And that will probably go on my gravestone.

Thank you to the teams at Michael Joseph and Ballantine. Publicity, marketing, designers. A lot of people make a book happen – and I work with the best (special mention to Jen for her patience in trying to teach me to use IG). Thanks must also go to my lovely international publishers. Being read across the globe never stops being a thrill.

The acknowledgements wouldn't be complete without a big shout out to my husband Neil and amazing daughter, Betty. I do this for me. But it wouldn't mean a thing without them.

I would also like to thank Talkeetna in Alaska – the

inspiration for the town of Deadhart. If you ever get a chance to visit, do. It's a weird, wonderful place and hanging out there for a few days really helped me flesh out my fictional town and its inhabitants. I made Deadhart a little wilder and more remote, but it still owes a lot to Talkeetna.

Finally, thank you to *you* for reading. Whether you're new to my stuff or you've been with me a while, I appreciate you taking the time. Let's do this again. Soon.